Praise for *Breach the Hull*,

Book One in the Defending the Future series

Winner of the 2007 Dream Realm Award

"There is more than enough great SF in *Breach the Hull*
for any true fan of the genre, military or not."
— Will McDermott, author of *Lasgun Wedding*

"I enjoyed this book and heartily recommend it."
—Sam Tomaino, *Space and Time Magazine*

"Pick up *Breach the Hull*. You're sure to find stories that you like."
—David Sherman, author of the *DemonTech* series
and co-author of the *Starfist* series

"[*Breach the Hull*] kicks down the doors in a way that allows
anyone access to the genre[. . .]it read like a bunch of soldiers
sitting around swapping stories of the wars. Fun, fast-paced, and
packed with action. I give it a thumbs up."
—Jonathan Maberry,
Bram Stoker Award-winning author

"[*Breach the Hull*] is worth the purchase. I normally don't partake
of anthologies as a general rule . . . but Mike McPhail has done
a great job in making me rethink this position."
—Peter Hodges, Reviewer

"*Breach the Hull* is full of excellent stories, no two of which are the
same. While similar themes crop up throughout, each writer has
managed to take the subgenre and make it his own."
—John Ottinger III, Grasping for the Wind Reviews

"A collection of military science fiction from a well mixed group
of authors, both new and established. Found it a good source
for some new authors to investigate."
—Tony Finan, Philly Geeks

The Defending the Future series

Breach the Hull

So It Begins

By Other Means
(2010)

BREACH THE HULL

Book One in the Defending The Future series

EDITED BY:
MIKE McPHAIL

Dark Quest, LLC
Howell, New Jersey

Special thanks to "Bob"
...It's All Your Fault!

Acknowledgments
"Cryptic" first published in Asimov's, April 1983. Copyright 1996 Cryptic, Inc.
"Black to Move" first published in Asimov's, Sept, 1982. Copyright 1996 Cryptic, Inc.
"Forgotten Causes" first published in Absolute Magnitude, #16, Summer 2001.
Copyright 2001, John C. Wright

PUBLISHED BY
Dark Quest, LLC
Neal Levin, Publisher
23 Alec Drive,
Howell, New Jersey 07731
www.darkquestbooks.com

ISBN (trade paper): 978-0-9796901-9-8
ISBN (eBook): pending

Previously published in another edition by Marietta Publishing ©2007.

Design: Mike and Danielle McPhail
Cover Art: Mike McPhail, McP Concepts
Copy Editing: Mike and Danielle McPhail
www.mcp-concepts.com
www.sidhenadaire.com
www.milscifi.com

Contents

This book is dedicated to the memory of:

Charles G. Weekes
1960 - 1992

United States Navy
A sailor and submariner
who served his country in its time of need.

A science fiction writer
who envisioned in the grandeur of galactic warfare.

Creator of:

Juan Carlos Mendez,
Commander of the Federal Empires',
Stateworld Class Galacticruiser
C2IOOD UCNS. Arcturus
(United Celestial Navy Ship)

CRYPTIC

Jack McDevitt

I T WAS AT THE BOTTOM OF THE SAFE IN A BULKY MANILA ENVELOPE. I NEARLY TOSSED IT INTO THE TRASH with the stacks of other documents, tapes, and assorted flotsam left over from the Project.

Had it been cataloged, indexed in some way, I'm sure I would have. But the envelope was blank, save for an eighteen-year-old date scrawled in the lower right hand corner, and beneath it, the notation "40 gh."

Out on the desert, lights were moving. That would be Brackett fine-tuning the Array for Orrin Hopkins, who was then beginning the observations that would lead, several years later, to new departures in pulsar theory. I envied Hopkins. He was short, round, bald, a man unsure of himself, whose explanations were invariably interspersed with giggles. He was a ridiculous figure, yet he bore the stamp of genius. And people would remember his ideas long after the residence hall named for me at Carrollton had crumbled.

If I had not recognized my own limits and conceded any hope of immortality (at least of this sort), I certainly did so when I accepted the director's position at Sandage. Administration pays better than being an active physicist, but it is death to ambition.

And a Jesuit doesn't even get that advantage.

In those days, the Array was still modest: forty parabolic antennas, each thirty-six meters across. They were on tracks, of course, independently movable, forming a truncated cross. They had, for two decades, been the heart of SETI, the Search for Extra-Terrestrial Intelligence. Now, with the Project abandoned, they were being employed for more useful, if mundane, purposes.

Even that relatively unsophisticated system was good. As Hutching Chaney once remarked, the Array could pick up the cough of an automobile ignition on Mars.

I circled the desk and fell into the uncomfortable wooden chair we'd inherited from the outgoing regime. The packet was sealed with tape that had become brittle and loose around the edges. I tore it open.

It was a quarter past ten. I'd worked through my dinner and the evening hours, bored, drinking coffee, debating the wisdom in coming out here from JPL. The increase in responsibility was a good career move; but I knew now that Harry Cooke would never lay his hands on a new particle.

I was committed for two years at Sandage, two years of working out schedules and worrying about insurance, two years of dividing meals between the installation's sterile cafeteria and Jimmy's Amoco Restaurant on Route 85. Then, if all went well, I could expect another move up, perhaps to Georgetown.

I'd have traded it all for Hopkins's future.

I shook out six magnetic disks onto the desk. They were in individual sleeves, of the type that many installations had once used to record electromagnetic radiation. The disks were numbered and dated over a three-day period in 2001, two years earlier than the date on the envelope.

Each was marked "Procyon."

In back, Hopkins and two associates were hunched over monitors. Brackett, having finished his job, was at his desk with his head buried in a book.

I was pleased to discover that the disks were compatible to the Mark VIs. I inserted one, tied in a vocorder to get a hard copy, and went over to join the Hopkins group while the thing ran. They were talking about plasma. I listened for a time, got lost, noted that everyone around me (save the grinning little round man) also got lost, and strolled back to my computer.

The trace drew its green-and-white pictures smoothly on the Mark VI display, and pages of hard copy clicked out of the vocorder. Something in the needle geometry scattering across the recording paper drew my attention. Like an elusive name, it drifted just beyond reach.

Beneath a plate of the Andromeda Galaxy, a coffee pot simmered. I could hear the distant drone of a plane, probably out of Luke Air Force Base. Behind me, Hopkins and his people were laughing at something.

There were patterns in the recording.

They materialized slowly, identical clusters of impulses. The signals were artificial. Procyon.

The laughter, the plane, the coffee pot, a radio that had been left on somewhere . . . everything squeezed down to a possibility.

More likely Phoenix, I thought.

Frank Myers had been SETI Director since Ed Dickinson's death twelve years before. I reached him next morning in San Francisco.

"No," he said without hesitation. "Someone's idea of a joke, Harry."

"It was in your safe, Frank."

"That damned safe's been there forty years. Might be anything in it. Except messages from Mars . . . "

I thanked him and hung up.

It had been a long night: I'd taken the hard copy to bed and, by 5:00 A.M., had identified more than forty distinct pulse patterns. The signal appeared to be continuous: that is, it had been an ongoing transmission with no indication of beginning or end, but only irregular breaches of the type that would result from atmospherics and, of course, the long periods during which the target would have been below the horizon.

It was clearly a reflected terrestrial transmission: radio waves bounce around considerably. But why seal the error two years later and put it in the safe?

Procyon is a yellow-white class F3 binary, absolute magnitude 2.8, once worshipped in Babylon and Egypt. (What hasn't been worshipped in Egypt?) Distance from Earth: 11.3 light-years.

In the outer office, Beth Cooper typed, closed filing drawers, spoke with visitors.

The obvious course of action was to use the Array. Listen to Procyon at 40 gigahertz, or all across the spectrum for that matter, and find out if it was, indeed, saying something.

On the intercom, I asked Beth if any open time had developed on the system. "No," she said crisply. "We have nothing until August of next year."

That was no surprise. The facility had booked quickly when its resources were made available to the astronomical community on more than the limited basis that had prevailed for twenty years. Anyone wishing to use the radiotelescope had to plan far in advance. How could I get hold of the Array for a couple hours?

I asked her to come into my office . . .

Beth Cooper had come to Sandage from San Augustin with SETI during the big move twenty years before. She'd been secretary to three directors: Hutching Chaney, who had built Sandage; his longtime friend, Ed Dickinson; and finally, after Dickinson's death, Frank Myers, a young man on the move, who'd stayed too long with the Project, and who'd been reportedly happy to see it strangled. In any case, Myers had contributed to its demise by his failure to defend it.

I'd felt he was right, of course, though for the wrong reason. It had been painful to see the magnificent telescope at Sandage denied, by and large, to the scientific community while its grotesque hunt for the Little Green Man signal went on. I think there were few of us not happy to see it end.

Beth had expected to lose her job. But she knew her way around the facility, had a talent for massaging egos, and could spell. A devout Lutheran, she had adapted cautiously to working for a priest and, oddly, seemed to have taken offense that I did not routinely walk around with a Roman collar.

I asked one or two questions about the billing methods of the local utilities, and then commented, as casually as I could manage, that it was unfortunate the Project had not succeeded.

Beth looked more like a New York librarian than a secretary at a desert installation. Her hair was silver-gray. She wore steel-rimmed glasses on a long silver chain. She was moderately heavy, but her carriage and her diction were impeccable, imbuing her with the quality that stage people call presence.

Her eyes narrowed to hard black beads at my remark. "Dr. Dickinson said any number of times that none of us would live to see results. Everyone attached to the program, even the janitors, knew that." She wasn't a woman given to shrugs, but the sudden flick in those dark eyes matched the effect. "I'm glad Dr. Dickinson didn't live to see it terminated." That was followed by an uncomfortable silence. "I don't blame you, Doctor," she said at length, referring to my public position that the facility was being underutilized.

I dropped my eyes and tried to smile reassuringly. It must have been ludicrous. Her severe features softened. I showed her the envelope.

"Do you recognize the writing?"

She barely glanced at it. "It's Dr. Dickinson's."

"Are you sure? I didn't think Dickinson came to the Project until Hutch Chaney's retirement. That was '13, wasn't it?"

"He took over as Director then. But he was an operating technician under Dr. Chaney for, oh, ten or twelve years before that." Her eyes glowed when she spoke of Dickinson.

"I never met him," I said.

"He was a fine man." She looked past me, over my shoulder, her features pale. "If we hadn't lost him, we might not have lost the Project."

"If it matters," I added gently.

"If it matters."

She was right about Dickinson. He was articulate, a persuasive speaker, author of books on various subjects, and utterly dedicated to SETI. He might well have kept the Project afloat despite the cessation of federal funds and the increasing clamor among his colleagues for more time at the facility. But Dickinson was twelve years dead now. He'd returned to Massachusetts at Christmas, as was his custom. After a snowstorm, he'd gone out to help shovel a neighbor's driveway and his heart had failed.

At the time, I was at Georgetown. I can still recall my sense of a genius who had died too soon. He had possessed a vast talent, but no discipline; he had churned through his career hurling sparks in all directions. He had touched everything, but nothing had ever ignited. Particularly not SETI.

"Beth, was there ever a time they thought they had an LGM?"

"The Little Green Man Signal?" She shook her head. "No, I don't think so. They were always picking up echoes and things. But nothing ever came close. Either it was KCOX in Phoenix, or a Japanese trawler in the middle of the Pacific."

"Never anything that didn't fit those categories?"

One eyebrow rose slightly. "Never anything they could prove. If they couldn't pin it down, they went back later and tried to find it again. One way or another, they eliminated everything." Or, she must be thinking, we wouldn't be standing here having this conversation.

Beth's comments implied that suspect signals had been automatically stored. Grateful that I had not yet got around to purging obsolete data, I discovered that was indeed the case, and ran a search covering the entire time period back to the Procyon reception in 2011. I was looking for a similar signal.

I got a surprise.

There was no match. There was also no record of the Procyon reception itself. That meant presumably it had been accounted for and discarded.

Then why, two years later, had the recordings been sealed and placed in the safe? Surely no explanation would have taken that long.

SETI had assumed that any LGM signal would be a deliberate attempt to communicate, that an effort would therefore be made by the originator to create intelligibility, and that the logical way to do that was to employ a set of symbols representing universal constants: the atomic weight of hydrogen, perhaps, or the value of pi.

But the move to Sandage had also been a move to more sophisticated, and considerably more sensitive, equipment. The possibility developed that the Project would pick up a slopover signal, a transmission of alien origin, but intended only for local receivers. Traffic of that nature could be immeasurably difficult to interpret.

If the packet in the safe was anything at all, it was surely of this latter type. Forty gigahertz is not an ideal frequency for interstellar communication. Moreover, the intercept was ongoing, formless, no numbered parts, nothing to assist translation.

I set the computer working on the text, using SETI's own language analysis program. Then I instructed Brackett to call me if anything developed, had dinner at Jimmy's, and went home.

There was no evidence of structure in the text. In English, one can expect to find a 'U' after a 'Q', or a vowel after a cluster of consonants. The aspirate is seldom doubled, nothing is ever tripled, and so on. But in the Procyon transmission, everything seemed utterly random.

The computer counted 256 distinct pulse patterns. Eight bits. Nothing recurred at sufficient intervals to be a space. And the frequency count of these pulse patterns, or characters, was flat; there was no quantitative difference in use from one to another. All appeared approximately the same number of times. If it was a language, it was a language with no discernible vowels.

I called Wes Phillips, who was then the only linguist I knew. Was it possible for a language to be structured in such a way?

"Oh, I don't think so. Unless you're talking about some sort of construct. Even then—" He paused. "Harry, I can give you a whole series of reasons in maybe six different disciplines why languages need high and low frequency letters. To have a flat 'curve,' a language would have to be deliberately designed that way, and it would have to be non-oral. But what practical value would it have? Why bother?"

Ed Dickinson had been an enigma. During the series of political crises that engulfed the nation after the turn of the century, he'd earned an international reputation as a diplomat, and as an eloquent defender of reason and restraint. Everyone agreed that he had a mind of the first rank. Yet, in his chosen field, he accomplished little. And eventually he'd gone to work for the Project, historically only a stepping-stone to serious effort. But he'd stayed.

Why?

Hutching Chaney was a different matter. A retired naval officer, he'd indulged in physics almost as a pastime. His political connections had been instrumental in getting Sandage built, and his assignment as Director was rumored to have been a reward for services rendered during the rough and tumble of congressional politics.

He possessed a plodding sort of competence. He was fully capable of grasping, and visualizing, extreme complexity. But he lacked insight and imagination, the ability to draw the subtle inference. After his retirement from Sandage, Chaney had gone to an emeritus position at MIT, which he'd held for five years.

He was a big man, more truck driver than physicist. Despite advancing age—he was then in his 70's—and his bulk, he spoke and moved with energy. His hair was full and black. His light gray eyes suggested the shrewdness of a professional politician, and he possessed the confident congeniality of a man who had never failed at anything.

We were in his home in Somerville, Massachusetts, a stone and glass house atop sweeping lawns. It was not an establishment that a retired physicist would be expected to inhabit. Chaney's moneyed background was evident.

He clapped a big hand on my shoulder and pulled me through one of those stiff, expensive living rooms that no one ever wants to sit in, into a paneled, leather-upholstered den at the rear of the house. "Martha," he said to someone I couldn't see, "would you bring us some port?" He looked at me for acquiescence.

"Fine," I said. "It's been a long time, Hutch."

Books lined the walls, mostly engineering manuals, a few military and naval histories. An articulated steel gray model of the Lance dominated the fireplace shelf. That was the deadly hydrofoil which, built at Chaney's urging, had contributed to a multi-purpose navy that was simultaneously lethal, flexible, and relatively cheap.

"The Church is infiltrating everywhere," he said. "How are things at Sandage, Harry?"

I described some of the work in progress. He listened with interest.

A young woman arrived with a bottle, two glasses, and a plate of cheese. "Martha comes in three times a week," Chaney said after she'd left the room. He smiled, winked, dipped a stick of cheese into the mustard, and bit it neatly in half. "You needn't worry, Harry. I'm not capable of getting into trouble anymore. What brings you to Massachusetts?"

I extracted the vocordings from my briefcase and handed them across to him. I watched patiently as he leafed through the thick sheaf of paper, and saw with satisfaction his change of expression.

"You're kidding, Harry," he said. "Somebody really found one? When'd it happen?"

"Twenty years ago," I said, passing him the envelope and the original disks.

He turned them over in his hands. "You're not serious? There's a mistake somewhere."

"It was in the safe," I said.

He shook his head. "Doesn't much matter where it was. Nothing like this ever happened."

"Then what is it?"

"Damned if I have any idea."

We sat not talking while Chaney continued to flip pages, grunting. He seemed to have forgotten his wine. "You run this yourself?" he asked.

I nodded.

"Hell of a lot of trouble for somebody to go to for a joke. Were the computers able to read any of it? No? That's because it's gibberish." He stared at the envelope. "But it is Ed's handwriting."

"Would Dickinson have any reason to keep such a thing quiet?"

"Ed? No. Dickinson least of all. No one wanted to hear a signal more than he did. He wanted it so badly he invested his life in the Project."

"But could he, physically, have done this? Could he have picked up the LGM? Could he have done it without anyone else knowing? Was he good enough with computers to cover his tracks?"

"This is pointless. Yes, he could have done it. And you could walk through Braintree without your pants."

A light breeze was coming through a side window, billowing the curtains. It was cool and pleasant, unusual for Massachusetts in August. Some kids were playing halfball out on the street.

"Forty megahertz," he said. "Sounds like a satellite transmission."

"That wouldn't have taken two years to figure out, would it? Why keep the disks?"

"Why not? I expect if you go down into the storeroom you'll find all kinds of relics."

Outside, there was a sound like approaching thunder, exploding suddenly into an earsplitting screech. A stripped-down T-Bolt skidded by, scattering the ballplayers. An arm hung leisurely out the driver's side. The car took the corner stop sign at about 45. A couple of fingers went up, but otherwise the game resumed as though nothing had happened.

"All the time," Chaney said. His back to the window, he hadn't bothered to look around. "Cops can't keep up with them anymore."

"Why was Dickinson so interested in the Project?"

"Ed was a great man." His face clouded somewhat, and I wondered if the port hadn't drawn his emotions close to the surface. "You'd have to know him. You and he would have got along fine. He had a taste for the metaphysical, and I guess the Project was about as close as he could get."

"How do you mean?"

"Did you know he spent two years in a seminary? Yes, somewhere outside Philadelphia. He was an altar boy who eventually wound up at Harvard. And that was that."

"You mean he lost his faith?"

"Oh, yes. The world became a dark place, full of disaster. He always seemed to have the details on the latest pogrom, or viral outbreak, or drive-by murder. There are only two kinds of people, he told me once: atheists, and folks who haven't been paying attention. But he always retained that fine mystical sense of purpose that you drill into your best kids, a notion that things are somehow ordered. When I knew him, he wouldn't have presumed to pray to anyone. But he had all the drive of a missionary, and the same conviction of—" He dropped his head back on the leather upholstery and tried to seize a word from the ceiling. "—Destiny."

"Ed wasn't like most physicists. He was competent in a wide range of areas. He wrote on foreign affairs for *Commentary* and *Harper's*; he wrote on ornithology and systems analysis, on Malcolm Muggeridge, and Edward Gibbon."

He swung easily out of his chair and reached for a pair of fat matched volumes in mud-brown covers. It was *The Decline and Fall of the Roman Empire*, the old Modern Library edition. "He's the only person I've ever known who's actually read the thing." He turned the cover of volume one so that I could see the inscription:

> For Hutch,
> In the fond hope that we can hold off the potherbs and the pigs.
>
> Ed

"He gave it to me when I left SETI."

"Seems like an odd gift. Have you read it?"

He laughed off the question. "You'd need a year."

"What's the business about the potherbs and pigs?"

He rose and walked casually to the far wall. There were photos of naval vessels and aircraft, of Chaney and President Fine, of the Sandage complex. He seemed to screw his vision into the latter. "I don't remember. It's a phrase from the book. He explained it to me at the time. But . . . " He held his hands outward, palms up.

"Hutch, thanks." I got up to go.

"There was no signal," he said. "I don't know where these recordings came from, but Ed Dickinson would have given anything for a contact."

"Hutch, is it possible that Dickinson might have been able to translate the text? If there had been one?"

"Not if you couldn't. He had the same program."

I don't like cities.

Dickinson's books were all out of print, and the used bookstores were clustered in Cambridge. Even then, the outskirts of Boston, like the city proper, were littered with broken glass and discarded newspapers. Surly kids milled outside bars. Windows everywhere were smashed or boarded. I went through a red light at one intersection rather than learn the intentions of an approaching band of ragged children with hard eyes. (One could scarcely call them children, though I doubt there was one over twelve.) Profanity covered the crumbling brick walls as high as a hand could reach. Much of it was misspelled.

Boston had been Dickinson's city. I wondered what the great humanist thought when he drove through these streets.

I found only one of his books: *Malcolm Muggeridge: Faith and Despair*. The store also had a copy of *The Decline and Fall*. On impulse, I bought it.

I was glad to get back to the desert.

We were entering a period of extraordinary progress, during which we finally began to understand the mechanics of galactic structure. McCue mapped the core of the Milky Way, Osterberger developed his unified field concepts, and Schauer constructed his celebrated revolutionary hypothesis on the nature of time. Then, on a cool morning in October, a team from Cal Tech announced that they had a new set of values for hyperinflation.

In the midst of all this, we had an emergency. One night in late September, Earl Barlow, who was directing the Cal Tech groups, suffered a mild heart attack. I arrived just before the EMTs, at about 2:00 a.m.

While the ambulance carrying Barlow started down the mountain, his people watched helplessly, drinking coffee, too upset to work. The opportunity didn't catch me entirely unprepared. I gave Brackett his new target. The blinking lights of the emergency vehicle were hardly out of sight before the parabolas swung round and fastened on Procyon.

But there was only the disjointed crackle of interstellar static.

I took long walks on the desert at night. The parabolas are lovely in the moonlight. Occasionally, the stillness is broken by the whine of an electric motor, and the antennas slide gracefully along their tracks. It was, I thought, a new Stonehenge of softly curving shapes and fluid motion.

The Muggeridge book was a slim volume. It was not biographical, but rather an analysis of the philosopher's conviction that the West has a death wish. It was the old argument that God had been replaced by science, that man had gained knowledge of a trivial sort, and as a result lost purpose.

It was, on the whole, depressing reading. In his conclusion, Dickinson argued that truth will not wait on human convenience, that if man cannot adapt to a neutral universe, then that universe will indeed come to seem hostile. We must make do with what we have and accept truth wherever it leads. The modern cathedral is the radiotelescope.

Sandage was involved in the verification procedure for McCue's work, and for the already controversial Cal Tech equations. All that is another story. What is significant is that it got me thinking about verifications, and I realized I'd overlooked something. There'd been no match for the Procyon readings anywhere in the data banks since the original reception. But the Procyon recordings might themselves have been the confirmation of an earlier signal!

It took five minutes to run the search. There were two hits.

Both were fragments, neither more than fifteen minutes long; but there was enough of each to reduce the probability of error to less than one percent.

The first occurred three weeks prior to the Procyon reception.

The second went back to 2007, a San Augustin observation. Both were at 40 gigahertz. Both had identical pulse patterns. But there was an explosive difference, sedately concealed in the target information line. The 2007 transmission had come while the radiotelescope was locked on Sirius!

When I got back to my office, I was trembling.

Sirius and Procyon were only a few light-years apart. *My God*, I kept thinking, *they exist! And they have interstellar travel!*

I spent the balance of the day stumbling around, trying to immerse myself in fuel usage reports and budget projections. But mostly what I did was watch the desert light grow hard in the curtains, and then fade. The two volumes of Edward Gibbon were propped between a *Webster's* and some black binders. The books were thirty years old, identical to the set in Chaney's den. Some of the pages, improperly cut, were still joined at the edges.

I opened the first volume, approximately in the middle, and began to read. Or tried to. But Ed Dickinson kept crowding out the Romans. Finally I gave it up, took the book, and went home.

There was duplicate bridge in town, and I lost myself in that for five hours. Then, in bed, still somewhat dazed, I tried *The Decline and Fall* again.

It was not the dusty rollcall of long-dead emperors that I had expected. The emperors are there, stabbing and throttling and blundering. And occasionally trying to improve things. But the fish-hawkers are there too. And the bureaucrats and the bishops.

It's a world filled with wine and legionnaires' sweat, mismanagement, arguments over Jesus, and the inability to transfer power, all played out to the ruthless drumbeat of dissolution. An undefined historical tide, stemmed occasionally by a hero, or a sage, rolls over men and events, washing them toward the sea. (During the later years, I wondered, did Roman kids run down matrons in flashy imported chariots? Were the walls of Damascus defiled by profanity?)

In the end, when the barbarians push at the outer rim of empire, it is only a hollow wreck that crashes down.

Muggeridge had been there.

And Dickinson, the altar boy, amid the fire and waste of the imperial city, must have suffered a second loss of faith.

We had an electrical failure one night. It has nothing to do with this story except that it resulted in my being called in at 4:00 a.m., not to restore the power, which required a good electrician, but to pacify some angry people from New York, and to be able to say, in my report, that I had been on the spot.

These things attended to, I went outside.

At night, the desert is undisturbed by color or motion. It's a composition of sand, rock, and star; a frieze, a Monet, uncomplicated, unchanging. It's reassuring, in an age when little else seems stable. The orderly mid-twentieth century universe had long since disintegrated into a plethora of neutron galaxies, colliding black holes, time reversals, and God knows what.

The desert is solid underfoot. Predictable. A reproach to the quantum mechanics that reflect a quicksand cosmos in which physics merges with Plato.

Close on the rim of the sky, guarding their mysteries, Sirius and Procyon, the bright pair, sparkled. The arroyos are dry at that time of year, shadowy ripples in the landscape. The moon was in its second quarter. Beyond the administration building, the parabolas were limned in silver.

My cathedral.

My Stonehenge.

And while I sat, sipping a Coors, and thinking of lost cities and altar boys and frequency counts, I suddenly understood the significance of Chaney's last remark! Of course Dickinson had not been able to read the transmission. That was the point!

I needed Chaney.

I called him in the morning, and flew out in the afternoon. He met me at Logan, and we drove toward Gloucester. "There's a good Italian restaurant," he said. And then, without taking his eyes off the road: "What's this about?"

I'd brought the second Gibbon volume with me, and I held it up for him to see. He blinked.

It was early evening, cold, wet, with the smell of approaching winter. Freezing rain pelted the windshield. The sky was gray, heavy, sagging into the city.

"Before I answer any questions, Hutch, I'd like to ask a couple. What can you tell me about military cryptography?"

He grinned. "Not much. The little I do know is probably classified." A tractor-trailer lumbered past, straining, spraying water across the windows. "What, specifically, are you interested in?"

"How complex are the Navy's codes? I know they're nothing like cryptograms, but what sort of general structure do they have?"

"First off, Harry, they're not codes. Monoalphabetic systems are codes. Like the cryptograms you mentioned. The letter 'G' always turns up, say, as an 'M'. But in military and diplomatic cryptography, the 'G' will be a different character every time it appears. And the encryption alphabet isn't usually limited to letters; we use numbers, dollar signs, ampersands, even spaces." We splashed onto a ramp and joined the Interstate. It was elevated and we looked across rows of bleak rooftops. "Even the shape of individual words is concealed."

"How?"

"By encrypting the spaces."

I knew the answer to the next question before I asked it. "If the encryption alphabet is absolutely random, which I assume it would have to be, the frequency count would be flat. Right?"

"Yes. Given sufficient traffic, it would have to be."

"One more thing, Hutch. A sudden increase in traffic will alert anyone listening that something is happening even if he can't read the text. How do you hide that?"

"Easy. We transmit a continuous signal, twenty-four hours a day. Sometimes it's traffic, sometimes it's garbage. But you can't tell the difference."

God have mercy on us, I thought. Poor Dickinson.

We sat at a small corner table well away from the main dining area. I shivered in wet shoes and a damp sweater. A small candle guttered cheerfully in front of us.

"Are we still talking about Procyon?" he asked.

I nodded. "The same pattern was received twice, three years apart, prior to the Procyon reception."

"But that's not possible." Chaney leaned forward intently. "The computer would have matched them automatically. We'd have known."

"I don't think so." Half a dozen prosperous, overweight men in topcoats had pushed in and were jostling each other in the small entry. "The two hits were on different targets. They would have looked like an echo."

Chaney reached across the table and gripped my wrist, knocking over a cup. "Son of a bitch," he said. "Are you suggesting somebody's moving around out there?"

"I don't think Ed Dickinson had any doubts."

"Why would he keep it secret?"

I'd placed the book on the table at my left hand. It rested there, its plastic cover reflecting the glittering red light of the candle. "Because they're at war."

The color drained from Chaney's face, and it took on a pallor that was almost ghastly in the lurid light.

"He believed," I continued, "he really believed that mind equates to morality, intelligence to compassion. And what did he find after a lifetime? A civilization that had conquered the stars, but not its own passions and stupidities."

A tall young waiter presented himself. We ordered port and pasta.

"You don't really know there's a war going on out there," Chaney objected.

"Hostility, then. Secrecy on a massive scale, as this must be, has ominous implications. Dickinson would have saved us all with a vision of order and reason . . . "

The gray eyes met mine. They were filled with pain. Two adolescent girls in the next booth were giggling. The wine came.

"What has *The Decline and Fall* to do with it?"

"It became his Bible. He was chilled to the bone by it. You should read it, but with caution. It's capable of strangling the soul. Dickinson was a rationalist. He recognized the ultimate truth in the Roman tragedy: that once expansion has stopped, decay is constant and irreversible. Every failure of reason or virtue loses more ground.

"I haven't been able to find his book on Gibbon, but I know what he'll say: that Gibbon was not writing only of the Romans, nor of the British of his own time. He was writing about us. Hutch, take a look around. Tell me we're not sliding toward a dark age. Think how that knowledge must have affected him."

We drank silently for a few minutes. Time locked in place, and we sat unmoving, the world frozen around us.

"Did I tell you," I said at last, "that I found the reference for his inscription? He must have had great respect for you." I opened the book to the conclusion, and turned it for him to read:

The forum of the Roman people, where they assembled to enact their laws, and elect their magistrates, is now enclosed for the cultivation of potherbs, or thrown open for the reception of swine and buffaloes.

Chaney stared disconsolately at me. "It's all so hard to believe."

"A man can survive a loss of faith in the Almighty," I said, "provided he does not also lose faith in himself. That was Dickinson's real tragedy. He came to believe exclusively in radiotelescopes, the way some people do in religions."

The food, when it came, went untasted. "What are you going to do, Harry?"

"About the Procyon text? About the probability that we have quarrelsome neighbors? I'm not afraid of that kind of information; all it means is that where you find intelligence, you will probably find stupidity. Anyway, it's time Dickinson got credit for his discovery." And, I thought, maybe it'll even mean a footnote for me.

I lifted my glass in a mock toast, but Chaney did not respond. We faced each other in an uncomfortable tableau. "What's wrong?" I asked. "Thinking about Dickinson?"

"That too." The candle glinted in his eyes. "Harry, do you think they have a SETI project?"

"Possibly. Why?"

"I was wondering if your aliens know we're here. This restaurant isn't much further from Sirius than Procyon is. Maybe you better eat up."

First published in Asimov's, April 1983. Copyright 1996 Cryptic, Inc.

PETER POWER ARMOR

John C. Wright

LET ME TELL YOU A STORY ABOUT A GIRL NAMED ETHNE. I DIDN'T LIKE HER WHEN I FIRST met her, but all that is changed now.

I found the power-armor I used to wear as a child in the wall-space behind my parent's attic, behind a door paneled to look like part of the wainscoting. No dust disturbed this miniature clean-room; no looters had found it here, not in all the years.

The fact that smooth white light filled the room when the silent door opened filled me with a premonition. I stepped inside and saw, (as I had not dared hope) that an umbilicus connected the little suit to sockets in the wall. The energy-box above the socket was stamped with three black triangles in a yellow circle.

Behind me, in the main attic space, I could hear the little brat named Ethne grunt a little high-pitched grunt as she picked up a crow-bar. A moment later there was a shivering crash as she tossed it through one of the living stain-glassed dormer windows. I remembered the day Mother had purchased those windows, grown one molecule at a time by a nano-mathematician artist. Those had been days of sunshine, and even the upper windows no one saw had been works of fine art, charged with life.

You see, Ethne was a naughty, silly girl. It is really not her fault. She was raised to be that way.

"Darling," I said, trying to keep my voice even. "Don't kill the windows. They are special. They were bulletproof, once, back before their cohesion faded. They're antiques, and cannot reproduce. It makes them the last of their kind."

Ethne was bright enough to ask a question: "So what? What makes them special?" It is always good to ask questions.

I said gently: "You see how the old building had their windows facing outward?

Not like modern buildings. Remember your school? All the windows only face inside, toward the courtyard. And your dorm is the same way, isn't it? You can tell a lot a about a culture by where they put their windows."

The courtyard-based construction of modern buildings reminds me of European designs. I don't really like Europe.

I heard little Ethne whine to the matron: "Mother Hechler! Mr. Paine is trying to oppress me again!"

It was not my real name. I always introduced myself as Thomas Paine, these days. No one ever caught the reference, not even people my age.

The chestplate of the power-armor was set with large phosphorescent buttons, with little cartoon-character faces to indicate the function options. I hit the Peter Power-Armor Power-on Pumpkin with my thumb. There was a goo-ga flourish of toy trumpet noise, a whisper of servomotors, and the suit stood up.

I know Ethne did not know her parents. I am guessing the age at about seven years old. Her mother, her real mother, had been a lovely, lively, caring woman, smart as a devil and with a sense of humor to match. That sense of humor managed to get her declared an unfit parent.

The father, Geoffrey, had been an environmental engineer. Very bright man. He had written papers, back before the Diebacks, questioning whether the trends showed a General Global Warming or a General Cooling. Those papers had cropped up again after Ethne was born. Geoffrey had been sterilized by the committee in charge of the First Redistribution; they believed in Global Warming. He had been made to vanish by the Second. They believed in Cooling.

And little Ethne was just not as bright as Geoffrey's daughter should have been. I knew the ugly reason why.

The helmet came only about to my waist, even when the armor was upright on its stubby legs. It looked like a miniature King-Arthur's knight, although I remember other attachments could make it look like a deep-sea diver's suit or a fireman. The smart-metal was made of a flex of microscopic interlocking strands, and I saw telescopic segments at the limb-joints and breastplate-seams, enabling the suit to expand to fit a growing child.

I heard, behind and below me, a soggy, heavy noise as the stairs whined under the bulk of Mrs. Hechler's footsteps. I heard her pant. She said, "Ethne!" she was calling up the stairs. Hechler was too inert, it seemed, to make it all the way. "Stop familiarizing with the People's Helpers. You are to call him 'Janitor' or 'Shit-sweeper.' We don't use his name, moppet: it makes them uppity."

Tiny xylophone-notes came from inside the helmet as the suit ran through its systems check. I could see the colors of a puppet-show reflected backward in the faceplate during the warm-up, as big-eyed rabbits and ducks in sailor suits pantomimed out safety messages as each suit function went through its automatic check.

It may seem absurd, but tears came to my eyes when Battery Bunny turned into a skeleton-silhouette surrounded by twinkling lightning-bolts above the words: KEEP FINGERS CLEAR OF THE RECHARGE SOCKET! Battery Bunny had once been a best playmate of mine, since I had had no real, non-virtual friends.

(Billy Worthemer was a real friend of mine. A real flesh and blood boy. Lots of blood. I will tell you about him if I have time. But, after Billy, no, after that I had had no real friends, except for Bunny. Well, maybe one.) Good old loyal bunny. How could I have forgotten him?

I wiped my eyes. At the same time, to cover the xylophone-noise of the suit-check, I was saying loudly: "Matron Hechler! The student-child is destroying property of the state! This may lead to bad habits later!"

Another soggy noise as Hechler climbed another step. She wheezed a moment, then said, "Let her have her fun. This stuff is from the Time of Greed. It's worthless. Go ahead, Ethne."

I heard a dull giggle, and then more smashing.

I twisted and removed the adult-override key from the armor's chestplate, picked up the remote handset from the socket, and thumbed the test button on the microwave relay. The LED lit up. I tapped my fingers on the handset and the little armored suit did a silent little jig of joy. Such elegant controls! Such a well-made machine!

Another button made Mr. Don't-Point-Me come out of his holster. I had forgotten, or I never knew, that the holster had a child-safety relay on it, which made an alarm-noise blatt from the handset. With one thumb I pushed the suppress button on the handset to kill the noise. With the other I reached for the larger, colored controls on the chestplate. I remembered that the Deadly Donkey button armed the lethal rounds. I hit Sleepy Sancho Pancake, and watched as a clip of narcoleptic darts was jacked into the chamber. The little armor twirled the gun on its gauntlet-finger and slid Mr. Don't-Point-Me back into the holster. I had programmed that little flourish in, when I was a child. I had seen Laser Cowboy do it on STV, and I had practiced and practiced in front of a mirror. That was my hand motion.

Hechler had heard the alarm. Her voice came nearer, sounding angry, "What's that noise?"

I said in a loud happy voice, "Ethne! Come quick!"

Ethne, sullenly, "What . . . ?! Is a machine? They're bad for you."

"Never mind," I called out. I heard her little footsteps coming closer. "I'll just keep it all for myself."

Ethne's footsteps sped up. Any adult who cannot outwit a seven-year-old should turn in his license.

I also heard the Matron's voice coming at a lumbering trot. Stairs squealed, and then the attic floorboards protested. "What—what's that light up there!"

I had to get her to come up. I said loudly, "It should be obvious what it is, you soggy old fart! I've found a working light. Don't you have eyes? I must say that I am continually amazed, now that each village and hamlet is divided into work zones and care zones for the communal raising and nurture of children, at the consistently low quality of the substitute parents involved."

Ethne was in the doorway, now. Her eyes grew big and round. I remember days when children often had such looks on their faces, at birthday parties, or at Christmas. Back when we had Christmas.

I took Ethne by the shoulder and guided her toward the armor. My other hand pushed the introduction menu sequence with the handset. The armor turned toward Ethne, evidently recognizing her as having the infrared profile and radar-silhouette of a child. It performed a perfect courtly bow toward her. She watched in awe as it took her hand and bent over it, pretending to kiss it.

And the little brat (her brattyness forgotten, or on hold) actually blushed and looked pleased, a modest princess. She was utterly charmed. I had to smile.

I continued talking the way I used to talk, in a loud voice, "But we cannot have a society where all child-rearing is public, without expecting it to end up in the same state as our public bathrooms. And what kind of low, common, ignorant folk will volunteer to serve as wardens for children not their own, whom they cannot adopt or make their own? Who would be willing to raise a child by rulebook? By committee? I suspect those who cannot get jobs as prison guards . . . "

But that was enough. Mrs. Hechler was here, red-faced, and angry enough that she had forgotten to use her radio-phone to call Jerry. Jerry, downstairs, was not a Regulator; he was an Infant Proctor, which was something between a Baby Sitter and the Bull. But I think he was packing heat.

Maybe she was too dumb to call him; too dumb to think I was dangerous. Or maybe her phone was broken again.

Her eyes grew round when she saw the lights, the atomic-power symbol on the wall, the brass-and-gold little armored figure. I do not think she recognized what the armor was; I think she thought it was a statue or a toy or something.

A woman raised in her generation, of course, could not understand the kind of folks people of my parent's generation were.

And so she stepped into the room. She did not know what kind of thing Peter was; or what kind of person I am.

Let me explain it to you. I don't know how much room is in the file: I'll try to be brief. But I have to tell you the way it was.

My dad was there the day the rules of war changed. He was about eight years old. He had climbed a tree, and found a little green-and-brown colored aerosol spray-can wedged into the branches, pointing over the sidewalk below. I remember him telling me how bright and sunny the day was, how the sidewalk sparkled, how the people looked so happy, so normal, when they walked by, walking dogs, carrying groceries, herding children, balancing schoolbooks on heads.

Every time someone walked by, the little aerosol can button went down. Activated by a motion sensor. Dad put his hand in front of the nozzle, and felt a wet invisible spray touch his palm. He sniffed it; it was odorless. He wiped the sticky wetness off on the green-and-brown label of the can.

His district was one of the few with a death toll under one hundred. A day or two later, a swarm of self-propelled smart-bullets, maybe launched from a passing crop-duster, maybe mortar-shot off the back of a flatbed truck, swept through the area, and homed in on everything which had been tagged by the invisible radio-active mist.

One of the bullets struck the aerosol can, of course, so that no further tagging was done, and the second and third wave of smart-bullets which came the next day, and the next week, found no targets.

Everyone who walked by on the sidewalk that day—Dad used to tell me their names, they were his neighbors and playmates—was gone.

When I was young, and played with my Dad, he used to pretend to be Captain Hook. His prostethic was actually a complex thing, that could open and close almost like a pair of fingers. But it did look like a hook.

The next generation of smart bullets were even smarter, smaller, and able to fly longer distances. With a shoulder-launched booster, a rifleman could throw a packet of smart bullets over the horizon.

And warfare wasn't warfare any more. No more gathering on battlefields, no more getting into big battleships, and steaming out to meet other battleships. No sir. Soldiers traveled in pairs, not in platoons. One rifleman to launch the bullets. He would sit in a tree, or wearing a diving suit and lay on the bottom of a lake or something. His partner, the forward observer, would walk into town with a laser pencil. He would sit on a park bench and pretend to eat a submarine sandwich or something, or smoke a cigarette—which was legal, back then—and point the laser pencil at a passer-by. A bullet from out of the sky would drop down and hit the target. In a crowd, who would hear the noise? Maybe he'd get two or three, he'd pack up his sandwich, walk down the street, find another bench.

You could launch smart bullets from a normal shotgun, or even a lead pipe. Heck, if you dropped one off a tall enough building, it could pick up enough speed for its lifting surfaces to get purchase, reach terminal velocity, and if your target was anywhere below the building, the bullet could angle over. There wouldn't even be the sound of a gunshot. Same thing dropping a boxful from a cropduster.

Those smart bullets were smart. They had memory metal jackets which could act like little tiny fins and ailerons, giving them some ability to correct their course in-flight when diving into the target. Some changed shape as they entered the target, swelling or dilating to change their cross-section. The could slim down their noses right before hitting bullet proof vests, to become armor-penetrating, and flattening their heads when they hit flesh to become dum-dums.

Mom told me her bridesmaid was shot during the wedding. The girl was standing too near an open window, and maybe her gown gave her a silhouette that some dumb smart bullet thought looked like a target. That was back when people still gathered in churches for weddings and stuff. Back when buildings still had open windows.

The pixel resolution on these weapons was not the greatest. Forty-nine times out of fifty they could not tell the difference between a school-child and a lamp-post, a passer-by, a shadow on the wall, a fire hydrant. So you'd have to shoot fifty-one bullets to make sure you hit a target.

Yes, I said a school-child. Target of choice, once the rules of war went away. Why? Well, the point of war is to use violence to terrify the enemy into submission; to break his will to resist. Right? The best place for violence was in a town; that's where the people are. The best place for terror is in a school; that's were the people gather all their children.

All their unarmed, unprotected, beloved, innocent children.

If you were a soldier, there was no point in looking for other soldiers to shoot at. They were all dressed like civilians, like you were, sitting on park benches, eating submarine sandwiches, or pretending to smoke. Or sitting up a tree thirty miles away;

or in a diving suit taking a rest on the bottom of a nearby lake, watching for a target-lock. No point in trying to shoot at soldiers. There were none to find.

I know what you're thinking. What about shooting the leaders? Assassinating the captains and colonels and commissars on the other side? Presidents, Premiers, Prime ministers?

Listen, honey, I'm running low on memory, so I'll try to make this quick, but it is complex—everything is tied into everything else. I'm trying to explain what kind of people your folks were, your real folks, and why they made a power- armored suit like this.

When the nature of war changed the nature of government changed. What is a government, anyway, besides a group of people in the business of winning wars and stopping fights, right? Even before when I was born, politicians had been using computer enhanced imagery to make their images on STV look younger, more com-manding, more handsome, less fat. Whatever. Guys with squeaky voices were given nice baritones. It was fake, but so what? We never minded if a politician did not write his own speeches, did we? Why should we mind what he really looked like, so long as he did his job?

Well, it was just a small step from cartoon-drawing over real politicians to replac-ing those politicians entirely with computer-generated talking heads. You see, the world when I was young was not divided into Haves and Have-nots. It was divided into Knowns and Unknowns.

When the nature of government changed, the nature of citizenship changed. The nature of wealth and power changed.

Not everyone was trying to shoot the kids, though. Thank God for that. When everything went away, when everything went bad, there were still some people who kept their heads. After my parents were killed, this family of Amish farmers found me, wandering the fields at night, still carrying my Mom's head. I guess I was out of my mind, a bit. Jeez! How old was I then? Younger than you.

My other real-time, real-life friend was Mr. Eister. He had taught me how to shoot, what to do during incoming-fire drills, how to check food for foreign substances after saying grace. I remember him as a tall man, tall as a mountain it seemed to me, who always wore an odd, old-fashioned wide-brimmed hat. When I was six, I had insisted the mansion-circuits make such a hat like that for me, which I insisted on wearing all the time, even to bed, even to church (we had churches back then.)

The only thing which could get me to take that damn hat off, was Mr. Eister him-self, when we were suiting up. I remember arguing with him that my helmet was big enough to allow me to wear the hat beneath it, if I scrunched it up a bit. He had ex-plained . . . once . . . that the extra fabric would prevent the helmet cushions from seating properly on my skull. When I hadn't listened he waited patiently till I suited up, then he struck me in the head with his gun-stock, knocking me from my feet and setting my ears ringing.

"English," (he always called me that,) "English, a hard-shot shell would conduct a thousand time more foot-pounds of force that that little tap." He had leaned over me to talk. "The only thing what keeps thy brains from being churned to jam during a fire-fight, lad, is that thy helm here can flex to deflect the shockwave into the exo-skeleton anchor-points. Which it cannot do if thee must wear thy hat; remove it."

Poor Mr. Eister. Someone posted a bounty on the Amish. Didn't like their ways, didn't like their looks, didn't like their farm carts blocking the road. Who knew why? Who gave a reason? I was in my armor when a flock of bullets dropped out of a clear blue sky and stuck the house, spreading jellied gasoline everywhere. I was cool and safe, surrounded by flames. Peter played jump-and-run music, so I could not hear the sound of my new family sizzling and screaming. I jumped and ran. With the Jack Rabbit toggle thrown, I could jump over a church steeple.

How could they get away with shooting at us?

It was the crypto, you see. Encryption. Encryption and digital money. Govern-ments did not bother raising and training armies. You did not need *esprit de corps* and unit cohesion to win a war any more. Governments just put out bounties over the Net, posted the reward and the bag they wanted on a public board in some neutral country. There was always a neutral country willing to carry the board.

The posting? Just a public announcement that decryption keys to a certain amount of digital cash would be sent out to anyone who could anonymously post a 'prediction' of how many people of a certain nation would be killed on a certain day. There was a third party verification system to confirm the kills, also encrypted both ways.

You see, with double-encryption, you could actually pay someone the digital cash, or even leave it laying around at a public bulletin board address, but anyone who picked it up could not spend it without unscrambling it. It was worthless and safe.

Each time someone downloaded a copy of your bag of cash to their personal sta-tion, a new unique key and counter-key would be generated automatically.

Let us say a hundred people, or a million, make copies of the scrambled cash. A hundred keys, or a million, are generated. Each personal to the person making the copy.

You send your counter-key back in to the government hiring you, along with what-ever proof you want that you've killed the number of people they wanted killed. You sent it in anonymously.

Once they have your unique counter key, they can publicly post the decryption for your unique key. They can shout the decrypt from the roof-tops; it doesn't do anyone any good but you. Unique means that you and only you can unscramble your copy of the cash bundle. Everyone else just has a string of garbled ones and zeros, meaning-less and worthless. You have a code which opens a credit line through a numbered Swiss bank account. You never meet your employer; he never meets you. The other party could not even help the police find you even if he wanted to.

And not just governments. Anyone who wanted anyone killed, for any reason or no reason. Someone posted bounties on black children. Someone else posted boun-ties on Ku Klux Klansmen. A retaliation? Who knew?

Someone else posted bounties on Jews. Someone else picked Witches. Someone else picked Christians. Homosexuals. Smokers. Non-smokers. Heterosexuals. Dog-owners. A zero-population group posted bounties on anyone. Anyone at all.

And it did not need to be one person posting the bounty. I contributed a few bucks myself, when I was in school, to have a certain famous entertainer who annoyed me bumped off. It was only a dollar or two; I meant it as a joke. I was drunk. But people kept adding to the fund. A dollar here, a gold gram there. After about five years, the bounty on the guy was half a million.

Now, I am not a murderer. That guy escaped. You see, that entertainer did not look like he looked in the See-vees. His picture was computer-generated. He was rich. He had friends. He was an Unknown.

Remember what I said about the difference between Knowns and Unknowns? It was the difference between life and death. Unknowns had all their money encrypted, overseas, stored as strings of scrambled numbers. You never met them face to face; you talked over the phone; and the picture and the voice on the phone could be someone, anyone, no one. But it wasn't them.

Remember I said governments changed? They were run by Unknowns. Appointed bureaucrats, some of them; others were just campaign finance contributors.

And taxes? Well, when everyone can hide their assets, there is no way to collect from them.

Tangible assets were different. Governments just seize them. They don't need a reason. They see a house or car they like, they take it. A piece of property, a publicly traded company. In the early days, they had to plant evidence of drug-dealing, or cigarette smoking, unauthorized public prayer, or gun ownership or something. Later, they just claimed the right of Eminent Domain and took what they needed.

How else could they be fed, those governments? How else could they continue?

It didn't bother the Unknowns. They just took out Seizure Insurance and kept most of their assets intangible. The ultra-rich sold or burned their cars after every car trip, and bought new ones before they went out again, just so they would have nothing on the highways to be seized. That was back when we had highways.

So how do you protect your children, in a time like that, with a civilization going to hell? You cannot negotiate with the assassins because no one knows who they are. Your rulers will not protect you. They are anonymous kelptocrats. The police? Don't make me laugh; everyone I knew kicked a few bucks into the kill-the-pigs kitty every time they got a traffic ticket, or had another car seized. The army? But there is no army. There will never be another army again.

A bullet-proof vest is not thick enough to stop a mid-sized smart bullet. And in order to have plate thick enough to shield your little child's heart and head from the assassins, you must mount it on an articulated exoskeleton.

I hated the stuff when I was young, and I always used to play with my faceplate open, so I could smell the free summer breeze. Billy Worthemer was the same way. Open faceplate. I talked him into doing it too, so he couldn't tell on me.

We were in the courtyard green-area. In a protected zone, with no line-of-sight to any taller buildings.

I remember seeing the targeting platform that painted us, Billy and me. It was just a motion sensor clipped to the collar of a puppy dog, with the sensitivity turned down so that only a body larger than a dog, but smaller than an adult, would set it off. Billy went over to pet the dog. I raced him to it to be the first one there, and picked up the dog.

I remember Peter Power Armor saved my life. I was hit in the shoulder by the round, but the shot did not penetrate. But the ricochet caught Billy in the face. He was turning around to say something to me; maybe to ask me to let him have a turn petting the dog.

I do not remember what happened to his face. I really do not. I remember the whine in my gauntlets when I pulled the innocent little puppy in half. Poor dog. I remember that. I do not remember what Billy looked like. Not at all.

I should erase that last bit. It has nothing to do with what I was saying. I am trying to tell you what your parents and grandparents were like. Are like. You're my granddaughter. It took me so long to find you. But I never gave up.

We are the kind of people who look after our kids. Having power armor for kids seems ridiculous, doesn't it? These days, it does. In the old days, it did not.

Everything you've been told about history is a lie. The People's Jesus did not come back to Earth and marry Mother Gaia, and appoint the First Protector of the Green People. That's not what happened.

The society I was raised in, the nightmare, could not last. The Unknowns could not last. They did not even know each other, did they? How could they help each other?

But what could stop the nightmare? Shut off the Net, you're saying. Cut the cables, arrest the Providers, take an ax to the mainframes, tear up the ground-lines. Easy enough. But who was going to do it? Not the multinationals; all their money was in the Net. Not the Unknowns; the Net was their universe.

In a society where everyone is being shot at, shot at any time and at all times, there are only two things you can do. Either you make sure everyone has a gun or you make sure no one has a gun.

The people West of the Mississippi chose the option number one. The people in the East chose option two.

The reality behind option two, of course, is that 'no one has a gun' actually means, 'no one but the authorities has a gun.' And that means, 'everyone but the authorities shuts up and does what they're told.'

The reality behind option one, of course, is that 'everyone has a gun' actually means, 'If you want me to shut up, tough guy, come over here and make me.'

The two systems are incompatible.

That's what the Second Civil War was really about; it was not about the Sacred Spotted Owl. And when the war got hot enough, and enough transatlantic cables got sabotaged, the Net went down. The Stock Market, all the stock markets, really, and bank records, personal records, everyone's identities, known and unknown, just went away.

The economy just went away.

And when that happened, the civilization's ability to feed the population of the world was cut roughly in half.

And the old-fashioned methods of warfare came back. We had soldiers again. I am not saying whether that was a good thing or a bad thing. They are brave, the soldiers these days; they wear uniforms, they do not hide and slink and sneak like soldiers from my day.

I am not brave. I am not like the soldiers of today. I am one of the old men of the days. My mission was to rescue you. I did it our way.

I was telling you about Peter Power Armor. I was telling you that I knew Mrs. Hechler would not know what it was. She had not lived through my grandfather's time, when fathers took their boys out into the woods to shoot squirrels. Or my father's time, when school uniforms were all woven with bulletproof material. My time I've told you about, the time of the Unknowns. The time of your mother (my daughter.) Her time was even worse; the time of the Diebacks.

Industrial collapse. No more computers, no more smart-bullets. War is more like the old days; men in uniforms who can see each other through the grass, in the trenches, shooting. The bullets aren't smart enough to pick their own targets any more. The nature of war turned back.

Your generation is so lucky. You don't know anything. Lucky, stupid, stupid, lucky fools.

A woman of Mrs. Hechler's generation would not believe any children's toy could be armed.

But Mrs. Hechler knew it was a machine, and machines of any kind were rare these days, and she knew the Correct Thought. "Ethne! Get away from that Satan-metal thing! Green Jesus and Mother Earth hate machines! Don't touch it!"

I said, "Darling Ethne; this is your magic fairy-tale knight-in-shining-armor, come to rescue you. Its yours, yours, all yours, your very own."

"Shut up!" Mrs. Hechler said to me.

I shrugged, putting my hands behind my back. "Oh, come now, you foul-smelling sack of lumpish fat. I am not the one who cannot control a seven-year -old girl. You signed the authorization saying we could explore this deserted old house to see if there was anything we could loot or sell for the communal kitchen. I'm not the one who will catch hell from the District Helpfulness Manager."

That directed her attention back to the child. 'Ethne Cornwall Delaplace! Ward of the State 142! Come here right now! Let go of that thing! It belongs to everyone!"

I said, "You are a princess, raised by trolls, who hate that you come from a high and noble lineage. This gentle knight-errant shall rescue you and take you to a free land across the Mississippi to the West. On your very life, do not let go!"

"Ethne! Come here! Don't make me call for Jerry downstairs!"

I said, "Free, Ethne. Freedom. No more equalization injections because you are smarter than other kids. Freedom."

Ethne smiled at me, looking very beautiful to me for the first time since I met her, just like her mother when she was a little girl.

And she said, "Please, sir. I want to be smart again, like I used to. I want to be free." And that was when I fell in love with her.

I think the mention of the F word did it.

Mrs. Hechler strode forward, huge and ponderous in her wrath. Mrs. Hechler grabbed Ethne by the arm. It was a good grab, swift as a snake, the kind of grip guards should learn to use on prisoners. And I am sure it hurt, because Ethne screamed.

I pointed the handset at the scene, opened the lens, and said carefully into the mic: "Child under attack."

It was amazing how surprised Mrs. Hechler looked when she fell. I had underestimated how loud the shot of the tranquilizer dart would be. I had not expected Jerry, who had been waiting outside, to come up shooting.

Jerry was not licensed as a cop, just as security. A baby-sitter. Regulations said he was not allowed to be armed with anything but a stunner. That hand-cannon he held was no stunner; it was shooting through walls, brick and plaster. Made a hell of a noise. Just like the old days, eh?

I had also underestimated how clever the power-armor's neural net had been programmed. It practically opened up in half and scooped Ethne into itself. Jerry really never stood a chance. It was very noisy and very bloody; not the sort of thing a child should see.

It is too bad you are unconscious. Peter sedated you because you were screaming and putting your hands in front of his gun barrels. I am recording this all through the hand-set into the suit playback for you to hear when you wake up.

Yes, I was wounded in the fire-fight. Wood-shrapnel from where a stray slug hit the door-frame. In my day, our doctors could have saved my leg.

I wish you could see what you looked like when you took off just now. It was lovely. You jumped out the window and over the next house. You should see the Seven-League-Boots program in action; each jet-assisted leap was two hundred yards if it was an inch.

I've already called in the escape over Mrs. Hechler's radio phone. The patrols are headed up north, into the swampland. In a minute, if I am strong enough, I'll send in a report that you were sighted down south, in the hills. All their equipment still runs off the old, old programs. Old as me. And I know the magic words to open the trap-doors and make my voice whatever CO's voice they need to hear.

I am a wizard, a warlock, a fraud, a gray old Prospero from a lost island, who never repented or burned his books or broke his wand. I have cast a spell on you, princess, and befuddled them.

They will not catch you. They will never catch you. I can just imagine the troopers on horseback, those of them who can afford horses, trying to catch you by lantern-light. I was the one who played hide-and-seek with my little friend Battery Bunny when I was eight, in that armor. One touch of the Mr. Frog button turns on the sneeky-peeky lowlight goggles, activates the aqualung, lets you to crawl along a river-bottom at night. The smart-metal is radar-invisible. If those barbarians still have any working radar sets. If they could get the bureaucrats in their organization to release them to the river patrol. Which I doubt. Which I doubt.

And Homer the Homing Pigeon who lives in the helmet is gyroscopically aligned and corrects himself by star-pattern recognition. So you cannot get lost or get turned around. I selected the map-program through the handset. It was the first thing I did before I started recording.

I do not mind going away. I was one of them, darling. An Unknown. That's why my name is not on the records. Dad gave me trapdoors into the computer systems that survived the Netcrash. That's why I was able to find my family. To find you. I am sorry for the things I did and I do not really mind dying. I've tried to make up for it.

What else do I need to say? I am getting sleepy now, and its hard to think.

I am the last of the Unknowns. I could make myself a fake ID. I could travel in the East on forged papers. I could give myself authorization to read the Child Safety and Domestication Bureau records, to unseal sealed files, and depart without a trace.

My magic. Left over from the old days. I wove a cloak of cunning mist and made myself invisible, while I was right in front of their eyes. Who looks at janitors? My papers were in order.

The job as a janitor at the Children's Center I got by hard work and sweat; something rare here. Tricking Mrs. Hechler into violating regulations and going to loot a deserted house in a public-owned area was simply not difficult. All serfs ignore regulations when they can; it's the only way they can live. There are just so many regulations, you see, no one can listen to them all.

Is there anything else I need to tell you, anything else I need to explain?

What they told you about the West is all lies too. We don't shoot each other down in the streets, we don't have gunfights in every bar. We do have bars, but not everyone drinks.

I do not know what went wrong with all the people back East, after the Diebacks. I do not know why they could not rebuild. The Western states are mostly empty desert. How come they got rich? I do not know. Maybe the Easterners did not have the will to resist when the People's Green Church of Mother Life came along. They certainly did not have the means to resist. They did not have anything like Peter.

But those deserts are so beautiful under the starlight. You'll see them soon.

Oh, God, let me stay awake long enough to tell you this.

Darling, I do not know the names of my contacts in the underground railroad. Remember I told you about encryption? You just go to any public phone once you are across the Mississippi, in the wide Western places they've remembered finally what a free country is supposed to be. They've also remembered how to set up a working Net again.

Another Net. Are the bad old days coming back again? I don't know. I'm very tired, and I just don't know. Maybe you can grow up and stop those bad things from happening.

Don't let me forget. Get to the phone. Push the button shaped like Puss-in-Boot. It's the crypto cat. It will turn on the circuit and make the phone call for you. It will call the nice people.

Get to a phone. Peter will know what to do. Trust Peter. He'll take care of you.

Peter loves you; I love you.

Goodbye, God bless, and Godspeed.

You mother is waiting for you in Austin. Your real mother. We got her out of the camps months ago. Her name is Roselinde. She was very pretty when she was your age.

WAYWARD CHILD

An Alliance Archives Adventure

Mike McPhail

THE YEAR WAS UC84 BY THE NEW CALENDAR—ULTRA CUNABULAM . . . BEYOND THE CRADLE, AS translated from Latin—now, only some eight decades after man first reached for the edge of space, fate gave them the key to trans-light travel. With it, he unlocked the gates to the heavens.

The towering canopy of Demeter's ancient forests cast a perpetual shadow on the ground far below. Against this shadowy landscape, the mind's eye easily imagined yet unseen creatures lying off in the nearby darkness; watching and waiting for that one pivotal moment when prey became victim.

As the brightness of Tau-Ceti's day turned into the all-consuming black of perpetually moonless night, the monsters of imagination took form; alien to this world, they roamed the darkness in an ago-old struggle: survival.

Two of these horrors moved over the root-covered ground with a deft bouncing motion; they negotiated the natural obstacles as if the blinding darkness that encompassed them held no domain. Their appearance brought to mind classic movie images of hellishly huge insects, with smooth carapaces, heads, and protruding mandibles. Their shapes and movements, however, were unmistakably that of man. It became all too clear at the sight of their angular Maschinengawehr-style weapons that these were men of war.

"Negative, we ran into another patrol, but managed to break contact," reported Sergeant Bauer, his tone grim; he looked briefly at his helmet's compass display. "We're moving along at one-ten from our initial contact point; with luck we'll swing around them, and then head toward the landing zone," he concluded with a burst of static.

"Acknowledged," replied the disembodied voice; with that the unseen squad leader's icon disappeared from the sergeant's helmet display only to be replaced by the comm's standby marker. As a team leader, Bauer was required to carrier an additional signal booster. Tonight he was more than thankful for the surrounding hilly-terrain played havoc with all but their short-range communications.

Stopping, Bauer half turned to survey in the direction from which they had come; in the space of a few heartbeats he was satisfied that there was no sign of pursuit.

Pivoting back, he could see on of his men up ahead. *We're not faceless machines*, thought Bauer at the sight of his fellow trooper; he understood the concept, but never truly felt it himself. Even if his suit wasn't linked to the others via the pac-scomp—the suit's integrated computer/squad-level communications—he knew he would still be able to recognize his teammates.

Through his helmet's display a bright green triangular icon topped with MGN was suspended ethereally near the other trooper; he didn't need the electronic identification, to tell this was Morgan. There was just no mistaking the fact that under all that body-armor was a woman; with her wiry-build, she moved more like a dancer than a soldier.

"Maybe that's the problem," he thought, as a wave of anger pushed at him. "Morgan," Bauer called.

"Sir," Morgan replied, still transfixed on the undergrowth, scanning for possible threats. With a snap of her head she briefly looked back toward him; he was double-timing it to catch up. As he closed the distance, he changed step to keep pace with her.

"What was your malfunction back there?" he demanded, getting up close until he practically loomed; only his discipline kept his emotions from coloring his words.

The question gripped Morgan, an unseen force reaching out and engulfing her whole body. It drove the air from her lungs, making it hard to catch her breath. Within a few paces she stopped.

She flashed back to the Legionnaire; through a red haze, she saw the face of the young man. Armed with a bullpup assault rifle mounted with an underslung 30mm grenade launcher, he had been outfitted as a soldier, with ballistic-mesh and plate body-armor. He was no hardened warrior, that had been clear in his nervous and almost confused actions; most likely a conscript, forced into service in this so-called war. His gaze had held terror as she eyed him over her own weapon's targeting reticle.

With her fingers poised against her weapon's electronic trigger group, she had depressed its safety; like a drumbeat, there was a sudden pounding in her head. She'd tried to concentrate on making the shot, but as she struggled to depress the trigger the pounding threatened to overwhelm her; not until she withdrew her fingers from the trigger guard did the sensation subsided.

"Your inactions . . . " the sound of Bauer's voice snapped Morgan back to present, " . . . put everyone at risk." The sergeant was standing right in front of her; she tipped her head back so that her helmet's side-mounted scopes could look up into his faceless visor.

Memories of her combat instructor, Major Stonebridge, push their way into her thoughts. The way he would scream in a put-on, typecast, British drill sergeant voice. "I don't give a damn about your crisis of conscience; when you're out there and some son-of-a-bitch is laying in fire on you and your men . . . " He would then get up close and personal with one of those standing in the ranks; and in an almost pleasant voice, " . . . you kill him, and keep killing him. You don't stop killing him until he's a pile of meat." At which point he would rear back and demand that they all shout in the affirmative, then in an almost fatherly way, "After all, do you want to look into the eyes of your comrades, and know, that when the time came . . . that you . . . You!" he said pointing off into the ranks. "That you cared more for that son-of-a-bitch . . . " he paused, " . . . than you did for them?"

Damnú, she thought to herself in the Irish curse her mother used to use. *I earned my chance to join the squads, and I've already screwed it up.*

After scanning back the way they had come, Bauer turned back to Morgan. "You had him cold. What stopped you from putting a dart through him?" It was more of an accusation than a question.

Fighting back tears, all Morgan wanted to do was beg for Bauer's forgiveness, but that would have put an end to her service in the ADF even faster than her screw up. "I have no excuse." She said as calmly as possible.

The sergeant just stood there for a moment; it was obvious to Morgan that he was considering her answer, and that her future may very well be decided in the next few moments.

With a sharp nod of his head in the direction they were heading, Bauer turned and started to walk, "Get moving, we'll de . . . " was all he had a chance to say as time slip shifted into slow motion. She felt the shockwave of a fired round and knew there was nothing she could do. Trapped in the moment, Morgan watched as the faceplate on Sergeant Bauer's helmet deformed around the point of penetration. Like a discharging strobe, the world around her disappeared with a brilliant flash of white light followed by intense darkness.

Within moments her vision returned. The return of sound was harsh in her ears as she stared in stunned horror at Bauer's body, collapsed to his knees, and only just starting to tip. The reality of the situation forced its way back into Morgan's consciousness. Stepping back on her left leg, she turning and brought her gauss rifle to the ready position, aiming in the direction where the shot originate. The rifle's targeting reticle hovered about in the ethereal space before her.

She saw nothing; in light-amp mode, her helmet-mounted imaging scopes could pick up enough trace light to turn the darkest night into false-color twilight. Despite that advantage, nothing . . . no one . . . was visible.

Her body was in motion before her mind officially gave the order; pivoting on her left foot, she drove herself back toward the massive tree trunk she had pass just moments before. With only a few paces until she reached cover, the air around her became populated by whizzing bits of glowing metal. They passed within inches of her faceplate each leaving a faint afterglow. Momentum took over and finished her bid to reach cover, but not soon enough.

She pressed her left forearm against the tree for stability and closed her eyes to help focus her senses; there was a smack to her right shoulder plate and a violent kick to the side of her helmet. She searched for the hot flow of blood pooling around her neck seal and found none; all she felt was a burning sensation to the side of her head. Static screamed in her ear. It was loud, almost loud enough to drown out the cracks and thumps as more bullets smacked into the tree, ricocheting off the ground around her.

Her heart pounded in her throat as she turned to look. Bauer was on his back, his knees bent and pointing up and away at odd angles; his head had rolled to the left as if looking to Morgan for help. His superimposed identification icon was now red and bordered by a time-stamp, indicating that his suit's pacscomp had declared him dead and beyond reviving. In response, it then fulfilled its priority-one programming and burned itself out, leaving only the recovery signal operational.

"Bauer . . . " She tried to speak, but her jaw was numb and apparently swollen beyond use; she felt isolated, and with a renewed burst of enemy fire, trapped. Panic pushed at her.

"When shite happens . . . " screamed Stonebridge out of the past, " . . . don't stand around mourning your fallen comrades. That is, unless you intend to join them." His face loomed large in her mind, his eyes burning with hatred. "Go and make those sons-of-bitches pay; and pay dearly."

"*Cac*," Morgan sub-vocalized in Gaelic. "Suit Mode, SIcom," she said through her inner-monolog; literally reaching out via the nano-scale wires in her brain that formed the lattice work that was the Synaptic Interface antenna.

As always, the suit's pacscomp AI picked up on the standardized keywords she used. "SIcom engaged," reported the all-too-relaxed voice of the computer. Taking a deep breath, she held it, and then let out a long exhale; it helped—a little. The stress was still there, but now more defined, rather than all-encompassing.

"Brennen from Morgan," she SIcommed, and waited as her pacscomp made contact and communed with her squad leader's. In the span of just a few heartbeats nothing happened; no burst of static over her comhood's headset, no surface thoughts, not even a confirmation icon on her display. Morgan suddenly felt like a small child who had just discovered that her parents were no were to be seen.

Pushing back against the growing stress, she tried again. "Bospher Comraden." She thought, using the new open-frequency code words; even if the enemy could intercept this message, they would have no immediate way of knowing its meaning. This from their pseudo-language Ty'Linqua; it meant "Greetings (to my fellow) troopers." In this case, it was a very polite way of calling for help from anyone who could both hear and understand; still nothing.

"Remember the difference between a Trooper and a warrior," she recalled from one of the Major's many lessons. But why this one? It only added to her confusion. Out of her memory, her instructor continued, "You fight as a member of a team, using all the skills and equipment your fellow troopers carry to the fight. A warrior fights alone, relying only on his own abilities and strength of arms."

"What are you trying to tell me?" she thought, "What warning are you . . . am I giving myself? Yes, I'm alone." That realization almost panicked her, but then she remembered " . . . fellow troopers and their equipment!" She looked at her team leader, "The signal-booster!"

"Gun, Auto," she SIcommed, and watched as the targeting reticle's quantifier-icon changed, confirming her instructions. Now on automatic, her weapon was capable of putting out some twelve hundred darts per minute—only about a fifth of the weapon's maximum potential—but still fast enough to consume a 90-round magazine in little over four seconds. Her gauss rifle was up and at the ready as she lowered herself to her right knee, its traction pad biting into the ground.

By definition, Morgan was left-handed, but long ago she realized there was very little difference in her abilities with either hand. With a practiced right hand, she reached across her abdomen and withdrew a smoke grenade.

Gripping the beverage-size can against her palm, she depressed the safety bar that ran parallel to its side; a green icon appeared on her helmet's display. Seating her thumb on the arming button on top, she drew back and shifted her body for the throw. She pressed down on the button. Click. The icon changed to red; in an overhand style that any soldier of Earth's wars would have recognized, she lobbed the two-pound cylinder just past the side of her tree, off toward the shooters. Quickly, she stood up and made ready for a second throw.

Some ten yards away the first one landed with a thump, setting off its impact sensor. The grenade deployed three spring-loaded legs that seemingly popped into existence, kicking the cylinder up on end. With a pop, a jet of white spray shot up, filling the air over the canister with a dense plume of slowly falling particles; the cloud ignited, and expanded a hundred-fold in volume.

As the icon changed to confirm the grenade's detonated, Morgan reared back for the long throw, trading accuracy for distance. The second canister arced toward the low-hanging branches, disappearing into the growing smoke screen.

The enemy's base of fire slowed and shifted onto the massive tree she was using for cover; they could no longer see her position, but obviously intended to keep her pinned down.

Now back on her knee and staying as low as possible, she held her rifle with the barrel pointing up and away from what she was doing; she reached out for Bauer. With her eyes fixed on the thermal smoke, she watched as passing projectiles momentarily extruded cone-like shapes from the glowing body of the cloud.

As she touched the all-too-familiar texture of Allied armor, she turned to look; her hand rested on Bauer's shoulder plate, just near his load-carrying harness. Wrapping her fingers around the strap, she tightened her grip and pushed back with her legs. As she worked, weapons fire tore into the side of the tree showering her with fast-moving splinters of bark and bits of hardwood; deflected rounds whooshed overhead.

"Damnu!" she mumbled through numb lips as she hunkered down into her armor, trying to make herself as small as possible; she was more angry than scared. Still kneeling, she released Bauer and grabbed for her weapon's foregrip; twisting herself, she brought the rifle up. The targeting reticle bobbed aimlessly before her, as she tried looking through smoke that for all intents was a visibly impenetrable barrier . . . or was it?

There! Movement! she thought. It was definitely someone trying to approach her using the smoke screen for cover; but it looked all wrong. It was like a miscolored thermal image: the soldier's face and head were the brightest parts, while everything else faded away through shades of deep red. The background was black with no detail at all, not even reflection from the glow of the target.

Shifting her weapon, she placed the reticle's aiming pip on the target; it failed to lock and just continued bobbing about. "Why can't you see him?" she demanded. "No target designated; range indeterminate." replied the pacscomp.

"Disregard," she thought. "Gun, fixed target," Morgan ordered. The reticle jumped across her display as it switched settings; like iron sights, it was now fixed to a point some three-hundred yards down range along the weapon's line of fire. She swung back on to the target, and with a gentle movement shifted to keep it under her sights.

With a squeeze of her left hand, she depressed the leading edge of the rifle's handgrip; Click. The safety was off and power made available. A pull of the two-fingered trigger would now launch a salvo of electromagnetically accelerated, armor-piercing steel darts.

Time slowed as she waited for the moment to fire; then, in the span of a heartbeat, she looked beyond the aiming pip, and like a rising wind before a storm she felt a growing emotional presence. The bastard Legion soldier, her target. "Noooo! Not this time!" she screamed past her swollen jaw as echoes of the earlier encounter threatened to slow her down. She fought her way past it and tightened her grip.

The world around her erupted in motion as a wave of brilliant white sparks danced across the Legionnaire's chest, dropping him on the spot. Subconsciously, Morgan released the tension on her index and middle fingers; she was up and at a full run before she realized what she had done. The sound of someone screaming pierced the crackle of static in her ears as she ran toward the smoke.

Her scopes went dark as she entered the cloud, but there in the distance—seemingly floating in a void—was another blob of red, another target. Morgan had him under her sights as she cleared the smoke. Through her imaging scopes the soldier was no more than a dark, bush-shaped mass; but to her eyes, the man within the camouflage was clearly visible.

At the last moment the Legionnaire turned toward the sound of her foot falls, but Morgan had him cold. A spray of hot particles was visible through her scopes, overlaid by flashes of white sparks at the points of impact. Beyond the screaming, she heard the crack of the gauss rifle's darts breaking the sound barrier, followed by the concluding thumps of the projectiles punching through mesh body armor, rending flesh and smashing bone.

 She continued to run; with her weapon held high and at the ready, she scanned the path with short movements of her head.

In the still air of the deep forest, her second smoke canister created a massive visual void. Its core was almost black through her scopes, only broken by protruding, leaf-covered branches, and partially obscured objects near its growing edges. No one was in sight.

The screaming stopped abruptly, only to be replaced by the woosh of her suit's air filters opening and closing against her deep breathing. Her throat was raw with the absence of the sound. The front of her comhood just below her lip was wet; not warm like blood, but cool. She was caught in an isolated moment of silence, oddly still amid the rush of combat.

It passed as the enemy renewed their base of fire. To her left an intermittent line of bullets emerged from the void of the cloud as if somehow spontaneously created within; each appearing as a blob of light trailed by its afterglow. The gunner was firing in groups of about five with a short pause in between. The weapon's report was in sync with its passing projectiles; he was very close.

Morgan swung her targeting reticle up and back along the line of fire, looking for the weapon's muzzle flash—or the red of it gunner—but nothing was visible beyond the smoke.

At a burst of enemy fire, Morgan answered in kind; in a sweeping motion she played out a stream of darts toward what she hoped was the gunner's position. Abruptly the fire stopped and the now-familiar red blur of a soldier came into view. Just as quickly the red again shifted into bright white, before fading away.

Morgan was just about to pass into the second cloud when another silhouette appeared. It was the outline of a soldier. He seemed to be sitting, one knee up with his elbow braced against it to support his weapon.

Once again lost in the void, Morgan saw her weapon's pip land on the center mass of the target; with a short burst of fire, a single flash of white exploded on the target, knocking it over.

"Ammunition expended," stated the pacscomp, as the targeting reticle's ordnance counter read triple zero.

"Cac!" exclaimed Morgan as she reached for her ammunition pouch. From the handgrip she thumbed the weapon's magazine release; a confirmation icon appeared indicating that the spent magazine had popped free. As she lifted the pouch flap to withdraw a fresh magazine, she approached the edge of the smoke cloud.

Boom! Morgan's reality flinched against the concussive force of the sound combined with the punch of a hypervelocity bullet passing thought the air just inches from her head.

The last Legionnaire she had shot now sat up against a tree just five yards away. Her scopes showed a hot spot on the left side of his chest just below his shoulder. I was slowly expanding. She watched his dark red outline grow brighter as white sparks danced and crackled along his shoulder and over his chest.

His weapon lay in his lap; he pulled back its operating lever, and with a soft ting, the weapon ejected the spent cartridge, which leaped into the air.

Morgan rushed him, not willing to take the chance that she could reload and bring her weapon to bear before he could; the fresh magazine fell from her hand as she grabbed for her weapon's foregrip.

The bloodthirsty screams returned as she fell upon the target, jaw clenched and her thoughts enraged. With the strength of both arms, driven by the mass of her body, she smashed the butt of her rifle into the now-upturned face of the Legionnaire. And again. And again. And . . .

"Morgan!" said the voice in her head.

She stopped; she was on her knees gripping the weapon's frame around the barrel of her rifle. Beneath her, the body of the Legion sniper lay on its back; its limp arms had obviously tried to protect itself against her mashing blows. The aura was no longer the deep-reds and sparks of white that Morgan had come to expect; shades of dark blue and black instead flooded her vision. Time seemed lost to her.

"Morgan, respond!" ordered the voice.

"Sir?" she mechanically replied via the Slcom; then she recognized his voice, "Brennen! I mean . . . Squad Leader." it was hard to focus; it was almost as if being awakened from a deep sleep.

Pushing back, using her rifle for support, she stood up; her mind started to clear.

"Morgan, we're five minutes out . . . " stated Brennen. With a growing sense of relief Morgan turned to look. There on her display were six green triangular icons. Her relief was short-lived as a red, time-stamped icon appeared. Sergeant Bauer . . . .

"Fall back to Bauer's position and standby. Acknowledge?" instructed Brennen.

"Set." Slcommed Morgan. With the somber realization that the person she had been was no more, she turned and walked back through the gently dissipating smoke. Not just returning to the body of her fallen comrade, but walking toward an uncertain future.

NOT ONE WORD

From the Chronicles of the Radiation Angels

James Daniel Ross

MY NAME IS TODD ROOK.
I was a Corporal in The Radiation Angels.
I was running for my life.

In my small rucksack was an avalanche drive, a one kilo mini-computer containing seven hundred terabytes of 'liberated' data. It contained enough evidence to finally put an end to court battles across this world. Worth thousands of years in prison for some, and trillions of credits in legal awards for others, it felt as heavy as a corpse in my pack. I shouldn't complain, I suppose, it was about all I was carrying anymore. I had been running forever, buildings slipping into shadow on every side, my lungs burning like a coal fire deep inside a mountain. I didn't know exactly what was on the avalanche drive, but it was obvious that the previous owners of the data were willing to kill a lot of people to get it back; including me. Especially me.

Bricks disintegrated over my head as steel-jacketed lead ripped through the air. I dove to the ground, thankful for the helmet that kept the refuse from the alley from piling up in my mouth as I slid into the detritus. Broken bottles shredded the cosmetic outer layers of my armored jumpsuit like a witch's claws. One shard of glass sliced through the strap on my rifle and it slipped away into the debris. I reached for it and veered into a trashcan. I rolled over just as engines shrieked overhead and vented superheated exhaust down upon me. From the mouth of the alley a massive mirrored cockpit stared at me like the accusing eye of a god. The man behind the windshield must have smiled as he squeezed his trigger unleashing a lead-hearted rain from his wing mounted guns. In the tight confines of the alley, the sound was deafening. The buildings on either side of the alley erupted into clouds of dust. I screamed.

I scrambled blindly for my rifle, unable to look away from the two-ton air vehicle that was trying to kill me. My gloved hands closed around the stock and brought the weapon up to my shoulder as the clouds billowed out and all but obliterated the flier from view. I sighted along the rifle and jammed down the trigger. Bullets snapped from the barrel, recoil punching the stock into my shoulder as I yanked down the front end to keep the weapon on target. I barely heard the high frequency cracks of shattering glass over the sound of Armageddon all around me. The sound seemed to go on forever, echoing in the alley and inside my soul. At the same instant my rifle clicked empty, the pilot stopped firing, and the jetwash of the four vertical engines cleared the clouds of brick dust.

There he was, hovering ten meters away, seven meters up. His windshield was scarred and cracked from my salvo, with a few small holes that had missed the pilot completely. I lay in the center of the filthy alley, terrified but untouched. We both realized his mistake at the same moment: While most of the buildings on either side of me had been badly masticated by steel teeth, his weapons were mounted on stubby wings on either side of the cockpit, too widely spaced to shoot straight down the alley.

The pilot yanked his control yoke back and forth, trying to give his guns a clear field of fire when I touched off the under-barrel grenade launcher on my weapon. The thick, slow projectile spun from the barrel with the sound of a base drum, arced up and punched a perfect hole through the weakened glass. I suffered a moment of horror and prayed that the grenade had traveled far enough from the barrel to arm before the world went white. A giant, uncaring hand swatted me further into the alley, bouncing me from wall to dumpster to doorframe. Pain erupted from every direction as the buildings around me wobbled back and forth. I came to rest deep in the darkness and just lay still.

The Angels were hired by the government of Goozner 3 to assault the KelRon datacenter and retrieve proof about a host of illegal activities; from corporate espionage and price gouging to financial information about rampant bribery and missing persons across the planet. We had counted on getting in, downloading the data, and getting out before the backup security teams or police showed up. We got in, but resistance was stiffer than expected. The avalanche drive had quickly copied the entire mainframe of data into tightly spooled bundles within seconds, but as we exfiltrated additional security forces had swept in from every direction.

These were not the normal retired-police-officer kind of security guard. In fact, the difference between KelRon 'security' and 'mercenary' was only semantic; they were carrying heavy weaponry, wore better armor, and were better trained than intelligence said they would be. We lost two fliers in the first exchange and I was separated from the rest of the team in the intense crossfire on the ground. Bullets and coherent light impacted on every side of me as I took cover behind some parked vehicles. I had to retreat under focused fire from all sides. I looked for a way to rejoin the fight when the order to Escape and Evade came down. I managed to find a hole in the combat and dive down a side street, but the respite never lasted long. It was as if they knew where the emergency hard drive was because every time I stopped security teams were there, snapping at my heels.

Now the world refused to focus clearly and my hands fluttered as I checked myself for broken bones or bleeding cuts. As each limb was inventoried, despair reached up like some dire thing from the bottom of a sea, and grasped me in cold coils. Tears welled up and stung my eyes. If something had been broken, maybe I could have rationalized just laying there for a few more . . . hours. I grunted and tested out my helmet-radio. Static crashed into my ears, a sure sign that some heavy-duty jamming was going on. There I was; alone, with no help coming and every muscle aching. Again I considered just staying put and going to sleep, a thought effectively shattered by another security flier crossing overhead at high speed.

I looked around and tried to get my bearings. My rifle was already a long forgotten memory broken and twisted somewhere in the trash of this slum. I also discovered that sometime in the last hour I had lost my pistol, the holster broken, hungry, and forlorn. I went further into the tight passage and turned into a spur as I heard the heavy metallic whine of another flier coming close. I managed to make it to the end and cross the street before the warble of a police flier's siren started up behind me. There was a flurry of cannon fire, the siren had its throat slit, and a resounding crash told the chilling story from two streets away. The police were not going to be able to come to the rescue and KelRon would brook no interference. I popped the virtual compass onto my HUD and shook my head as the world tried to go all black and squishy again.

. . . I don't remember kneeling, but I must have. I took deep breaths and fumbled for the thigh pouch with my medical pack. I took out two disposable syringes and plunged them between the armor plates on my thigh. The world snapped into focus and I tried to get my bearings again. I took a metallicized nylon map and crypto-voltage box from my shoulder pouch. I set the coded keys to the correct power level, and touched it to the map, revealing the correct map and rendezvous site in glowing blue lines. If I was anywhere near where I thought I was, the emergency pickup RV was to the west, near the river. I reset the box to all 0's and stored the bundle away. Ammunition entombed in the burning wreckage at the end of the alley began to cook off like popcorn, bringing me back to the here and now. I had to move. I had to do it now.

On legs progressively more steady, I stuck close to the fronts of the ancient rowhouses. I kept near the walls, eyes sweeping for the telltale cloud of an RPG launch. I crossed streets quickly, keeping to shadows and hiding every time a flier screeched by. Across the city, the sounds of warfare were spreading. I limped along in silence, without the benefit of audience or sound track. War is discordant. It has no theme music. Truthfully it has no theme, no overriding feel and it is filled with weird holes saturated with nothing but the sound of your own heartbeat. I stopped in a doorway and ducked into a puddle of gloom as a pair of shadows walked by. I waited silently, unmoving, until they had turned the corner out of sight. The moment they disappeared, I continued onward, leg feeling better for the brief rest. Urban warfare is the worst for this kind of thing. It is infused with the randomness of people trying to help, harm, or simply go about their lives as you search for death around every corner . . . and sometimes, death searches for you.

I crept down one brick and concrete corridor after another, discipline forcing me to keep track of every turn, every door, every dumpster that could act as an element in escape, cover, or attack. It was a habit drilled into me, but it was new enough to still be distracting, and slow the passage of time to a crawl. The fog of fatigue, and probably a concussion, started closing in on me again and I began to question if the mental effort was worth it.

Light flooded down the alley, spearing me in place like the pin of a giant bug collector for just an instant. I leapt two steps back and flung myself at a door. My hundred kilos of nineteen-year-old muscle collided with the metal door and snapped the lock free of the weakened frame. I was dumped on the floor of a nondescript hallway and managed to pull my legs out of the alley as metal wasps scraped at the ground where they had just been. Arms protesting, legs crying, I vaulted to my feet and slapped on the low-light sensor on my helmet. The black hallways became a murky, trashy green, lined with peeling wallpaper and cracked vinyl flooring. It was a straight shot to the front door, its starred glass glowing like a misshapen maw. I dove through it at a sprint, trusting the twenty kilos of ceramic and laminate metal armor to break the window's teeth. Glass erupted around me in a volcanic spray and I tumbled through the air into something only barely softer than concrete. Something that whuffed, cursed, and wiggled. I opened my eyes. What I saw did not make me happy.

Training kicked in like gravity; nothing to think about, just do it. I rolled off the security goon I had accidentally tackled and snapped my foot into the kneecap of the woman to his right. There was a slight bit of resistance before the joint bent with a distinct wet pop and muffled crackle. She collapsed, screaming and holding the ruins of her leg as a sharp pressure slammed into my shoulder blade. I spun, gritting my teeth, and leading with an elbow, aimed instinctively to catch the poor bastard just under his chin. My armored elbow plate, hard and unyielding, crashed against the soft ballistic cloth over his Adam's apple. He went down, trachea collapsed, his last seconds of life gurgling away wetly.

And then I was running, crossing the street with well-practiced strides as bullets impacted all around me. Stairs came out of nowhere, materializing out of the darkness only when my foot went looking for hard ground and found none. Again I fell, world spinning. Air exploded from my mouth, diaphragm and lungs slapped as I landed flat on my back in a pile of loose trash. My shoulder erupted into full scale agony. The sloppy pile of boxes half collapsed around me and I couldn't breathe, had to breathe, must breathe . . .

. . . My shoulder was still on fire. I must have passed out for a moment; as it turned out it was a moment I didn't have.

Like every animal ever given birth, I froze as my natural enemies began pouring past me in an endless wave. One or two missed the first step, but those behind saw those in front and managed to double time the stairs just fine. They raced down the alley, lights stymied by those in front, creating daylight through the upper half of the alley, but bodies blocking light to cast the floor in shadow.

And there I sat, half-covered with stained boxes, ruined clothes, half-eaten sausage, and broken toys as they ran past in ranks without number. Then, they began to slow, and trickle, until one, lone man came jogging behind. Without a light of his own, and without any real sense of urgency, he descended the steep flight of stairs carefully. Then he looked ahead, fumbled with armored fittings to expose his fly, and took a leak on an innocuous pile of trash.

He kept watch in front and behind, clearly more worried about discovery by an ally than an enemy, and I toyed with the idea of murdering him right here and now. The problem was every soldier in the area was now south of me, giving me a straight shot to the RV as long as I didn't leave a fragging corpse to point to where I really was. So I stayed as still as the grave, bit my lip against the burning in my shoulder, and let him piss all over me.

I finally decided to start officially hating both this planet and everything on it.

It seemed like forever, but soon enough he zipped up and jogged after his comrades. I forced myself to slowly count to one hundred before I moved. A quick glance at my improvised bed revealed a dark, bloody pool near where my head had lain and I cursed. Someone must have gotten a lucky round off. I made it to another alley and another shadow before breaking out the powdered coagulant and pouring it over my left shoulder. I couldn't exactly see what I was doing, so I was generous. I scrabbled with the bandage for minutes before figuring that there was hump-all I could do about taking care of this myself. I reached around to the small pack and felt the avalanche drive there, safe and sound. I had to keep moving.

I headed west, the world taking on harsh angles and severe lighting, a paranoid genius' eye lending the feel of reality to this gruesome nightmare though the lens of his camera. I blinked furiously, righting the world for a second before it began to swim again. I was probably still losing blood. Lord knows if my brain was swelling inside my skull. Everything felt a little broken and a little off kilter, somehow distorted. I rechecked the map, stowed it and popped one street to the north. I snuck a peek out onto the main boulevard, looking out onto the gently arcing downhill grade that fluttered down for a kilometer or so to the shore of the river. It all looked so peaceful.

I reached for my gun, and found it was still gone.

Without any other real choice, I moved out. I fooled myself into thinking I'd actually make it, too, when another light enveloped me, followed by shouts and shots. I sprinted for the mouth of another nameless alley, and turned to crash though the door to another cheap, dingy apartment block. I made the stairwell before the enemy made the front window, and I vaulted up the stairs as holes sprang up on all sides. Bullets made their tinny, cracking music as a more subtle backbeat began to brush my brain. I made the first landing and slung around the banister, turning one hundred eighty degrees before launching myself up the next flight.

And the next.

And the next.

I burst onto the roof, shattering the door with my good shoulder and setting my bad shoulder screaming again. Footsteps thumped behind me, ghostly bass bounced on all sides, I looked around the roof and realized it was, indeed a roof. I wasn't sure what my brilliant plan had been, but roofs aren't generally known for having an abundance of escape routes. I saw the building to the west and instantly decided to do something I haven't done since I was a boy. I jogged to the east edge, spun on one heel, and put everything I had into the soles of my feet.

The memory of a hundred million steps flashed through them, the remembered prayers for safety and speed. Thick boots bit into the gravel like the claws of a wolf, and thighs contracted in perfect harmony, pushing faster and faster. I grew up in a place where, the strong preyed on the weak, the good were eaten by the bad, and law was lynched by the criminal. It was a place where you avoided the cops, for they always wanted something from you, it was a place where there was no self defense, only murder and murder again. It was a place with no armor, no help, no hope, where the only safety lay in speed. I grew up to be fast, very fast. And sometimes, just sometimes, those who wanted to use you as entertainment would chase you onto a roof. And there would be nothing left to do but fight, jump, or die.

Three security goons burst from the stairwell behind me. One managed to open fire as my right foot caught the edge of the roof and gave one last push, a wrenching, roaring, screaming push to propel me up and out, further, further. And for a second, just a second, I was free. Free, as the air washed all fear from me, as gravity gave me a moment's respite, as my enemies saw me and were amazed.

Thirty meters stretched beneath me, rendered into infinity by vertigo.

The far building came closer, closer.

I stopped rising and began to fall.

Right foot, strong foot, stopped wheeling ineffectually, reached out.

I was dropping fast. Too fast.

I pulled my leg up tight to my chest and held my breath.

My right foot caught the edge of the building, slamming my knee backward into my chest. The roof of the building even with my crotch, I lunged forward, desperate to roll away from the endless edge of oblivion. Gravel scraped underneath me as I rolled and skipped, scrambling behind the west building's stair penthouse. I sat and gave a breathy sob as bullets careened ineffectually against my cover. I took the chance to breathe. Just breathe.

The bass beat was stronger here, a physical force, a current just under my skin as the building resonated with the sound. I steeled myself for a dash around the stair's cupola to the door when I realized it was on my side. I pulled and found it was unlocked. Suspicious of any help from fate, I opened it only a crack. Even so, music hit me in the face like a physical force, squeezing my ears to the center of my head and rumbling inside my chest. I crept downward into a cacophony of sound.

I exited the stairs on the third floor, and burst into pure chaos. Lights played whimsical games of sex and violence on the walls and across hundreds of gyrating bodies. Electronic rhythms crashed, flew, bounced, and slid on every side, infiltrating my head and taking up residence. Suspicious eyes glared at me on every side and I swept my helmet off and held it at waist level. I passed into a bar area, music only slightly muted, where drinkers took note of my holsters, packs, boots, and blood. I had better things to do than blend in. I took the stairs down to the bottom dance floor and I saw KelRon Security pushing their way past belligerent bouncers. Suddenly, becoming invisible was much more important.

I made my way to the edge of the dance floor and grabbed an overlarge, purple coat off of a wall-mounted hook. The owner of the coat must have been truly gargantuan of proportions, because the whole thing fit over me, my pack, and my armor. I put it on and disappeared into the crowd, looking for a window, a door . . . any way to get out. As I disappeared into the dancers, KelRon security was close at my heels.

Then I saw Her.

Hair splayed out like the spray of a fountain, clothes so tight they could have been genetically engineered, She moved like a cat as the music flowed through Her.

Inside Her was a tsunami, fierce and fantastic as She projected it in every direction in expressions of anger, joy, sadness, and ecstasy. I couldn't stop staring, caught as a bug in amber, as She moved. Then She looked at me and I forgot about anything else in the universe except Her eyes. I glided toward Her, crowd parting on either side like the Red Sea. And still, She stared at me, lips barely parted, eyes wide. I noticed She had stopped breathing. So had I.

I glanced back, and saw my hunters dive into the press of bodies, grabbing people and roughly turning them around for a good look. As each was eliminated as a suspect, they continued toward me.

I spun to increase the distance between us, and came face to face with the dancing girl. She and I came closer and closer, drawn together through forces nobody can claim to understand. Even in the press of bodies I could smell Her, vanilla and sandalwood hitting me like a rockslide. For a panicked instant, all I could think of was the scents coming off of me: blood, cordite, sweat, and urine. But then She reached out, placed a cool hand on my cheek, and pulled me close. The heat between us built into fission, two bodies of significant mass glowing ever more brightly with a light nobody else could see. The whole world faded out, urban drums sliding away as we began to move, pulled like puppets by the tensions between us. Amidst the shadows of gyrating bodies, we pressed together tightly. Then She stopped and glanced down at the rest of me, wondering why I was so hard and angular.

The world slammed back into my consciousness. Music swirled around me in a violently angry flood, the heat of the dance floor seared me, faux drums rumbled in my skull. I tried to explain my armor, who I was, what I was doing . . . but my words were lost in the eddies of an electronic symphony and She shook Her head sadly. She pulled me close again and whispered something in my ear that was swept away like a loved one in a riot. I tried to talk, She shook Her head and shrugged . . . And then Her eyes went wide. Something pressed into my back and a commanding glove closed on my good shoulder. I dropped my helmet and went backward with an elbow, connecting with a face that crumpled under the force of the blow. His weapon tumbled to the floor and he went down on top of it. KelRon security had found me.

I reached out and grabbed another guard, still dealing with another dancer, by the front of his armor. His eyes focused on me as my steel-toed boot snapped up into his groin. The hard armor codpiece did its job perfectly, stopping my hard steel-toed boot from mangling his privates, but it did nothing to eliminate the raw kinetic force of the blow. He bent over and I brought my knee up to meet his jaw. He sprawled backward into his remaining partner. He turned with a curse on his lips, a curse that changed into a scream as I launched over the falling body of his comrade. We went down in a pile. With one hand I slapped up his visor my other fist jackhammered into his face over and over. His nose disappeared in a smear of blood, the constant shocks up my wrist kept time with the schizophrenic music. Every pain, every frustration, every moment of fear and hatred unleashed upon his too-fragile skull through my hand. I felt it seed, grow, and begin to consume my sanity in an orgy of conflagration until a soft touch, as gentle as a breeze, as strong as steel, alighted on my shoulder. Like cool water, it drenched the storm inside my soul and I glanced back onto the face of Her. Instead of knowing love, or beautiful radiance, She was looking at Her hand, dripping with my blood. My damn shoulder must have come open and soaked through the stolen jacket. I got off the mauled guard.

I wanted to explain, I tried to explain, but the music wouldn't let me. Worse, the crowd was losing its dance trance as it noticed the three sprawled bodies bleeding on the floor. In a few seconds someone would get frightened, someone would summon the bouncers, who would call the cops, which would alert KelRon, bringing them down on my head. I grabbed a guard's rifle and my helmet, feet prepping to bolt when I was stopped again by light hands of unimaginable grace.

She was frightened. She was terrified, but whatever I was feeling staring into Her endless eyes, She must have felt it too; She was not ready to abandon me just yet. She pulled me through the crowd toward the back of the building, opening a door marked 'employees only' and led me down dark stairs into the relative quiet of the basement. I stumbled on a loose plank, saving myself from another fall by leaning into the wall. A wall hook dug into my injured shoulder and I stifled a scream as my legs went all weak and wobbly. I forced the world to stay in focus through will alone, and made it to the bottom of the stairs without collapsing.

And She was there, opening a hatch into the earth.

I walked to the opening, favoring the side nearly paralyzed with singing pain, and glanced downward. It led into a tight utility tunnel, the kind that wandered underneath nearly every city in the galaxy. It would be a tight fit, in fact I would have to crawl, but I knew it would drastically increase the chance of me making it out of here alive.

I turned to my savior and tried to speak, tried to vocalize the apocalyptic tempest of emotion that burned, froze, healed, and killed all at once. She placed a hand over my mouth, Her eyes breathing life into mine. Then She leaned in and kissed me. Most people go their entire lives without ever finding someone they can fall in love with from across a crowded room. Most people will never know someone utterly, completely, wholly from looking into the other's eyes. I had traveled millions of light years and dodged gunfire to be here, with Her. Now I had to leave. And She knew it. It was a beautiful kiss. Beautiful and sad, a tender moment that said both 'I love you' and 'goodbye.' It killed me and buoyed me to the surface of my emotions all at once, a baptism that washed away the fire and pain. She turned and left. I fed my stolen rifle into the hole, stripped out of the awful purple long-coat, and followed behind my weapon, chest threatening to collapse around the vacuum inside.

The passage was even tighter than I had thought. I crawled on my belly for most of a kilometer before I could find an access hatch to the street. I shot the lock off with the rifle and crawled back into the open air. Stiff hands unfurled the map, and I confirmed my position. I managed to find a fire escape and lever myself up, one rung at a time, to the top of the dilapidated office building. There, in the cool air, I looked over the fallen stars of the city and sent out three letter codegroups to The Radiation Angels, telling them to come and get me.

I should be checking carrier signals. I should be finding cover. I should be scanning the streets below and sky above for the next wave of KelRon security. Instead, all I did was sit, and bleed, and think about the astronomical nature of chance, about love and life, about men gurgling and dying, about the billions of bits in my backpack screaming out silently for justice.

I heard the engines of a flier coming close. I crept to my feet like an old man, looking into the sky and tracking the two tons of steel racing toward me on four pillars of flame. I hoped for painkillers and a medic, but I'd take the former over the latter to be honest. I managed to scrounge up enough strength to wave at them before the machine guns opened fire.

Adrenaline dumped into my system from all directions as my feet found purchase. I dove through the air, demonic sparks flying up from all directions as bullets screamed in to drink my blood. I rolled behind an air conditioner unit and bounded outward again as enemy fire punched through it as if it were tinfoil. The big craft slewed around again, touching off automatic fire that flashed in my path like a solid wall of lead. I skidded to a stop and fell over backwards. I dropped the rifle and it was shredded as it passed through the deadly rain. My back arched, bringing my full weight down upon my wounded shoulder. My helmet came loose and launched into the night. The world swam, fluttered, and came back into focus. All I could see was the KelRon flier, lining its guns up for a final volley.

I closed my eyes and thought about those eyes, Her eyes. Of all the random cruelty of this night, of the entire galaxy, one thing pierced me like a misericorde: I was going to die without knowing Her name.

There was an explosion. Heat ran along me like the hand of a devil. It tossed me like a rag doll in a hurricane . . .

. . . I came to, hanging half off of the building and looking straight down to the street below. Blood dripped through my short hair and ran down my face, leaping from my nose and slapping into the pavement stories below. I rolled away from certain death and laid on my back, looking up into the sky where a new flier hovered warily as the wreckage of a KelRon flier burned the roof across the street. My vision swam, and I swear everything went black and white for a second, but through the haze I saw the sword, wings, and trefoil of The Radiation Angels emblazoned on the side.

For what seemed the thousandth time, I took inventory: Everything hurt. My ears registered only ringing. I was bleeding from a few places I could see and untold number I couldn't. But nothing felt broken. Nothing refused to work when called upon. And it appeared that the avalanche drive was still in my backpack. All of which meant it was time to stop goldbricking and get back on the job.

The flier came down low and popped the cargo hatch, exposing four tethered Angels reaching out for me, shouting words of encouragement my wounded ears could not hear. I stumbled toward them, but they still had to bring the flier dangerously close to the building and half drag me into the rear hatch. They hauled me in, closed the hatch and the pilot punched the engines.

Once the speed stabilized, a medic came over and shined a light in my eyes. He mouthed some more words at me. Events unfolded on every side, but I felt disconnected from them all. One woman, whose name I knew I should know, took the avalanche drive and secured it . . . somewhere. Other soldiers, each name blurrier than the one before, strapped me into my seat. They kept asking questions, so I pointed at my ears and shrugged until finally they left me alone. The medic inserted an IV of something into my arm and hung it on my seat above my head. We went ever higher, caught between the peaceful stars of the sky above and the violent stars of warfare below. The pilot angled the flier, preparing to fire off the nuclear reaction engines for our flight into space.

I closed my eyes as tears leaked from them freely. I knew that soon I would be asked questions, and I would have to answer. They would ask what had happened, and I wondered what I could say. What HAD happened? What was real? Nothing seemed real except for Her. I tried to envision Her, explain Her, categorize Her, but nothing could encompass the smallest of Her features. It was like trying to fathom the mind of God.

I tried to comfort myself with the idea that I had survived, but my thoughts dwelled on the next few hours, to my debriefing, where they would ask me questions and I would have nothing to say.

Not one word.

FORGOTTEN CAUSES

John C. Wright

I WOKE UP TO A BEAUTIFUL WOMAN'S VOICE WHISPERING DIRECTLY INTO MY EAR: "WE ARE now in a secure mission posture. All information hereafter will be on a need-to-know basis."

I was in zero gravity, warm, comfortable, floating. No doubt I was back aboard the Ship, safe at the perihelion of some wide elliptic orbit, nice and far, far away from the deadly danger of the Suspects . . .

Wait. What Suspects? Who were they? And . . .

And who exactly was I again? I seemed to have misplaced my name.

Furthermore, there was an irksome pain in my arm, a stabbing pain, as if the intravenous needle built into the elbow-joint of my armor had missed the vein.

Funny. Why would I be wearing my full kit heavy battle-armor if I were back asleep in my little brain-womb aboard the Ship?

I pried an eye open and saw a grand, stately movement of blue and white swirls slowly passing across my face-plate screen. To one side, as I rotated, was a pretty flower-shape of blazing red with arms of floating black.

It took me a moment to focus. Blue ocean. White clouds. Flaming wreckage formed an expanding cloud out from me. Smoking shards of hull-ceramic spun giddy trails of smoke. No. Not 'out from' me. Up. I was in an atmosphere. A planet. I was at least a thousand feet up. And I was in free-fall only because I was freely falling.

Hey—Was that my landing craft that just got shot down?

My limbs jerked, trying to grab something. But nothing moved. A coffin would be roomy compared to power-armor with the power off. Imagine having a ton of composite alloy wrapped skin-tight around each limb. I was trapped.

"Where the hell am I? Who am I?"

A beautiful woman's voice, like the voice of an angel. It was the Ship. "I'm sorry, but you are not cleared to know that at the present time. The mission has assumed a secure posture and all information hereafter will be on a need-to-know basis . . . "

A good marine probably would have just said, ma'am yes ma'am! Ready to splatter! Wilco! But I just screamed and swore a blue streak.

She said: "You are apparently fully conscious. I am returning battle-suit control to you."

Now my limbs moved. Joint motors amplified my panicky flailing so that I began to roll and tumble. Reflexes took over. I spread my arms and triggered altitude jets. And kicked the switch with my chin to snap the airsickness bag over my mouth. I had to remember to thank the Designer back on Earth for that one.

If I could remember who the hell the Designer was. And why did a sensation of cold desolation creep up my spine at that thought?

The Ship's lovely voice: "Attention. You have three targets approaching mach 4.1 north-northeast. No confirmation exists that these are hostile forces . . . "

With a shock, light exploded into my eyes. No. Not my eyes. It only seemed that way. There were a dozen pin-point cameras dotting the hull of my battle-suit; the information from all those points of view were flooding directly into my visual cortex.

" . . . You may fire in your own self-defense if you or your mission are threatened. Avoid collateral damage where possible . . . "

There were a dozen more cameras and reader-heads in the noses of little micro-rocket remotes which were fanning out from the wreckage of my downed lander. Think its hard to integrate the viewpoint of two eyes into proper perspective? Try doing it with two dozen.

" . . .You are not, I say again, not required to commit suicide to avoid capture. . . "

I could see the radio-noise and thermal exhaust radiating from the bodies approaching. They had hard radar-reflective surfaces. The favorite object a marine ever sees: Big, hot, slow, and made of metal.

" . . . The amnesia drug has removed those memories tagged with security neuro-linkages from your brain . . . "

I directed (how? just by wishing it, like pointing a finger) two of my remotes at each target, to get overlapping fields of fire, and I set their idiot-brains on DefCon two, which is, shoot if they change energy levels, alter course, or open fire. Then I sent two more remotes toward the group at high-speed, instruments cranked over to high-sensitivity, active scan, double-readings. Were the incoming bodies armed?

" . . . You may cooperate with your captors in any way which does not endanger the mission."

My brain had been tampered with. No one can interpret visual images from twenty viewpoints on twenty bands of the spectrum, infrared, IR, UV, radar, magnetic anomaly. What else had been done to me . . . ? What else had the Designer done to me . . . ?

(Just the word made me recoil slightly. I wondered then whether the Designer was an It, not a He.)

But I didn't let the prospect of imminent death in battle distract me.

"Ship! Am I going to be rescued, damn you? Where are the other members of my . . . " I was going to say 'my squad' or 'my unit' or something. But I stopped. The words sounded wrong.

Loneliness. Terrible loneliness rose like bile in my throat. I knew what she was about to say before she said it.

She said: "There are no other human beings."

That sentence seemed to hang in my ears for a moment, echoing.

The lead incoming aerospace craft (old-fashioned, using a ram-jet and rocket combination for low-troposphere to high-atmosphere theater) blossomed with heat in the armpits of its stubby triangular wings, and fired two beam-guided missiles in my direction.

"What's my mission?"

"I am not certain if you are cleared to know that. Please stand by while I consult instruction scenarios . . . "

My remotes had already sliced the lead enemy craft from stem to stern, and issued an electromagnetic pulse powerful enough to scramble any avionics and sterilize any unshielded men aboard. The other two remotes were beeping plaintively for instructions; their simple-minded threat-response software couldn't decide if the other two craft were 'part of' the first craft's attack.

I toggled them over to DefCon One (which is, shoot if they sneeze.)

My altimeter alarm went off. I had been deceived by my Earthly instincts. The globe was smaller than Earth; the horizon closer; and the surface was a hell of a lot closer than I thought.

The helmet monitor lit up: Deploy chute? Yes/No.

"Damn you, Ship! You told me not to do anything to endanger the mission! To carry out that order, you've got to tell me what the mission is—"

The craft on the left sneezed. Remotes three and four blotted it out. A smear of oily flame and radioactive debris unrolled across the sky.

"Your mission parameters are: Determine if the suspect world is responsible for the destruction of the surface biosphere of Earth. If so, execute suspect world, regardless of civilian collateral damage."

My mind went blank. Earth dead?

In that stunned blankness, one little thought asked plaintively: Who would do it? Who would or could launch an attack to a target light-years away? An attack which would not arrive till their great-grandchildren had died of old age? It was insane . . .

There could not be that many suspect worlds. Multi-generation colony-ships were very big and very expensive and very slow. And it was very, very hard to find volunteers. Besides, within a thousand light-years of Earth, only six planets were capable of sustaining human life.

And evidently I was falling toward one of them.

Her voice continued: "If not, determine if suspect world has any weapons or weapons technology capable of large-scale interstellar attacks. Disarm suspect world. Use any means necessary. Inform the population of the Law."

"The Law . . . ?"

But I knew the Law. Thou shalt not kill worlds.

The third incoming aerospace craft wasn't what it seemed. When it flinched, the particles beams from my remotes bounced off its inner hull, which was made of something a damn sight tougher than the phony outer hull; and then it swatted half my remotes out of the sky with a sweep of hard radiation.

The nose tilted up till the craft was vertical. The stubby wings fell off; a column of white light and white noise erupted out of the engines. My neutrino counter ran up to five digits 99999! and burned out. Whatever the hell they were burning wasn't old-fashioned chemical rockets.

I could see, on higher wavelengths, beams like searchlights drop into synch with the tight-beam shining from the radio-laser horn of my helmet. The beam pointed up. The super-rocket or hell-craft or whatever it was shot straight up. Same direction. My remotes didn't have a chance of keeping pace.

And remember those two big, dumb slow rockets coming for me? They suddenly got a lot faster, and they peeled open into segments almost as small and almost as hard to see as my remotes.

An automatic circuit in my battle-suit began jinking me back and forth with random bursts from my retroes. Yanked up, jerked left, swatted right, knocked spinning. Instantly, I was one huge bruise across my whole body. This was supposed to keep me safe?

My counter-electronics flashed. Screaming little super-missiles flashed to my left and right, missing the target, or got tricked into exploding early.

Deploy chute? Yes/No. (WARNING Chute cannot deploy while retroes are firing.)

"Ship! Ship! What the hell do I . . . "

A man's voice, in a language which I somehow knew, broke in: "Terran! The Military Arm of the Avernian Collective requires your immediate surrender!"

What the hell? Were they asking me to surrender? Me?!!

I decided then and there that I knew one thing about myself. I didn't give up.

The Ship: "This channel is compromised. Do not break radio silence. Out."

It was true. They were tracing my communication beam. The hell-craft had climbed almost out of the range even of my godlike sight. It was headed to some spot in low orbit, the source of the lovely female voice which was my only link with my life. Whoever the hell I was.

The man's voice was still talking to me: "Shut down your active systems! Let your energetic and nucleonic radiations drop to equal background readings to display sub-mission! This is a necessary ordainment!"

The on-board computer in my suit flashed good news: Enemy signal protocols algorithm solved. Engage signal falsification routine? Yes/No.

And bad news: WARNING Below safe descent ceiling. Initiate emergency crash-landing procedures? Yes/No.

(Yanked left, jerked up, swatted down-left, knocked right.)

They must have done something to my brain. I was able to see what no one could see; I was able to know things I knew I didn't know. I saw that fast little super-missiles mugging me were being guided by beams pointing at me from some distant source. (And I knew that the guide-beams were coming from six kilometers away, a large metallic craft 50 meters below the ocean surface.)

And when I wondered if my suit could impersonate those guide-beams and point those fast little bastards at some better targets . . . (For example, at the disappearing hell-craft up above closing in on my siren-voiced Ship. Or at the source of the beam-guides themselves. Or toward the source of the irksome voice asking me to surrender. Or at all three . . .) I wondered; I knew; I willed it.

It happened.

And the nasty little super-rockets, now my toys, flipped 180 and screamed away. Fast enough, maybe, to get the hell-craft.

Then, it all happened at once:

Man's Voice: " . . . willing to recognize your absurd claim to be the Terran emissary, Marshall Lamech . . . " (Lamech! My name was Lamech!) " . . . and extend you grant of ambassadorial immunity, if only you will stop these brutal and unprovoked attacks on Avernus and her satellites . . . "

Unprovoked? My lander was shot down! (Had my lander been firing? I had a dim memory of a streamlined dart of a machine, every forward surface studded with weapon-tubes, launch-ports, deflection and evasion arrays.)

Deploy Chute? Yes/No. WARNING You are below safe descent threshold.

Ambassador? Did he just call me an Ambassador? (And I thought they arrived in limousines, not in Armored Assault Re-Entry Vehicles.)

WARNING Incoming particle beam weapon from submarine source. Outer ablative material breached. Return Fire? Yes/No.

And then roaring, fire, pain, light, noise, confusion.

And then darkness. I don't remember what happened then.

Isn't it funny how you dream in black and white?

In the first part of the dream, I was sinking, sinking, numb with shock, all my bones were broken, and my helmet was filling up with blood.

In the second part of the nightmare, I was crawling along the ocean bottom, along the muddy floor of some sea-trench sunlight never reached, and slow clouds of murk swirled between the fingers of my gauntlets as I moved. Lamp-eyed transparent fish and blind insects swarmed in my face, attracted to my helmet-lights.

I screamed each time I moved, because it wasn't me moving. The joint-motors of my power-armor were running on automatic. Pull right arm; drag left knee. Pull left arm; drag right knee. Every time my limp limbs were yanked by the metal sleeves through the movements of that painful crawl, I could feel the jagged bone-ends grinding together inside me.

And then some huge armored machine, like a bathysphere on treads, rose up from the mud and gloom and speared me with a spotlight. A manipulator-claw reached out . . .

The third part of the nightmare was worst of all. I was strapped to some sort of morgue-slab or inquisition rack or something, and some sort of torture surgeons, faceless shapes in gray, were tearing off my skin, flaying me alive. Except it wasn't my skin they were tearing off, but my armor, prying me like an oyster out of its shell.

Days or years of pain went by; the room changed size and color once or twice, or maybe I was moved. Then, voices I could somehow understand:

"Officer-surgeon of the Collective! Observe here. Neural actions. The Envoy Lamech is awake—!"

"Illogical. Cortex tissues were destroyed with a number-five laser-scalpel. Nervous tissue does not regenerate."

"Yet, see, Luminous One!"

My eyes were open. Some sort of instrument clamped around my eyelids kept my eyeballs moist with drops of mist. Nice of them.

'Them' consisted of gaunt, tall figures in gray airtight suits, with faceplates of mirror-white. A battery of blinding lights, like a nest of snakes, coiled from the overhead, and writhed to peer across their shoulders, turning as they turned, pointing lamps whatever direction the figures glanced. The one on the left had a set of cables and medical appliances, clamps and probes and scalpels, growing in place of his right arm.

The other one—evidently a superior officer—was speaking. "Recall that our ancestors were modified to survive this planet, and modified again to serve the Collective. He is not Homo Sapiens Superior Eugenicus. He is merely a Human Being. Some quirk in his atavistic neuro-chemistry might account for these readings."

"Yet, ponder, Sagacious One, how long ago our ancestors set out from the Once-Home-World, and how slow the giant ships! The science of Earth may have grown in one hundred centuries! He could be infested with nanomachines, bodies in his cell fluid too small for our instruments to detect, programmed to repair his tissues. Even brain tissue."

"Nanomachines are a myth. Earth is a myth. Dead tissues and dead worlds do not spring to life again!"

"Yet look at the readings, All-Imposing One! He stirs; his eyes track our movements! I implore you! Look! Look!"

"Hm. Even so, with all his weapons and armor removed—what can he do? We are safe."

"Sir! This is an Earthman!"

"Ah. Perhaps you are right, loyal one. Sign the death-warrant in my name, and note the time. Stun him with six hundred volts of neuro-suppressor. I will apply a lethal impulse directly into his skull."

So the guy on the right picked up something like a shiny pistol and leaned over me.

I raised my arm (I had to jerk—my hand was stuck for a moment) and took the pistol (funny how his fingers just came apart in my grip, like bags of jelly, like dry twigs) and pointed the business end at his head and pulled the trigger.

When his brains exploded all over me, they were yellow, gray and red. Bright red. And I thought you couldn't see colors in dreams.

I was distracted for a moment by my hand. My wrist was dangling with severed cables and broken chains thick enough to bind an elephant. I watched the broken chain-ends swinging idly. Did I do that . . . ?

What the hell was I?

The other guy hit a switch or something before I could move. The snake-necked lamps ignited with a strange blaze of blinding energy. It felt like a sledge-hammer with a red hot head slamming home into my skull.

Out again. (Maybe that was good. If I had been awake, I would have been pretty miffed about being knocked unconscious every few minutes.)

Waking up was more fun the next time. I was floating again, nice and safe in zero-gee. In free-fall . . .

I shouted and grabbed for something to hang onto, some weapon to shoot. I got a handful of water and splashed myself in the face.

Blinking my eyes clear, I saw I was floating in a garden-pool. An inflatable pillow supported my head and shoulders. A white box—a medical servo of some sort—floating nearby, with intravenous tubes running to my throat and elbow, and wires attached to disks on my chest and head. Perhaps the pool-water had been salted with something to increase its buoyancy; or maybe the gravity here was lighter than standard.

A circle of fruit trees surrounded the little pond, and terraced hedges of ferns and flowers rose up to my left and right. Beyond that was a wall. Above was not sky, but a ceiling of blue glass, criss-crossed with a trellis of lacy supports. This garden was in-doors.

I stood up, kicked aside the box, and yanked the needles and wires away with a sweep of my arm. It hurt, but it made me feel good. Maybe I don't like having machines to whom I haven't been properly introduced sticking their little things into me.

At first, I thought I heard the Ship's Voice, beautiful and feminine. "We estimate the year on Earth, correcting for relativistic effects, to be AD 12705, the One Hundred Twenty Eighth Century. Are you aware of what that implies?"

It was my language. Or, at least, it sounded sort of familiar.

So I turned around, stark naked, with blue pool-water still dripping from my parts, and the loveliest woman I had ever seen or imagined was walking toward me. Floating toward me, it seemed like, since her step was as graceful as a ballerina's. She wore a dress of white, pinch-waisted to accent her figure, with an elegant long skirt swinging in counterpoint to the sway of her hips. Her hair was raven-black, her cheek-bones high, her lips full and red, chin delicate. Her eyes were slanted and exotic, and as green as glass.

Her eyes held the clearest and most intelligent gaze I'd ever seen. On the other hand, they were, at the moment, the only pair of eyes I could ever remember seeing, so I guess I didn't have much of a basis of comparison.

A real marine would have engendered triplets on her on the spot. Me, I just stood there, dangling, wearing a dumb look on my face. Finally, I managed to say, "What the hell's going on?"

She smiled a half-smile, and looked at me sidelong. Did I mention how long and lush her lashes were? How green her eyes, like mirrors of emerald? "You mean, why are you still alive?" (A beautiful voice, soft and soprano, but not the voice of my Ship.)

I nodded. It did indeed seem to be a fine question, and one well worth pondering. Why the hell was I still alive?

"So tell me," I said.

A quiet smile graced her lips a moment. "We hope to reason with you. You have crossed six hundred and eight light-years from Sol; at least a thousand years have passed, Earth-time, since your launch. Whomever or whatever sent you out so far is long, long dead. Why continue this struggle? Whatever your reasons—and I'm quite sure that they were good reasons at one time—they are now defunct, meaningless. Your orders are out-of-date. And we are not your enemies; we are not monsters. Come, look!"

So I climbed out of the pool. It was warm in the garden, and she didn't seem to mind the way I was (or wasn't) dressed. Maybe buck-naked was the way prisoners of war were kept, here. Or honored ambassadors and other guests of state. Or monsters from another star. Or whatever the hell I was.

The touch of her hand on my elbow thrilled me. With delicate, nymph-like step, she moved up the little terrace-slope and past the hedge. I felt her warmth, smelled the hint of her perfume, as she stepped past me.

The grass was cool on my bare feet, pleasant, and dew-drops from the tall ferns near the hedge touched my neck and shoulders with icy dots of shock as I pushed through them.

She gestured to the wall beyond the trellises. A large section of wall faded into transparency.

I was looking out an expansive window which was halfway up a cliffside. Facing it was another cliff, equally as tall, studded likewise with windows. Between the two canyon walls, a little strip of gray-blue sky showed high above. The canyon was crossed by a hundred bridges and aqueducts. Odd-looking people strolled the lanes or rolled on wheels. Some were animal-headed or were part-machine. They were slender and tall, almost bird-like; perhaps a side-effect of the lighter gravity. Everyone wore cloaks (or were they wings?) of muted colors, mauve, tan, blue-gray, tawny, brown.

I stepped closer to the huge window.

From the window, I could see a park underfoot, bright with shrubs and flowering green bushes. Several waterfalls cascaded from nearby aqueducts, formed little brooks across the lawns, and gathered at a central pool. Children frolicked in the pool. I saw a mother dangling her baby above the water, and it smiled and splashed its little toes.

I was very conscious of the woman at my shoulder.

She pointed at the scene. "We are the men beyond mankind; we are post-human; we have re-engineered our minds and bodies to survive the harsh conditions here on Avernus. Our minds have been restructured; we exceed old human limitations, selfishness, greed, individualism, disloyalty. Does that make us forfeit our right to live in peace? These are the people you tried to destroy. Look at them; wives and husbands, mothers and children, boys and girls. Has the force which sends you justified its evil acts to you? If so, that is an explanation we are all eager to hear."

"I don't have an explanation," I said. "You've medically examined me. You must know I don't remember a damn thing." A note of bitterness crept into my voice: "I don't even remember who I am."

She nodded, looking not a bit surprised. "I will remind you. What you are, Marshall Lamech, is a remnant of the far past. You are the forgotten left-over of some ancient war. An unexploded bomb. A dormant virus. A relic. You come from a world long dead.

"For forty years we watched the flare of your ship's deceleration as you approached from deep space. We welcomed you, but your ship would not land. By radio, you accused our ancestors of some long-ago attack against the Earth. You demanded we accept you as our police and prosecutor, judge, jury, and, if need be, executioner. Yet you had no right to stand in judgment over us.

"Then you attacked us, killing and destroying. That is fact, which no regret, no dwelling on the past can alter or ameliorate. Now we must concentrate on the future. Do you wish to have a future? We are prepared to offer you a life useful to the Collective, a role within our society, material comforts and . . . pleasures."

My imagination was all too eager to fill in what kind of pleasures I'd like to get from her. But I tried to keep a stony face. "Yes..? Providing . . . ?"

" . . . Providing only that you cooperate. Radio your ship, arrange a rendezvous. We wish to inspect this ship of yours. Any men, material, or technology aboard will be turned over to the Collective and used for the public good."

"And—just for the sake of argument—let's say I refuse. What then?"

"Pain and torment, agony and death . . . "

"Gee. Why am I not surprised . . . ?"

"Not for you. I don't know what would happen to you. But I will have failed in my mission. You must have noticed my body-form is not proper." She gestured again at the slender, birdlike not-quite-humans gliding on the bridges and balconies outside. None of them looked like her. "I was designed for you. For your environment. I cannot live outside this museum, this terrarium. Without you, I have nothing . . . "

"Designed . . . ?" I wasn't sure I liked the sound of that.

She smiled again. It was a sad, soft smile. "We had forty years in which to prepare. There were genetic archives, old records from the Once-Home-World."

"You are a slave?"

"I do my duty and I obey my orders. Are we so different from each other?" When she smiled, she had dimples. "But why dwell on unpleasant things? Happiness and joy awaits all who are loyal to the principles of the Collective. But you must not delay in deciding! For, see: the Correction Instructors grow impatient!"

I turned. Coming up the grassy slope behind us, pushing through the flowery hedges, came four tall, angular machines, like oversized preying mantises. The robotic carapaces were covered with thorns and hooks. Their thoraxes held turrets. Some of the weapons I recognized: rail-guns, hard-shots, flamers, neural whips. Others, I did not. Nothing looked pretty. But they were quiet as cats, and they stalked closer.

I jerked my thumb at the approaching monsters. "So they are 'bad cop', I take it?"

She huddled close to me, as if for support. Automatically, by instinct, I put my arm around her. It felt good. She looked up at me with her wide, green eyes, and she said in a troubled voice: "What makes you hesitate? You yourself admit that you recall nothing; if there is a reason for you to be loyal to your mission, you have forgotten it. Is there any point in dying for a forgotten cause?"

I pushed her around behind me, put my foot on a nearby tree, and, with a grunting shrug, tore off a branch. I turned to face the approaching machines, branch held in both hand, like a club. Little green leaves floated down from my impotent impromptu weapon.

The machines stopped and pointed their various barrels, lenses, and muzzles at me. There was a metallic snap as the lead unit jacked ammunition into its chambers. I heard the hissing ultrasonic whine of plasma-magnetics charging. With a loud clatter, gas-shells and flame cartridges slammed into gun-breaches. Little red dots from aiming lasers floated on my naked chest.

I felt about as stupid as a man can feel.

But, hey, the way I figured it, I'd rather fall weapon-in-hand instead of hands-up. Even if the so-called weapon is nothing but a green stick.

"You will be led now either to a bridal chamber or a torture chamber, Marshall Lamech," came the soft voice from behind me. I could feel her soft hand on my back, her scented breath on my ear. "Defiance is pointless, unless, of course, your goal is to ensure both our deaths. But why fight? Do you remember any reason to fight on?"

Her other hand, no doubt, was readying some small-arm from her pocket. What was the reason I had turned my back on her again? To protect her from . . . whom? Her own allies? Her own superiors? (I think I've mentioned how stupid I felt just then.)

"I need some answers first," I said.

A masculine voice issued from all four robots at once: "Little time remains! In a few minutes, your ship's orbit lifts her above the here-now horizon. We do not wish your ship to have direct line-of-sight with this area; her energy-silhouette indicates a particle beam weapon is ready. We are directing radio-signal toward her, but she will not respond to us. Call! Order your ship to stand down! You need but speak aloud; we can convey your words to the broadcaster. We are all one system."

The Ship had told me it was OK to cooperate with these people here, provided it did not impede the mission. But did this hinder the mission?

And was the cute emissary behind me right? Did I even care about the goddamn mission?

I spoke: "Who killed the Earth?"

I felt the breath of the girl behind me in my ear : "What does it matter? The question is entirely academic. Earth is long, long gone. And what do you care even so? You are not from Earth. The medical evidence shows that your body is only a few weeks old. You were constructed, fully grown, from genome records, during deceleration. You think you are a human being, but you are not. There are no human beings."

I decided I didn't like having the girl behind me, so I stepped sideways to put her in my view. As I thought, her right hand was in her skirt pocket, clutching something heavy and rectangular.

Unfortunately, the robot on the far right now glided forward, so that it was behind me. I didn't like that much either.

And it got dark. The sunlight was failing. But it was not dusk. A glance at the window showed that some roof or blast-panels were sliding over top of the canyon outside, closing all the city under a giant lid. I saw people rushing, but no panic, no show of emotion, except that some of the babies in the park were crying. What was odd about the scene was that all the people were in step. They were marching double-time but they were clearly in step, all being controlled by one mind, one will.

Like a chorus, four copies of the same masculine voice came from the robots: "The decision horizon reaches unity! The unintegrated organism known as Lamech must proffer cooperation behavior! Order your ship into close orbit, weapons stand down, shut off reaction drive, open airlocks, prepare to be boarded. This course of behavior leads to reward! All other courses lead to corrective penalty! Speak now!"

The girl spoke softly, her green eyes looking deeply into mine as she swayed forward. "If you are not a human being, what would it matter to you if the home planet of the human beings had been destroyed? Besides, there is nothing you can do about any of that now. That issue is dead. A thousand years dead. Only your life matters now. Doesn't it? Doesn't it?" Then, more softly, she whispered: "It matters to me, if not to you."

But I noticed she did not step between me and the mantis-robots. In fact, they were both in motion, she daintily stepping forward, eyes soft and pleading, and perhaps a trifle afraid for me; and them, creeping catlike on their twitching spider-legs, gun-barrels and projectors swinging to track me, fanning left and right to cover possible avenues of escape.

Funny how they stepped that way. It was little things that attracted my attention, such as how her head moved ever so slightly to the left while the upper launcher from the killer-robot nearest her slid ever so slightly to the right, so that spent shell-casings from its ejectors would not graze her hair once it started firing. Very smooth. All choreographed.

All controlled by one will.

I said, "I don't believe you."

She said, "Ask your ship. Talk to it. Simply speak out loud."

"Ship! Are you there?"

I counted. One Mississippi, Two Mississippi. Then, the beautiful, beautiful Voice of the Ship answered, as placid and perfect as only unliving voices can be: "Message received. This line is not secure. Switching to encryption. Please confirm if you understand me." This last group of words was somehow different, but I still understood them.

About two seconds delay between signal and response. So that ship was roughly 186,000 miles away. Rather high for a firing orbit. The bad guys implied she had opened her weapon-parasol, and powered her particle-beam weapons. Was she going to fire a directed energy beam from that far away? Through the atmosphere?

"I understand you," I said, and the way the words came out hurt my throat.

Really, I understood almost nothing that was going on in this whole mess. But I did understand that the Ship was preparing a volley against satellite targets, something in high orbit, near her. Otherwise, her posture did not make sense. The target satellite had to be emerging from what was (relative to the ship) the planet's communication shadow.

I noticed the cute emissary had taken her hand out of her pocket and was holding her ears.

I said, "Give present target orbital elements."

That was when I realized that what was coming out of my mouth was not words; it was some sort of strident whining noise, a mathematical set of hiccup and shrills. It sounded terrible.

The Ship: "Requested information cannot be broadcast on non-secure channels. Switching to secure channel . . . "

The noise of the Ship's Voice coming out of the speakers was the same hiccups and shrieks. An encryption. The bad guys were passing it back and forth between us, but I doubted that they could decipher it.

They must have doubted it too. Maybe they had given it a try, and given up, for then they said (all four in unison, just like a boy's choir:) "Interrupt! Private communication is selfish, irregular, impermissible! Unadapted Lamech-entity continues to conspire against the Unity! His actions do not conform!"

The girl put her hand back in her pocket, now that I wasn't making an ear-splitting squeal. She said to me, "What were you talking about with your ship? Did you ask her whether you were human? Did you ask her why you were here?"

The robot-quartet chimed in: "Consult with central dogma! Formulate a danger-assessment of Marshall Lamech's character, extrapolate, react! Awaiting verdict."

The girl flushed. She looked actually angry or upset. "Wait, masters, I beg you! He may still be willing to help us! Give him time to think! Stop treating him like the enemy; he is as much a victim here as we are!"

The robot crew actually stepped back. Certain weapons were holstered; others powered down. I heard the ticking of the energy-direction barrels cooling, the whine of multiguns going into standby-cycles.

Was that supposed to reassure me?

She turned back to me. "Please! There are more lives involved here than just yours! You've got to believe us! We are not your foes, how could we be? Whatever happened to Earth happened thousands of years before we were born!"

I saw how her eyes glittered; she seemed about to weep; and her bosom heaved with passion, her cheeks were blushed with fear.

Good acting. I almost bought it. Almost.

I wondered were they had gotten the algorithm to mimic human body language, nuances of gesture. I wondered how, just working with mathematical code and old records, they had been able to match up specific gestures with specific emotions. The sheer genius of it was even more impressive if you figured they did not know what "emotions" were anymore, not really; they must have been judging states of mind by statistical analysis.

They? I should say 'it.' It seemed to be one system.

And evidently its knowledge of body language gesture algorithms was very exact. At that moment I "heard" a high-frequency communication-burst, coming from a point outside the building, reach out and touch receiver cells in the four robots, and, yes, also in the nervous system of the girl. The so-called 'girl'. The message ran: "Bio-chemical gestalt reactions of unincorporated Lamech unit display rejection-behavior. Probability 89% disbelief; he will initiate aggressive-defensive complex motif shortly. Neutralize. Terminate experiment. Log expended resources as wasted . . . "

I must have sped up then. The sound in the room dopplered down the scale, and I felt a familiar burning heat in my limbs as my muscle pressure increased, a dizzy moment while high-speed superconductive strands took over the signal-transmission from my nervous system. And I jumped into the middle of the damn fighting robots.

Yes, I hit one with the green stick in mid-jump, and, yes, the blow struck the joint where the slugthrower was coming up out of its cleaning holster, so that the shell went past my head rather than into it, and hit the robot behind me in the magazine box. And yes, my skin turned mirror shiny where the aiming lasers touched me, reflecting them away, so that the beamriding smart bullets (which followed those beams) popped their tiny retroes and slammed back toward the third machine they had been shot out from, sending lines of gunfire stitching up the sides of two of the fighting units. One of them was hit in its target-finding lens-array and vomited napalm in my direction, but missed me by a country mile. I ended up with my foot broken where I struck the fourth machine, but I toppled it from its legs.

Yay and hurray for me. And no, being knocked over did not stop machine number four from shooting a smart-grenade into my guts, or taking off my left leg below the knee with a fan of energy. The grenade did not go off for some damn reason (counter-electronic built into my goddamn belly-button?) it just passed through me, but that was enough to uncoil some ropy blood-colored spaghetti all over from inside of me, (amazing how weird and ugly intestines look, when they're yours) and for me to lose all sensation in my legs, and for hydrostatic shock (which should have killed me instantly) to blow out my eardrums and crack several teeth. I was slapped to the grass by some immense force (or immense clumsiness) and the ungodly pain which wracked my every torn muscle, the disgusting weakness and nausea, the sensation of freezing and burning convinced me that I had about two seconds left to live.

And what a goddamn stupid life it had been. How old was I? An hour? Less? Not counting time when I was asleep. My first memory was falling from a blown-up landing craft. If I had had any life before that second, if I was going to have any life after this second, well, you sure as hell could not prove it by me.

It is amazing what it feels like when your blood pressure drops to zero, or what it is like to see a red flood sweep out from what had once been your midsection all across the pretty grass and pretty flowers. (How long can a brain keep thinking once severe blood-loss cuts all its oxygen off?) Even the weeds were going to last longer than I was.

I was still sliding across the grass, actually, still being carried forward by the momentum of my original kick, or maybe I was being blown back by the shot that killed me. The whole combat had not taken an entire second to run its course.

My body (I could feel it dimly) was still jerking, like a slab of meat being slammed by a fire-poker. That was small-caliber antipersonnel shot coming out of machine number three, which was hunching over me like an eager spider, two pair of twin-barrels hammering away. Blue smoke trembled from hot barrels. The sound seemed so dim. I wondered how I could hear it at all, me with my eardrums blown out. It should have been impossible for me to hear anything. One more unanswered question in a short, strange, stupid, pointless life. One more impossible thing.

Damn liars. They had been telling the truth all along. I guess I was not a human being. Not even close.

But was I still alive . . . ? Maybe for a second or two longer. Alive.

And that just made it too damn early to quit.

So I reached up and thrust my fingers in a knife-hand blow into the weak undercarriage of machine number three, where the leg-action elements joined the main power-box. The force of the blow rocked the war-machine backwards enough to elevate the blazing gun-barrels. Machine number four got a friendly dose of friendly fire.

My hand went through the armor into the interior of the machine. Then my fingernails touched the power-core, the computing center, and signals from the bio-circuits in my hand started to trace the communication channels back to the main brain running the whole show . . .

I began to see numbers in my head . . . timing synch information, addressing data, code/decode couplings, protection switch commands . . .

Then, nothing. I flopped like a puppet with its strings cut, falling back, all my limbs dead and numb, paralyzed.

Cutie-pie, the girl emissary, had taken that long (her nervous system was biological, remember, not photoelectronic) to twitch her thumb. I "heard" the signal come out of the box in her pocket and "saw" it touch some foreign metal objects implanted along my spine and hindbrain. Just some nerve blocks they had put in, simple as a pass-interrupt switch. Prisoner pulling garbage you don't like, and zap, all voluntary nerve trunks cut. Even if the prisoner has some sort of gee-whiz-wow wonder-junk built into his body by the miracles of modern science, so what? Doesn't matter what weapons he has in his hands or built into his armpit; if he can't fire them, he's a meat bag.

So I lay there, one leaking meat bag. Still conscious, even though the little black sparks were getting brighter every heartbeat, and the scene around me was getting dimmer. Funny how it felt like I was floating, falling. Funny how you don't need conscious control of your nervous system to drool blood all over yourself. Blood was coming out of my nose also. I bet I looked all yummy and kissable.

She said, "The experiment has confirmed our suspicions; when put under pressure of immediate death, subconscious pre-conditioning took over. His reaction was to attempt to seize a communication node, and link into our mental system. The coded addresses his probes began to form were for deep-archives, for history data from the estimated launch-dates had the attack on Earth been ours. His mission was investigatory, not unlike the others . . . "

Others . . . ? What the hell others?

"We conclude that the Earth-ship will not destroy us without proof of culpability." I noticed her lips were not moving. I noticed I was deaf. This was not coming in through my ears.

"Can he hear us on this channel?" A high-speed zap of communication flickered through the room. Where was it coming from?

"Yes. Note the electrochemical changes in auditory nerves; his brain interprets this as speech." Her voice was still pretty, or, at least, my dying brain was hearing it that way.

"How? We still do not detect any machines or electronic circuitry. No antennae. We removed all the energetic cells and manipulators our micro-probes detected in his nervous system."

"Others may have been too small to detect. Or they grew back." She sounded thoughtful.

"Grew? Grew?! It has only been a few minutes!"

And my brain was interpreting this as if it were a conversation. It was not. It was one mind talking to itself; an internal monologue.

One system, one collective, housed in many brains and neural nets, biological or not biological, as needed. A system old enough to have done the deed?

If so, what had been the motive? Who would fight a war across the uncountable distances and meaningless emptiness of space? The damn nothingness is so damn big and so damn empty that everything men dream about doing. every cause they dream about fighting for, or against, means not a damn thing; not a damn thing at all; not hatred, not revenge, not anything.

The part of the collective mind I thought of as the cute girl was saying to her other selves: "We have no information about the sciences of Old Earth, or what developments might have taken place, over the centuries. Without information, it is premature to form expectations, irrational to be surprised."

She turned to me: "Call off your attack! We have been forced to hurt you only in our self-defense, because you continued to resist. Surely that is legitimate! You cannot prove us guilty of the ancient crime against the Earth; we are not your subjects, you are not our king. Call off your ship."

I could not talk or move and I was bleeding—bleeding heavily—bleeding to death. So I merely thought to myself: "How do you want me to do that, babe? Am I supposed to be able to talk to my Ship just by thinking at her?"

Without any fuss or bother, the Ship's Voice came softly into my brain: "That is within the operational parameters of your present somatoform and body-system. Unless that was a rhetorical question, Marshall Lamech?"

I thought: "This channel is not secure."

The Voice of the Ship: "Analysis of the initial code-address packages you retrieved, before contact was cut, from the deep archive communication system has been fed to the targeting computer. The main energy source-points for communication throughout the Avernus Collective appear to be grouped in a centralized bunker beneath a range of tectonicly stable mountains to the West of your present location . . . "

Wait. What was going on now? Had the Ship somehow read my mind? Or some subconscious part of my mind had acted without my knowledge, and broadcast to the Ship just the tiny beginnings of what I had tried to steal from the Collective communication node. So the Ship now knew where the enemy HQ was hidden.

If they were the enemy . . .

The beauty of the Ship's Voice came again: "Firing solutions are obtained for central communications bunkers and for the high-level satellite arrays which house the main neural network of the Avernus Collective. There appear to be no secondary or back-up systems present; therefore this single operation should win unparalleled strategic advantage."

The Ship was talking about a blow which would lobotomize the Collective's hive-mind, and maybe kill off everyone on the planet.

Was that a good thing or a bad thing? I could not help but picture all those babies out there, once their robot-nurses keeled over, crying and crying for milk . . .

The Ship: "We are in go/no-go situation. As the only human member of staff command, and therefore supreme commander-in-chief of all armed forces of Earth, the decision must be yours. Awaiting instructions."

The ignorant amnesiac who had maybe a few seconds left to live? I was not exactly in the best shape to be weighing evidence and making careful judgment-calls. "Return my memory to me so I can make the goddamn decision . . . "

"Unable to comply. This mission is still on a need-to-know basis, and you are a prisoner behind enemy lines . . . "

I gave her an order which was anatomically impossible and probably illegal in most jurisdictions.

And the Ship replied: "I will interpret that as an order to restore bioconductive neural strand linkages to your command, since this action would be necessary before any sexually reproductive features can be initiated . . . "

The bad guys must have broken the encryption on my communications just as I raised my head, because I overhead three high-speed zaps of communication flicker through the room, one part of the Collective talking to another part.

First message: "His ship will not fire without his command. All of our assumptions were wrong: this is not merely another man-shaped expendable war-unit; he is the real Marshal Lamech! The original template! He will not issue the firing-order even in the extreme of death, since he cannot kill the innocent, and he does not know if we are guilty . . . "

Second message: "His internal nervous system has changed its configuration; the nerve-blocks are being penetrated by an unknown signal, or he had grown by-pass tissue . . . "

The answer: "The experiment is an utter failure. Kill him at once."

And maybe the Collective was not so collected and centralized as I had thought. Because when the girl heard the kill-order come down, she shouted, "NO!" and stepped into the line of fire, trying to protect me.

I did not see any signal traffic when she did it. It was not an outside order. It was just her.

I swear to God I do not know how it was possible for me to jump to my feet with my guts still hanging out. I was sure my nerves were dead; bioconductive strand must have been getting instructions from my brain and jerking dead muscles. Sparks making a severed frog leg flex, I guess. Red intestines slapped against my legs like a wet towel, and I drove my hand through in into the control processor of machine number three, same hole I had made before, but this time I had all the commands ready. On my fingertips, so to speak.

One group of my orders took control of war-machine three and had it open fire on its friends with every gun and energy-antennae. A second group bollixed the local communications net, so echoes of false orders were reproducing themselves, shouting back and forth across the room in a little chorus of chaos, setting off sprinklers and opening and shutting doors. A third group demanded answers from the archives.

But the archives were closed; the lines were dead. The Collective was too fast for me. I could detect some local system traffic in the area, though, and I could see a huge number of channels turn over a huge number of orders to something in the area, even if I could not read those orders . . .

Even though I was deaf, when treads a yard wide tore up the soil, I could hear it through my broken teeth. Nine or ten heavy armored vehicles had been buried under the gardens here, and now they rose up, saplings and hedges toppling from their upper turrets, yards of green turf sliding away, fountains and statues being shouldered aside, earth crumbling. Not little police units like my four preying mantis friends here. No. These were the big boys. Battleship guns swung my way and centered on me.

I assume they opened fire with everything they had, throwing out a few thousand pounds of shells per second in my direction. I also assume that some sort of primary assault orbit-to-ground directed-energy fire from the Ship cut through the roof blocking the canyon outside at that same point in time, shattering the huge plate glass behind me and burning away all the antennae and periscopes of the supertanks (and perhaps of few chucks of melted outer armor.) Because I assume they must have been blind not to hit me.

I also assume that the inside Earth-normal air pressure was somewhat higher than the native Avernus outside air-pressure. I assume that is what picked me up and flung me headlong backward out the window.

All this is assumption. What I remember is those huge battleship guns swinging to cover me, and then, after a moment of noise beyond noise, I woke to find myself floating again. A nice safe, comfortable sensation, falling is. Reminds me of zero-gee.

I still had the robot, fighting machine number three, in one arm, and, somehow, I had the girl in the other arm, who I was beginning to believe was not a robot. She did not seem that hurt. Not compared to me. The wind whipped her long black hair around her as we fell, and her eyes were all white in their sockets.

We were falling though the beam of sunlight which slanted down from the huge melted circle, lipped with white-hot molten stuff, which had appeared in the metal roof over the canyon. Windows and windows slid past us, and not-quite-people-shaped silhouettes stood and watched us fall.

I could feel her warmth in my arms, I swear I scented the perfume of her hair, despite the stinks and burnings and vapors we fell through.

With no eardrums, the whole scene was ghostly quiet. Eerie, actually.

I said to myself, "Ship! I am feeling sort of like an indestructible god at the moment. This techno-crap the Designer stuffed into my body can doing fucking anything, right? Tell me how I can save the girl."

Really, I wasn't too worried about the three hundred yard fall. I was assuming, after what I'd just been through, that my super-body could let me hop out of any crater I made and just dust myself off, smirking. But the girl might not be so lucky.

The Ship Voice came loud and clear, as if she were right by my ear. I wondered why the signal was so strong. "There is no parameter for that operation, Marshall Lamech. The concussive force from a fall from that height, given the frail construction of her body, will most likely result in death. However, a communications bio-filament inserted immediately into her central nervous system should allow a read out of brain-cell charges sufficient to construct a mnemonic read-out . . . "

"You mean I can suck her soul out and put it somewhere else? Give her a new body, new life?" I had already stuck my finger into her ear, and I felt my fingernail dissolve into a swarm of tiny assemblers, sending strands into her skull.

"Not at all, Marshall. It may provide us with some useful postmortem infor . . . "

I hit the ground and the lights went out for me too.

More floating sensations. This time it was because I was stunned.

When I came to, I was still standing within sight of the place where I fell; I could see it through remote cameras. I was on a green hill, with pools and fountains gathered around the foot of the hill, and chunks of broken canyon-roof armor were toppling with slow vast grandeur to the gardens to each side. One whole side of the canyon had had all of its windows blown out. The sunlight was slanting in through several holes melted in the roof.

The signal traffic in the area was a hash. The Collective was sending unsynchronized squawks from one segment of itself to another, all up and down the canyon-metropolis. Arguing, contradicting itself. I saw some war machines firing at each other, surrounded by toppling building-structures and broken glass. When one started to turn its guns toward me, an intolerable flash like the wrath of God smote down through a hole in the canyon roof-armor and burnt it like a bug under a magnifying glass.

It all made sense. The reason why the Voice of the Ship had been so loud and clear had been because she had infiltrated and subverted the communications satellites. Her directed-energy main battery had been making pin-point shots far beyond her unassisted targeting range. Not a problem if the local satellites acted as spotters, and sent her targeting info.

Which all mean that the Ship was in a position to give the Collective a lobotomy. She had the planetary mind by the balls as long as its intercommunication was going through a satellite system we now controlled.

I was in armor again. Parts of the armor were boiling and seething, but not hot. And the hue of the metal seemed familiar. I could 'see' on a microscopic level, all the little assemblers and disassemblers which had poured out of my intestinal tract were fitting the cannibalized crystals of metal, stolen from war machine three, into place, one quick molecule at a time. My insides, without asking me, had just been programmed to turn that machine I had been holding under my left arm into raw materials and to manufacture a new battle-suit. Swell. Nice engineering. I also assume my body had been programmed to keep fighting while I was unconscious, because there were a half a dozen corpses and pieces of wreckage scattered across the slope below me.

And my body also must have had some programming inside whatever circuits the Designer had seen fit to install in my groin. My he-man instincts were still good; because the girl was still in my arms.

So I can even kick ass in my sleep. And rescue the girl. So I'm that good.

Or maybe not.

Rescued? I did not think so. She was covered with blood. My blood? I was amazed it did not eat her like acid or something. Maybe it was hers.

I put her down gently, and her dark hair spilled across the green grass.

As I did, signals reached me. The tiny Collective-cells in her nervous system were broadcasting.

"All records of the crime, if there had been a crime, had been erased . . . " her 'voice' was dreamlike, soft and sweet and sad. I thought it was the loveliest thing I had ever heard. "We knew ourselves guilty of some crime, because of the gaps in the memory records, the world-wide deletions from all libraries, the uniform wreckage of space-stations which no records showed had ever been built . . . "

The little machines living in my bloodstream had also manufactured another brace of remotes, and I had one, no bigger than a dragonfly land between her breasts and take a reading. No breathing; no pulse. No real brain activity, only an electronic ripple through the girl's nervous system.

Her voice came again: " . . . Refueling stations for some large vessel, perhaps a two thousand years ago or more. But why had we destroyed our own memories? Erased all knowledge? Only because we feared the coming of the vengeance of Dead

Earth. A terrible vengeance. Once we heard your name, we knew. From the oldest records. From the Bible of the Judeo-Christians."

I knew the words. They were in my memory. Ancient words. I said them aloud: " 'Adah and Zillah, hear my voice, for I have slay a man for wounding me, and kill a youth for striking me, and if Caine shall be revenged sevenfold for any wrong done him, truly Lamech shall be avenged seven times sevenfold . . . '"

I shook her shoulder. "But why? Why did your Collective help send an attack against Mother Earth? Six Hundred Eight light-years away! It would take a thousand years for the weapons-mass to travel, and then six centuries after that for any signal to reach you telling you you'd made a strike. Why?"

The Ship's Voice was loud and bright in my ear: "Marshall Lamech, the subject is clinically dead. What you are hearing is not her speaking to you, but is the last few random discharges of her brain cells, being stimulated and read by the strands you injected earlier."

"You mean I killed her. By injecting her brain with brain-eating gunk."

"Not at all. She suffered cardiac arrest when several bullets severed her spine, and suffered additional trauma from heat-discharges, the fall, and from exposure the atmosphere of Avernus, for which her lungs were not adapted."

And yet, dead as she was, the girl answered my question. Maybe the words had been in her dying thoughts anyway. Or maybe the Ship did not know everything about the human soul.

The ghost-thoughts touched me: "Only our rulers enter true one-mind unity of the Collective. Officers receive instructions and communion. The rest are work-thralls and serfs. We are not whole. The Collective promises true unity will be achieved on the day all are unselfish enough to serve without reward; and says no other system, no other form of living, is desirable or possible. But Earth, Mother Earth, kept speaking to us.

"The radio signals from Earth made lies of everything the Collective promised. Where were the riots of Earth? The starvation? Where was the tyranny and evil caused by individualism? Why were the machines of Earth the servants and not the masters? Why were they wealthier than we were? Even six hundred years out of date, each broadcast displayed new marvels. And anyone who could run up a simple short-wave radio antennae and point it at the stars could hear.

"And so the Voice of Earth had to be silenced. Yes, we knew the Voice of Earth knew nothing of us, was not speaking for us, but was sending signals to some colony further distant still. But the mere fact that hope and freedom and individuality existed anywhere, anywhere in the universe, was enough to condemn them. The Collective could not tolerate the knowledge that anyone, anywhere, was not as we were, and lived in greater happiness than anything we knew . . . "

The ghost-voice grew silent. I shook her again, gently, by the shoulders, hoping that might stimulate the dead brain cells.

I caught a wisp of last thought, perhaps something from her childhood. " . . . I am not like the other girls in the dorm. The air is bad, and I am sick all the time. I was made for another world . . . I was made for another kind of man . . . Lamech . . . made for Lamech . . .

Then: " . . . I hope he likes me . . . "

I opened my faceplate and kissed her on the forehead. Then I laid her out as gently as my rough hand could on the grass.

"Ship," I said, "I assume the Collective cannot talk to itself right now, but has broken down and is fighting itself."

"Each regional command in the local area is asserting supreme command. On the other continents of the planet, Collective communication is uninterrupted. However, subversion of their satellite array does not allow them much strategic response. If the Collective wishes to survive as an intact entity, it will be able to do so only on such terms and conditions as you wish to impose."

"Well. There are going to be a few reforms; I can say that much. I may not remember what things were like back home, but this place . . . this place sucks."

"We are no longer in urgent mission status, Sir. You are cleared to have access to secure information. Would you like your memory back?"

"Just hold on a moment."

"Standing by."

"They mentioned 'others.' I was not the first mission down. Don't tell me, let me guess. I sent out clones of myself. I am the only human being left alive, right? So they must have been grown out of me."

"Would you like you memory restored, Sir? Standing by."

"And those missions failed. I guess those had been actually my sons, weren't they? Maybe not in the eyes of the law, but actually, really. Soldiers under my command. My boys. Grown in a tube or something, but my babies and I was responsible for them. Right? Dead now, I assume, because of me."

"The Avernus Collective was willing to stand down their orbital defenses to allow you to pass, once they suspected you were the true mission commander, that you alone had plenipotentiary powers to spare or to condemn the planet. You knew it was a trap, but were confident you could elude it."

"But why send anyone down here at all? Why not just command all the operations from orbit? From where it is safe?"

"An excellent question, Sir, and one to which I wish I had received an adequate answer."

"What did I give as my reason? If I am actually the CO, risking my life on a ground op is just absurd. It is against all military principles."

"You said there were other principles. You said your mission was more than just a military one, Sir. You said no judge should weigh the evidence without seeing the accused, no jury should pass sentence on a prisoner without given them a chance to be heard. You said no executioner should kill the condemned without first looking into their eyes."

"But these aren't the real condemned. It sounds like they aided and abetted. They helped refuel and resupply some interstellar vehicle originating somewhere else, another colony."

"That is consistent with what I have recovered from their redacted archive records. Standing by to restore your memory. Will you give the order, Sir?"

I sighed.

"Tell me if I am human, first . . . "

"Due to weight considerations, the Designer thought it best to minimize payload, and ship merely a cryogenically suspended brain with instructions to grow any needed body or body-systems upon reaching target. In order to deceive the Avernus Collective, it was thought that a human-shaped body, but equipped with certain . . . "

"No. Belay that order. Shut up. I am really not sure I want to know the rest just yet."

I sighed again, looking down at the poor dead girl. I did not even know her name. Maybe they did not give out names on this damned world. I wished she had had a nice-sounded one. The only other Homo Sapiens alive but me, it seemed, grown from museum-stock for my benefit. What a waste.

"Ship, there are how many colonies of Earth? Not including this one."

"Five have broadcast radio signals between 50 and seven hundred fifty years old."

"And one of them is the suspect planet now, As soon as my memory is back, I'll be under orders again, right? We'll have to race off and go smite someone else, I suppose."

"It will take thirty years to build the equipment to create the conversion fueling station in near orbit about the local sun, Sir. But, yes, the instructions from the Designer require we not take undue time at non-mission related tasks, lest our purposes be forgotten."

"Great. But, at the moment, I'm not in dereliction of duty yet, am I? So, to answer your question, no. Leave me ignorant for now. As soon as I recall what is really going on, I'll know whether or not this mission was worth doing, or whether this whole thing was a thundering clusterfuck, won't I? And while I don't know I can still hope that all this mess was somehow worth it. So leave me alone for a while. I'll tell you when I am ready."

I had part of my armor grow itself into an e-tool, and I set about to dig a grave, right there on the flowering hill. It seemed like a nice enough spot.

I was standing in a half-dug grave, when I looked up and said. "By the way, Ship . . . ?"

"Yes, Marshall Lamech?"

"What the hell is the point of this anyway? Revenge a thousand years out of date? Why did the Designer build you and me to do this?"

"You yourself are the Designer, Marshall Lamech. I assume you will recall your purposes when you ask for your memory back. Standing by. Will you give the order?"

I looked down again. "No. Let me finish this first. I just can't stand seeing a job half-done."

"On that we are agreed, Sir."

First published in Absolute Magnitude, #16, Summer 2001. Copyright 2001, John C. Wright

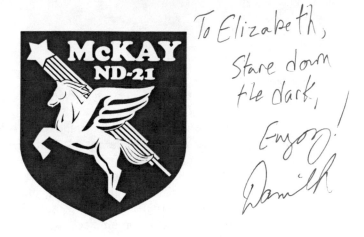

IN THE DYING LIGHT

An Alliance Archives Adventure

Danielle Ackley-McPhail

Earth Orbit: 42.05.18 – 0715hrs

ON THE COMMAND DECK OF THE STELLAR CLIPPER *McKAY*, FIRST OFFICER USHIMI YAKATA RAN the final checklist before third shift ended:

> Duty Log: **42.05.18 – 0715hrs**, Yakata, U.
>   Reactor status – nominal;
>   O2 levels – optimal;
>   Power – five percent over-consumption.

She frowned at the last item as she printed out a hard copy of the entry. We're going to have to watch our calculations, she thought. We haven't even left orbit and already the systems are running hot.

It was that damn shuttle Corporate had them balancing on the *McKay*'s nose. They were hauling the spacer's equivalent of a luxury yacht over twelve light years to Demeter just so some CEO could tour his colonial facilities in style . . . There were so many more important payloads they could have taken with them. Of course, it was the "pay" part that decided things in the end; the rates for transporting luxury items to the Tau Ceti system were ten times that of necessary goods.

Behind her a clunk and a soft whoosh announced the arrival of her replacement. A whiff of licorice drifted from close by her ear. She'd stopped counting the times she'd told Karl Dunn not to crowd her. That was one of the reasons they had a history, and no future. She'd had doubts about signing him for this cruise. They had been close once, very close. But not anymore. And with only a nine-man crew, she had no hope of avoiding him.

Her lips pressed in a tight, thin line, Yakata dropped her hand to the toggle by her hip and shifted the command chair back along its track, away from the control panel.

"Hey! Watch it!"

She brought the chair around, her grey eyes leveled at Karl dead on as he rubbed his abdomen where the chair smacked into him. Only his grip on the nearby tether bar kept him bobbing in place.

"Excuse me." Her tone was cool and formal. "I didn't realize you were so close."

Any comment Karl would have made was interrupted as the flat, persistent tone of the proximity warning sounded through the cabin. They both forgot their personal conflict, their attention riveted on the sensors.

Toggling the command chair back into place, Yakata automatically scanned the ship's attitude and power consumption on the screens flanking the main monitor. At the same time, she called up the isometric collision display. The flashing alert icon vanished from the screen in front of her. In its place appeared a wire-frame sphere with a representation of the *McKay* in the center. Something was coming up from behind, closing on the ship at a fraction of a meter per second. They had about thirty minutes until it came into range over their drive section.

"Dunn, reach over and activate the aft camera," Yakata ordered as her fingers danced in and out of the button depressions on the control panel. At her command, the main display switched from short-range to long-range scanning. She had to be sure whatever approached was not the forward edge of a meteor storm or something else their ablative hull plating could not handle.

Her scans told her nothing more. She called to Karl, "Crewman, do we have visual?"

Silence.

"Crewman . . . " Her short, sharp tone telegraphed impatience. "Do . . . we . . . have . . . visual?"

She whipped around, spearing him with a glare. He remained oblivious, his feet tucked into the boot docks and his gaze riveted on the image on the external monitoring station.

What the hell? Yakata had never seen him like this. He looked stunned . . . horrified. What could be out there?

Remembering the fate of her father's freighter, the *Tyler*, she felt a shiver of dread. Not another wreck . . .

She couldn't tell; Karl's body blocked the screen. Impatiently, she released the restraint keeping her in the command chair and drifted out. Once she was clear of the panel, she rotated and pulled herself toward Karl.

"Step aside, crewman," she barked. His intent gaze snapped to her. Emotions rippled violently across his face. His deep brown eyes looked nearly black with them. It unsettled her, but Yakata didn't back off. Dunn's moods were nothing new to her. He had always been too on edge, his emotions close to the surface; like he picked up on random vibes in the air that no one else could feel. In their time together, she had never been able to tell what a given situation would trigger. Now she told herself she didn't really care. She kept her expression impassive and her gaze sharp. "Move it . . . now."

The muscles along Karl's jaw twitched and his eyes fell out of focus. He closed them and gave his head a little shake. She could see the tension drain away. When he opened his eyes again, they reflected faint confusion. Without a word, he gave the standard heel jerk to free his feet from the workstation's dock and drifted off to the side.

She gave him a measured look before redirecting her attention to the screen. The camera was deployed, the high-power, ten-optical zoom fully engaged. The view was stunning. Distant stars glittered like metallic flecks on a field of raw black silk and muted colors added an unexpected depth to the starscape. She wasn't interested in pretty sights, though. She scanned for her objective with an intensity that mirrored Karl's earlier stance.

The projectile headed toward them wasn't some random bit of space debris; it was clearly manufactured. The shape was something like a squat pillar or obelisk, and appeared about the size of her head. It was too far away to make out much more, though the camera hinted at intricate detail.

Rogue thoughts of her father swarmed her mind once more. In his last letter to her, he mentioned a similar find. She'd lost him long before the letter ever reached her. Neither her father, nor the object was retrieved. Burned into her memory, as clear as yesterday, was the image of his shattered helmet floating in the vacuum of space. She still had that helmet.

She banished the thought. Turning back to Karl, Yakata caught his eye and held it. "Assume your post. I'm heading up to the rendezvous station to retrieve the object."

He was silent a moment. His jaw ticked and his gaze flickered from the aft display to her face.

" 'Ta . . . " he began, but she cut him off.

"Excuse me, crewman, how did you address me?"

"Ma'am," he ground out through clenched teeth, frustration snapping in his eyes. "Respectfully, I'm not sure that you should . . . something feels really wrong about this."

"I have to do this."

The knowing look he gave her was disconcerting. If anyone understood, he did. Yakata didn't like that familiarity or the self-betraying warmth she felt at his concern. "I said get to your post. Start the pre-hyperdrive checklist," she ordered. "The Captain wants to jump by 0800."

She pulled her communications hood up over her close-cropped ebony hair and triggered the overhead hatch. With the grace of frequent practice, she hauled herself up through the shaft. Propelling herself past the T-junction that branched off toward the cargo bay, she opened the second hatch into the rendezvous station. She closed it behind her before drifting toward the aft window. Yakata pressed the activation button on the left side of her comm hood. "Command deck . . . "

There was a sharp chirp before Karl's slightly staticy voice responded. "Go ahead, Ma'am."

"I need an update on the incoming object."

There was a pause. While she waited, Yakata peered out into space, as if she had any chance of pinpointing the object without the aid of the cameras. It was getting closer, but not that close.

Another chirp brought her out of her distraction.

"Ma'am?"

"Go ahead, crewman."

"The object is ten minutes out and closing."

"Acknowledged," she responded, and cut the connection.

Ten minutes. Barely enough time to deploy the arm. She snapped her boots into the dock and engaged the control panel. Powering up the arm, she then hit the sequence instructing it to retrieve the grappling attachment. While the mechanism prepared, she triggered the cargo bay doors. The strident warning klaxon sounded as a large segment of the ship opened to space. The arm rose from its cradle in slow, precise movements. Her teeth gritted and her muscles tensed as she watched. It had to move faster or she would miss the interception point. With her free hand, she depressed the activator on her comm hood once more.

"Command deck . . . "

"Go ahead, Ma'am."

"Feed me the trajectory of the object."

On the panel in front of her, a micro-display came to life. The information played across it. It was going to be close. She deployed the grappling net to intersect the flight path and held her breath. The object crested the drive section in a gentle arc, and seemed to flare as it came into contact with the sun's rays, bathing the ship and arm in a startling green glow. It faded in the shadow of the arm. Yakata leaned into the console. She was afraid her prize was going to overshoot the net. Reaching for the joystick in front of her, she extended the assembly as high as it would go over the drive section.

Her breath hitched. It still looked as if it was going to skim past. This was ridiculous. It was space debris. There was no reason she should be so upset. She tried shifting the joystick even further, but the arm was fully extended.

Her father's face drifted unbidden across her thoughts. It felt like she was failing him. She clenched her teeth and forced the thought away. Furious blinking cleared her vision, but she could hardly believe what she saw: the object changed trajectory. It was a slight alteration; barely perceptible except for the drive section being there as a point of reference. Still, Yakata had to wonder if she had really seen it. There was no way the thing could have changed its trajectory. Short of mechanical means or an outside intervention, an object moving in space would continue along the same path until it encountered another force. And yet, as the artifact plowed into the grappling net, she forgot all about the laws of physics. The net closed, locking the object into place.

"Yeah!" Her cry was loud and unbridled in the seclusion of the rendezvous station. Only the boot docks kept her from bouncing around the compartment. "Oh, yeah!"

A burst of unexpected static crackled from her comm hood. She felt the blood drain from her face as she went still.

"Hey! Knock it off!" Karl's amused voice came over the connection she'd forgotten to close. "You want to rupture my ear drum?"

"My apologies, crewman," she responded with a degree of dignity she did not currently feel. "The object has been retrieved. I'm locking down and securing the salvage."

She cut the connection.

Shoving embarrassment aside, Yakata input the sequence that returned the arm to its cradle. Another rapid set of keystrokes, and the cargo bay doors closed. She was impatient with the drawn-out procedure. Recklessness in vacuum, however, could get a spacer killed.

Once everything was locked down, she retreated to the antechamber to climb into her protective constrictor suit. She waited for the green light from the automatic systems check before securing her helmet and engaging the O_2 tanks. Prepped for EVA, Yakata cycled through the airlock into the cargo bay.

She grabbed an empty storage container and hauled both it and herself down the length of the armature. Once there, she anchored the container to the deck and pulled herself up the handholds along the wall until she was even with the grappling attachment. She hit the release and worked the fingers open.

Her hands twitch over the surface of the artifact and she had to resist the urge to draw off her suit's skin-tight gloves. The object demanded to be caressed.

In shape it resembled a short, squat obelisk. It tapered slightly from top to bottom and had three columns of unfamiliar symbols running up and down each side. It was metal . . . apparently old metal, given the deep, dull sheen. The color had a greenish tinge, like ancient bronze. Only this was no metal she recognized. It seemed smooth, almost soft, other than the etching. Otherwise, there were no seams or depressions.

It took extreme effort to lower the thing into the bin. Now was not the time to examine it. She had less than ten minutes to get herself secured for hyperdrive. Unhitching the container, she hefted it to her shoulder and propelled herself toward the airlock. In the antechamber, she slid her burden into a storage locker by the cargo bay hatch and keyed it to her personal code. It would be safe until she could take it down to the lab.

Duty Log: 42.05.18 — 1100hrs, Kinney, Captain J.
   Reactor status — nominal;
   02 levels — 98 percent;
   Power — ten percent over-consumption
         Note: Schedule diagnostics of ship's systems upon arrival at Demeter, *McKay* exhibiting systems-wide reduction in efficiency despite recent overhaul. Power fluctuations ship-wide, stabilized. Malfunction of atmospheric filters in compartments 8A through C, corrected. Electrical fires between bulkheads 10 and 11, section 5, contained; damage minimal.

Cargo Bay Antechamber: 42.05.18 — 1100hrs
Yakata struggled for hours to get some rest. She just couldn't do it, though. The artifact haunted her thoughts. She would almost say it called to her, but that was as nuts as thinking it had changed its trajectory. She tossed and fussed until Jones and Pittman, the crewmembers trying to sleep in the billets flanking hers, begged her to give up.

That was why she was again climbing down into the cargo bay antechamber. Captain Kinney, in position on the command deck, had given her a considering look, but didn't question her. She'd already briefed him about the events that occurred at the end of her shift.

All thought of anything but the artifact fled her mind as she pushed open the last hatch and continued down the ladder, which in orbit had been the floor. She hated the way hyperdrive and the artificial gravity it created turned reality perpendicular to orbital conditions. Kneeling down, she punched her code with rapid jabs and hauled open the storage locker at her feet.

Any thought of spatial geometry evaporated.

Yakata half expected the artifact to be a dream. But there it was, nestled in its bin. She tried to draw it out of the locker.

It wouldn't budge! In the weightlessness of the orbiting ship, the artifact had been nothing to move. Now that they were under drive there was artificial gravity again. Not earth-norm, but enough that they could walk on the deck. If the obelisk was this heavy in three-quarters grav, she didn't want to consider what it would be like under normal conditions. It had to be denser than gold.

No! Yakata straddled the opening, flexed her knees, and inch by inch pulled the container up, until sweat ran into her eyes and her muscles screamed. She wasn't going to wait forty-eight hours until they were in orbit. The bin was coming out now.

Personal Log Entry: 42.05.18 – 1230hrs, Dunn, K.

We retrieved something today. 'Ta . . . excuse me . . . First Officer Ushimi hasn't told me what it is. Don't think she even knows. While I was on shift, she took it to the storage bay Captain had temporarily converted into a lab. She talked O'Neal, the metallurgist we're shep-arding to Demeter, into helping her try to figure out what it is.

She goes on shift in seven hours, but they're still holed up in that lab. She's going to be a real bitch on deck tonight if she doesn't get some sleep, but she's obsessing on that bit of debris.

Of course, I can't stop thinking about it either. It's gotten under my skin. It shouldn't be on this ship! It has me so freaked, and I can't even tell why. The first half-hour of my shift is a lost memory. All I know is that it feels like we are in for a major shitstorm.

Temporary Science Lab: 42.05.18 – 1230hrs

"What in the world made Corporate think it was worth the 100-million-dollar ticket to haul you up here?" Yakata growled through clenched teeth.

Bastian O'Neal, world-renowned metallurgist, lowered his instruments to the work surface and gave her a long, silent look. The dignified expression on his ebony face didn't change, but his hazel eyes were disapproving. He didn't answer. He looked away and took up the artifact in both latex-covered hands, repositioning it for another documenting photograph.

She'd strained to haul her prize down here; he seemed to toss it about as if it were cotton candy. Part of that was due to his clearly prosthetic left arm; but part had to be because of his own innate strength. He was developed enough that someone who didn't know better could be excused for thinking he mined metals, rather than studying them.

The metallurgist set aside his digital camera and picked up the item once more. He turned it in his hands until he'd looked at every side, his finger lingered over the engraving. She wanted to snatch it from his grasp. Uncontrollably, a muscle in her forehead twitched, as did her fingers. How dare he manhandle her salvage like that, hefting it with an ease that she couldn't? She tensed and fought not to scowl at him. What was wrong with her? The stress was scrambling her circuits.

Yakata tried to shake it off. This was O'Neal's field. She'd come to him for help and he was kind enough to give it. She should be grateful and respectful, at the very least. It wasn't like her to behave this way. She took a deep breath and forced herself to calm, to smile and be pleasant.

Finally, he set the artifact down. Yakata expected to relax. Instead, she tensed even more; ready, in fact, to hurry forward and grab the obelisk away. But then O'Neal spoke, distracting her.

"I can't identify it."

"What do you mean you can't identify it?!"

"The tests were unable to determine the age or composition of the material."

Her resolve to be polite evaporated. "What did Corporate do . . . send you up here as a tax write-off?"

Seething with frustration, Yakata grabbed for her artifact.

O'Neal stepped in her way.

"If you're done insulting me?"

"There's one more test I can run, but I need some equipment from the storage bay. My imaging spectrometer is our last option on-ship."

She glared at him and had to force her negativity down. It was getting harder to do. Without a word, Yakata moved to the terminal set into the chamber wall, her feet straddling the boot docks.

The muscles in her shoulders bunched and tightened as she keyed in the commands calling up the ship's manifest. He was watching her. Surely plotting to take her salvage for himself.

Whoa! Where did that paranoia come from? She forced it away.

Finally, she located his equipment and requested immediate retrieval. Closing out the screen, she whirled to face him. For a moment, everything held a greenish tinge like the one she'd noted when the object crested the drive section. The sense of looming increased with the glow. It faded so quickly, though, that she had to wonder if it were her vision causing the effect. That would explain the flickers out of the corner of her eye. Yakata clenched her eyes shut and popped her neck. It sounded like several rounds of gunfire.

"Sorry, O'Neal, can't imagine why I'm so edgy. Jones will bring your spectrometer down in short order. Why don't you head to the mess for some coffee . . . I'll comm you when the equipment gets here."

"That's okay. If I'm here when it arrives I can hook it into the ship's systems quicker. This has already taken longer . . . "

"O'Neal," Yakata cut him off, her tone sharp and brittle, even to her own ears. "Go get some coffee. I'll have the spectrometer rigged up when you get here."

For a moment, she thought he would refuse. Her suspicions flared brighter and she had to consciously force her fists not to clench. She didn't trust him here; didn't want him here, unless he was in the middle of a test. Even then she had issues.

Her gaze again locked with his. She read concern in his eyes. But was there something else lurking beneath that? Something sly? Calculating? Damnit! She couldn't tell! It took more effort to mimic something of a reasonable tone. "I have to be here to sign off on the retrieval. If you don't want any coffee, could you at least get me some? I'm dying here."

Temporary Science Lab: 42.05.18 – 1245hrs
Yakata vibrated with impatience as O'Neal finished calibrating the spectrometer. She wanted to snatch his hands away from the knobs and buttons and yell at him to get on with it. It wasn't just an overwhelming need to know. That she could have handled. No, it was more like whatever lurked behind her was drawing closer, just out of sight, just out of hearing range. Always there, always watching . . . Some part of her equated it with the artifact. She had to know what it was now, but the technology would do them no good if it weren't set up properly. She understood that.

Then why was she ready to scream when he slipped a common bit of steel in the spherical sample chamber and fired up the machine?

She couldn't restrain herself any more. "Come on, already!"

"Do you want accurate results, or do you just want me to go through the motions?" O'Neal's voice came out a low, controlled rumble, contrasting sharply with her outburst. "If you don't care if the results are true, you're wasting my time and I'm out of here."

His response made Yakata want to scream even more, but he was right. What was wrong with her? Her impatience did not serve either one of them well and she couldn't afford to have him abandon the test. She could probably figure out the machine, but the data it spit out would be indecipherable to her. Taking a deep breath, she forced herself to calm.

"Sorry."

It took a lot of effort not to fidget as O'Neal watched her closely a moment. The concern had returned, along with a thread of irritation. He clearly wanted this to be done as much as she did, even if their reasons were different. Without a word, he turned back to the spectrometer.

"Okay, we're ready."

Yakata's pulse sped up. She reached for the artifact, only to flinch back as a mild static arced between it and her fingertips. It seemed to cling to her hand like the persistent suction of vacuum through a hull breach. Like she was being sucked out the tiniest hole, only the hard surface of reality kept her from going through. Before she could say something, the pull abruptly released and a surge of rage and frustration swelled over her. She shook it off. Looked up in a daze. O'Neal had lifted her prize away and slid it into the chamber in place of the metal bar. He made no comment and Yakata saw no sparks when he touched it. Had the phenomenon been her imagination? She couldn't resist creeping forward to glance at the operator's display as the spectrometer charged up to pulse full-spectrum light at the object from four points within the sphere.

The hum of the machine seemed to come up through the deck plates until she expected her entire body to vibrate with it. A flaring light intensified abruptly until it engulfed the machine and the room. There was a power surge and the deck plates vibrated more violently beneath Yakata's feet. Both she and O'Neal flinched in that instance of brilliance before they were engulfed by utter darkness. The only sound was a sharp gasp. She couldn't tell which of them it came from. She could no longer hear the spectrometer or any of the ship's normal background mechanical noises. Other than their nervous breathing, silence dominated the pitch black.

Yakata struggled not to panic. Where was the hum of the hyperdrive? The click of relays opening and closing? The sizzling snap of the coms? Sounds every spacer took for granted; their unrealized security blanket in everlasting night. Yakata shuddered.

The darkness seemed to last forever; in truth it was less than twenty seconds before systems re-engaged with a whir. Not even long enough for them to fall out of drive.

Right on the heels of everything powering up, all coms within hearing distance gave a strident chirp.

" . . . eport . . . All crew, report!"

She reached for the comm on the console and toggled the activator to respond to Captain Kinney.

"Yakata here. O'Neal and I are in the Science Lab."

"What the hell was that?"

Yakata didn't have an answer. She couldn't have gotten one in, anyway, as a stream of responses came over the com. All crew were accounted for.

"Everyone to stations, run full diagnostics. Let's figure out what the deal is before it happens again," Captain Kinney ordered before closing the comm line.

Turning to O'Neal, Yakata was struck by the confusion on his face as he looked at the read-out from the spectrometer.

"What? Something go wrong?"

O'Neal turned toward her, his head shaking. "The test completed before everything shut down, but this doesn't make sense."

She walked over and read the printout:

Processing Error 021:
Spectral Anomaly – Negative Scan

"*Kuso shite shinezo!*" Yakata hissed through clenched teeth.

O'Neal was looking at her odd. "I don't know what you just said, but it sounded painful."

Yakata flushed. Among spacers it was one thing, profanity was a part of their make-up. But in front of others she was generally more circumspect. She was just grateful the man did not speak Japanese.

"I apologize for my rudeness. But, damn!" She slammed her hand down on the casing of the machine. "All of that and it's unidentifiable!"

"Not just unidentifiable . . . it's like nothing's there. The machine didn't even register the walls of the chamber." His expression grew considering. "It's as if the artifact absorbed the light. But to do so this completely . . . it's impossible for none to have gotten past it."

"Malfunction?"

"Not one I've ever seen, but there's one way to find out."

Captain had ordered everyone to their stations. But she had to know. She could always double-time it to the command.

O'Neal opened the chamber and reached for the artifact. He hissed sharply, as if in pain. His body arched and shuddered. The look of terror in his eyes sent panic through Yakata. It must be the prosthetic. She remembered the static that had clung to her hand when she'd touched the artifact earlier.

Yakata yanked an equipment bag toward her and rapidly rifled through it. Tucked in the bottom was a set of insulated gauntlets. She donned them and braced herself against the workstation. With all her weight behind the effort, she hauled on the obelisk until it left his grasp. It came away with the sound of metal scraping metal. Yakata landed in a heap across the compartment, the obelisk heavy on her chest. O'Neal collapsed across the table, greenish static arching and popping along the length of his arm. He shook his head and groaned. After a moment, he leveled a glare toward Yakata.

Perhaps it was the sparks, or perhaps just the light, but as he stared at her in silence, it seemed his eyes reflected the green hue. He slowly stood and stalked across the room to where she lay. When he reached out his hand, her eyes went wide, expecting pain.

She searched his face for some clue as the man remained silent. His eyes darkened and she couldn't read the swirl of emotions dancing through them. She shivered. He closed his eyes with a sigh. When he opened them all she saw was impatience in their green depth. Green eyes? But . . . .

"The gauntlets . . . "

She yanked them off and held them up, never taking her eyes from him. He donned the gear and lifted the artifact from her chest. She gasped as breath flooded back into her lungs to full capacity. Damn, that thing was heavy, she swore to herself.

O'Neal turned his back to her. He deposited the obelisk on a metal tray on the table and reinserted the control element he'd used to test the machine initially.

The second reading of the steel bar was identical to the first.

Without a word, Yakata returned the artifact to its storage locker. Using her body as a shield, she keyed the lock with her personal code.

She turned and found O'Neal staring at her. Yakata carefully slipped past him and hurried from the compartment, trying to ignore the faint odor of scorched latex lingering in her nostrils.

Personal Log Entry: 42.05.18 – 1250hrs, Dunn, K.

McKay's systems just flatlined. Everything's back up, but talk about freaking out. What the hell is going on?

Haven't felt like this since I was four and Da took me to the reptile house at the Bronx Zoo. I zoomed all over that place. Couldn't stay still . . . until I came to the king cobra. Something had pissed it off. It mantled and swayed three feet high in the air, right up close to the glass. It kept up a hiss, low and menacing. Don't know how long I stood there watching its tongue flicker in and out above me, but I couldn't move. Not even when it struck. Lightning-fast it slammed into the glass. To this day, I swear its fangs left long grooves in the surface, dripping with venom.

I still remember the stench of terror. Right now it's strong in my nose . . . a hundred times stronger than it was when I was four. And I have that feeling again . . . like death is hovering above my head and I'm not sure if the glass is going to hold.

Damn . . . Captain just called duty stations.

Command Deck: 42.05.18 – 1310hrs

The silence was tangible as Yakata hauled herself through the command deck hatch from the *McKay's* main shaft. The passage ran the length of the ship and was fitted out with a ladder that doubled as a track for the slow-moving utility lift. The track could either be climbed or used for crewmen to pull themselves along, depending on the ship's attitude. She had scaled it at record speed, but apparently she hadn't been quick enough.

"First Officer Ushimi . . . the comm system may have been affected by the anomaly. My order to report to duty stations doesn't seem to have reached all compartments." The captain's words were even and void of tension. His gaze was not. The look he gave her was harder than the artifact she'd left in the lab. "With this sudden glitch, I'm concerned that diagnostics might not show up all malfunctions. I'll need you to conduct an on-site inspection of every comm station and hood on the *McKay*."

Yakata flinched on the inside. "Yes, Sir. Right away, Sir."

Captain Kinney was known for his swift and fitting discipline. Actually, she'd gotten off easy; she should have been the first on the deck, not counting those who were already there.

There was a sound beneath her feet. She stepped aside to clear the hatch. An acrid aroma preceded Dunn as he clambered to his post.

"Ah, very good." The Captain's smile was not very pleasant, though his tone pretended to be. "Crewman Dunn will assist you."

Drive Section Service Module: 42.05.18 – 1700hrs

This was it. The final comm station. Yakata sighed as she pulled out the checklist and ran the last test. Carefully, she removed the housing and used a maglite and a telescoping mirror to visually inspect the wiring. Then she tested the connections. Finally, she closed the unit and toggled the activator.

"Dunn . . . "

"Go ahead . . . "

"Drive section comm inspection complete, how are you coming with the Engineering unit?"

"System's green to go." Dunn's voice was even but Yakata detected an edge to it. It was barely perceptible, but his breath was coming out in quick, shallow huffs. She waited for him to report something catastrophic, but he remained silent.

"Okay, that was the last one. Wait for me at the main shaft." Yakata cut the link and toggled the activator again. "Command deck . . . "

"Go ahead." The captain's voice came through the relay sharp and precise. Yakata winced. He would remain on deck until she relieved him. That was part of what drove home the lesson. Her failure to follow orders affected everyone, right up to the captain, whom she respected more than anyone alive. Nothing, short of a fatality, would have made her feel worse about her lapse in protocol.

"On-site inspection of the communications system complete," Yakata responded, keeping her voice neutral.

"Acknowledged. I'll be waiting to hear your report."

"Yes, Sir." Yakata groaned as she cut the link.

With haste, she secured her maintenance kit on her hip, slid the maglite into its belt loop, and left the compartment. The sensors flanking the door registered her exit. The drive room went dark and the dim, stand-by lights of the causeway brightened. After nearly a decade of service, she generally took the lighting system for granted. Today she newly appreciated the comfort it represented. Even without the recent system's failure, Yakata was uneasy. Her nerves vibrated beneath the surface of her skin and her eyes ached from trying to penetrate the dark spaces around her. She'd yet to spy anything staring back. Her skin crawled though as she imagined a thousand pairs of eyes creeping forward into the now-darkened room behind her. Clenching her teeth, she cocked her head from side to side until the vertebrae ceased to pop. To her left, she thought she heard the faintest sound from somewhere near the pressurized tanks. Probably a loose valve. She made note of the section where she suspected the leak, and set off for the main shaft.

Dunn was not at the rendezvous.

Toggling the activator on her comm hood, the barest edge of anger sharpened her tone. "Crewman Dunn, report . . . "

Silence.

"Dunn, what is your location?"

Still no response.

What in the world was going on? Their personal comm hoods were the first to be tested. Both had operated fine. She went to the comm screen in the main shaft wall. With a couple of jabs she input the protocol that instructed the system to display the current location of all crewmembers.

She glanced down the list of names and locations: Captain Kinney and Crewman Suarez – Command deck; Crewmen Jones and Chapman – Environmental Control Compartment; Specialist O'Neal – Temporary Science Lab; Crewmen Pittman, Jenks, and Gunter – Mess hall; and Crewman Dunn . . .

Port lateral airlock! Yakata powered down the display and set off back the way she came at a hard clip.

Bad enough they'd both drawn discipline duty, being late back was going to make it impossible for the captain to gloss over this time. She tried her comm hood again, activating it with such force she could feel the surrounding fabric pull. "Crewman Dunn . . . respond . . . "

Nothing. She put on a little more speed through the shaft. A tight sensation took root in her gut. She tried again, "Come on, Dunn, talk to me. What's going on?"

No answer. The airlocks came into sight. Even in the dim light of the corridor, she could see a dark smear on the floor.

"Dunn! Damnit, Karl! Answer me!"

Yakata closed the last few meters. Dropping to one knee, she touched a finger to the slick spot. It came away bright red, the sweet, metallic tang unmistakable.

What happened? And where was Dunn? Sensors indicated the port airlock, but both chambers were dark. There should be lights. Lighting was automatic. She stepped to the side of the hatch portal and reached for her maglite. The high-powered beam cut through the black pit beyond the glass.

Yakata gasped. For a second she could do nothing but stand there and stare at the horror revealed by the light: an EVA suit sprawled against the far wall, blood a solid curtain across the faceplate of the helmet.

A burst of static reminded her that the comm hood was still active, on stand-by. The sound was enough to snap her out of the shock.

"Command deck . . . " She was surprised how low and calm her voice remained. The rest of her was trembling. "Command deck, acknowledge . . . ."

The only response was another burst of static.

She moved to the comm unit in the corridor wall and tried again. Again static hissed and crackled through the corridor, echoing through her comm hood. She moved back to the airlock door.

The beam of light glimmered on the helmet like sunlight through rubies. She could make out nothing beyond the faceplate. Swallowing hard, she swept the airlock with light as far as she could from side to side. Nothing. Not even more smears. No movement. Still, something did this. Yakata was acutely aware of the blind spots to either side of the hatch.

She punched in the sequence to open the airlock. The keypad didn't respond. She tightened her grip on the maglite. It was awkward manipulating the manual release one-handed, but, with determination, she managed it. The hatch opened smoothly. Out wafted the heavy, copper-penny scent of blood and something else, something bitter and sharp. The lights still didn't engage.

"Dunn, can you respond?"

She peered into the room, her head just past the collar as she flashed the light into the corner to the right of the door. Nothing.

As she brought her light around to the other side, the comm hood gave a more energetic hiss. She flinched back at the unexpected sound. A blur of motion from the left caught her eye. Metal slammed against metal. From the shadows, hoarse breathing punched up into a roar. She now recognized the acrid odor in the air. She'd smelt it on the command deck, when Dunn came up the hatch.

There wasn't time to call out to him. There was only time to move. An industrial-grade spanner crashed into the airlock door just millimeters away her head. Again, the weapon rose. She couldn't continue to evade; the space was too restricted. She brought the maglite up to block the spanner's descent and allowed her body to fall back upon the deck. The move cost her the maglite, which went spinning away, but her bones were intact.

She stared up into Dunn's face. He was barely recognizable. His eyes were wide and wild, a long, bloody scratch marred his face, and sweat stood out in hard beads on his forehead. The rest of him was coated in blood. He did not seem to recognize her. She watched as a tremor ran through his body. No matter what had passed between them, she didn't want to hurt him, not even to get away. She would, but she didn't want to. She prayed he was coming out of it.

"Dunn . . . Karl, what happened to you?"

She held her breath. For a moment his pupils expanded. Recognition floated just beneath the surface. Then her comm hood hissed. His echoed in response. She had most of a second to watch him retreat behind the terror.

"Oh shit!" Yakata braced herself. This was going to hurt. Her only hope lay in the leverage of her position and her greater lower-body strength. The spanner came down full force. She dodged her torso as best she could, taking a glancing blow to her shoulder. Her left side went numb on impact. She wrapped herself around the spanner with her good arm and drew her legs up sharp. Snarling, she planted both feet in Dunn's gut and shoved for all she was worth.

The weapon remained in her posession, though it was close. Dunn went flying. Yakata winced as he slammed against the lockers, landing awkwardly on the sprawled EVA suit. She bit her lip at the fresh smear of blood across the dented metal. Bit harder against the impulse to go to him. Instead, she rolled to her feet and slammed the airlock hatch. Using the spanner, she wedged the door closed as best she could. It wouldn't hold long. She headed for the main shaft at a hard clip. Within the first five strides, the pain in her left arm triggered a grey haze across her vision. Gasping, she stopped running immediately.

Yakata blinked furiously, forcing herself to take slow, deep breaths, until the haze went away. Behind her she could hear banging, furious and violent.

Gritting her teeth against the pain, she loosened her web belt and slipped the wrist of her damaged arm into the gap between belt and pants, angled across her stomach. She hissed with the pain and the sounds from the airlock increased in intensity.

She forced thought of Dunn out of her mind and tightened the belt against her wrist, immobilizing the damaged arm as best she could. Once again, she set off, this time at a gentler, swinging lope. Her gut clenched. As she left the cacophony of the drive section behind, the faint sound of a warning klaxon could be heard elsewhere on the ship.

Yakata toggled her comm activator again. "Command deck . . . Come in, Captain Kinney." Not even a hiss sounded in her ear. "Deck officer, respond."

No answer; and her comm went dead, completely dead.

Abandoning her gentle pace, Yakata ran full out for the transport. The lift was slow, but one-handed, she would be even slower hauling herself up the ladder to the command deck. Her eyes locked on the lift mooring as it came into sight. The knots in her shoulders eased the slightest increment. The platform was there. She added another burst of speed.

Her steps faltered as she drew close. Something was not right. The lift wasn't seated properly in the track. It hovered about six inches off the mooring. She stopped where she was and tried to peer beneath it.

How had she missed the thin, crimson rivulets snaking across the deck? The fine, meandering tributaries flowing from the crushed body of Crewman Mory Chapman? Yakata fought the urge to be sick.

Was Dunn responsible? Was this why he wasn't at the rendezvous? Why he didn't answer her hails? Her throat spasmed and she had to swallow hard as she moved closer to examine the mechanism.

The body was tangled in the power couplings, bits of it pulped by the gears. Even if she could get the lift into motion, it would shred what was left of him. Only his face was untouched. His expression would haunt her.

A sound echoed up the corridor. Cursing, Yakata re-tightened her belt against her injured arm and climbed onto the lift. Her added force caused the platform to drop another inch. There was a sickening crack as something organic gave. She clenched her teeth and closed her eyes, emptied her mind of everything, and started up the lift. Before it had gone more than a few meters she slumped to her knees.

Central Shaft, Upper Utility Lift Mooring: 42.05.18 – 2100hrs
The lift locked into its upper mooring. Before her was the command deck hatch. She should get up. She had to report. The captain was waiting for them. Them. Not just her. Reality came rushing back. Yakata yanked herself to her feet with her good arm and gripped the ladder-track for balance. The hatch was open and the deck lights were at standby dim.

Every nerve in her body pricked. The command deck was unmanned. It was never unmanned. Leaning into the ladder, Yakata braced herself. She released her grip with her good hand and reached down into her maintenance kit. Near the bottom, she found the telescoping mirror she'd used earlier. Taking the reflective end carefully between her teeth, she angled the head and drew out the handle as far as it would go. She then edged the tool around the hatch. There were no bodies on the deck, and there were none walking around, either. Not that she could see, anyway.

The lights flared higher as she pulled herself through the hatch. She squinted against the sudden brilliance. It took a moment for her eyes to adjust. Pulling the hatch closed, she keyed the lock with her personal code. Dunn wouldn't corner her again. Her shoulder throbbed in agreement. With a grimace, she settled into the command chair. The display in front of her was completely lit up. Alerts flashed over nearly every inch of the ship, a confusing dance of flood, fire, and vacuum. Sometimes all three at once in the same compartment. How much of it was real?

Clearing the screen, she prayed nothing would go critical before she could get this sorted out. She ran diagnostics, keying in commands one-handed. Half of the alerts disappeared. Next, she toggled the comm on the console. Nothing. Not even static. She had to try, though.

"Yakata to all crew, report." She set the hail to repeat and went back to diagnostics. It was halfway through and there were no major malfunctions yet. A host of minor ones, but those they could survive. Of course, that assumed the diagnostics system wasn't fried as well.

She then input in the command to identify the locations of all on board, just as she had when she was looking for Dunn. It took longer this time. The computer spit out multiple conflicting responses. There was no way to tell which one was accurate.

While she waited for diagnostics to complete, Yakata moved to the emergency kit. She selected an analgesic patch. After tearing it open with her teeth, she palmed it and slipped it past the collar of her coverall. It was cool, instantly soothing her battered shoulder. That taken care of, she settled back into the command chair.

Diagnostics was at ninety-five percent. Another alert went off as the logarithm completed. Yakata's eyes moved from the diagnostics display to the main console. It was the proximity warning. It shouldn't have gone off when they were under hyper-drive. She stood and went to the external monitoring station. Nothing appeared on the fore view. Yakata activated the aft cameras. Her finger trembled as she depressed the button. Her vision greyed out one moment, only to telescope into sharp focus the next. Something drifted by the lens out by the drive section, caught in the electromagnetic pocket of e'space surrounding the ship. Several somethings, in fact. Yakata swallowed against the acidic tang climbing her throat. Visions of her father's helmet overwhelmed her, eclipsing the images she didn't want to see. She distanced herself through extreme willpower and zoomed in on the debris.

" . . . all crew, report."

"Shit!" Yakata yelled as her own voice suddenly called out through both her comm hood and every speaker on the deck. Communications was back. She killed the auto repeat and sent out a fresh hail.

"Command deck to Captain Kinney . . . "

Her voice trailed off as she tweaked the settings on the monitor. The objects had come into focus. Her eyes slammed closed. But even with them tightly shut she could still see the empty gaze of Captain Kinney staring at her from the vacuum of space.

Personal Log Entry: 42.05.18 – 2230hrs, Dunn, K.

FUCK YOU! I don't know what you are, but I know what you're doing now, so fuck you! You made me hurt her. I would never hurt her. She is the only one who cares. Who still means something to me . . .

I know you can access what I'm writing here, because you knew how to mess with my head. Well access this: You will NEVER get me to hurt her again. You will never touch her again. I will destroy you.

Duty Log: 42.05.19 – 1230hrs, Yakata, U.

Reactor status – indeterminate;

O2 levels – fluctuating;

Power – data unavailable.

Note: SC *McKay* operating under emergency conditions. Ship-wide malfunctions worsen. Member or members of the crew unstable. Captain Kinney; deceased, means unknown, body expelled from ship by unidentified personnel. At least three others likewise expelled, positive id cannot be made. Crewman Chapman; deceased, accidental or by design. Crewman Dunn; unstable, violent, temporarily restrained in port lateral airlock. Remainder of the crew; status unknown. First Officer Ushimi Yakata assuming command.

Out of habit, Yakata printed a hard copy of the duty log. Events must always be documented. Not that she expected anyone would ever read this account. As she tore the sheet from the printer, her eyes drifted across the page. She cursed and jerked her hand away. The page drifted to the deck, bold, black letters stared up at her. They're all dead. You're all dead. Die already, Bitch.

There was the faintest of sounds behind her. She whirled. O'Neal came through the hatch across the command deck, the one leading to the cargo bay and rendezvous station.

She took in the metallurgist's appearance: his coverall was torn, and dark stains across his chest glistened wetly. There was no sign he was the party injured. At his side, his prosthetic arm slowly flexed, as if the motion were unconscious. Yakata met O'Neal's gaze. She did not recognize the man staring back at her. His eyes were cold and hard, alien and bereft of humanity. His expression was neutral; as if she wouldn't notice something else lurked beneath. *There was so much wrong with this picture,* Yakata thought fleetingly.

"You plan to do what you're told?" he asked in a slow draw, nodding toward the slip of paper on the floor.

His tone was as flat as his expression. Yakata's eyes flickered to the printout.

"I don't take orders from a piece of paper," she growled. "And I sure as hell don't take orders from you."

"We all have to answer to someone."

"Yeah, well the only person I answered to is drifting out by the engines," Yakata spat back at him. "Who do you answer to?" She moved to the side as she spoke, edging toward the hatch.

"You'll meet soon enough." The neutrality was gone. Pure evil crept through O'Neal's voice. He followed her movements like a raptor tracked prey.

Forget that, Yakata told herself. With the line of her body to block the action, she lowered her right hand back into her maintenance kit. Very carefully, she eased out her utility knife, her hand through the wrist strap and the hilt solid in her palm. She depressed the release button on the pommel and the blade silently deployed.

Yakata's muscles rippled beneath her skin. She braced herself, poised to react to whatever move O'Neal made. Her only real option was evasion. If he got a hold of her with that prosthetic, he would crush her before she could even flinch.

As the metallurgist advanced, a tremor went straight through Yakata's body. It took her a moment to realize it wasn't internal. She sucked in a sharp breath. Her gaze flickered away from O'Neal to the main display. Alert icons flashed, one by one. The system was losing power. Within moments they would no longer have enough to sustain hyperdrive. There was a boot dock just behind her and a tether up and to her right. She was going to need one of them shortly.

It would have to be the boot dock; she had too few functioning hands to grab a tether and use the knife. She edged herself closer. Let him think she was afraid of him; that she futilely distanced herself.

She was ready when the bottom dropped out of the universe. The ship shuddered as the electrogravitic drive envelope disintegrated. Simul-taneously, she leaned back and jammed her heel into the dock. She was barely secure when there was a pop and a flash as intense as a hundred strobes going off right there in the room. Yakata squeezed her eyes shut just in time. From the heaving sounds, O'Neal had been caught unaware. She opened her eyes as reality uprighted itself in an orbital orientation. O'Neal floated in an uncontrolled sprawl on the far side of the command console. Around him floated globes of acrid vomit. As he bumped them, they burst into a dozen smaller globes, minus what clung to him. Feebly, his hand reached for the edge of the console.

Yakata grinned. In this state, he was no threat at all.

He groaned, and she laughed. She couldn't help it.

She went somber quickly, though, as hatred sharpened his gaze. Smelt it as the stench of malevolence overpowered the odor of bile. He looked ready to launch at her. Yakata tightened her grip on the utility knife. Let him try. He was a ground-pounder. Vacuum was her element, and this was her ship.

There was a clunk and the manual release on the command deck hatch spun toward open. Yakata froze. Once she'd keyed the lock, even the manual release required her personal code to open the hatch. Only one person onboard had the slightest chance of figuring it out. Dunn.

Confusion infiltrated the evil glint in O'Neal's eye. She watched fury flood his expression as the hatch swung out. The open portal remained empty.

Yakata didn't relax. Now she had to be on her guard on two fronts, and her ex was no rookie in vacuum. He must have been the one to disable the drive system. He certainly had the knowledge.

"Don't just stand there, 'Ta!"

Dunn peered around the edge of the hatch as he snapped at her. The scratch across his face was crusting over. His expression danced between violence and panic. She shifted her grip on the utility knife and turned her body so that her good arm could strike at either O'Neal or Dunn.

From the far side of the command console, O'Neal let out a serpentine hiss. She resisted the urge to turn to stare at him. Dunn was the more potent threat at the moment.

She watched the muscles of his face clench and twitch in response to the sound O'Neal made. Dunn's breath quickened. The massive spanner he'd used earlier came into view. She braced herself, ready to yank her heel out of the dock the second she knew which direction to propel herself. But his attention wasn't on her. Dunn's eyes were locked with O'Neal's. Her gaze flickered from one to the other. Between them, they blocked the only ways out.

"Will you move it before he figures out how to get both of us!"

Yakata jumped, startled as Dunn spoke in rapid Japanese. She'd forgotten he knew her language. It wasn't something they'd used often. They both knew that O'Neal didn't share their knowledge. The entire crew was required to familiarize themselves with his profile before he came on board. She was surprised Dunn had enough of a grip on himself to use that knowledge.

"What . . . and I'm supposed to trust you over him?" She slashed back in the same tongue. "He's not the one who tried to cave in my head!"

"Just move it, 'Ta!" Dunn continued in Japanese. Sweat gleamed on his forehead and his eyes were wild.

Before she could dodge aside, he lunged. His free hand latched onto her belt. She snarled as he jerked her loose from the dock. Yakata gasped with pain, her damaged arm wrenched about by his handling. Her head spun at the sharp, sudden movement. Dunn angled her toward the hatch with practiced ease. At the same time, the hand gripping the spanner swung out, aimed at O'Neal's head.

There was a solid thunk: the sound of metal against flesh. Silence followed. Threat floated thick on the canned air. Yakata shifted her head to look back at O'Neal. His green eyes glowed with malice. She cursed and lost the thought as her quick glance took in his unbloodied head and Dunn's spanner caught by the metallurgist's flesh hand. Some oddly detached part of her brain wondered why he hadn't just grabbed it with the prosthetic.

Her answer was a strangled gasp from Dunn. With no visible effort, O'Neal's cybernetic limb crushed Dunn's wrist, the one holding the spanner.

The sight refocused Yakata's rage in an instant. She tried to wrench away from Karl's grip, throwing herself back as far as his tethering hold allowed to lash at his attacker with her utility knife. The tip sliced through O'Neal's shirt, barely scratching his shoulder. He didn't even flinch.

Her curses cut off abruptly as Dunn shook her hard.

"Go! Now!" Karl snapped. Pain glimmered in his eyes, brilliant and jagged. Beneath that, he wordlessly pleaded with her. She stopped struggling, her brow drawn down in confusion.

Executing an effortless turn, she used the tip of her toe to propel herself off the overhead toward the hatch. She torpedoed through the opening, dropped the utility knife to hang by its strap, and caught the hatch collar with her good hand. Behind her there was a sick grinding sound.

She pivoted, catching sight of Dunn on his knees, his captured arm bent impossibly high behind his back. She growled and started to draw herself back onto the command deck. She couldn't leave him to this.

"No! I said go! One of us has to get away . . . head for the Cans, now!" Despite his obvious pain, he continued speaking in Japanese. Yakata hissed in objection, but she dipped her head in a brief, sharp nod before pivoting around to zip down the main shaft. Behind her, she heard a loud snap and the sick sound of laughter drifted through the hatch. She had to fight the impulse to turn around and tear O'Neal to shreds.

"Yes . . . do run, little rabbit . . . I'll be along as soon as I'm done here. Shouldn't take long."

Yakata's blood thickened and her heart froze. O'Neal had just spoken to her in flawless, textbook Japanese.

An agonized scream came from the command deck. It rose sharply before an abrupt end.

Her good arm burned nearly as bad as her injured one. She ignored it and grabbed another rung of the ladder-track, slingshoting herself down the shaft. The echo of Dunn's final scream followed her. It filled her head until she heard nothing else. She tried to force the memory into the fading recesses where it belonged. It resisted.

The flickers of movement were back. The flashes of light behind her, just to the side of her vision. Halfway down the shaft it got to her. Growling deep in her throat, she turned to confront the phantoms that stalked her. A practiced flick of her wrist sent the utility knife back up into her grip and a moment's pressure deployed the blade. Her momentum sent her colliding with the substructure. The impact to her damaged arm sent true sparks across her vision, followed by a grey haze. She blinked it away and cursed.

The shaft behind her was empty. There was nothing behind her, and nowhere anyone might hide. She retracted the knife and let it drift at the end of its strap. With a little more care, she turned and continued to haul herself along, both arms throbbing as she went.

Her comm hood gave a sudden burst of static. Yakata jumped. Another growl filled her throat to pulse against her jaw. She nearly snatched the comm hood off to shred the delicate wiring.

"What the hell are you doing?!"

The unexpected outburst stayed her hand. Dunn. How . . . ? Her gaze snapped to the command deck many stories above her head. She couldn't see him. He must be watching her on the monitors.

"I told you . . . to get out of here! Get to the Cans . . . now!" Dunn's voice was thin, strained.

"What happened to O'Neal?"

"Don't know . . . I passed out. He's not here." Sounds of movement filtered through the com; rustling, a sharply drawn breath. What might have been a sob . . .

"Dunn? Dunn!" Yakata's suspicions disintegrated beneath a fresh wave of concern.

"Don't yell, 'Ta." Karl's voice was low and weak. "You're making it hard to think.

"He left me for dead, which means he's after you."

"I don't understand what's going on here," she whispered.

"It's that damn artifact," he snapped back, but his voice quickly lost its strength, slurred and lost focus. "None of this started until we salvaged that thing. It's screwing with our minds. It's screwing with the ship. Somehow it's infiltrated the system . . . and . . . " Static disrupted him in sharp bursts. " . . . anything electronic . . . nly use manual overr . . . only. Not malfunc . . . deliberate."

"The artifact! I have to get the artifact!"

"No! . . . amnit! Get the hell off this ship. Now!"

Immediately, uncertainty sank firm fingers into her thoughts. She had more reason to doubt Dunn than to trust him. And O'Neal had already proven their attempt at speaking covertly had failed.

"Move!"

No. Perhaps O'Neal left him for dead . . . or not. Dunn had attacked her once already. She couldn't help but wonder if this was a trap.

She was getting her artifact, and then she was getting off this ship. It was foolhardy to continue to the airlocks, though. That's where they expected her to go. Besides, the Cans—as the escape pods were called by any spacer with experience—had precious little reserve, and almost no maneuverability. The distress signal was a joke. She wasn't ditching this ship just to suffocate slowly in space.

Like a swimmer doing laps, Yakata flipped end over end and hauled herself the way she came. The pods weren't the only option. There was that payload attached to the forward coupling, the inter-orbital shuttlecraft meant to transport Corporate big-wigs to their facilities surrounding Demeter. Even if O'Neal knew about it, he wouldn't expect her to try and escape that way. Transports were shipped dry, no fuel, no external tanks, and just enough juice to power the maneuvering thrusters and internals. Right now the shuttle was a big, floating box. But—most important for her—it was a big, floating box with enough air to support seven adult males for fourteen days, without cracking the reserve tanks. That . . . and a state-of-the-art distress beacon.

All she had to do was reach it. Yakata renewed her efforts, keeping her eye on the reflectors as she went. No one threatened to come through the hatches ahead of her. As she neared the hatch leading to the Temporary Science Lab, she again glanced both ways down the shaft.

Wherever O'Neal had gone, he wasn't stalking her.

Yakata opened the hatch and dove inside. She thanked God that the drive had not reengaged. The only blessing in this whole thing: weightlessness certainly made it easy to get around. Not to mention the obelisk would have been a dead weight if the ship were still under gravity.

Lights flared as Yakata slipped into the compartment where the artifact was stored. Immediately she noticed the door to the locker hung open, and nothing remain inside.

"No!" Yakata hissed with rage. She looked around, her gaze darting frantically, as if the obelisk might be sitting right in front of her. But it was useless. It was gone. She slammed the locker door and whirled, her anger taking over. The spectrometer still sat affixed to the table. It mocked her. She'd known O'Neal was out to screw her over. Her good hand snapped out, denting the housing of his costly machine. She let it fly again. It felt good. She took aim once more, until a reflection in the battered metal caught her eye.

O'Neal! She dove away from his raised fists, certain that any moment she would feel the crushing blow from his prosthetic. None fell. She twisted in midair, fighting to control her motions, to palm her knife and deploy the blade.

As she came to rest against the far bulkhead, Yakata felt a ripple of laughter seize her throat.

"What the hell?" she murmured aloud. The room was empty. No O'Neal hovered, ready to pummel her to pulp. Yet . . .

Yakata gripped her knife tighter and propelled herself toward the spectrometer. Had she truly lost it? Or was this proof of the sinister force Dunn claimed now possessed the ship? She tapped the dented surface with the tip of her utility knife. Tapped it right over the reflection of O'Neal. The micro image flinched back. Yakata giggled. The sound had a jagged edge.

That was it then: she'd gone over the edge. She giggled again and chased the figmentary O'Neal around the spectrometer with rapid taps of her utility knife. She laughed full out and tasted salt drip over the rim of her lip onto her tongue. A sob slipped out next. The knife drifted down to its strap and she rested a gentle hand against the reflection.

"I'm sorry . . . I'm so sorry . . . "

She brought her face right up near the metal, noticing the terror on that tiny man's face. He didn't look at her, though; his gaze stared off into the room. It took her a moment to realize there were now two O'Neal's trapped in the metal. Perhaps it was an accumulative thing: the longer she stared the more the image would multiply. Her next giggle bordered on a wail.

That was when the ching of flexing metal reached her ears. Her eyes went wide. She leaned against the machine. Clarity seeped back into her own reflection. The memory of the last time she and O'Neal had been in this room came to her. He'd taken the artifact out of the spectrometer and gone into painful convulsions. Her gaze snapped to the tiny O'Neal with the hazel eyes, somehow trapped within his own machine while some thing went around in his body. He gave the slightest nod. "I'm sorry," she whispered as she snaked her hand around the housing.

With a mighty heave, she flung the machine at the O'Neal creeping up behind her, the one with something alien peering out of stormy green eyes.

Connections snapped. Metal collided with metal in a satisfying crunch. The creature's roar deafened her.

As she rocketed past, aiming for the hatch, she spared half a glance for her would-be attacker. The spectrometer was drifting away from him. Massive bruises shadowed O'Neal's already dark shoulder. The prosthetic attached to it was crumpled, but the fingers flexed, if somewhat haltingly.

Her aim was off. She'd meant to cave in his head.

There was an odd gleam in O'Neal's eye as his gaze locked with hers. She jerked her eyes away and maneuvered out of arm's reach.

She was nearly clear when he lurched up. His flesh hand shot out and grabbed her ankle. Screaming with rage, she flicked her wrist and palmed the dangling utility knife, the blade still deployed. She lashed out. The edge bit deep into the back of his hand.

She kicked out with her unfettered foot at O'Neal's still firm and bloodied grip on her ankle. He laughed up at her. The trapped O'Neal pounded furiously from the far side of his reflection; the evil one raised his battered prosthetic and caressed her calf with deceptive gentleness.

Frantic, Yakata tried to yank her foot free. She succeeded only in drawing him closer. Again the prosthetic stroked her leg, this time higher.

"Shh . . . it will be okay . . . " he mocked.

Her vision went dark and flat. Nothing had depth or shading. Nothing was as crisply clear as his grip on her leg. Nothing mattered more than freeing herself from that hold. Without a second thought, she brought her knife around and impaled O'Neal's hand . . .

. . . straight through to her ankle. More blood filled the room.

"Augh!"

O'Neal laughed over her scream as he tugged his hand away from the blade, bisecting his own flesh. The damage did nothing to hinder his movements. But for her, the motion sent shafts of breath-stopping pain shooting from her foot to the top of her head. The knife remained lodged in the muscle just above the ankle.

"Bad girl . . . you were supposed to head for the Cans."

Yakata whimpered. Clenching her teeth, she yanked out the blade, sending pearls of blood spining through the bay. The strap went back over her wrist. The hilt locked in her grip. Again armed, she kicked off toward the hatch.

From just inside the room, O'Neal's laughter stole her breath. She waited for him to haul her back. She could already feel his fingers locked around her. Not again! She sent herself rocketing with reckless force. Her body careened off the interior walls. She slammed against the hatch collar with her bad shoulder. Her injured foot snagged on the door. The agony was nearly crippling. Her vision clouded and a buzz filled her ears.

It wasn't enough to drown out O'Neal as he called after her. "Run, rabbit, run . . . it's so much fun to catch you."

Despite O'Neal's taunt, there were no sounds of pursuit. She was under no illusion it would remain that way. Tumbling into the main shaft, Yakata planted her good foot against the track and shoved off, bulleting toward the nose of the ship. She cursed at the lights. Some sections activated as she passed, others went out, plunging her into darkness. She ignored it. After all her years on this ship, a little darkness wasn't going to screw her up.

As she neared the command deck there was a faint green ambient glow, like that given off by digital displays in the dark. It was impossible to make out if anyone was there. O'Neal was somewhere behind her, but what happened to Dunn? Intense sorrow gripped her heart as she remembered the last time she saw him. Yakata forced it away. He was either dead, or a danger to her.

Cautiously, she eased past the command hatch, keeping to the far side of the shaft. It was slow going, but she made it to the staging bay two levels up without incident. A glance behind her revealed no obvious motion, but her nerves vibrated with tension.

She turned back to the open hatch of the staging bay. The mechanism to seal the two-meter wide opening could close in less than thirty seconds. She released the knife and reached into her pouch for a spanner, wedging it into the grating where the retractable hatch was housed. It wouldn't hold long, but should another . . . malfunction occur, the obstruction would give her a little extra time to get clear.

Reaching just past the opening, she felt around for a tether bar to haul herself through. Something brushed against her hand in the darkness. She jerked back and palmed the knife, bracing herself for an attack. A whisper of sound taunted her ears. Her grip on the knife tightened even more, but nothing else came at her out of the dark. Yakata breathed out a growl.

Fine, she thought. *I'll do it the hard way.* She flung herself through the hatch, rocketing past the opening and deep into the bay, her body angled to intersect with the lift track. Instead, she collided with something soft and yielding. It was impossible not to scream as arms came around to encircle her.

No! She would not be caught so easily! Yakata brought up her knife and thrust brutally into the one blocking her way.

"'Ta . . . " The whisper was faint, and right by her ear. Yakata moaned and her knife hand jerked back. Warm globules bounced against her skin as the blade did more damage coming out than going in. The pinpoints of warmth sent her trembling.

No! Oh, God, no! Please no! Yakata's thoughts were frantic. She released the knife as if it were a contagion. Her now-empty hand scrambled around in her maintenance pouch as the knife bobbed on its strap. *Where was it? Where, damnit?* She forgot all about escape as she searched for her spare light among the jumbled tools. As her hand wrapped around it, and she depressed the button, a sudden clang from the direction of the hatch startled her. She fumbled the light. It made eerie arcs as it spun in the darkened bay, revealing small slices of her surroundings. Her gasp echoed through the compartment as the rotating beam briefly illuminated a blood-coated hand. Yakata lunged for the maintenance light. Before she could bring the beam around, there was a deep, rumbling chuckle behind her. She whirled and the main lights flared to life in the bay. She flinched and squinted against the sudden brilliance.

"My . . . and haven't you been busy?" O'Neal rested against the lift track, his arms crossed over his chest as he watched her. She noticed his gaze sweep the chamber. He frowned faintly as he looked right, but he made no move toward her or the room.

The last thing she should do was take her eye off him. The impulse, however, was irresistible. Yakata pivoted until she could see the whole of the bay.

The blood rushed from her head. She barely heard O'Neal's malicious laughter. Around her floated three bodies. Her unaccounted-for crewmen . . . She immediately recognized the one to the right as Dunn, much bloodier, but still clearly him. The closest to her, however, was John Pittman. From his gut streamed a trail of ruby-red bubbles.

She was overcome by the urge to fling the utility knife from her, only that would have cut her probability of survival down even lower. It was an effort to tug her eyes away, to get past the horror. She told herself he was already dead. Beyond Pittman floated Anita Suarez, her expression softer, more feminine in death than it had ever been in life. Old spacer that she was, she looked like a frightened child now. A frightened child frozen in intense and unbearable pain.

Yakata refused to look more closely at Dunn.

She cursed and turned on O'Neal once more, her knife in her hand, though she didn't remember flicking it up. O'Neal continued to laugh.

"'Ta . . . no . . . ."

Again, the bodiless whisper by her ear. No . . . from her comm hood! Dunn was the only one to ever call her 'Ta. She glanced sideways, trying to catch the subtle motion breathing alone would have caused. It was so hard to tell at this angle.

"Damn it, 'Ta, come . . . get this thing . . . " The strained whisper was no product of her imagination. He 'drifted' ever so slightly; just enough to reveal the outline of a line-gun hidden in the curve of his body. Behind him was the half-open storage locker the tool had come from.

Without another thought, she braced both legs against the wall. Pain rippled from her ankle, but she needed equal force to keep herself headed straight as she launched herself forward. O'Neal arrowed toward Dunn, as well, but Yakata was closer.

Grasping the gun and using her momentum to pivot the rest of her mass, she braced the improvised weapon against her body and jerked the release.

There was a whoosh and a thud. O'Neal went rocketing across the bay toward the opposite wall. His head slammed into the hull and then the only motion was his body recoiling from the impact.

Numbness set in. *Could that be it? Was it that simple?* She thought as she drifted where she was, the gun still gripped in her hand. Beside her, Dunn moaned and it barely reached where her psyche had retreated.

The steady tug on the rope, though . . . that went right to her nerve centers.

"Oh shit!" She let go of the line-gun and wrapped her good hand in Dunn's vest.

"N-no . . . you have to survive," he murmured, batting away her hand. "Can't do that hauling my ass behind you."

"Bullshit!" she growled. "You made it this far, I'm not leaving you here to die."

"I'm . . . I'm d-dead, either way."

She ignored his failing whisper, and pushed off, sending them past the bodies. Her mind shut down as she did so, focused on one goal: freedom. Nothing existed but the nose dock of the *McKay* and the payload it led to.

And suddenly, they were there.

She let go of Dunn's vest to work the manual release. The hatch clanged open and she reached for Dunn once more. He gripped her hand back. His hand trembled violently. She turned to look at him, to gauge how much distress he was in.

"No!" she shouted, as she spied O'Neal past Dunn's shoulder, raising the retracted line-gun. But it was too late. She felt the impact as the hook embedded itself in Karl's back. "No . . . no . . . " she sobbed. Not Dunn. Not when she . . . "No . . . I I-love you! No!"

Tears streamed down her face as she watched the awareness faded from his eyes. *No.* But this protest was silent, weak. *Did it matter now,* she wondered, if she got away? But the tug of the line decided her. She roared with rage and yanked back. O'Neal and whatever rode him would not have Dunn.

She brought up her utility knife and severed the line. Grabbing Karl's vest, she tugged him through the forward airlock. He bobbed behind her as she cycled the hatch. Yakata was numb as she took them through the yacht access. She gave him a gentle nudge to send him drifting deeper into the cabin as her hand danced automatically through the manual release sequence for the docking ring.

As they separated from the *McKay*, she could swear she heard the ghost of laughter.

She dropped into the driver's seat of the luxury yacht, barely noticing the sensual caress of fine doeskin leather. Her only concern was powering up the systems. Lighting and atmospherics engaged, followed by the exterior cameras.

The numbness faded as she realized how near Demeter they were. There was hope of rescue. A solid chance for survival. Her hand hovered over the distress beacon, but drew back, leaving the unit inactivated. Why bother? Dunn was gone.

"No . . . you must survive."

Yakata shivered as Dunn's earlier words whispered through her thoughts. Clenching her eyes against the heartache, she brought her hand back and slammed it down on the distress beacon button.

Rescue would come now. And she would have to go on. Alone.

As that realization hit her, she watched the *McKay* fire its engines. She deftly manipulated the contoured joystick controlling the external camera, panning it in the ship's wake.

What was he up to now? she wondered, unable to turn away. The *McKay* angled further to the left and the display in front of her blazed fiercely, blinding her a moment. The system adjusted the filters until the brilliant sun was no more than a distant, glowing disk marred only by a rapidly diminishing black speck.

"Enjoying the show, Ms. Ushimi?"

Yakata jerked as O'Neal's voice came over the yacht's speakers. She cursed herself for forgetting to disengage the remote sensors connecting the two ships.

"Why?" she hissed.

"Where's the terror," he purred, "if there's no one left to know exactly how fucked you all are?

"Oh yeah, and thanks for the ride."

As his words faded, the yacht's lights flickered out, plunging Yakata into darkness. She fumbled with the control panel, frantically trying to reengage them, to no avail. Her only illumination was the display in front of her.

She couldn't hold back a whimper. She was no longer comfortable with the dark. O'Neal's disembodied laugh wrapped around her just before he closed the link. She was so shocked it took a moment for her to realize the *McKay's* hyperdrive had engaged.

Horrified, she watched the ship's graceful arc; was mesmerized by the shimmer of its electrogravitic drive envelope. Yakata held her breath. She could still see the glittering trail streaming behind the transport, but knew it had, in fact, already plunged into the sun. Eight minutes later, the sunlight contracted, the glowing ball getting smaller and smaller.

O'Neal's voice echoed in her head. An old memory from when he had still been himself and the spectrometer had fed them an impossible reading on the obelisk: *It's as if the artifact absorbed the light.*

She shuddered and watched as the star died, its fire eaten up by an ancient evil no larger than her head.

Yakata was left in complete darkness with her dead.

Dunn. The spaced crew. In her panicked mind, she pictured each of them in a mask of her father's face.

Her breath came in rapid huffs and her body shook until she had to grip the console to remain in the chair.

How long before we all die? she thought, staring in the direction of Demeter, an entire planet suddenly and inexplicably plunged into bitter-cold darkness.

The comm hood crackled and Yakata's heart seized.

"Yummy," O'Neal's voice whispered malevolently in her ear. "Want to come get us? We'll do dessert . . ."

Yakata screamed.

BLACK TO MOVE

Jack McDevitt

MAYBE IT'S JUST MY IMAGINATION, BUT I'M WORRIED.
The roast beef has no taste, and I'm guzzling my coffee. I'm sitting here watching Turner and Pappas working on the little brick house across the avenue with their hand picks. Jenson and McCarthy are standing over near the lander, arguing about something. And Julie Bremmer is about a block away drawing sketches of the blue towers. Everything is exactly as it was yesterday.

Except me.

In about two hours, I will talk to the Captain. I will try to warn him. Odd, but this is the only place in the city where people seem able to speak in normal tones. Elsewhere, voices are hushed. Subdued. It's like being in a church at midnight. I guess it's the fountain, with its silvery spray drifting back through the late afternoon sun, windblown, cool. The park glades are a refuge against the wide, still avenues and the empty windows. Leaves and grass are bright gold, but otherwise the vegetation is of a generally familiar cast. Through long, graceful branches, the blue towers glitter in the sunlight.

There is perhaps no sound quite so soothing as the slap of water on stone. (Coulter got the fountain working yesterday, using a generator from the lander.) Listening, seated on one of the benches at the fountain's edge, I can feel how close we are, the builders of this colossal city and I. And that thought is no comfort.

It's been a long, dusty, rockbound road from Earth to this park. The old hunt for extraterrestrial intelligence has taken us across a thousand sandy worlds in a quest that became, in time, a search for a blade of grass.

I will remember all my life standing on a beach under red Capella, watching the waves come in. Sky and sea were crystal blue; no gull wheeled through the still air; no strand of green boiled in the surf. It was a beach without a shell.

But here, west of Centauri, after almost two centuries, we have a living world!

We looked down, unbelieving, at forests and jungles, and dipped our scoops into a crowded sea. The perpetual bridge game broke up.

On the second day, we saw the City.

A glittering sundisk, it lay in the southern temperate zone, between a mountain chain and the sea. With it came our first mystery: the City was alone. No other habitation existed anywhere on the planet. On the fourth day, Olzsewski gave his opinion that the City was deserted.

We went down and looked.

It appeared remarkably human, and might almost have been a modern terrestrial metropolis. But its inhabitants had put their cars in their garages, locked their homes, and gone for a walk.

Mark Conover, riding overhead in the *Chicago*, speculated that the builders were not native to this world.

They were jointed bipeds, somewhat larger than we are. We can sit in their chairs and those of us who are tall enough to be able to see through their windshields can drive their cars. Our sense of the place was that they'd left the day before we came.

It's a city of domes and minarets. The homes are spacious, with courtyards and gardens, now run to weed. And they were fond of games and sports. We found gymnasiums and parks and pools everywhere. There was a magnificent oceanfront stadium, and every private home seemed filled with playing cards and dice and geometrical puzzles and 81-square checkerboards.

They had apparently not discovered photography; nor, as far as we could determine, were they given to the plastic arts. There were no statues. Even the fountain lacked the usual boys on dolphins or winged women. It was instead a study in wet geometry, a complex of leaning slabs, balanced spheres, and odd-angled pyramids.

Consequently, we'd been there quite a while before we found out what the inhabitants looked like. That happened when we walked into a small home on the north side, and found some charcoal etchings.

Cats, someone said.

Maybe. The following day we came across an art museum and found several hundred watercolors, oils, tapestries, crystals, and so on.

They are felines, without doubt, but the eyes are chilling. The creatures in the paintings have nevertheless a human dimension. They are bundled against storms; they gaze across plowed fields at sunset; they smile benevolently (or pompously) out of portraits. In one particularly striking watercolor, four females cower beneath an angry sky. Between heaving clouds, a pair of full moons illuminate the scene.

This world has no satellite.

Virtually everyone crowded into the museum. It was a day of sighs and grunts and exclamations, but it brought us no closer to an answer to the central question: where had they gone?

"Just as well they're not here," Turner said, standing in front of the watercolor. "This is the only living world anyone has seen. It's one hell of a valuable piece of real estate. Nice of them to give it to us."

I was at the time standing across the gallery in front of a wall-sized oil. It was done in impressionistic style, reminiscent of Degas: a group of the creatures was gathered about a game of chess. Two were seated at the table, hunched over the pieces in the classic pose of the dedicated player. Several more, half in shadow, watched.

Their expressions were remarkably human. If one allowed for the ears and the fangs, the scene might easily have been a New York coffeehouse.

The table was set under a hanging lamp; its hazy illumination fell squarely on the board.

The game was not actually chess, of course. For one thing, the board had 81 squares. There was no queen. Instead, the king was flanked by a pair of pieces that vaguely resembled shields. Stylized hemispheres at the extremes of the position must have been rooks. (Where else but on the flank would one reasonably place a rook?)

The other pieces, too, were familiar. The left-hand Black bishop had been fianchettoed: a one-square angular move onto the long diagonal, from where it would exercise withering power. All four knights had been moved, and their twisted tracks betrayed their identity.

The game was still in its opening stages. White was two pawns up, temporarily. It appeared to be Black's move, and he would, I suspected, seize a White pawn which had strayed deep into what we would consider his queenside.

I stood before that painting, feeling the stirrings of kinship and affection for these people and wondering what immutable laws of psychology, mathematics, and aesthetics ordained the creation of chess in cultures so distant from each other. I wondered whether the game might not prove a rite of passage of some sort.

I was about to leave when I detected a wrongness somewhere in the painting, as if a piece were misplaced, or the kibitzers were surreptitiously watching me. Whatever it was, I grew conscious of my breathing.

There was nothing.

I backed away, turned, and hurried out of the building.

I'm a symbologist, with a specialty in linguistics. If we ever do actually find someone out here to talk to, I'm the one who will be expected to say hello. That's an honor, I suppose; but I can't get Captain Cook entirely out of my mind.

By the end of the first week, we had not turned up any written material (and, in fact, still haven't) other than a few undecipherable inscriptions on the sides of buildings. They were even more computerized than we are, and we assumed everything went into the data banks, which we also haven't found. The computers themselves are wrecked. Slagged. So, by the way, is the central power core for the City. Another mystery.

Anyhow, I had little to do, so yesterday I went for a walk in the twilight with Jennifer East, a navigator and the pilot of the other lander. She's lovely, with bright hazel eyes, and a quick smile. Her long tawny hair was radiant in the setting sun. The atmosphere here has a moderately high oxygen content, which affects her the way some women are affected by martinis. She clung to my arm, and I was breathlessly aware of her long-legged stride.

We might have been walking through the streets of an idealized, mystical Baghdad: the towers were gold and purple in the failing light. Flights of brightly-colored birds scattered before us. I half-expected to hear the somber cry of a ram's horn, calling the faithful to prayer.

The avenue is lined with delicate, graybarked trees. Their broad, filamented leaves sighed in the wind, which was constant off the western mountains. Out at sea, thunder rumbled.

Behind the trees are the empty homes, no two alike, and other structures that we have not yet begun to analyze. Only the towers exceed three stories. The buildings are all beveled and curved; right angles do not exist. I wonder what the psychologists will make of that.

"I wonder how long they've been gone?" she said. Her eyes were luminous with excitement, directed (I'm sorry to say) at the architecture.

That had been a point of considerable debate. Many of the interiors revealed a degree of dust that suggested it could not have been more than a few weeks since someone had occupied them. But much of the pavement was in a state of disrepair, and on the City's inland side, forest was beginning to push through.

I told her I thought they'd been around quite recently.

"Mark," she said, staying close. "I wonder whether they've really left."

There was nothing you could put in a report, but I agreed that we were transients, that those streets had long run to laughter and song, that they soon would again, and that it would never really be ours.

She squeezed my arm. "It's magnificent."

I envied her; this was her first flight. For most of us, there had been too many broken landscapes, too much desert.

"Olszewski thinks," I said, "that the northern section of the City is almost two thousand years old . . . . They'd been here a while."

"And they just packed up and left." She steered us out of the center, angling toward the trees, where I think we both felt less conspicuous.

"It's ironic," I said. "No one would have believed first contact would come like this. They've been here since the time of Constantine, and we miss them by a few weeks. Hard to believe, isn't it?"

She frowned. "It's not believable." She touched one of the trees. "Did you know it's the second time?" she asked. I must have looked blank. "Twenty-two years ago the Berlin tracked something across the face of Algol and then lost it. Whatever it was, it threw a couple of sharp turns." We walked silently for several minutes, crossed another avenue, and approached the museum. "Algol," she said, "isn't all that far from here."

"UFO stories," I said. "They used to be common."

She shrugged. "It might be that the thing the Berlin saw frightened these people off. Or worse."

The museum is wheel-shaped. Heavy, curving panels of tinted glass are ribbed by polished black stone that is probably marble. The grounds are a wild tangle of weed and shrub anchored by overgrown hedge. A few flowering bushes survive out near the perimeter.

I laughed. "You don't suppose the sun is about to nova, do you?"

She smiled and brushed my cheek with a kiss. Jenny is 23 and a graduate of MIT. "It's going to rain," she said.

We walked past a turret. The air was cool.

"They seem to have taken their time about leaving," I said. "There's no evidence of panic or violence. And most of their personal belongings apparently went with them. Whatever happened, they had time to go home and pack."

She looked uneasily at the sky. Gray clouds were gathering in the west. "Why did they destroy the computers? And the power plant? Doesn't that sound like a retreat before an advancing enemy?"

We stood on the rounded stone steps at the entrance, watching the coming storm. Near the horizon, lightning touched the ground. It was delicate, like the trees.

And I knew what had disturbed me about the painting.

Jenny doesn't play chess. So when we stood again before the portrait and I explained, she listened dutifully, and then tried to reassure me. I couldn't blame her.

I have an appointment to meet the Captain in the gallery after dinner. He doesn't play chess either. Like all good captains down through the ages, he is a man of courage and hardheaded common sense, so he will also try to reassure me.

Maybe I'm wrong. I hope so.

But the position in that game: Black is playing the Benko Gambit. It's different in detail, of course; the game is different. But Black is about to clear a lane for the queenside rook. One bishop, at the opposite end of the board, is astride the long diagonal, where its terrible power will combine with that of the rook. And White, after the next move or two, when that advanced pawn comes off, will be desperately exposed.

It's the most advanced of the gambits for Black, still feared after three hundred years—.

And I keep thinking: the inhabitants of the City were surely aware of this world's value. More, they are competitors. They would assume that we would want to take it from them.

"But we wouldn't," Jenny had argued.

"Are you sure? Anyhow, it doesn't matter. The only thing that does matter is what they believe. And they would expect us to act as they would.

"Now, if they knew in advance that we were coming—"

"The Berlin sighting—"

"—Might have done it. Warned them we were in the neighborhood. So they withdraw, and give us the world. And, with it, an enigma." Rain had begun sliding down the tinted glass. "They're playing the Benko."

"You mean they might come back here in force and attack?" She was aghast, not at the possibility, which she dismissed; but at the direction my mind had taken.

"No," I said. "Not us. The Benko isn't designed to recover a lost pawn." I could not look away from the painting. Did I detect a gleam of arrogance in Black's eyes? "No. It doesn't fool around with pawns. The idea is to launch a strike into the heart of the enemy position."

"Earth?" She smiled weakly. "They wouldn't even know where Earth is."

I didn't ask whether she thought we might not go home alone.

One more thing about that painting: there's a shading of light, a chia-roscuro, in the eyes of the onlookers. It's the joy of battle.

I'm scared.

First published in Asimov's, Sept, 1982. Copyright 1996 Cryptic, Inc.

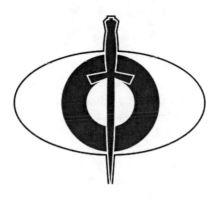

KILLER EYE

James Chambers

THESE DAYS ALL OF CAPTAIN ELL CAMDEN'S DREAMS WERE SILENT. IN THEM, PEOPLE moved their mouths without speech, questions materialized stillborn on Camden's lips, and everything transpired in eerie tranquility. In one dream Camden witnessed a jump plane crash. The graceful, silver craft plummeted into an open field where it erupted in a ball of fire and black smoke; but without the expected roar and shriek, the explosion seemed to billow outward in slow motion. Often Camden dreamt of walking through a bright meadow where a whisperless wind swayed the chest-high grass all around him. Flowers speckled the landscape like a fluorescent snowfall. Roses grew everywhere, rising on long, thorny stems laden with heavy, blood-red blossoms that bobbed and nodded at Camden as he passed. He felt them watching, straining toward him; he tried to call out, but the stillness devoured his cry. He awoke from just such a dream on the morning the kill orders came.

Snapping to consciousness, his body electrified with tension, Camden pawed the clutter on his nightstand until he unearthed a pack of stimarettes, then popped one between his lips and cracked its seal. Stimulating vapors cooled his throat and calmed his jittery nerves. He glanced at Lieutenant Ginny Nakata sleeping next to him, tangled in the bed sheets. Her black hair protruded in blunt spikes, and her torso rose and fell with her steady breathing. This was the ninth morning in three weeks he'd woken up beside Lieutenant Nakata, and he knew the others—Major Davis Wyle and Captain Marnie Ambrov, and even Nakata herself—wondered if he were becoming attached. Mission protocol allowed sex for physical and psychological release, not to foster romantic distractions that could jeopardize their mission. Camden knew he was due for a warning from Major Wyle, probably with orders to sleep alone for awhile or go to bed with Captain Ambrov to restore the balance. He didn't care. All that mattered was that his dreams didn't unsettle him so much with Ginny beside him.

Camden was one of four soldiers assigned to *Chang* Station. Selected for their skills and their psychological classification as "emotionally self-contained," they were natural loners who required only passing social contact to satisfy their human need for companionship. They were killers, as well, weapons primed and waiting to be triggered. They'd been on duty for two years already or for more than a decade if you counted the nine-year journey from Earth to the Weed system. Two more years and they'd ship back home, assuming there was still an Earth to return to then.

Chang Station was one of thirty-five human outposts in the Weed system, each part of Operation Killer Eye, each home to four soldiers on the same twenty-two-year sniper stint. Most teams consisted of two men and two women, some of four soldiers of the same gender. All of them were trained to monitor Arbor, the Weed homeworld, and operate their outpost's weapon: armaments ranging from cluster bombs to nuclear missiles, grav phasers to particle beams. *Chang* Station stood embedded in the rocky surface of Freeloader, a moon in orbit around the gas giant Vegas Strip, one of five planets in the system. The other planets, their moons, and the asteroid belt that spiraled through the system harbored the other thirty-four KE stations.

With an hour to kill before reporting for duty, Camden slid from bed and ambled into the adjoining observation chamber. The viewport offered a perfect vista of silver dust and craggy rocks. Pale amber and green light crested the horizon, heralding planet rise for Vegas Strip, named after the stormy, Technicolor cloud bands that lit it like infinite rows of neon lights. Camden finished his stimarette and tossed it into a waste bin. He reclined and waited until the emerald edge of Vegas Strip crept above the horizon like a cooling sun. Afterward he headed for the shower unit, and a short time later, clean and alert, he dressed in his uniform and gently roused Lieutenant Nakata. She smiled as she slipped from the sheets, pulled on the sweatpants and T-shirt she'd left crumpled on the floor, and padded away.

The room felt emptier without her, a sensation Camden had only begun to notice these past few weeks. He'd never minded being alone before. In fact, he'd often preferred it. The change heralded a potential problem for someone with two years left in his solitary tour of duty. From the top drawer of his nightstand, he took the photo plate he'd brought in his small allowance of personal items and activated the slideshow. It contained a handful of pictures of his parents and his brother, Varrow. He and Varrow had tried to stick together after they were orphaned by a plane crash, but bureaucratic artifice had forced them apart. Over the years they'd kept in touch, helped each other when possible, until they'd both enlisted, and the military separated them for good. Ell hadn't heard from his brother for more than a decade when the news came six weeks ago—already 13 months old—that he'd been captured with a hundred others during a skirmish with the Weeds and was presumed dead.

Ell imagined his brother fighting and falling, being dragged off and trapped like a lab rat in an utterly silent starcraft piloted by alien beings. The Weeds had earned their name for their appearance: lanky stalk-like bodies and multiple, asymmetrical limbs that resembled branches and leaves, topped by a bulbous head like a cross between a rose blossom and a human brain. Their ships were said to be deathly still and quiet because the Weeds communicated telepathically.

That was one reason for the war. Because their telepathy didn't extend to humans, the Weeds failed to recognize people as sentient beings, classifying them instead as something akin to ants or beetles, pests to be exterminated and driven out of civilized places. That was one theory, anyway, cooked up by experts after decades of study, although no one could say for sure.

It was Weed telepathy, though, that also gave humanity its only edge in the conflict. It worked across vast, even interstellar distances, and so the Weeds had never developed any form of audible or electronic communication. They traveled in silent ships, lived in silent cities, and sent no signals through space. Thus they were unable to intercept or interpret human communication via radio, laser, or subspace comm, a weakness that allowed humans to infiltrate the Weed system and keep contact without exposing themselves. And so Camden had come to live in a cramped and Spartan base on an airless moon, where his sole task was to maintain a directed energy weapon, dubbed "the torch," and wait to fire it when ordered.

He clicked off the photo plate and put it away. It was time to go on duty.

Heading for the command deck, Camden felt grateful for the dull tapping of his footsteps, for the tinny clang when he knocked on the bulkhead, for the presence of all the small sounds that filled *Chang* Station. He was midway down the ladder between levels when the alert siren sounded, and his heart leapt at the raw, dizzying wail that filled the cramped corridors. He dropped the last few feet of the tube and darted along a short passage to the command deck. Major Wyle stood there, his face taut with worry.

"Pre-signal, code Foxtrot-Kilo-3-1-Niner," he announced, then looking up, "Morning, Captain Camden."

"Major," responded Camden as he took up his post and launched the mandatory diagnostic check of their decrypting array. "System check," he said, then when a green light flashed, added, "All channels open and clear."

"Pray for good news," said Wyle.

In anywhere from fifteen minutes to two hours, a message, already as much as a year old, would follow the pre-signal, traveling from the Killer Eye command ship four luminal months out from the Weed system. Communications with command were infrequent; the last had been the required notification to Camden, as next of kin, of his brother's death.

Captain Ambrov entered the command deck, moved to the gunner's station, and initiated the priming sequence for the torch.

"What's the word, boys? We going live?"

"Don't know, yet," Wyle said.

Regulations required all stations to be manned during communications transmissions. A moment later, Lieutenant Nakata joined them.
"Captain Camden, your turn to call odds," she said.

"Right," said Camden. "Okay, given we're still technically under cease fire, I'd say 500,000 to 1 we're getting kill orders. 50 to 1 it's a war report, 20 to 1 it's just a morale booster."

"What about peace?" asked Ambrov. "The last war report sounded promising for further negotiations."

"That had to be spin. How far do you think they can get with the Weeds by trading holographic projections of mathematical equations?" asked Wyle.

"Gotta start somewhere," said Ambrov.

"All right," interjected Camden. "Odds on peace are a million to 1. Get your bets on the table."

"Wait," Nakata said. "What about a false signal? The last war report also warned the Weeds might be catching onto our communications tech. Maybe it's a trick."

"Rumors, that's all," Wyle said. "Something to keep us on our guard."

"Rumors from almost two years ago," said Nakata. "Could be the Weeds learn fast. Captain Camden?"

"Fine, 100,000 to 1 it's a ruse," offered Camden.

"Better odds than peace or a kill order," commented Nakata.

"Yeah, because you're making me paranoid. Now, open channels with our sister stations for verification," Camden said. "We should find out if anyone else is activated."

Each soldier scribbled an amount on a scrap of paper and tossed it into a small depression on the central command table. They'd started the no-limit betting game and kept a running tally in honor of Vegas Strip, and they bet on just about anything they could. Captain Ambrov was up $653,486 over everyone else, and she insisted that she aimed to collect every cent of it when they were all discharged.

After placing her bet Nakata arranged the controls to relay between the four nearest stations. Camden listened to the steady hum of the machinery that surrounded them and the tinny beeps from Ambrov's monitor as she powered up the torch. The directed energy weapon could be aimed to strike a target as small as a single Weed or as sprawling as a city. The Killer Eye program was meant to give humanity a chance to hurt the Weeds badly enough to end the conflict. Fighting head to head, the Weeds seemed unbeatable. They'd been a spacefaring race longer than mankind; they had faster ships and better weapons. And communications at the speed of thought let thousands of them act as one in executing battle tactics. Humanity's only chance was to remain unpredictable and attack by surprise. The Navy had been forced back almost all the way to Earth before the latest cease-fire. The next time hostilities reached a fever pitch the Killer Eyes would certainly be activated.

Lately it seemed more and more imminent. Observations of the Weed homeworld indicated they were constructing a new type of starship that would dwarf their other battleships, one possibly intended for a final assault against Earth. Expert analysis estimated a decade at least before it could make an attack. Most of the human population held out hope for a peace agreement before then, but two previous cease-fires had failed, and the current one seemed destined for stalemate.

The Weeds simply rejected the concept of humans as being equal to themselves.

Camden wondered if his brother were truly dead. Because no one taken prisoner by the Weeds had ever been recovered, military policy declared those captured as killed in action after thirty days. But maybe Zarrow still lived, caged in some silent prison where the Weeds studied him. Or maybe they'd dissected him alive. Or incinerated him. There were hundreds of stories about what the Weeds did to prisoners, but not a shred of evidence to prove any of them.

The uncertainty somehow made the loss all the more painful. A military death declaration worked to close the files, but for Camden it just emphasized how alone he was now with his entire family ushered into oblivion. All he had left was the military, and they'd made him into more of a machine than a man. His physical needs were rigidly satiated, his emotional needs neatly cataloged and accounted for. They'd been told they were special, that as Killer Eyes they were granted responsibilities and privileges beyond those of common soldiers. But the freedom, the self-reliance, the isolation were illusions crafted to disguise that fact that KE soldiers were no more than carefully chosen, strictly trained triggers—extensions of the military intelligence machine. With minor variations, the soldiers on all thirty-five Killer Eye stations were exactly the same, as if they'd been stamped out of clay on a factory line. They ate, they slept, they excreted, they copulated, but mostly they did their assigned duties and spent as much time alone as possible. There was no need for discourse or debate; they were all perfectly attuned to each other. Like members of a cult, it had recently occurred to Camden, and for the first time in his tour of duty it bothered him. He hadn't considered it much before his brother died, before the dreams started, before the scent of Lieutenant Nakata's sweat began to linger in his memory for days. But now the irony seemed inescapable—to fight the Weeds they'd shed their humanity and become in some ways exactly like their enemy.

Camden's gaze drifted to Lieutenant Nakata. He wondered if she felt any of this, if she'd been drawn to him like he'd been to her, or if she were just going along with him out of duty.

"Comm channel check. Confirm status," Nakata said, snapping Camden out of his thoughts.

He ran the program and scowled. "No contact with our sister stations."

"How can that be?" asked Nakata. "Interference?"

"Between us and all four of our sister bases simultaneously? Unlikely," replied Camden. "Besides, all readings are clear, and we've had minimal sunspot activity for three weeks."

"Maybe technical failure?" she offered. "Our comm gear is due for maintenance in two days."

"I'm checking that now," said Camden. "And all equipment appears fine. Could be failure on one of the other bases but not all five simultaneously. Do we have line of sight with any of the stations?"

Nakata summoned a fresh display on her monitor. "*Philip* Station will be in position in forty-five seconds. Go to Morse laser for contact confirmation?"

Monitoring the conversation, Major Wyle glanced over Nakata's shoulders at her screen, and said, "We've never used the signal laser, Lieutenant Nakata. It's meant as a last resort. The Weeds could see it. How long will we have line of sight with *Philip* Station?"

"Approximately nineteen minutes before planet rise puts Vegas Strip between us and them," Nakata told him.

"Then, let's wait and see if our orders come through," said Wyle.

"Major Wyle, all D-E-W systems active," Captain Ambrov announced. "Targeting systems operational. The torch is primed and ready to light."

"Thank you, Captain."

The alert siren blared back to life with dizzying urgency. Wyle darted to his station, while Camden and Nakata managed the incoming signal.

"That was fast," Nakata observed.

"Record time," said Ambrov. "Anyone else getting a bad feeling about this?"

"Quiet," Wyle snapped.

Camden's fingers clacked over his keyboard, assigning computers to the decrypt their orders and route them directly to Major Wyle's station. A cold draft of tension crept through the room as each soldier waited. The signal transmitted for several minutes then ended. Major Wyle's eyes remained glued to his monitor as the decrypted orders scrolled across his screen. He read them over twice and cross-checked them against his mission journal.

"Is that it?" he asked.

"Yes, Sir," answered Camden. "It cut short."

Wyle turned to Nakata. "Status of comm channels, Lieutenant?"

"Still off-line, Sir."

"Line of sight with *Philip* Station?"

"Open for another nine minutes."

"All right, activate the laser. We need confirmation," Wyle ordered.

"Sir?" asked Nakata.

"We have been assigned a target and ordered to fire," Wyle told them. "I want confirmation."

"What is our target, Sir?" asked Ambrov.

Wyle tapped his keyboard and relayed the decrypted portion of their orders to the other stations. On each monitor appeared: "Arbor Spaceport Omega, 09:00." It was a prime target in the planet's southern hemisphere.

"That's it?" asked Ambrov.

"It came in segmented and heavily coded. There might have been more to it, something that got truncated," said Camden. His fingers crawled over his console. "More was embedded in the transmission, but the signal ended before we received the final close code, so we can't decrypt the rest."

"Then our orders are incomplete," noted Wyle.

"I'd say they're pretty clear, Major," Nakata said.

"We could be missing something important, like a secondary target, or a firing condition," Wyle countered. "I don't like proceeding on half-baked information."

"The rest of it was probably just a war report," said Camden. "An update on negotiations."

"Or lack of them," added Ambrov.

"We don't know that for sure," said Wyle.

"Commencing signal to *Philip* Station," Nakata announced.

The four soldiers waited, outwardly still, yet each of them running mental drills as their battle training swept them into fight mode. They imagined the strike and the inevitable Weed retaliation; they wondered what had happened to bring about activation of the Killer Eyes. If one base acted alone, it was almost certain the Weeds would locate and destroy it. Only if all of the KE stations fired simultaneously to utterly devastate the Weed world could any of them really hope to survive. But there was always the possibility that command needed just one heavy attack to make a point to the Weeds, to win an advantage in negotiations, or to eliminate a critical target. For that, a single KE station was expendable.

"No reply from *Philip* Station," Nakata reported. "Their sensors should've sighted our laser by now."

Wyle stood and rubbed his forehead with his thumb and forefinger. "Captain Camden, you care to give odds on whether or not *Philip* Station still exists?"

"No, Sir," Camden said. "Bets are already on the table."

"Consider this a new hand," Wyle replied. "Because we all know what happens after we light the torch. Unless it's a prelude to an all-out attack against the Weeds, there's no doubt they'll find us and destroy us. For all we know, that's what happened to *Philip* Station. Maybe they received orders before us and acted. Or maybe something just went wrong over there and *Philip* Station is down by a quirk of fate. They could've been gone for weeks. Our last communication with them was—what?"

"Seven months ago," Nakata supplied.

"But the loss of radio communication with the other stations suggests something more at work," Wyle said.

"Like maybe the Weeds are jamming our transmissions," said Camden. "The kill order could be a trick to flush us out. The truncated signal would camouflage the fact that the Weeds don't have the close codes needed to authenticate the orders. They're hoping we'll overlook that and give ourselves away."

"So, they're fishing," said Wyle. "Could be they've got an idea we're here, but they don't know for sure."

"Which might also explain the silence from our sister stations," interjected Nakata. "Maybe they figured this out ahead of us and went dark."

"So, of course, we go blundering in with the damn Morse laser," said Ambrov. "Great."

"Not likely the Weeds'll notice our laser with Vegas Strip so close by," said Wyle. "Anyway, we've got bigger problems to worry about."

"Such as?" asked Nakata.

"Do we fire?" said Wyle.

"We have orders," said Ambrov.

"But our orders are incomplete and unverified," Wyle pointed out. "The absence of a close code aborts authorization. For all we know, this could be a drill or a targeting test—something that would've been disclosed in the portion we lost."

"Or KE command could've been destroyed before completing transmission," said Camden. "When have we ever gotten orders so fast after a pre-signal? They were rushing. There had to be a reason."

"You think the cease fire broke?" asked Nakata.

Camden shrugged.

"How long would it take to replace KE command?" said Ambrov.

"Eighteen months at least before another ship can be moved into position," said Wyle. "If that's the case then we're now under the direct command of General Cuidera."

"Which leaves us with a three-year turnaround if we request confirmation," said Camden. "And our orders are to fire in just under two hours."

"Reassess the transmission, Camden. Maybe we missed something," said Wyle.

"I've checked it six times, Sir. We've gotten everything we're going to out of it."

Major Wyle settled into his seat and peered at his monitor while he replayed the full transmission, watching the progress bar track across the width of his screen only to halt and freeze just before the end, leaving him with nothing more than a jarringly succinct time and target.

"All right," he said, turning back to the others. "We're cut off and it's up to us to decide. Anyone have a problem with that?"

"We have our orders right here," said Camden, tapping his screen. "What's there to decide? At 09:00 we fire."

"So you're not worried it might be a Weed trick?"

"Does it matter? We take out one of their key spaceports, give them a black eye," said Camden.

"And give ourselves away," said Wyle. "Maybe even blow cover for the whole KE program."

"It won't matter if all stations fire."

"We don't know that will happen," Wyle argued.

"Listen, if the orders are legit, then all stations probably received a target. Maybe some of them even received the full transmission. And if it's a trick—if the Weeds are out there fishing—then somehow they've gotten their hands on some radio gear and they're jamming our communications and transmitting blind. That means everyone's getting the same message, the same orders. They'll fire."

"Not without verification," said Wyle. "Absence of verification negates an order. Effectively we have no kill order. That's protocol. We're out here on our own, connected by the slenderest of threads to the rest of the military. We are not a bunch of cowboys. Procedure is the only thing that holds us together. It's been that way since day one, and that's how it has to be now. Captain Ambrov, power down the D-E-W."

"Wait," said Camden. "Have you forgotten what we all enlisted to do? We're here to defend Earth."

"We won't do that by launching an unauthorized attack that could jeopardize our entire mission," said Wyle.

"What if they're counting on us?" Camden asked. "Waiting for us to soften up the Weeds before bringing the fleet into position?"

"We'd have received a war report and orders," replied Wyle.

"We just did," Camden insisted.

"No, what we've got is an unverified signal from an unidentified source. Less than an hour ago, you—yourself—called better odds on it being a deception than a kill order," said Wyle.

"Yeah, and Ambrov really thinks she's going to collect her winnings from us after our tour," Camden said. "You can't take that seriously."

"What I take seriously is that I'm not willing to gamble with our mission," said Wyle. "Captain Camden, report to your quarters until further notice. I will not have you brewing dissent."

Camden stiffened as though he'd been struck. He clamped his mouth shut, saluted stiffly, and then exited the command room, pausing to glance back once at Lieutenant Nakata. Her worried expression burned like a bonfire in contrast to the pale passiveness on Captain Ambrov's face, and though he wasn't sure why, Camden took comfort from it. Then he was in the well and climbing to the upper level.

He bypassed his room and headed instead to the observation chamber. Vegas

Strip filled the sky with saccharine ribbons of color, a sight Camden had seen many times, but one of which he never wearied. He knew that if he ever returned to Earth, this of all the things he had done and seen since his enlistment would remain brightest in his memory. The mesmerizing whorls of color swirling through bands that seemed to be spinning like the cutting edge of a power saw. The light and dark flashes of storm activity. The contradictory sensation of serenity that such wonderful chaos fostered in him. This proof of the sheer wonder of the universe. This reminder of the magnitude of humanity's accomplishments in challenging cold, harsh space and conquering it. He wondered if the Weeds saw Vegas Strip the way he did, if any single living creature among them was capable of looking upon the planet and experiencing the awe it inspired in him.

On a whim, he rose and went to the door control panel. He punched in his access code, called up the past six months' entry records, and scrolled through the list. His own code appeared over and over again, sometimes two or three times a day, and here and there he saw Lieutenant Nakata's, and less frequently but still regularly Captain Ambrov's. Major Wyle's appeared only once, logged in eight weeks ago barely a minute after Lieutenant Nakata's, suggesting a mood-setting rendezvous, something done out of facility rather than desire. Why did Wyle never come here, Camden wondered. Was the sight lost on him? Did he truly prefer to be sequestered in his quarters doing whatever he did to pass the time? None of the KE soldiers were much for socializing, but a thing as raw and powerful as Vegas Strip possessed a gravity that tugged at something deep and primal in human nature, something that, perhaps, Major Wyle had lost or forgotten or, worse, feared.

Camden spared a last glance at Vegas Strip's stunning luminosity. Then he left the observation chamber and moved to the armory. He selected a shotgun and a pulse rifle to complement his uniform sidearm and prayed he wouldn't need to use any of them. Then he steeled himself and returned to the command deck.

It surprised Camden how calm he was when he stepped through the entryway and leveled the shotgun in Major Wyle's direction. No one spoke for several seconds. In that time, the color leached out of the Major, just as his bearing seemed to turn quite brittle. Captain Ambrov rested her hand on her sidearm but didn't draw it, and Captain Nakata regarded Camden with pure shock.

"Ell," she said.

The way she said his name, the way she breathed it as though it were part of the elements that sustained her life sent shivers down Camden's spine, and in that moment, any flagging doubt remaining within him evaporated.

"Captain Ambrov," Camden said. "Power up the D-E-W and prepare targeting coordinates for Spaceport *Omega* at 09:00."

"I'm sorry, Captain, but no. I already have my orders," she replied.

"Yes, you do, and Major Wyle won't object now if you follow them. He's gotten a little confused today, but we're going to help him through it," said Camden.

"This is mutiny," Ambrov said. "It's insane. Put the weapons down before someone gets hurt."

"Sorry, Marnie," Camden said, watching Ambrov's face crinkle at the sound of her first name. "But mutiny is when you don't follow orders. Now you can do as I told you or I will fire on Major Wyle."

Moving with fluid speed, Ambrov drew her sidearm and aimed it at Camden. "Then I'll have to kill you where you stand."

Camden hadn't expected her to be so fast, hadn't anticipated that she'd take Wyle's side. Her hatred of the Weeds was almost a running joke, and he'd assumed she'd leap at a chance to hurt them. But she was disciplined, moreso than himself probably, and Camden considered again the possibility that he'd made a fatal mistake. He didn't want to kill Wyle, wasn't sure he could act against Ambrov before she killed him; but they had their orders and something deep inside Camden urged him forward, insisted that at 09:00 hours their weapon must be fired. As much of a gamble as it was, as much of a risk as it presented, instinct told Camden it was right.

"I'm sorry, Marnie, but I intend to see that weapon fired as ordered. If you need to see Major Wyle and myself dead to prevent that, that's your choice," said Camden.

"Two people can man this station as well as four," said Ambrov. She cocked her weapon.

"No!" Lieutenant Nakata's voice shattered the icy tension. In a second the balance shifted, and with Nakata's sidearm prodding her torso, Captain Ambrov shuddered and lowered her gun.

"Ginny," said Camden. "Don't. I didn't mean to involve you in this."

"It's all right, Ell. I trust you," Nakata said. "I really do. It's like those dreams you told me about. Maybe they mean something. Maybe you know something the rest of us don't. I don't know. But I know you. Better than these two at least. I know you're a real person."

Nakata prodded Ambrov with her gun barrel. "Now, power up the D-E-W, Marnie."

Ambrov grimaced and complied. Camden inched across the room and gently removed Major Wyle's sidearm and tucked it into a pocket of his uniform. The Major did not resist.

"Have a seat, Major," said Camden. "This will all be over soon."

"What if you're wrong?" the major asked.

"Think about it," Camden replied. "If the orders are legit, then we're doing what we're supposed to. What's the difference if they're not? If the Weeds have caught on to our communications tech, then we've lost the last hope we have of keeping one step ahead of them in this bloody war. If they track us, interfere with our communications, then we're lost, and we need to hit them hard with everything we've got right now—before they get their act together."

"What do you mean?"

"If the signal is a Weed ruse, it's a clumsy one. A kill order broadcast blindly? And the jamming signal? Maybe they've got an idea how the tech works, but they don't understand enough yet to really use it against us. They're like children picking up a telephone for the first time. They get the idea, but they keep trying to talk into the ear piece because that's where the voice comes from. But they'll learn. They'll get better at it, and they'll take away our only edge in this fight. So that means, no matter where the signal came from, it's now or never."

"I hope you're right," said Ambrov. She backed away from the control deck and sat beside Wyle. "D-E-W is primed, firing coordinates programmed."

Nakata confirmed the gun settings, and all four soldiers settled in to wait. It was 08:36.

Camden tried to clear his mind, tried to think of what position Vegas Strip would be in now, tried to summon the vision of Ginny in his bed this morning and the way her hair and skin had smelled. He tried to recall the sound of his brother's voice and the rough way he shook hands. And then he dove back deep into memories of his parents whom he had known for precious few years. He wondered what they would have made of his life and Varrow's, whether they would've been proud or horrified, and whether or not their presence would've made things turn out differently. The time passed too quickly, not at all like Camden had expected, and when the moment came, he strode to the gunner's station and eased Nakata aside. This was his decision, his act, his lashing out at the inhuman enemy that confronted him, at the inhumanity that jeopardized mankind's survival. If there were one like him on every KE station, then perhaps there really was a chance, he thought. As the digital countdown ended, he entered the execution order and then—listened.

Unseen machinery whirred and vibrated. The entire station quivered with a deep, basso thrumming that ran through the soldier's bodies and set their teeth chattering. The entire place throbbed like a beating heart, its pulse building on the rising whine of energy pooling in the chamber. Camden listened to the others breathing: Wyle taking in air in curt, staccato inhalations; Ambrov huffing with frustration; Nakata panting with shallow gasps. Camden realized he was silent, holding his breath, immobile. He exhaled in a long stream and let his chest begin to rise and fall once more.

The external hissing of the torch firing lasted for several minutes, and then in a moment, it ended.

Camden imagined the searing blast of ivory fire pouring out of the dark structure of steel and titanium embedded in Freeloader's harsh granite, pictured it slicing through space, progressing minute by minute, second by second until it reached its target with merciless and incinerating fury. The blast would strike ground at 09:12, and when the time came and Camden knew the act was done, the order fulfilled, he dropped his weapons, slumped in the gunner's chair, and sighed.

Minutes passed and nothing happened.

No one moved; no one spoke.

They sat motionless, draped in a corrosive quiet that Camden despised.

"Did..." Nakata finally uttered, "Did the other stations fire?"

Ambrov swiveled to the nearest keyboard and summoned up the sensor outputs. "Everything's flat," she said. "No, wait! I've got an incoming signal."

The radio comm crackled as Ambrov shunted the transmission over to speakers.

"*Philip* Station to *Chang* Station," a voice said. "Come in, *Chang* Station."

Tendrils of ice crept through Camden's mind.

"Come in *Chang* Station," the voice repeated.

"This is *Chang* Station," Ambrov responded. "We read you *Philip* Station. What is your status?"

"*Chang* Station, our status is active. We are at war and have fired upon a target," the voice repeated. "We have confirmation from *Addams* Station, *Lodi* Station, and *Tesla* Station. Please confirm weapon discharge."

"Discharge confirmed," Ambrov breathed into the mouthpiece. "*Philip* Station, our order signal was cut short. Can you confirm orders?"

"Negative," came back *Philip* Station. "Orders were false. Repeat. Orders were a false signal from the Weeds, combined with a jamming transmission. We have destroyed the source, but the situation has left us no choice but to act. Check your radar, *Chang* Station, because we are not done fighting yet."

Nakata moved to a work station and ordered up the radar display.

"Ships," she said.

"Hundreds," muttered Ambrov. "Some of them are huge."

"Looks like the Weeds finished their new destroyer ahead of schedule," said Camden. "Marnie, can you get a bead on one of the big ones with the torch?"

Ambrov nodded and dashed around to the gunner's seat.

"You were right, Ell," said Nakata. She reached for the scraps of folded paper in the center console. Camden placed his hand on hers and stopped her.

"It doesn't matter," he said. "Gambling only counts when you've got something real to lose."

Ambrov ignited the torch again. *Chang* Station sang with energy and the strain of cold metal shifting and churning together. The hum of the blast filled everyone's ears. Camden turned to a keyboard and began plotting their next target. In his mind appeared the image of the energy beam lancing through space, cutting the darkness, destined to claim the lives of hundreds, even thousands of Weeds—and silent all the while. Silent in its glory; silent in its devastation. As silent as Camden's dreams and the forever stilled lips of his parents and his brother.

COMPARTMENT ALPHA

Jeffrey Lyman

COMMAND TO ALL AFT GUN BATTERIES." THE XO'S MESSAGE FLASHED ACROSS MY MIND on the ship's neural link. "Alert, five minutes to flares away. Countdown to Operation Slowdown begins now."

Alarms brayed for general quarters across the *Glory*. A five-minute countdown timer ran behind my right eye.

There was a lot of chatter on the neural link and I tuned it out. My nerves were tight enough. The engineers had struggled to keep us elevated in hyperspace his long. We should have fallen out hours ago, but they were milking the batteries for all they were worth. Forty-seven hours and counting, and now we were out of time.

I was the gunnery sergeant in charge of the aft, port gun, nicknamed "Annie". I hadn't left her remote feeds for all of these forty-seven hours. Other avatars came and went, quick as a wink, checking on our pursuit, but I remained at my post. I had stayed awake for longer periods before. With our bodies suspended in the core of the ship we didn't require much downtime from the link, and I needed to keep my eyes on the enemy. Our sister gun-cruisers had died getting us this far.

Square in Annie's sights sat Bandits 1 and 2. The *Aylin* destroyers glowed in the dim, roiling light of hyperspace. They weren't gaining and they weren't falling back; they were biding their time. They knew we would fall out of hyperspace before we reached inhabited space.

It had taken twenty-nine gun-cruisers to bring down four of their destroyers and three of their big carriers, so what could the *Glory* do alone? We had lost *Upsilon* Station, we had lost the Tarish system, and that was only the tip of the *Aylin* incursion. We had to warn Fleet. We had to survive in realspace long enough to launch a message-drone. That was the captain's orders.

Operation Slowdown was a crazy scheme cooked up by the navigators. It relied on the accuracy of the *Aylin* tracking computers. Those computers were waiting for us to drop out of hyperspace. They could calculate the emergence-time for a ship of our mass vs. a ship of their mass and drop in behind us with guns firing. We wouldn't have enough time to launch the message-drone. Unless we could somehow drop into realspace faster than their tracking computers calculated.

The navigators were going to hook us on a heavy gravitational mass, use it as a momentum yoke, and drop into realspace half a second faster than standard. The destroyers should over-shoot us by a kilometer. Then our forward and midship gun-batteries would rake them from behind while the message-drone sped away. The Captain made it clear we were protecting the drone. He didn't mention survival. So I remained at my post, unable to take my eyes off my killers.

"Eight-five seconds," I said to my targeting techs. "Let's push these flares up their noses."

Back in basic training I used to fantasize about being a hero. I figure everybody does at some point. Now at my final battle, my entire contribution would be a bunch of EMP flares.

I masked my fear. There was already a strange combination of calm and fear smoking up the neural link. Some resignation, some eagerness. Battle fever simmered.

My two techs crunched a thousand calculations a second in their heads and fed me preliminary vectors. Augmented humans are better than computers in hyperspace, but I still didn't trust the data. You just can't target in hyperspace. I prayed that one of our shots would come close enough to cloud the *Aylin* tracking computers. Give us a margin of safety.

My two ordnance jockeys limbered up their remote servos beside the breechings of Annie's twin, ten-meter long barrels and unloaded her 150mm warheads. Our only warheads! We had been ordered to ship them to the forward guns since aft guns would not be involved in the final firefight.

I began to elevate Annie's barrels based on the targeting vectors. I could hear echoes of the other gunnery sergeants prepping their crews. Bits of static that must have been nerves. Then the conveyers kicked to life and the steel balls housing the EMP flares rolled up from the armories.

The Gunnery Officer's voice came down from Fire Control. "Aft guns, load flares. You have been allotted twenty each."

I would have shrugged if I were in my body. Twenty flares, thirty flares, it didn't matter. We would send them on their way and then sit idle while the other guns tried to save our asses. I was desperate to shoot something. I didn't want to die with my barrel empty of warheads. Not after the *Mariah*.

The *Mariah* was the reason we escaped into hyperspace. She was behind us, shielding us, when an *Aylin* rocket caught her amidships. The cores of our gun-cruisers are so compartmentalized that we can operate with multiple hull-breaches. The *Mariah's* aft section continued to maneuver and fire long after her forward section had sheered off and exploded. She bought us an extra twenty seconds. This time, my barrels would be empty of all but flares. There would be no heroes at the aft guns.

"Command to Navigation and Propulsion: ninety seconds to reentry." The XO's voice was crisp and calm. The Captain's voice followed immediately. "Good hunting. I'm proud of the way this crew has manned the *Glory*. See you when they wake us up."

It was a joke, but it felt good to hear him say it. They couldn't wake us up until we were back in homeport on Earth and they had offloaded our bodies.

"Here we go," I said to my crew, happy that my voice was calm on the link. Our countdown was at ten seconds and we did have a part to play. A hundred avatars from other departments joined us at the aft feeds to watch. "Final vectors received," I said when my targeting techs sent me their best estimates. " . . . four . . . three . . . two . . . Releasing."

I cut power to Annie's magnets and the EMP flares rolled serenely down her barrels. You don't waste warheads in hyperspace because you can't aim, but flares had a much wider effect-radius. Eight flares dropped silently away from the four aft guns. Immediately my jockeys loaded new flares and I let them roll, adjusting Annie's barrel.

As the flares fell further behind the ship, they gyrated and twisted in the fluxes of hyperspace. The timers on the first wave went off and they detonated brightly, some near the destroyers and the rest spread across 180 degrees of view. The second wave detonated similarly. Not close enough. All of the guns changed barrel-elevations again, striving for accuracy.

"Mipship guns," the XO's voice came down, "begin rotation forward to Position-Gamma on my mark."

All avatars vanished except those required to be here. Engineering returned to nursing the FTL batteries. Navigation prepared the momentum yoke. The forward and midship gunners sat on their 150mm warheads like chickens on eggs. I continued releasing flares as fast as my servos could load.

"Mark." The XO's voice was accompanied by a neural signal and the four midship guns began rotating forward in unison on their gimbals. If one gun turned off-speed, it would change our center of gravity. The bow-shock would tear us apart. There is no turning in hyperspace.

I ignored the thought and stared down Annie's barrels, watching the flares detonate, praying for a miracle. As the reentry-timer counted down I pulled up a ghost image off the bow feeds. I needed to see the destroyers overshoot us when we dropped into realspace. I needed to be with the forward guns when they fired. If a compartment breached and a gunner's body died, my avatar might be rotated forward to take over a gun.

The XO's voice counted down to reentry. " . . . eight . . . seven . . . "

"See you when they wake us up," I said to my gun crew. We always say it. Superstition. We continued to roll flares down Annie's barrels until the countdown fell to zero. I hoped we had done enough to disorient the *Aylin* tracking computers.

I struggled against something wet and slippery and snake-like. I couldn't breathe. I panicked. I was blind and deaf. Something hard and cold shoved me. I tumbled, flailing. All of the voices on the link, my constant companions for a year, were gone. I was alone in a muffled shell of cottony thoughtsilence.

An electric cable arced below me bright and loud as I spun. I couldn't feel my legs. I hit a wall hard and someone grabbed me. A hand wiped liquid away from my face and I sucked air, coughing violently. Steel groaned and popped.

Where was our neural link? How could the neural link go down? Where were the destroyers?

The hands that held me rotated me. A face loomed in the dim light, inches in front of my eyes. A man with his hair wet and slicked back, wearing a taught skin-suit. He slapped my cheek and I grabbed his wrist.

"Are you awake, Sergeant?" he shouted in my face. My ears roared. "Focus on me, Damn it! We've had Catastrophic Decoupling. Get these people out of their containers. Disconnect yourself and go! Now, Sergeant!"

I gaped at him as he turned to rescue someone who was drowning in a ball of suspension fluid. The fluid that had cushioned our bodies for so long in our containers was clinging to her head in zero-g like a ball. I understood. Catastrophic Decoupling. The *Glory*'s main computers had gone down. The link was gone. The failsafes had pumped us with adrenalin to cold-start our bodies, then thrust us out of our containers and into the core of the ship where there was oxygen. We'd practiced Decoupling drills in basic. Most people 'died' in the simulations.

I started yanking quick-releases on the wires and tubes connected to my leg-flanges. My legs ended in metal cuffs at mid-thigh because Fleet removed our legs to make the suspension containers smaller. Smaller containers, larger crew. They would have regrown our legs if we made it home.

I turned away from the man who'd saved me and started down the open, two-meter wide core-tube towards a bulkhead, hauling myself on handholds. Opened containers and gobs of suspension fluid surrounded me. Bodies tumbled and flailed in the dim light, tangled in tethers or caught in pockets of liquid.

The worst part of Decoupling is the disorientation. I couldn't think. My cybernetic implants were down and I felt slow. I hadn't been in my body in a year and I couldn't coordinate my fingers.

I grabbed a twitching woman and wiped slime from her mouth. She didn't inhale, only continued to twitch, so I spun her around and gave her a clumsy Heimlich. She spat and gasped and I left her. I didn't have time for more. Most people die from Decoupling in the first two minutes. Drowning in space. It sounds funny until your first simulation.

I bypassed the next man. His neck was tilted wrong and he was limp. I kept moving; kept wiping and yanking and slapping people. It took two of us to pull one poor bastard out of the tangled mess of his life support wires. Suddenly I was at the bulkhead. I turned, resting my hand on the lagging riveted to the metal surface. I was panting. Maybe a minute had passed.

The tube stretched six or seven meters away from me to another bulkhead. The space was crowded with people staring wild-eyed. There were bodies. Many survivors shook from adrenaline overdose. All of us were coated in fluid and wearing tight skin-suits marked by stripings of rank. All of us had bright, stainless steel leg flanges glistening in the rows of emergency lights that were still flickering and coming to life.

The man who had first rescued me floated at the far bulkhead, and I rotated my body so that both of our heads shared a common 'up'.

"Listen to me," he yelled unnecessarily and all heads swiveled. "I'm Lieutenant Commander Jacobson, and we've undergone Catastrophic Decoupling. This is not a drill, but I don't have to tell you that." I stared at him and realized that he looked just like his avatar, only legless. He was our resident compartment officer.

They randomly divide up personnel between compartments so that no matter how many compartments are breached, any remaining compartment will have a full skeleton compliment.

"By the numbers," the Lt. Commander continued. "Everyone get into your masks. The oxygen in here won't hold out much longer."

I peeled a mask out of a wall socket, not wanting to fight my way back down to my home container. A hose stretched from the mask to CO_2 scrubbers in the wall.

"By the looks of our lights," the Lt. Commander continued, "the ship has lost main power and we're operating on local batteries. We've taken a bad hit. Maybe the destroyers have left us for dead. Maybe they're coming around again."

I could hear rivets groaning and I gripped the lagging tighter. I hate confined spaces and the tube seemed to be getting smaller and smaller. In the consensus reality of the neural-link, the ship seemed huge. Not here.

"Sergeant," he said to me, "what is your name?"

I lifted my mask. "Gunnery Sgt. Kirchov, Sir!" My throat was hoarse from disuse. I was thirsty.

"Glad to have you aboard. What is the status of the compartment adjacent to you?"

I turned to the gauges at my elbow, squinting. "I read 27 Kelvin, zero atmospheres, Sir."

"Then we have had at least one compartment breach, possibly more. The compartment behind me is the FTL drive chamber. It also contains an emergency shuttle that can provide life support if needed. Roll call, starting at the back. If the person next to you is dead, return them to their stasis container."

I was shivering. The temperature was dropping, but maybe it was the adrenaline shot and the dislocation of waking up. I missed Annie. If we were adjacent to the FTL chamber, then we were Compartment Alpha behind the bow. I was a long way from my gun.

In the end we had thirteen living and seven dead. My old drill sergeant would have called that unbelievable luck. None of my gun crew was here, and I hoped they survived somewhere in another compartment. We did have one surviving ordnance jockey and a maintenance tech. The telemetry tech was dead. I shut her eyes before closing her container.

The life support officer worked with the tube engineer to divert what power they could from the emergency systems to improve the CO_2 scrubbers. They initiated a full air change, and the remaining bubbles of suspension fluid were drawn out through drains with a terrible sucking sound.

The communications tech and the electrician's mate got the local network up and running in relatively short order, and I blessed whatever genius had installed a LAN in each compartment. We jacked in through wall ports and suddenly my world was back. Twelve minds swirled around mine. I damped their fear because mine didn't need any help and tried to access external ship-feeds. They didn't respond. We were isolated.

"I haven't heard any secondary explosions," the Lt. Commander said, "but we don't know what happened. Someone's going outside. Mr. Liu," he looked at the hull tech, "you will be my eyes. Who else?"

I volunteered immediately. I had to get out of here. Better to die out on the hull than in here where the walls were closing in. Mr. Liu and I unracked our compartment's two EVA suits

My new jockey, Michael, and maintenance tech, Leona, helped me on with the suit. My leg flanges clicked into place on the suit's cybernetic leg-jacks and suddenly I felt like a whole man again. I could feel my feet.

"Who's your gun," I said to my two new crewmen.

"Lucky number Seven," said Michael. "Midship, starboard. We call her Betty. Veronica's her sister gun on the ventral side."

"Number Two," Leona said. "Forward, port. Clotilde."

"Did either of you get off a shot?" They lowered the helmet over my head.

"No," they both thought to me on the LAN now that the helmet was on. "We caught a split second of realspace and then nothing."

"Good luck," said the Lt. Commander.

I turned and Mr. Liu was floating right behind me, looking calm. Hull techs are born to crawl the outside skin of ships like lice. He clapped me on the shoulder, pushing me down to the deck because I hadn't been holding a handclasp.

"Shall we?" he said.

We shoved chest to chest into the auxiliary hatch and Leona closed the door on us. The only light was the tiny headlamp we carried. Eleven avatars took up residence in our helmets' feeds. I closed my eyes. This tiny space was worse. What if the hatch didn't open? What if I died in here? C'mon, c'mon. Open the hatch.

"Close your glare shield," Mr. Liu said. "We could be next to a star."

I flipped down the shield as the outer hatch opened. Stars drifted by. The *Glory* was rolling. Suddenly, the brilliant rim of a star flared into view. We were close. Our ship was in orbit around the monster. Roiling reds filled the hatch mouth with harsh light and I lowered a second glare shield. Then I pushed out. Hard wires connected to the LAN played out behind me, keeping the avatars connected. Just being outside I began to relax. I checked the suit's O_2 levels. With the rebreather, I had nearly two hours supply.

"Sgt. Kirchov," the Lt. Commander said, "find those destroyers while Mr. Liu checks the hull." I attached myself to outside handholds while Mr. Liu started climbing.

The overwhelming glare of the star made searching difficult, but at last I located one of the destroyers. I had to lower a third shield to focus on her. I could only make out her black silhouette, but she was listing at a much lower orbit that we were. Some of our guns must have gotten a shot off to cripple her that badly. She was on a decaying orbit. The *Glory* rotated away from the star and I saw the second destroyer.

"She's coming back around, Sir," I said.

"Tap into Mr. Liu's feeds," the Lt. Commander said. "She's not going to bother with us."

I switched to Mr. Liu's feeds and stopped aghast. Our communications arrays were gone. All of the dorsal guns were gone. The docking hatch. Our hull was crushed from bow to stern.

I scrambled up the side of the hull, past the hulks of powerless loaders and maintenance 'bots. I needed to see for myself. And I stopped short at Mr. Liu's side, directly on top of our compartment. The only surviving compartment. A rip extended from just a few meters shy of our feet all the way to the aft drive pods. The hull gaped open; the edges of the wound were coated in frozen fire-extinguishing foam. I took another step and looked down through the double hull and shattered hulks of hyperspace batteries into our adjacent compartment. The stasis containers must have flash frozen, but I could see that the failsafes had opened some. Bodies hung partially out, entrained in frozen globules of suspension fluid. Fourteen compartments, two hundred and eighty men and women.

"I wonder if they felt anything," I said.

"What do we do?" Mr. Liu whispered. "The ship is gone. The communications arrays are gone."

"The *Aylin* destroyer must have come out of hyperspace right on top of us," our surviving navigator said in awe over the link. "They didn't overshoot us."

"Write that up in your report," I said. "Sir?" I called to the Lt. Commander, "You are now the ranking officer of the ship."

"Affirmative," the new Captain said. I couldn't feel a lick of his emotions. He was that controlled. It solidified my resolve.

We rotated back around and the second destroyer came into view again. She was slowing down, probably on a rescue mission to her crippled sister below.

"Some of our guns must work, Captain," I said, watching the long, sleek ship drift past. Hundreds of thousands of tons of steel, waiting to be popped. "I can aim without telemetry at this range. Give me one shot into her main drive section."

There was a long silence. Finally, "How many shots do you think you can get off before they fire back?"

I sent a thought down to Michael. "Can you load quickly without the computers?"

"I placed third in the military games running a loader just from my implants. Never jammed a shell."

"Captain," I said, "they've already scanned us and found that we're cold iron. They must have seen oxygen venting from every compartment. They're done with us. All of their attention is below. I'm sure I could get in four, maybe five shots."

"Sergeant, our former Captain's orders stand. We must get a message back to Fleet. Fire as many shots as you can. Your primary mission is to draw their attention away from the drone."

"But they'll fire back," someone said. "We'll be destroyed."

I could feel horror crackle across the LAN as realization descended. I bowed my head. At least we would go down fighting like the *Mariah*.

"I'm sorry," the Captain said. "Yes, we'll be destroyed. Many of us will die, but not all. I'm sending out the emergency shuttle with the drone. It has limited FTL capabilities, but only six suspension containers. Sergeant?"

"Yes?"

"I need you to stay and man the gun. Select a gun crew to assist you."

"Aye, Aye, Captain," I said slowly. I felt the frightened attention of the avatars turn to me. Damn it. "We'll need more EVA suits."

"Mr. Liu," the Captain said. "Go down into that failed compartment and retrieve their two EVA suits. Bring them here, then return to the next compartment for additional suits. We will suit everybody."

I felt cold. Then hot. I stared at the destroyer. I had memorized her over the past forty-seven hours. There were three gun batteries up the starboard side and three on top. There would be an equal number on the far side. There were many smaller cannons. I had to get through that and strike her fuel cells somehow.

I sent down to Micheal and Leona: "Looks like we're it. Can I count on you?"

Michael answered right away, "I'll be out as soon as I get the EVA suit." Leona took a longer time in answering. "Yes, Sergeant."

In the end I only requested Alex, the electrician's mate, to help Leona jury-rig a gun to temporary batteries. I couldn't command anyone else to die. That left nine people for six seats. The Captain would have to decide.

Our ship rolled away from the destroyer and I sat in the cool darkness and waited. I liked it out here. I wouldn't mind dying out here, watching the cold stars shine. Watching the giant star rotate by. Maybe I should have been a hull tech instead of a gunner.

Three times the destroyer rotated back into view before Michael, Leona, and Alex joined me. They stopped next to the rent hull just as I had and stared in.

"At least they never woke up," Leona said.

"Let's get to Betty," I said. "We've got a lot to do."

"Why can't we use Clotilde?" Leona asked.

"I don't want to use the forward guns. Without attitude control, they'll twist the ship. The midship guns might roll us faster, but we'll stay straight."

We followed handholds along the edge of the torn hull. I tried not to look inside in case I recognized someone. A nimbus of sheered metal around the ship was all that remained of the dorsal guns and primary communications arrays, but Betty and Veronica were still pristine. They still held a 150mm egg in their baskets. Their loading servos still clutched a second egg at ready, waiting for the shot that had never come.

"For our lost crews and for the survivors," I said. They all nodded. "We'll fire every warhead we've got and hope a couple get through. Michael, I bet that star is putting out a lot of interference. The *Aylin* may not detect our warheads if we don't fire up the rockets. Can you recalibrate the shell firing control for just enough burst to clear the barrel? I want to send them in cold."

"I haven't run a system directly since the military games," he said. He inserted a neural wire from his helmet into the back of the loader.

"Can you do it?"

He saluted. "I can do it, Sergeant."

Leona and Alex began reconfiguring wires, directing battery power into the loaders and into my barrel adjusters.

"Sergeant," the Captain said across the LAN, "what's your estimated firing-time?"

"Rough estimate of fifteen minutes, Captain. How are you doing on suits?"

"We're short one, but that'll be resolved in a minute. We're going to the shuttle now."

I switched to a private band and sent down to him. "Who's staying?"

"I'm staying. And Ensign Earl and Second Lieutenant Savron have volunteered to stay."

"It's a shame we survived the crash and still have to die, Sir. Come on up when the shuttle's out. Enjoy the show with us here."

"Affirmative, Sergeant."

The LAN shut down as the nine people below exited Compartment Alpha for the FTL chamber.

I started moving Betty as soon as Leona got me an ounce of juice. I used the rough bore-site down the barrel. I doubted it had been used since she was first aligned and test fired at the dockyards, but it would serve me. The destroyer was directly above her crippled sister now. Through visual filters I could see that her shields were crackling irregularly. There was interference. And she may have been trying to extend her shields around her sister to lend some protection. A warhead could get through that.

"How we doing on juice?" I asked. I was growing eager.

"If our hands weren't so weak, we'd be done rewiring by now," Leona said. "I need my tech-servos just to work on the tech-servos." Showers of sparks leapt from her torch and out into space.

At the bow, nine people gathered. The shuttle lifted slowly into view, ejected from the *Glory's* nose on spring-jacks. Six people climbed inside. Three crawled in our direction.

"How long 'til sufficient power," I said.

"Two hundred and eleven seconds," Leona said.

I started a countdown. Yellow lights flashed on Michael's loader.

"I have fifteen warheads, Sergeant," he said. "That's it. The rest were distributed for Operation Slowdown."

"Fifteen it is." I laughed and flexed my fingers. I had often pressed simulated buttons to fire Annie. The manual firing buttons on Betty's control arm were the real thing, and they felt real. I could just imagine the recording from the shuttle, sent back to inhabited space. Me, standing at the back of a ten-meter gun, firing manually. This was the stuff of Recruitment Holos.

"The *Glory* will roll out of range in twenty seconds," I said. "I'll commence firing when the target returns to view."

I dropped Betty's barrel as low as it would crank. The initial shots would have to fly directly across the hull, straight past Veronica. The debris field around the ship made me nervous.

I flexed my fingers again. "Are we good?" I said to Michael.

"The rockets have been reprogrammed, Sergeant. You are good to fire."

"Firing in fifteen, fourteen . . . "

The three castaways from the shuttle took up station behind us and joined into our tiny LAN. I gripped Betty's control arm and grinned. The star came back into view.

"Alpha Mike Foxtrot, Ladies and Gentlemen," I said and fired. As promised, the rocket flared and immediately went dead, flying swiftly and quietly from the end of the barrel. "One away."

I calculated lead-times through the group-LAN and our cumulative cybernetic implants, compensating as the *Glory*'s roll grew slowly greater. I fired as fast as I could, adjusting Betty's elevation. Her long barrel rose to ninety-degrees-high as the *Glory* turned, then began dropping again to port. Fifteen warheads leapt out and then we stood in silence. We had done all we could. The rim of the star passed from view and it was dark and cold.

"How long?" Ensign Earl said.

"They aren't moving that fast because we didn't light the rockets."

We rotated back into the harsh light. Both destroyers still sat below us, unaware and unreacting. I couldn't see the warheads; their tiny silhouettes were lost in the glare. We began to rotate away again.

"Strike near the bow," someone shouted.

I whooped when I saw the explosion and the gout of ejecta. I had aimed for her bridge, hoping to incapacitate her. We rotated away and I couldn't see any more.

"Captain to shuttle, light your engines now! Get away from us! Move!"

The shuttle's drive pods sprang to life and the ship nosed up agonizingly slowly. They had to get away. Beside them, the messenger-drone's rockets also flared up and the tiny 'bot sped away.

"What's happening?" Alex said. "Their rockets are faster than ours, right?"

"There's one now." I pointed up. An *Aylin* rocket flew past like a shooting star, speeding into deep space. Interference or not, they couldn't miss us at this distance. Four more rockets flew past in a cluster. I gripped Betty's control arm, my skin crawling. Soon. The shuttle pushed farther and farther away. Another rocket streaked by our drive pods.

Twenty seconds. Forty seconds. Seventy-eight seconds without another *Aylin* rocket. We rolled back into view.

"What the hell happened?" Michael said.

I zoomed my lenses in on the destroyer. "We knocked them into each other," I said, understanding suddenly.

I replayed the recording from the shuttle over and over later.

The healthy destroyer had dropped in extremely close to her crippled sister. My first lucky shot pushed her bow down and they collided. Their autonomous defensive systems kicked in and launched rockets, aimed at our warheads, not at the *Glory*.

My second lucky shot hit near the tail, pushing her farther into her sister. All the rest of my warheads were intercepted. It was the collision that, in the end, destroyed the ships. When the drive pods impacted, dense yellow flames burned at the edge of the star's red.

Now we wait.

The shuttle's been gone two weeks, but only took four people. The rest of us chose to stay here, on the *Glory*. Trying to get the stasis containers working again so we can sleep until rescue comes.

Alex repaired the conduits bringing power from the radioisotope thermal generators and he's slowly powering up the undamaged batteries. The oxygen generator and CO_2 scrubbers are working fine in our compartment, and we have heat. Leona and Mr. Liu have some hull 'bots working, and they're patching the rent hull as best they can. We want the *Glory* in good enough shape for a tow home when rescue comes.

The gyros are spinning again and they stopped our roll. The pilot turned the hull breach away from the star to protect us from the UV radiation.

I keep our guns ready. Michael and I distributed a few warheads to each of them.

And when I'm not helping with the hull repairs or with wiring, I sit on Annie's barrel. I've seen this view a million times through the remote feeds, but this is the first time I've seen it through my own eyes. After the rescue, I may never get another chance. I never get tired of watching the cold stars.

DEAD END

John G. Hemry
(a.k.a. Jack Campbell)

FROM THIS DISTANCE, THE MOON ORBITING THE FIFTH PLANET AROUND THE RED DWARF sun wasn't visible to the naked eye. On the screens of guidance computers installed on twenty asteroids, the moon flared as a brilliant white dot. Commander Jane Devries checked the maneuvering solutions, checked the green status lights for the directed-thrust parasite drives also installed on the twenty asteroids, then gave a thumbs-up to Captain Franco. "Ready for launch, Sir."

"Is everyone in the landing parties back aboard?" Someone, rumor held, had once left a landing party on an asteroid when they launched it. No one wanted to be the ship to make that mistake again.

"Yes, Sir. All personnel confirmed aboard."

Captain Franco grinned, the skin of his face stretching into a grotesquely wide smile. "Launch."

"Launch, aye." Commander Devries punched one button, then a second. "Confirm all parasite drives activated. Confirm guidance systems providing input."

Very slowly, but gradually accelerating, the twenty asteroids began moving on a path which would bring them to the moon around the fifth planet in a few months time.

"Take that, you bastards," someone muttered.

Captain Franco's smile somehow widened a little more. "Navigator, you have the course laid in to reach that *T'kel* base?"

"Yes, Sir."

"Then let's go." Accelerating far more rapidly than the asteroids, the *Chesapeake* headed into the red dwarf's system. "Commander Devries, make sure every possible weapon is ready when we come within range of that moon."

"Yes, Sir."

"And make sure we're watching for any ships trying to escape before we get there."

"Yes, Sir." Devries reviewed the status of the *Chesapeake*'s weapons and sensors, no emotions stirring within her. "None of them will get away."

"Excellent. Did they actually think they had a chance of hiding this base? In a few months our rocks will be ripping that moon apart."

Devries nodded.

"And they'll just have to sit and watch our rocks coming, because we're going to destroy everything on that moon that can lift. Go to hell, you bastards."

A momentary quiet settled on the *Chesapeake*'s bridge, before being shattered by a rapid beeping. "Incoming message, Captain. High priority."

Franco's smile vanished. He chewed his lip as he waited for the communications system to decode the message. The voice which finally came out sounded weary. "All units in the Fleet of Humanity. The *T'kel* have hit our orbital station codenamed *Phoenix Twelve*. All spacecraft destroyed. Incoming asteroids have been detected, with an expected arrival time of five weeks. Any ship able to reach *Phoenix Twelve* and evacuate personnel and equipment before asteroid strike arrives respond immediately."

Captain Franco's lip twitched. He stared at Commander Devries while she ran the calculations, then slowly shook her head. "We can't make it, Sir."

"Damn. Pray to our dead ancestors that someone else can. Alright, then, let's go get these *T'kel*. We may lose *Phoenix Twelve*, but they'll lose this moon. And every one of their scum infesting it."

All weapons ready, with a swarm of asteroids in its wake, the Second Battle Squadron of the Tenth Combat Task Force of the Mars Flotilla of the Fleet of Humanity headed inexorably for its target. Commander Devries gazed outward, seeing no other ships on her display. Just her ship, the *Chesapeake*. For the *Chesapeake* was the last surviving ship of the Second Battle Squadron. If the Tenth Combat Task Force should gather, only four ships would be present. The Mars Flotilla, at last count, could still muster twenty ships. How many ships still made up the total Fleet of Humanity was known only to the very highest commanders of mankind.

Devries shifted her gaze to the nearby bulkhead. The pictures were fastened there, as they were on every ship which remained of Humanity. The first showed a blue and white dappled globe, home to teaming billions. The second showed the shattered remnants of that world, after the *T'kel*-launched asteroids had come swarming down from the outer edges of the solar system. Empty of life, once home to the human race, Earth lived only as a motivator for the vengeance represented by the next two pictures, the before and after for the *T'kel* homeworld, after mankind-launched asteroids had impacted there. *T'kel* billions had died then, too.

Then we lost Mars. They lost Ghald. We lost Titan. They lost Haf'g. And so on. We smashed a *T'kel* Task Force at Daniel's Star. They smashed a lot of our ships at Dragon One. And so on. The fleets get smaller, the planets and moons and bases die every time either side tries to establish anything in a fixed orbit situation. Commander Devries tried to summon up sorrow, but she'd lost the ability to feel anything a long time ago. What else can we do?

✦

The refueling point had a code-name. *Apache*. Were there any *Apaches* left in the Fleet of Humanity? Devries had heard the smaller ethnic groups were virtually exterminated already. Only those groups which had started with large numbers were still represented in the Fleet's dwindling ranks.

The tanker flashed into existence. Tense minutes followed as the two ships matched courses and began transferring fuel. They were following a predictable trajectory now, which meant they'd be vulnerable until the transfer was complete.

"Captain! There's movement near the second planet."

Franco checked his own display, cursing under his breath. "There's something coming out. Fast."

The *Chesapeake*'s combat system chirped as it identified the object. "Asteroid, Captain. Point-three-four klicks in diameter. Speed—. What the hell?"

Commander Devries jerked the watchstander out of the way to read the data. "It's coming in very fast. Collision course. One point six hours."

"That's impossible!"

"That's what it's doing. The *T'kel* must have improved their parasite drives."

"By a goddamn order of magnitude! They must have finally cracked the Baker Algorithms. Can you spot a base in there, or a *T'kel* ship?"

Devries shook her head. "Nothing, Captain. It must be an automated mine, planted here in case we popped into this system. If we could just figure out how to rendezvous in deep space we wouldn't have to worry about this kind of attack."

"And if we could figure how to stop asteroids we could finish the *T'kel*. How long until fuel transfer is complete?"

"One-point-one hours."

"Can we out-accelerate that thing at that point?" Captain Franco left off the obvious, that the *T'kel* mine would probably attempt to alter its path to intercept them.

Devries ran some calculations. "If we head off at a high angle, it shouldn't be able to follow us. That extra speed means the mine can't maneuver as well." Not that any asteroid could maneuver well.

"Good." The minutes dragged, the *T'kel* mine coming closer. Jane Devries watched the visual display, where Humanity Eyes planted in the system were able to track the asteroid as it flashed past. Humanity Eyes were everywhere, watching everything, transmitting reports whenever suspected *T'kel* activity was detected. Mines, human and *T'kel*, were everywhere, too. *I wonder how many mines we've planted here? No worlds left worth trying to build on. What was the second planet called? Faeroe. It was pretty cold there. Before the T'kel rocks hit. And those moons around the third planet. Two good ones. The T'kel got to them first. Our rocks got to the T'kel.* She scanned the displays again. *Dead system. We helped make it that way.*

"Transfer complete. Breaking links to the tanker."

Captain Franco's smile was back. "Good. Get us going."

The *Chesapeake* began to flee, angling away from the path the asteroid had targeted.

"Captain? The tanker's got a problem."

"What?" Franco stared at the displays. "What problem?"

"Maneuvering systems dropped off-line. They're trying to get them up again."

"They've got a rock heading for them! Can we tow them out there?"

Devries checked her data. "No, Sir. No time." More minutes crawled past. *Everything's getting older and older. Less reliable. More prone to failure just when you need it.* "If they don't maneuver pretty quick, they won't be able to get away."

Franco's face had gone ashen. "Get them off it. Order them to abandon ship."

"Sir, we need that tanker!"

"I don't care. Get our people off of that thing." Alarms began sounding as the asteroid closed on the tanker. "Where's the lifeboats? I told them to evacuate."

"They think they can get it going, Captain."

"No! It's too late. Repeat the evacuation order."

"Yes, Sir. Acknowledged, Captain. They're headed for their boats."

Devries watch the track of the *T'kel* asteroid mine heading on a perfect intercept trajectory with the tanker. Small objects began fleeing the tanker, lifeboats each carrying a few humans. The crew of the *Chesapeake* could only watch, praying the lifeboats would get clear of the danger area before impact.

"Time to impact five seconds. Three. Two. One. Impact."

Humanity Eyes near the tanker recorded its destruction. Against the mass of an asteroid that size, the tanker had simply been smashed. The last two lifeboats out failed to get free, also getting caught by the asteroid as it swept past.

Captain Franco stared blankly at the display. Commander Devries spun on the bridge crew. "Let's get in there and pick up those boats. Make sure we do it fast, before that thing can manage to make it back."

They'd picked up the surviving lifeboats and started accelerating out of the system before Captain Franco came out of his daze. "Notify the Task Force commander that the tanker was destroyed along with one third of its crew."

"Aye, aye, Sir." Commander Devries began coding the message. The Tenth Combat Task Force was down to three ships.

Commander Devries left the bridge, walking slowly through the battered passageways of the *Chesapeake*. *Time and hard use had taken its toll everywhere. Even inside me. When did I stop caring? Please don't let me start caring again. I'll go insane if I do.* She stopped at Captain Franco's cabin and knocked politely.

"Come'n in." Captain Franco sat sprawled in one of the worn chairs which graced his cabin. A near-empty bottle sat on his desk. Reaching for it, Franco took another swallow.

"Captain, you shouldn't be drinking that crap. The crew distills it out of all kinds of junk. It'll kill you."

"Now or later. What's the diff'rence?" Franco gazed into the distance. "Got a question, Jane. What's the name of that tanker?"

Devries frowned. "I'll have to check. I think it was the *Baltic Sea*." *Ships named after pieces of a world. The real pieces of that world were gone. The ships remained. A few of them, anyway.*

"I nev'r knew. Didn't care. Didn't wanna know. All dying. Now. Later." Captain Franco drank the last liquid from the bottom, started to hurl it away, then carefully sat it down. *You didn't break anything on purpose. Not any more.* "We can't last.

Need bases to build ships. Mines for raw materials. Factories. Places for cities. Not enough kids in space. Too many miscarriages. Y'know."

A chill entered the dead place inside Devries. "I know."

"Can't do it. Can't build anything. Damned *T'kel* just rock 'em."

"We rock theirs back."

"Yeah." Franco brooded for a moment. "Figured out how to make sure they lose."

"Sir?"

"Yeah. Gotta plan. Bet the brass buys it."

Jane Devries eyed Franco with growing curiosity. "What is it?"

"Reserve worlds." Franco hiccupped. "Y'know. Habitable planets we've stayed off of so the *T'kel* wouldn't rock 'em. Someplace to rebuild humanity after we win. *T'kel* got 'em, too."

"I know. So what?"

Franco smiled again, an unnerving sight. "We put our people on *T'kel* reserve worlds. They'll have to rock their own worlds to stop us. Wipe out their chance to ever rebuild. Make sure they die. All of 'em."

"But they'll do the same thing to us! They'll plant *T'kel* bases on our reserve worlds. We'll have to rock them!"

"So what?"

Devries stared at Franco, feeling something stirring again inside where she'd thought everything long dead. "Without those worlds, we can't survive. We've lost too much. We need them after we win."

"Ain't gonna win, Jane. Gonna die. You know it s'well as I do. Gonna make sure we take 'em down with us. Brass gonna like my plan. You see. Finish those *T'kel* bastards."

"Captain, what's the point?" The stirring inside of Devries came out in a scream. "What's the point of us both being wiped out?"

Franco focused on her with some difficulty. "Got no choice. They started it. R'member? Earth. We hit 'em back. Not enough. Now all gone. Earth, Mars, New America, Celestial, all gone. Still got fleet. What's left of it. Gonna kill 'em."

"At what point does who started it begin to lose meaning? I hate the *T'kel*! They've killed everything and everyone I'd ever loved! But why does humanity have to die killing them?"

Franco frowned for a moment. "Only way."

"There's got to be another. Some new weapon, some new—."

"They's workin' on somethin' on *Phoenix Twelve*. Gone." Franco tapped his head with one finger. "Gotta new idea. Gonna work. Kill 'em all. Fleet brass gonna go for it. You know."

Jane Devries stared back at Franco. They will. *We and the* T'kel *will use most of what we've got left to establish bases on each other's reserve worlds, and then we'll both rock each other's worlds into lifeless rubble. Will anything else ever come here? Any other race exploring and finding star system after star system full of dead and destroyed planets, and wondering what kind of homicidally insane races did this to each other?* She got up and stumbled out of Franco's cabin, leaving the Captain mumbling to himself.

The torn insulation on one bulkhead fluttered near her face as Devries leaned against the bulkhead for support. *There's almost nothing left. Soon there'll be nothing left. We've spent almost a century destroying each other, smaller and smaller fleets of ships roaming endlessly to avoid the asteroids that smash anything with a predictable course through space. What would it be like to live on a planet? I never saw Earth. There's nothing left.*

A hatch nearby drew her gaze. The *Chesapeake*'s sole remaining long-range shuttle. Nothing. Commander Devries threw herself against the hatch, punching in her authorization code. Access lights winked green and the hatch cycled open. Nothing. Systems powered up. Alerts would be displayed on the bridge now, warning the *Chesapeake*'s crew that the shuttle was preparing to launch. They'd be trying to find out what was going on. Who was in the shuttle. Nothing. Her boards green, Devries hit the emergency launch button and moments later blacked out from the force of the shuttle blasting away from the *Chesapeake*.

It had once been the *T'kel* home system. Jane Devries had figured if there'd be any place likely to have a *T'kel* ship lurking about, it would be that system. And when the shuttle jumped into normal space, she saw one.

She methodically shut off the shuttle's offensive and defensive systems. One by one, her shields and her swords dropped off-line, until the shuttle was no longer a warship, but just a target, brightly visible to anyone tracking it.

The *T'kel* ship had sat watching as Devries' shuttle came deeper in-system. Fearing a trap, no doubt. Hours passed. No asteroid mines came after her. The *T'kel* ship remained silent and passive. Surely a trap. Surely some attempt by humans to lure them in.

But, for all she hated them, Jan Devries knew the *T'kel* had the same curiosity as any other form of intelligence. They'd be wondering why she was here. They'd want to know the answer.

More hours. Devries napped several times, starting awake to stare around in confusion each time, before she remembered where she was.

The navigational system beeped. An inbound object, closing on her course. Devries bit her cheek and tasted blood. Had the *T'kel* grown tired of waiting?

"It's one of their shuttles." It took a moment for Jane Devries to realize she'd spoken out loud. The move made sense. The *T'kel* shuttle had its combat systems active. It had the *T'kel* warship backing it up from a safe distance. If this was a human trap, the *T'kel* were prepared for it.

Slowing as it approached Jane's own shuttle, the *T'kel* shuttle carefully nudged itself into contact, the emergency airlocks mating thanks to flexible seals designed to handle any possible hatch configuration. Humanity had been throwing together ships as fast as possible before the last shipyards were rocked. Standardization hadn't been a concern at that point.

Thumps and thuds sounded. Jane Devries stood up as her shuttle's hatch began to cycle. A moment later, the hatch opened and a *T'kel* stepped inside.

The *T'kel* resembled a cross between an alligator and a dolphin which had evolved into a four-limbed sentient life form. Its large eyes regarded Jane, but she could read nothing in their depths. Moving slowly, Jane reached down, unbuckled her holster, drew out her sidearm with one finger, and pushed it as far away as she could.

The *T'kel* watched, not moving. Minutes passed.

"Well?" She pointed to her sidearm. "I'm disarmed. Either kill me or talk to me, damn you."

A long pause, then the *T'kel* brought out its own sidearm, and shoved it toward Jane's. "What?" it asked, the voice sounding like gravel washing together.

She shook her head. "I don't know what. I don't know why. Haven't enough died?"

More silence, then the *T'kel* made an odd gesture. "Dark."

"Dark? The light shouldn't be bothering you."

"Go to Dark."

"Who? Who goes to Dark?"

"Worlds." Jane still couldn't guess at the expression on the *T'kel*. Colors rippled across its belly. "Light. Go to Dark. *T'kel* worlds."

"And human worlds." Her voice came out as harsh as that of the *T'kel*. "Human worlds were Light and now they're Dark."

"Light is *T'kel*."

"Why can't we share the Light?"

"Light is *T'kel*. Hu'ans go."

Jane Devries sagged down into her seat. "I don't know how much the *T'kel* have left. Probably about as much as humanity does. How can we go? Every habitable world with range of our ships is dead. Dark."

"*T'kel* the Light."

"No. Don't you get it? *T'kel* the Dark."

"Hu'an not the Light. Hu'an go."

Jane buried her face in her hands. *What was I thinking? When we met the* T'kel *we tried talking to them. We never understood them. After Earth was destroyed we stopped trying. Why did I think I could somehow communicate meaningfully with creatures who've baffled all of humanity since first contact?* "We're dying. We're about to do something . . . something suicidal. There's no other word for it. Do you understand? Can you understand? Humanity is planning to force your hand. The war will end. We'll both be destroyed. Both races dead. Is that what you want? How can you want that? The Light will be gone."

"*T'kel* the Light."

"*T'kel* the Dark!' She screamed it, wondering how the *T'kel* would take that. "Your race will die."

The *T'kel* didn't seem affected by Jane's words or her actions. "*T'kel* the Light. *T'kel* the Dark."

"You stupid, insane race of . . . of . . . mass murderers! You want to die? You want us to die? Fine. You'll get that. *T'kel* the Dark and humans the Dark!"

The *T'kel*'s belly suddenly swirled orange. "*T'kel* the Dark!"

"And humans the Dark!"

"*T'kel* the Dark! Hu'ans go!"

"We can't go. We'll stand and die because there's no longer any alternative. And we'll take you with us. *T'kel* the Dark and humans the Dark."

"No!" Jane stared, startled by the word. The *T'kel*'s belly had shaded into red. "No hu'an the Dark!"

"Sorry, you son-of-a-bitch, we're going down together." Seeing the *T'kel* apparently get increasingly agitated, Jane Devries savored hurling the words at it again. "*T'kel* the Dark and human the Dark!"

"No. *T'kel* the Dark."

"You can say it as many times as you want. It won't change anything. Understand? Both our races have reached their limit and now we're going beyond it. We'll both die out. I hope you bastards are happy." Jane looked away, the deadness beginning to fill her again. "Go ahead and kill me now. It's just a matter of time anyway. Franco was right." She jabbed one thumb at her chest. "Me! The Dark! Go ahead."

Jane Devries closed her eyes and waited. Nothing happened. Finally she looked back at the *T'kel*. Its belly had darkened until the red was almost black. The eyes swung wildly from side to side. Finally focusing back on her, the *T'kel* raised one arm. "*T'kel* the Dark!"

"When you kill me, I'll go to the Dark. Just like all those dead worlds. Go ahead."

"Hu'an the Dark?"

Jane Devries stared at the *T'kel*. "Of course. What did you think? If we don't . . . if humans and the *T'kel* don't have the Light, we'll have the Dark. Both our races."

The *T'kel* suddenly spun around and headed into the hatch. Jane watched it go, wondering why she was still alive and what was bothering the creature. *We never understood them. They never understood us. And now we never will. I guess it's planning to blow my shuttle from its own ship. Fine. Get it over with.*

But the *T'kel* shuttle kept going, back to its ship. Jane watched for a long time, then shrugged. Her shuttle carried some rations. She chose a few and ate them, not tasting anything, wondering how long ago they'd been packed away, if some might even have come from Earth. She slept again. Woke and ate some more. At some point she finally noticed that the *T'kel* had left so hurriedly that its sidearm had been abandoned in her shuttle.

After a long time, the *T'kel* shuttle came back. It may have been carrying the same *T'kel*. Jane couldn't tell. The *T'kel* stood in her shuttle, its belly dark red, then slowly extended one arm carrying some sort of document. Jane reached out at the same careful speed, taking the papers from the *T'kel*'s hold, feeling a slight shudder inside at even that indirect contact.

The papers contained *T'kel* writing on one side, standard English on the other. Jane looked at them, perplexed, then back at the *T'kel*. "What is this?"

"Take? Hu'ans take?"

"I don't understand. Take what? These papers? Of course I'll take. I mean, yes, I took them."

"Hu'ans take. Hu'ans the Light."

Jane's eyes widened as she looked down at the papers. Words from the English text leapt out at her. 'Coexistence.' 'Cease hostilities.' 'Joint worlds.' "Is . . . is this a peace treaty?"

"Hu'ans the Light." Somehow, Jane thought the *T'kel* sounded resigned. *"T'kel the Light. T'kel and hu'an not the Dark."*

"Oh, God." She sat down and cried, shaking, not able to move for a long time as the *T'kel* stood watching her.

"What happened, Commander Devries?" Fleet Admiral Chang leaned toward her. "What happened when you met the *T'kel*?"

She glared back at him. Approaching a human ship had been a long, drawn-out process, with the crew of the *Arabia* watching for any sign of a trick. She'd been isolated, quarantined, searched, tested, and probed. Only after assuring themselves that neither Jane nor her shuttle carried any traps or weapons of any kind did the *Arabia* bring her here, to the Flagship. The *Terra*. "You've seen my records. The shuttle recorded every moment of the meetings. Audio and video. Why are you asking me this?"

Leader Owen raised a calming hand. The many factions of humanity had never been able to agree on a title for a single political leader, so Leader she became. "We've seen the recordings. We don't understand them. What happened? Why, after all this time, have the *T'kel* agreed to share space with us?" She held up the documents the *T'kel* had given Jane. "Commander Devries, they're actually saying they want our bases and their bases located close together on habitable worlds. Why?"

"Oh, I've figured that out," Admiral Chang noted. "That way, it'd be impossible to rock the planet without taking out your own people. It's sort of like exchanging hostages."

"That would work. But it still doesn't explain this." Owen walked toward the large display on one bulkhead, where stars glittered against the blackness. "We're so tired. Humanity is on its last legs. We're facing extermination with no way out. And then you show up with a miracle. A peace treaty from the *T'kel*. How is this possible?"

Jane Devries started laughing, then stopped before the laughter became uncontrollable. "Oh, it's very simple. Really, it's very simple. I stumbled across it purely by accident. Purely out of despair. The *T'kel* are agreeing to coexist with humanity for what to them is a very good reason."

"What possible reason could there be? The *T'kel* have never even agreed to separate areas of control, let alone sharing planets or orbital locations with us. They've pursued a genocidal war against us, just as we've waged one back against them. So why now? Why are they finally agreeing to some sort of co-existence? Why are they now willing to let humanity live?"

Devries stared at the star display. "I discovered that they want to die in some kind of Armageddon. Maybe it's religious or maybe it's something else we can't begin to understand. But they want us to kill all of them in a great war and they were going to keep killing us to keep us hitting back at them until we finished exterminating their race. What they hadn't taken into account was that they might exterminate us as well."

"Why does that matter?" Owen demanded.

"Because there's one thing more important to them than whether or not they share the universe with us."

"And what is that?"

"They don't want to share hell with us."

BROADSIDE

Bud Sparhawk

C APTAIN FARADADDIE CHECKED THE BRIDGE AS SOON AS HIS HEAD CLEARED FROM THE dizziness of blink transfer but before the headache started. Everybody looked all right for a change.

"Ship approaching," Navigation reported as the long-range detector pinged. "Three thousand klicks and closing at eight hundred."

"No SIFF, Sir," Communications said. "Rebel for sure."

"Coming on screen," Visuals reported and zoomed the cameras on the approaching ship.

"Sir, we've got identification. It's *Invincible*," Intelligence said. "Heavy cargo hauler. Ten million tons. Armed and armored."

Faradaddie swore. He'd hoped they'd engage with one of the rebels' ships, but not this one. She out-massed *Pride*, one of the Fleet's warships, which meant she was a lot slower. Maybe there was a chance he could get her back. The more ships they captured, the sooner the colonial trade war would be over.

The rebel forces had captured *Invincible* only a month and a half ago. How could they possibly have gotten one of Earth's capitol ships ready for combat so quickly? Where had they found enough crew to learn how to operate her systems, let alone fully man it? For that matter, how in the name of everything holy had they managed to capture it?

He examined the grainy, magnified image carefully. "No sign of external damage, Sir," Intelligence confirmed his observations.

"Unless it's somewhere we can't see," he corrected. They could have gotten it by stealth, or a hundred other ways, but most likely was that they'd breached the hull to capture it. Nothing else made sense.

"Weapons armed," Guns reported. "Tracking."

"Still closing at eight hundred," Navigation reported.

"Battle stations," the Chief blared over the general net. "Lock down sections." Immediately the sounds of blast doors slamming into place echoed through the huge ship, sealing each section into an independent unit to minimize damage.

"Let's pass on her anterior side," Faradaddie instructed the helm. If the breach was on the side he couldn't see perhaps they could take advantage of it. "Get as close as you can. Guns, aim for the steering jets as we pass."

"Give us two hundred meters separation, minimum," Navigation confirmed as Helm made the adjustment as Guns adjusted range on the cannon.

"Spin the ship to ten rotations per minute," Intelligence advised. "That will be enough to put the marines in place."

Faradaddie turned to the Chief. "Tell your marines to get ready."

The quantum probability drive gave mankind the stars. It allowed ships to travel multiples of light-years in an instant. At the same time, it did have a few drawbacks. For one, the maximum distance one could travel in a single blink was limited to two light years. Ships disappeared when they tried to go further and, some contended although no one could prove it, that they were destroyed. Others thought that they were simply unable to return. It meant the same thing, regardless. No ship's captain in their right mind would dare go beyond two lights in a single blink.

The QP drives were enormously expensive. Each ship represented a major investment of a world's economy. As with other capitol projects such an investment was not to be wasted. A colony was rich if it could afford two ships, fabulously wealthy if it had four, and only the resources of the entire Solar community could muster the resources for more than five.

The second problem with the QP drive was that light-year blinks were not kind to the human body. Roughly ten percent of the crew became deathly sick on a long blink. One in a hundred died on a one light year blink. Regardless of distance, nearly everyone experienced headaches, dizziness, or threw up when the drive engaged. You could not stand two blinks in a row without being violently ill.

"How are your men?" the Chief asked over the intecom, four seconds after coming out of blink.

"Armed, ready for action, and mean as hell," Sergeant Tsu replied immediately. It wasn't strictly true, coming out of blink made him feel as bad as the morning after a really good liberty.

Four of his marines were on the deck, puking their guts out and two were sitting down, shaking their heads in confusion. Some of the others looked pretty green around the gills, but what the hell, marines can survive anything. He just wished that he had their youthful constitutions.

He'd been in this stupid war since the beginning, had four boardings under his belt and had fought hand-to-hand a half dozen times. He just hoped this attack wouldn't be his last. He was getting too old for this, too old and maybe too lucky. He prayed his string of luck would last until the damned idiotic trade war was over. It was the only way of getting out with his ass intact.

He felt the ship lurch. It must have been a pretty violent movement because nothing else could have overcome the ship's artificial gravity. There was somebody shouting in the corridor. Tsu couldn't make out what they were saying. He mentally kicked himself: Pay attention to what you are doing. Let the god-damned Fleet officers worry about the ship.

Concentrate, he reminded himself as he walked among his troop, fifteen good men, even though three of them were women and one was, well, different.

"Snap that faceplate," he warned a young 'cruit who looked like she just stepped off the freaking farm. He tugged the straps on another's pack, adjusted the air flow on one man who was hyperventilating, and nodded approvingly at the way the newbie caHenrath was holding her torch with one finger resting on the guard, not the damned trigger. Good thing, too, the way her hands were shaking. He'd seen some Firemen blow off their legs when they forgot basic safety. Rough way to learn a lesson.

He pulled Wilkerson from the deck. "I'm all right, Sarge," the boy said as he knelt to help another get to his feet. Tsu nodded. It looked like they were all reviving from the blink.

"Get ready," came the word from the bridge. "We're spinning to give you a tangential boost on launch."

"All right, form up," Tsu ordered. "Time to do or die for the fucking politicians."

The lock's inner door slammed shut three seconds later, cutting off the noise from the corridor. "Systems on," he shouted as he slammed his own faceplate closed. His ears popped as the lock's air was evacuated. His suit pressure quickly compensated.

His troops had already formed their pods; two grapplers with each torch bearer. They all knew the drill and were lined up, ready for launch. He dreaded what they would face on the other side of that lock.

He took position at the lead, lifted his right arm, and waited for the red light. When the lock hatch opened he saw the stars whipping past as the ship spun on its axis. Christ, how many mps were they going to give the launch?

"Go!" The light came on, his arm fell, gravity disappeared, and fifteen marines were thrown into space, each pod flocking to ensure maximum survival as they approached the projected path of the other ship.

In the distance he saw the other groups flying as well. One was ahead of them and the other delayed by fifteen seconds.

He prayed that the ship had timed their own launch properly.

Fireman Third Class Susan caHenrath could practically hear her heart pounding as she stood before the hatch for her first combat. Her head still ached from the damned blink and there was a sour taste in her mouth. Her stomach felt empty and cold and she had to pee really, really badly. Why was time going so slowly? What was all that shouting in the corridors about? It was as bad as the time she and Phil Crenshaw had tossed the . . . Oh God, she hadn't thought about Phil for months and now she was . . .

The light blinked red, the hatch flew open, and there were ten million stars racing by and somebody was yelling. She was thrown away from the ship as gravity disappeared and followed her two grapplers into the dizzying whirlpool of stars.

Sue clutched her torch tight to her chest as they all flew away from the ship. She prayed that the officers had calculated their jump correctly. If so it would place them above the enemy's hull just as it passed.

Would she see the approaching ship? Wouldn't it be moving too fast? What if it changed course and hit them? What if they missed it completely? Would their own ship come back for them? Hell, would those dumb sailors be able to find them? What if the . . .

She glimpsed a huge metal wall as the enemy ship suddenly flashed by, just a few meters away. There was a snap at her back and, suddenly she was accelerating as she was yanked at right angles. She twisted her head and saw her two grapplers busily gathering their skeins that had stuck to the ship's hull. They were reeling in the lines like fish that had caught a boat.

She released the safety on her torch before her feet hit and looked around for the color tag that Sarge used to mark her spot. There! She checked the seam he'd identified. It looked as if there had been a repair to the armored plating. She tilted her torch, made sure the others were not too close, and fired.

The other two firemen began working on the opposite side of the plate. Their torches threw an actinic light on the entire group. Several of the grapplers were ducking to avoid the gobs of molten metal that flew off the burn. They already had their lines secured to the plate's center.

"Clear," Tsu radioed the instant the firemen's torches completed their circuit of the plate. Sue stood back as the grapplers pulled it free and let it fly away.

She quickly began burning through the insulation, deck plates, and miscellaneous cables and pipes that they'd exposed. The entire section exploded as soon as someone made the final cut that weakened the structure. Air rushed out in a cloud of debris, along with an unlucky, writhing crewman.

She had no time to dwell on the dying rebel as he flew past. She brought her torch to cross arms and dropped into the hole. Her grapplers followed, their small arms already swinging around to fire on anyone in sight.

The location on the door said "B-34." That was pretty close to the bridge. "Follow me," Sarge said as soon as everyone was inside. She followed close behind him into the corridor.

The amount of control Earth had over its colonies diminished as the colonies became more self-sufficient. Soon commercial ties began to grow between the scattered worlds and too, the desire of some colonies to control others. A strange sort of war emerged, with capture and control of the ships that traveled between the worlds being the key.

Capturing an enemy ship had two purposes. First, it denied the enemy of its ability to traffic with other worlds, thus striking an economic blow. Second, it kept that ship from being used to capture other ships and often meant taking that world out of the war entirely.

Both could be accomplished by destroying a ship, but every combatant knew the cost that represented. No one wished to waste such a valuable resource. Capture was the only alternative.

But how does one capture a ship that has the ability to jump light years? Detection was still limited by light speed so a quarter-light jump's destination could not be detected for three months at least.

The strategies that emerged were to either lie in wait near the approach lines to a world or to boldly attack another world in hopes that its ship, or that of its allies, was there.

The battles that emerged were more like seventeenth century naval battles than twenty-second century duels. Ballistic weapons were fired to disable the opposing ship. Boarding crews were sent to take command by whatever means they could.

And men died horrible deaths in the process.

Sergeant Tsu checked the deck panel. "B-34. All right troops. We need to get down one and up thirty to reach the freaking bridge." His troops immediately began moving up the corridor, arms at the ready. One of the firemen burned through the first blast door quickly and died in a burst of enemy small arms.

"Shit, they're armed!" One of the grapplers shouted before he too went down in a splatter of blood and guts.

Tsu's remaining men immediately dropped into file formation; the front two providing covering fire while the second two bracketed individuals over their heads. Another of his marines went down. He saw one of the rebel squad swing his rifle toward him. Is this it? he wondered even as he started to duck.

Wham! A chunk of the rebel's helmet blew off and, with it, a rush of snow as the moist air inside the man's suit evacuated. Tsu hoped nobody had a patch handy. That would be one less rebel they had to contend with. "Good shot."

"Thanks, Sarge," Wilderson said as a shot blew away a patch of wall next to his rifle.

Despite her training, despite the endless drills and simulations, despite everything she'd been told to expect, Sue caHenrath was still scared. None of it had prepared her for the sight of someone she knew being cut in half by enemy fire. It could easily have been her. What was she supposed to be doing now? Oh lord, everybody was shooting and Sarge was shouting and she couldn't think and her hands were shaking and she thought she might have peed.

Images of her little dog, her friend Phil, her mother, and a thousand other minutiae of her short life before joining the marines flashed unbidden through her mind. The marine in front of her fell forward with most of his back gone.

A surge of intense anger overcame her. She wouldn't let these bastards kill her. And there was no way she was going to let them kill her buddies! She screamed and hit the torch's trigger before she even realized what she was doing. Immediately the corridor burst into flame. The firestorm incinerated the bodies on the deck, scorched the paint off the walls, and did gods-knew-what to the enemy squad.

Oh God, what had she done?

Tsu saw his faceplate blistering from the intense radiation before he realized the source. He threw an arm out and pushed the fireman aside, ready to chew her out for firing a torch in close quarters, when he realized that her action had saved all their lives. "Drop the damn torch and use your Goddamn rifle," he ordered as he slapped caHenrath's helmet.

The firestorm had cost them. Four of his marines had flame-damaged suits, one was wounded from the firefight, and the three who'd been shot first were now cinders on the deck. That left him with twelve effectives. Christ, one of them could have been him! "Weapons?" he commanded.

"One torch, nine rifles, one side arm," Schilling called out. The other arms were molten lumps. Tsu kicked a smoking rifle aside as he pushed forward over the seven blackened stumps that used to be men.

"Coming about," Helm cried as *Pride*'s steering jets fired and the big inertial gyros twisted the ship on her axis. The stars wheeled around on the screens as the ship turned toward Invincible.

"Sixteen minutes," Intelligence warned. That was the estimated time remaining until *Invincible*'s drives had enough charge built up to blink away.

"I think we hit the dorsal steering jets," Guns reported.

"Captain, we've got a hull breach amidships," Chief reported. "Damage control in action. Small arms, we think."

That meant a boarding party, for sure. "Any damage from shot?"

The Chief checked. "Some hull impacts. No penetrations." That was good news. Invincible's cannon could easily destroy his small ship.

Captain Faradaddie ran a quick calculation to see how much time it might take for his own marines to reach their objectives. They would probably take five to eight minutes to breach the hull, another twelve or fifteen minutes to fight their way through the corridors and compartments to the bridge, engineering, or life support objectives. That gave them only five minutes to render her ineffective before she could blink to safety. That is, if they weren't all killed before then. There was damn little slack in that schedule.

"Fire main engines as soon as we're lined up for another pass," he ordered. Velocity was what he needed. Momentum. Every extra meter per second he could add to the ballistic cannon's shot counted.

"On screen," Visuals called. Faradaddie looked up to see that Invincible had changed direction and was heading away on an oblique angle.

"Son of a bitch. Alter course to intercept."

"Right thirty, up twenty," Helm acknowledged. As the mains fired the image of the other ship drifted off the center of the screen.

"Correct that damned precession," Faradaddie ordered and felt the thrum of the steering jets firing through the soles of his feet.

Tsu was down one more rifle, a grappler this time, lost to a shattered faceplate. Some rebel smart-ass had evacuated all the air in the corridors as a defensive measure. Probably expected them to be stupid enough to open their suits.

CaHenrath was still lugging that damned torch along like it was her fucking baby. He hoped there was no charge left in it. Gods, she could kill them all if she fired it in these confined spaces.

He checked their location. B-3. Good, that meant they had to go down one and just a little bit forward to reach the bridge. Piece of cake, that is, once they got the damned troops guarding this passage taken care of. He checked the time. Chief had said he had twenty minutes, plus or minus three, to reach the bridge and he had already wasted eighteen.

They were on borrowed time.

On board *Invincible* Captain Zaggat fumed. The smaller Fleet ship was being clever, turning to track their new tack so quickly. "How much time left?" he asked.

"Two minutes," Navigation replied.

"Spinning up," Engines reported.

"Target set," Navigation said. "Quarter light."

That should be enough to get out of this damned pickle, Zaggat thought. It was a bad piece of luck, running into the enemy just as they were departing. He hardly had enough weigh to turn to meet them and get Guns to shoot before the bastard went whipping by. Well, *Invincible* was ready now and God help him when he tried that passing maneuver again.

"Target acquired," Guns said quietly. "Full load."

"Automatic fire," Zaggat ordered. "Set a two-second bracket. Three loads." There was no way they could avoid running into that much armament. "Steering jets and engine," he ordered. He wanted her knocked out of the battle, not destroyed.

"On screen," Visuals said. The other ship was racing toward them, its image expanding as he watched.

"Twelve thousand meters," Navigation reported and, a few seconds later. "Ten, now."

Zaggat smiled as he looked at the track projections. Their closing speed was close to five hundred meters per second.

No fucking way they could miss.

The two ships approached to within one-fifty kilometers.

"Are our drives spun up yet?"

"Aye, Sir. Set for one-quarter light. Dlink on your command."

"Stand by." With less than a minute to go he had to assume that none of his marines had reached their targets. "She changed course awfully fast. Guns, are you sure you hit those steering jets?"

"Confirmed, Captain," Guns replied. "She can't turn to one side."

Faradaddie wondered which side that was. They'd noted *Invincible* rotating as they passed. If so, in which direction was she vulnerable now? He peered at the screen, hoping to get some visual indication.

"Go beneath her," he said.

"Aye," Helm replied and adjusted their track with a microburst of the steering jets.

Navigation counted off the seconds. "Thirty seconds. Twenty-nine. Twenty-eight . . . "

They were still too far apart. What if *Invincible* blinked away before the shots at her reaction engines impacted? Crap, if only there had been more time.

"Fifteen. Fourteen. Thirteen." Three bright flashes from *Invincible*.

"She's fired on us. Blink!" he ordered.

The universe contracted to a pinpoint and immediately expanded again into light so bright it made him wince. The headache hit immediately this time. It was a throbbing, pounding agony that originated behind his forehead and extended along both temples and down into his shoulders.

"Condition?" he shouted and listened as Guns, Helm, Navigation, Visuals, nd all the other bridge members reported in. Good, there were no losses to blink syndrome. "Check Engines, Chief," he said. "Make certain they can still think straight."

They had jumped a quarter of a light year, although the headache made it feel as if it had been further. Had *Invincible* blinked as well or had it remained long enough for his shots to do some damage? Well, they'd have to wait for their own drives to charge back up before they could go back to find out.

One of the crewmen handed him meds and a drink to wash them down. Hydration and pain relief were the only sure remedies for blink syndrome. He wished the drink were something stronger than distilled water, but he'd drink anything he could to rid himself of this headache.

"Stand easy until we can spin up again," he said.

Captain Zaggat on Invincible was also nursing a headache, although this one was in the form of four marines who were too close to the bridge. "What's the situation," he asked the Chief.

"We captured the ones headed for the drives," Chief Sanchez reported. "Our men are still holding off the group at life support. We're sending a contingent to circle behind them. It won't be long now before they're neutralized."

Which left the pesky foursome outside the bridge. They were in a secure position, backed up to the blast hatch, which they'd managed to render inoperable. That meant nobody could get behind them. It also meant that nobody could get off the bridge, either.

"They have a torch," the Chief remarked grimly. "If push comes to shove . . . " He left the rest unsaid. Zaggat knew that, if the situation got desperate enough, the four just might torch the corridor, fry the defensive forces, and melt the relatively thin bridge hatch. If they did that, it would kill everyone on the bridge with a fiery hell. That tactic wouldn't do the four enemy marines any good either. In those narrow confines they'd be just as incinerated as everyone else.

"Should we parlay?" Sanchez asked. "What can we offer them, besides their lives?"

"I'm not sure they'd accept. They've just seen their comrades killed. Probably expect the other squads to have done no better. They know their own command will be able to locate this ship even if they manage to render us inoperable. If they're suicidal they could fire that torch." He couldn't risk them being sensible enough not to suicide.

"Spin up to one light," he ordered Engines without further thought. "Blink when ready and without my command."

It was a hard decision, but the right one. A blink that far would knock out many of *Invincible*'s crew, possibly kill a couple, and drive a few others out of their minds.

But those four marines in the passage had to be tired and worn down by what they had gone through. A one-light blink wouldn't be easy on them. If he was lucky, it might even kill one or two.

Even if the blink didn't disable the four, they couldn't avoid noticing the blink. They couldn't help but realize that much displacement would put *Invincible* beyond recovery.

The Chief looked puzzled. "A one-light blink, Captain?" Zaggat nodded. "Yes sir. I'll warn the crew." He reached for the intercom.

"No, they might intercept. I want the blink to hit them by surprise." He just hoped the marine with the torch wasn't one of those who went insane.

Even a small, short blink is a long distance. The wave front of a ship coming out of blink at any distance would take days, weeks, or months, standard, to be detected. If Fleet knew the *Invincible*'s escape vector, they could take short hops to catch the wave front. But that tactic would mean waiting in each location for the wave front to hit them. That was a waste of precious time. By the time they detected anything, *Invincible* would have long departed.

The only hopes they had to catch *Invincible*, or any other rebel ship, was to keep watch near the planets. Every ship had to refuel, restock, and deliver or pick up cargo. Cargo was the main reason for the ships to ply the ways and cargo had to be delivered. That's what the damned war was all about, wasn't it?

Earth's own ships, like Faradaddie's, were no different. She was a Fleet ship, but she carried substantial cargo as well. She still had to service those colonies that remained loyal.

At the same time, they had to protect Earth's ships from harm, make deliveries to the loyal outposts, and the get back to the home planet.

"I guess we lost them, didn't we?" the Chief asked.

Faradaddie didn't need to reply. Whether the Chief was asking about the *Invincible* or those poor damned marines mattered little. He had lost both. "We'll get another chance," he promised.

Sergeant Tsu tried to figure out what had gone wrong and how he had managed to survive with only a busted leg. He'd been told that most of the damned rebels couldn't fight worth crap and much of what they had as weapons were pathetic.

These guys, the ones who'd chopped his troops into mincemeat, were nearly as good as his marines. They'd made effective use of cover, managed to force him into a defensive, but escape-proof, position, and were preventing him from doing anything less than suicide.

At the moment they were at a stalemate. He had twelve centimeters of hardened armor at his back, a narrow field of fire before him, and enough weapons left to hold this position for days, if need be. They could only get to him in single file, allowing him to pick them off at leisure. Impasse. Yeah, that was what the Captain would say. How much time was left now? Had they blinked already?

He didn't expect the stomach churning, wrenching, dizzying wave of nausea when it hit. Damn, they must have spun up again, he thought, and a big blink too.

Shit, caHenrath was down again, puking her guts on the deck. Shilling was looking blank. There was a line of drool coming from the corner of his mouth. Wilkerson was completely out—dead or unconscious.

"We've blinked a full light year," a voice blared over the emergency channel. "Your ship will never be able to find us now."

"What the hell?" he said in reply. "How did you manage to get on a secure channel? Screw you." But had the voice said a full light year? Holy crap. He was right. There was no point fighting any longer. They'd never get back now.

He tried to hold back the tears he felt for all those damned wasted deaths, all those dead marines and rebels. It had all been for nothing – a pointless battle in a fucking trade war. He was sick of it. .

"Listen. You don't have choices. You either give up or you'll die."

"Who the hell are you, anyhow? How did you manage to tap into this channel?" Was this the end? Was he actually going to die?

"This is the Captain," the voice responded. "Name's Zaggat."

Tsu started. His leg really hurt bad. "I shipped under a Captain with that name. Big ugly sucker, thought he was so damned smart." Were the defenders going to rush them now?

"And wouldn't let the marines piss in the corridors, is that right?" the voice chuckled. "Yeah, that was me."

Tsu was taken aback. His entire worldview turned over. How could one of Fleet's officers go over to the rebel side? No, it had to be a trick.

"I don't want to see any more people die," Zaggat continued. "All I want is to get *Invincible*'s cargo delivered."

Tsu considered his options. Wilkerson was still down, he didn't like the way caHenrath was looking, and Shilling had gotten a wild look in his eyes and was stroking his rifle like it was a payday whore. "My men need medical attention." He didn't mention his own shattered leg.

"They'll get it. Throw out your weapons if you mean it."

Tsu carefully peeled Shilling's hands off his rifle and then plucked the torch from the ineffective caHenrath's hands. He skidded both along the deck and then tossed his own with them. "There you go," he said and crawled out, leaving a trail of blood behind him. As far as he was concerned, the war was finally over.

And he was still alive.

THRESHER

Lawrence M. Schoen

ERCUTIO'S GHOST CHECKED ITS MATH AND MUSED THAT A LIFE OF PIRACY IN THE middle of an interplanetary war was no life for a physician. The math checked; the Folio's outbound course from Varuna would carry it through the Kuiper Belt, with an eye toward creating the appearance of just another trans-Neptunian object, too small for even a MarzCraft with full sensorial to bother noticing. Its piracy piloting done, the doctor portion of the ghost took over and accelerated its time sense several hundred fold. This burned up the larger share of its temporary lifespan, but gave it the next ninety subjective hours to search for a cure for the Captain.

In the war between Erth and Marz, the Old Man had put himself smack in the middle. Only ErthCraft sported ghost crew. Their ships could produce key decisions several orders of magnitude faster than MarzCraft. Only MarzCraft pilots had access to the sensorial that let them see and taste and touch and hear every iota of information within an AU with utter clarity. A sensorial ship could usually see an enemy vessel coming with enough lead time to get away safely. A ghosted vessel almost invariably outgunned an opponent running with real-time targeting. All that fine technology was proprietary, and neither side had both kinds, at least as far as anyone knew. But Captain Book had both the knack and the means to acquire tech through unscrupulous channels, which made him a natural to command a pirateship.

Mercutio's ghost's current medical effort failed, as all its predecessors had. Disappointed but unsurprised, it dilated its time sense back out to human norm. Varuna had receded far behind the Folio. The ghost once more reviewed the course Mercutio had prepared to Ixion, then fired off an acknowledgment to the First Mate's ghost lurking elsewhere in the system.

The MarzGov mining ship Declaration would soon be leaving Ixion, its holds laden with tholin and other precious heteropolymers not found on either Marz or Erth. The Captain wanted those heteropolymers, and by extension so did Mercutio, which meant his ghost did too. Time then to get to it. The ghost hurtled back through the system arriving at the interface plate that led to its origin, jumped the gap, and merged its memories with its flesh and blood creator.

In his cool bunk, Mercutio, pilot and ship's doctor, blinked and yawned as his ghost roused him from the chill of suspension and dumped the experience of its brief life into his mind. Piracy wasn't his first calling, it wasn't even his second, but circumstance had taken him this way and complaining wouldn't change things. His body warmed to real time and he winced as he reviewed the particulars of another unsuccessful research session. He could only try again; so long as the Captain lived, it was his duty. Mercutio pressed his face firmly against the activation plate, generated a fresh ghost, and unhooked himself from the harness of the ghosterizer. He swung himself out of his bunk and went to check on the Captain.

"Still no luck?" said the speaker grid on Captain Book's cool bunk as the doctor entered the tiny ship's infirmary.

Mercutio stepped within range of the Captain's acuity sensors and nodded. The Old Man's bunk was colder than his own, though not so cold as the crews'. The First Mate had rigged it to chill the Captain's brain, but allow him to remain conscious all the same. "No, Sir, but I've started another run. Meanwhile, I wanted to see how you're doing." More than two dozen ceramo-magnetic diagnostic beads covered the Captain's body, like glowing red eyes that gave the darkened bunk a demonic feel. Each beamed its readings to the infirmary's computer, which in turn displayed a summary to a wall display. Mercutio studied that summary and frowned. Despite the trickling pace of the Old Man's metabolism, the meds he'd administered had already stopped working.

"I have faith in you, son," said Book. "But then, what other choice do I have?"

"You could abort this run, Sir. Tell the First to let me plot us a course out of the Belt. We can run the distance to Erth or Marz on hard shields. You've got letters of marque from both sides. You'll get a parade as a privateer either place."

"What do I need with a parade? And I'm only a privateer because neither side knows I work for the other. We have business to do out here, Mercutio, pirate business. I'll see Erth, sure, but not before we liberate all the Ixion tholin on that MarzCraft."

"You'll never see Erth then, Captain. The thresher will kill you long before then."

"You're sure of that?"

"I am. Even with maximum chill slowing your body, the drugs haven't been able to suppress your reaction to the field. I've already had to amputate your left leg. Another limb could develop Sagan's fasciitis without warning, and only the cool bunk is keeping organ failure at bay. As long as we're in the Belt we can't turn off the thresher without killing everyone. The hard shields aren't enough to protect the ship here."

Book whistled faintly, summoning a glowbug from the communication console and directing it to land on the trio of gold rings hanging from his left ear. "Then you'd best set aside my share of the haul for my funeral costs," he said. "I want to go out in style."

Every ship in space, whether ErthCraft, MarzCraft, or Indy-made, used a thresher. The machine was as ugly and awkward a sight as a lust-crazed bull mounting a groundcar, and about as big, but the field it generated made space travel possible. The thresher pushed a ship out of Probabilistic space, freeing it from the constraints of Euclid, Einstein, and Chaos. As an added bonus it laughed in the face of conservation and boosted velocity without any messy acceleration issues. And all the while the field protected everything within it from radiation and normal matter up to the mass it contained.

Transition back to Probability dumped the gained velocity but otherwise had no effect on inorganics. Usually it didn't affect flesh and blood either. But every now and then, one time in ten billion, a body came back into normal space changed. The smarties they called it, and the luckless spacers who got it had the choice to either leave space quickly or die there. You could live, assuming you never stepped inside a thresher field again. Otherwise the disease progressed with lightning speed, killing you in a burst of brilliance as your brain spun off millions of new connections while every organ in your new genius body failed. Smart death, but death all the same.

Mercutio had diagnosed the Captain's condition before they'd gone to ground on Varuna, and immediately put the Old Man in a cool bunk. Then he'd set about using the limited resources of the *Folio* to do what the best medical minds on two worlds hadn't been able to do. He'd failed. The ghosterizer had only let him fail faster and more thoroughly.

Mercutio owed the Captain his life ten times over, and the most he could do for him now was to plan his funeral party.

"That's it then," said Prospero as he and Mercutio sat in the mess. The man fastidiously nibbled the full crust perimeter of a toasted cheese sandwich as he spoke. "We make way near Ixion as planned, liberate the tholin as planned, and leave them Marzies with the final tale of Captain Book."

"And then what?" said Mercutio. He sniffed and frowned, the First Mate had engineered the foodstation to manufacture curds that went beyond pungent and well into stench.

"Then I'll be captain," said Prospero, "and you'll quicken such crew as need it. Those that choose to sign on under me, as they did for Book, can stay and it will be as it has been. Those what don't, can leave the *Folio* with their full shares as expected."

Mercutio sighed. "Then off we go, on another thrilling pirate adventure."

Prospero finished the last of the crusts and smushed the remainder of the sandwich between his hands, rolling it into a tight ball of melted, smelly cheese and toasted bread. He popped it into his mouth as he regarded the pilot. He chewed silently for a full minute, swallowed, and pointed a greasy finger at Mercutio. "What about you? I know we haven't gotten on well, but I'm hoping you'll stay. You're a passable doc and a better pilot, and I'll need both."

"Right now you're still just ship's engineer and first mate," said Mercutio. "The Captain's not dead."

The First nodded. "Not yet, but my ghosts are in the system same as yours, and they talk to one another, usually more than we manage face to face. I know the status of things same as you. We're cruising your camouflaged route through the belt towards Ixion, the thresher's running at full, and if the Captain ain't dead by the time we crack open that MarzShip, it won't be for lack of trying."

Sixty-seven hours and a dozen failed medical simulations later, tumbling along its seemingly haphazard route, the *Folio* fell into position an hour away from where it would cross *Declaration*'s vector and rendezvous with the unsuspecting mining ship. Mercutio informed the Captain, who in turn ordered the First to prepare an assault, who then sent word to Mercutio to quicken a boarding party.

As both pilot and ship's physician, moments like this required Mercutio to be in two places at once, a situation which the ghosterizer made possible. He spun off a pair of them, one to actually pilot the *Folio*, and one to stand ready to relay messages between that spectral pilot and himself as near to instantly as human synapses could manage. Then he went to thaw the crew.

He quickend MacBeth first. While not an officer, the man had seniority among the crew, and at one time or another had beaten each of them senseless as part of some initiation ritual they all seemed to regard as a rite of passage. Mercutio didn't pretend to understand; he'd merely set the bones and provided the necessary stiches. If it contributed to crew loyalty and boosted morale he had no cause to complain. The cool bunks accelerated healing anyway.

MacBeth, like half of the crew, was classic Marz stock, and stood a foot taller than Mercutio. Generations of Marzian eugenics had made him lean, muscled and golden-skinned. The Captain had named him MacBeth, just as he had given all the crew their names. It didn't do for pirates to know one another's birth name. The nominal Scotsman quickened swiftly and with none of the grogginess that the cool bunk often imparted to the Erthborn. The instant his eyes opened he locked Mercutio's gaze and asked, "How soon?"

"Less than an hour. Give me a hand rousing the others."

MacBeth rolled naked from his bunk, and pulled open the storage locker with his gear. He dressed with quiet efficiency while Mercutio moved on to the next cool bunk, and then joined him. Over the next five minutes they revived the others, Horatio, Benedict, Katrina, Antony, and Romeo.

"Look lively you lot," said MacBeth to his men. "Don't be thinking it's only a mining craft and going all soft. We'll be giving them the hard bump this day, same as we'd give any vessel as Captain Book sets his desire upon. Clear?"

"Aye," said Romeo, and Katrina and Antony nodded in time.

"Bump," said Benedict, who'd taken a blow to the head during their last raid and hadn't been quite right since. He grinned and punched his brother, Horatio, in the shoulder.

"Hard bump, aye," said Horatio, and punched him back.

"Anything else we ought to be knowing, doc?" asked MacBeth.

Mercutio shook his head. "It's a big ship, but mostly automated for all that. A MarzCraft, so no ghosts. Three man crew, according to specs. If they've picked us up on their sensorial, they're still thinking we're a small rock that will pass right through them without touching."

Horatio barked with laughter. "Until our thresher bumps theirs."

"Hard bump," said Benedict, and punched him again.

"All right you lot, head for the lock and suit up." MacBeth waved them toward the exit. "Every man carries a grapple, two cables, and a stunner. No one tries anything fancy and we all come back richer than when we woke up. Now move."

They shuffled out, amidst a raucous chorus of "Bump! Bump! Bump!"

Mercutio put a hand on MacBeth's arm, holding him back a moment. "Why 'bump'?" he asked.

"Cuz the good lord won't be delivering them," said MacBeth.

"Huh?"

"I don't know from ghoulies, but you officers are ghosties and we've our share o'long-legged beasties. And space is as dark as any night I know of."

"Huh," repeated Mercutio, finally recognizing the reference. "I've always thought of space as daytime. The sun's always shining."

MacBeth grinned at him. "You think too much, doc," and he turned to follow his men.

The boarding was especially anticlimactic. Trusting to their own thresher field to spare them impact from anything smaller than themselves, *Declaration* didn't clue to the *Folio* being more than a stray stone until the pirate vessel tumbled within a kilometer and matched vectors. By then it was too late. As the *Folio* drew closer, the two thresher fields merged, pulling the ships together. Mercutio's ghost had used the sensorial on precision settings to line up their locks with perfection. It signaled the First's ghost to begin the swiftly completed raid.

It was over almost before it began. MacBeth and company forced the lock, boarded the ship, rounded up, and efficiently disarmed the trio of personnel by the time Prospero and Mercutio followed them onboard. The doctor set the men to converting *Declaration*'s ward room into a temporary brig, while the First began preparing their prize for transit.

Half an hour later Mercutio joined Prospero on *Declaration*'s bridge. It smelled of sweat and boredom, a result of someone always being at the helm. The First aimed to fix that. He lay on his back, waist deep in the guts of a computer relay, installing a spare ghosterizer to the mining ship's sytems. "We've got quite a haul," he said, the acoustics making his voice reedy.

"You're not usually one to get misty about money," said Mercutio.

"I've never had so much of it from one job. Between the payoff from the heteropolymers, and with what we'll get selling this ship back to MarzGov, I'm thinking maybe it's time to get out of piracy and become a business man."

Mercutio laughed. "Don't go spending your shares quite yet. This job's a long way from done. We can't sell this ship until we've ransomed her crew."

Prospero slid out from the relay, pulled the panel closed, and sat up. "Don't be getting naïve on me, Mercutio. This isn't a military ship like we normally target. There's no ransom to be had for this lot. We'll be spacing the crew before we head out."

Mercutio paled. "Piracy is one thing, but I won't be party to murder."

Prospero smirked. "That's for the Captain to decide now ain't it?"

Mercutio returned to the *Folio* and went straight to the infirmary; Prospero trailed behind chuckling to himself, but stopped when they discovered their Captain had left. His modified cool bunk lay open, his diagnostic beads scattered upon the floor like marbles.

"Where could he have gone?" asked the First, following the doctor into the infirmary and joining the search.

"C'mon," said Mercutio after assuring himself that Captain Book hadn't fallen behind the cool bunk or hidden himself away in a supply cubby. "We'll check his cabin, then yours, then mine. Mind the beads as you go."

"Why would he be in either of our cabins?"

"Why would he have left his cool bunk?" said Mercutio. "It was the only thing keeping him alive."

The Captain's own quarters were empty, everything organized and shipshape as they'd been since he'd gone into the infirmary for treatment. They moved on to the First's cabin, found it less tidy but no less empty. To the doctor's horror and relief, Captain Book proved to be in his cabin, sprawled head-first, half in and half out of the active cool bunk. He'd died there, his body wracked by spasms as opposing muscle groups contracted simultaneously, tearing flesh free from bone as his cortical functions froze. Blood, now dry, had trickled from ears and eyes, and the Old Man had bitten through his tongue as well.

"Well, at least we know why he came here," said Prospero. He sat at the doctor's workstation, and gestured to an active screen. "He was running some kind of biomedical analysis using your gear."

Mercutio stared at the screen and nodded.

Prospero scowled. "This makes sense to you?"

"Yeah. As soon as he left the cool bunk the smarties kicked in. He was trying to use it to find a cure before it killed him. He must have given up and tried to get back in a bunk to buy himself more time, and didn't make it." Mercutio glanced at the body and then back to the screen. "It will take me weeks to figure out how close he got."

"Not close enough," said Prospero. He stood, and regarded Mercutio and then Book. "Move his corpse back to the infirmary; chill it for now. Once we've sorted the mining ship, then you can prepare the body for a vacuum burial; I know it's not what he told you he wanted, but he doesn't get a say any more. Now, if you'll excuse me, I've got to go talk to the crew."

"What are you going to tell them?"

Prospero paused, one hand on the door of the cabin. He spoke without looking back. "That Captain Book is dead, and that there's a new Captain. As we discussed." He walked out a different man than he'd entered.

"I think I'm being generous," said Captain Prospero. Two hours had passed and he'd assembled everyone in *Declaration*'s ward room. Mercutio knew the man had already made his decision; this was all for show.

"Your physician's oath won't allow you the expedience of killing our three captives, and I respect that. I think my solution is quite elegant."

"You're taking my shares, in violation of the code," said Mercutio.

"No, I'm giving you your shares, and our late captain's too, and then I'm swapping them back and trading you the *Folio* for them. And I'm throwing in the captives you're so squeamish about. Keep them as crew or keep them in cool bunks until you drop them off, I don't much care.

"Time's change, doctor. The letters of marque are in Book's name, not mine. Sure I could likely get one or both transferred, but there's more wealth and less risk in mining than in pirating. MacBeth and the rest of the crew agree. Not much need for a pilot of your talents, nor a doctor for all that. So it works out well for everyone."

"You're cheating me," said Mercutio, "and you're trying to be rid of me. You've already ripped out half the cool bunks and most of the armaments."

"I need 'em, and you don't," said Prospero. "And as for being rid of you, as Captain I'm within my rights to kill you outright and there's not a man here that doesn't know it."

Mercutio gnawed his lip a moment. "That'd be true," he conceded, "if you were still a pirate and not a miner. But fine, let your last act of piracy be robbing me of my fair shares. I'll take the *Folio*, and chart a course where I can give Captain Book the send off he wanted. And I'll take your prisoners and see they find their way somewheres safe."

"That's it then," said Prospero, "save one last thing. Your word, that you'll not prey upon this ship and crew of innocent miners in the future."

"No bump," said Horatio.

MacBeth eyed the doctor solemnly and nodded, "Aye, no bump," And looked away.

"You've my word on it," said Mercutio. "Give me an escort to get the prisoners over and safely stowed; I'll ungrapple and be gone in under an hour." Without waiting for confirmation he turned and headed to his ship.

The former crew of *Declaration* looked to slip into their new cool bunks almost willingly, given brutal murder was their only alternative. Mercutio sealed them in, and went to his own quarters next. The Old Man had asked not to be jettisoned into space, as was pirate tradition, but to have his remains drowned for all time in the seas beyond Old Britannia. Mercutio had no other plans. After his ship had tumbled away from *Declaration* he slid into his own cool bunk and connected to the ghosterizer to spin off a simulacrum to plot a course for Erth.

The ghost he'd left running in the system greeted him first. "You're not going to believe this," the spectral Mercutio told the original.

"Believe what? Merge and let me know what you're going on about?

"Now where would the fun be in that?" said his ghost, speaking around a grin, and in a deep and familiar voice.

"Captain? I didn't think you had a ghost in the system, not since you took ill."

"Crazy system, having to talk through your ghost," said the Captain. "But he's been very helpful. You know a lot more about medicine than you've let on, son."

"Captain, you do understand that you're dead?"

"Well, we both saw that coming, now didn't we? But never mind me, did you get the heteropolymers?"

"Yes, Sir. Only, well, what with you being dead and all, Prospero named himself captain, and with the rest of the men decided to take the mining ship and give up piracy. It's just me here, Captain. We've no cargo."

"Not a problem, doctor. Between your ghosts and mine, the *Folio* will do fine.

"About that, Sir. I saw your notes, I get what you were trying to do, but even with the smarties hyping your brain there just wasn't time to work out a cure. It would have taken you months at least."

"You might have told me that," chided the ghost. "It would have saved me at least three minutes. But no harm, I had time to get to your cabin and plug in. I'm not an old spirit. I've filled your buffer with a couple dozen fresh ghosts."

Mercutio paused a moment, trying to wrap his head around the notion of his ghost channeling the ghost of his dead captain. "Why? Captain, no offense, but that doesn't change things. You're still dead. Are you planning on haunting me?"

"No, son, I'm planning on finding a cure. My ghosts are copies of me, so they're smartie ghosts."

Mercutio wiped at his eyes, half surprised to find them wet. "Nothing like that has ever been done," he said.

"But even if it doesn't work, well, I just want to say I'm glad to have you back, Captain."

"Of course it will work. All my buffered copies are dialed down as low as their time sense can go. They're more suspended than any cool bunk could slow flesh and bone. When this ghost nears its limit, I'll wake up another and so on. Now if you'll excuse me, I've work to do. I'll let you get caught up and get us bound for Erth. If you have any questions, you know where to find me."

Mercutio nodded to himself as his ghost merged and a flood of wild and ragged medical conversations poured into his memory, more than his conscious mind could process at once. But that wasn't a problem. It would all get sorted out in his unconscious while he slept. His goals as a pirate and a physician had merged as neatly as he had with his ghost. There was medical adventure ahead, a course plotted for the unknown, and treasure the like of which no man, be he doctor or pilot, had ever beheld. He pressed his forehead against the activation plate, generated a replacement ghost to handle navigation, and let the cool bunk take him down into dreamless sleep.

ALLIANCE

Bud Sparhawk

HOW'S YER HEAD?" I OPENED MY EYES TO BLINKING LIGHTS AND THE SOUNDS OF A compressor rattling loudly near my ear. Sheila Foster, the Captain of the ship we highjacked was leaning over me. I had vague memories of headlong flight down a corridor and a struggle to get her through the lifeboat lock before something hit me in the back.

When I tried to sit up cords cut into my legs. She'd tied me to the bunk. "Did you have to pull them so damn tight?"

"If y'knew how tight, y'know why, y'damn fool." A while back she'd been our prisoner and now I was hers. Why hadn't she shot me while I was unconscious? Merchant captains were not known for kindness toward hijackers.

"Here," she said and dribbled a ration of water between my parched lips. It hurt when I tried to smile. "Sorry I've no salve for yer burns. Nor for my own, y'see." I took another look at her face and saw the ring of blisters where her face mask hadn't protected her from the blast that had hit us just as we reached the lifeboat.

"My back hurts," I said and tried to turn, hoping she would loosen the cords.

"That's yer burns from the blast," she said. "Naught I can do, y'see, until we get rescued. They can fix yer burns when they pick us up. Then it's off to prison with ye, I'd wager."

That was a certainty. Had the lifeboat ejected before we blinked or after? If afterward, had there been another blink to get away from the Fleet ship? If so, we could be stranded anywhere within a light year of where we'd been discovered.

"More likely Fleet will dump me out the lock instead of bothering with prison. I guess that would give you a bit of pleasure—the revenge, I mean."

"Revenge? For stealing my ship, y'mean? *Pfaugh*, While it might give me a jot of joy to see y'spaced it'll do nothing to fill my empty wallet. No, I figure yer smart enough to bargain clear by telling where Fleet might find yer shipmates."

"I'd never tell the Fleet a damn thing," I protested.

She shrugged and stood up. "In that case, yer out the lock and good riddance. I might need the water and food y'would otherwise consume until rescue comes." As she reached over to loose the cords that held my legs immobile I tensed my muscles, ready to strike out.

Her hand hesitated and then pulled back. "No, best I not be judge and jury. Besides," she smiled wickedly and poked my thigh, "I might need fresh meat if things get too bad."

"Why y'be a pirate," she asked the next day after we'd shared a biscuit and another dot of water. "Why y'prey on we poor merchants?"

"We needed your ship," I said. "It's the only way we can become independent. Earth won't sell us transports. That's why we needed yours," I said and wondered about the extent of the damage Fleet might have inflicted on her ship.

Seeing her puzzled expression, I explained the reasons. "Don't you know that Earth restricts what they send to the colonies? Oh, they send a trickle of medicines, trace minerals, and low-technology gadgets while they hold back the tools that would let us build quantum drives."

"The corporations have a right to protect what they own," she said, but there was a note of doubt in her voice.

"Protect the exorbitant fees they extract, you mean? Listen to me! The worlds of the Alliance want to craft their own destiny. They want to trade freely instead of having Earth dictate every damn thing. What's the good of having interstellar travel if we're prisoners of our systems?"

"That be the dumbest pile of crap I ever heard," she sneered. "There's free trade aplenty, so long as y'follow the rules."

"It's Earth's rules we object to," I countered. "We want to build our own drives so we can ship our own cargo. It's the rules that are keeping us tied to Earth's obsolete, failed economic system." Quite unintentionally I was shouting angrily instead of maintaining a calm, reasoned voice.

"The rules protect us all, y'damned fool. Have y'any idea of how yer economies would fare were Earth not regulating trade? Do y'think the weaker colonies share the dreams of the rich ones? Don't y'see how disruptive free trade would be? If it weren't for Earth yer be at each other's throats in a heartbeat."

"Easy for you to say, while you merchants make a tidy profit off us."

"That's a bloody lie," she yelled back. "After the fees, I barely make payments on my ship and crew, much less make a profit. Y'think we merchants sell dear? Well, it's a fairer price than y'd get from the other colonies, I'd wager."

"Earth propaganda!"

"Rebel lies!"

"These cords really hurt," I said to change the subject. "Look, there's nothing I can do with my arms tied. Why don't you at least untie my legs so I can sit up?" I hoped that we had gotten to a point where she saw me less of a threat. "Besides, what could I do? We're stuck together in this lifeboat, like it or not."

She nodded. "Yes, that's so and y'don't seem a bad sort, for a pirate, I mean."

Still, she held a stunner on me as she loosened the cords.

"Thanks," I said. "I'm actually an Alliance officer." There was no sense hiding my identity. The Fleet would learn that much when they showed up.

"Pirates have ranks?" she shrugged. "Well, I guess it makes y'feel legitimate."

"Stop calling me a pirate," I answered. "I'm a Lieutenant."

She grinned. "The Alliance isn't exactly a real military force. It has what—a half-dozen ships?"

That hurt. "We're growing," I answered, hoping my crew still had her fat transport.

"Much as I might sympathize with yer plight, I've my own worries. Insurance won't cover all the costs, y'know and the corporations are not known to take kindly to those that lose their ships."

"I did save you," I reminded her. "I could have left you behind."

"I'd be an ungrateful fool if I forgot that," she said. "But why?"

"Two reasons," I replied. "First, I admired your spunk and didn't want to see you killed."

She cocked and eyebrow at the compliment. "And the other reason?" A flirtatious smile played on her lips.

"You were the only one I had time to get to."

The smile disappeared, but not completely. I started to think that waiting for rescue with her wouldn't be unpleasant and, if I played my cards right, she might start thinking the same way.

I'd work on that.

A week later the proximity alarm shrilled. Sheila jumped from our bunk. She looked puzzled. "Can't be Fleet or there'd be a hail."

I doubted that it was my shipmates either. They wouldn't come back for a junior lieutenant. But, if it wasn't them or Fleet who could it be? There weren't many others out here.

An abrupt shift and a commotion at the lock told us that we'd been pulled aboard another ship. Sheila glanced at me. "Best we be prepared whichever way this goes," she said. "If it's Fleet, yer my prisoner, and vice versa."

"I won't tell if you won't," I promised as the hatch opened.

A man with a bushy red beard came through. "Well, I'll be damned. If it isn't my old friend Hart Kapor and, what's this? Brought your girlfriend along, did you?" he said.

"Nice to see you too, Spratt," I replied bitterly. "Sheila is," I hesitated for a second and then continued, "a passenger of mine."

Spratt cocked an eyebrow. "And when would it be that an Alliance raider took on passengers? No, Hart, I think she's something other than that, say, the missing Captain from that hijacked ship Fleet was after? What say we check her name against the registry?"

"Yeah, y'be right," Sheila answered. "I was ship's master; that is, the former master, New Caledonia bound from Earth until yer pirates grabbed her." She turned to me. "Well, I guess I lost the gamble, Hart. At least remember that I didn't space ya."

Spratt laughed. "Better for me if you had, my dear. Would have saved me the trouble of doing it myself."

Sheila spun about and stared at me. "I though he was another damned pirate."

"Hardly," I answered. "A while back you told me Earth was concerned about war breaking out between the colonies. Well, it's happened. Say hello to Pitr Spratt of the Eagle Consortium. He's my worse nightmare."

My cabin was bare, save for the fold-down bunk and a single toilet. I had been locked up for a few days, but it was hard to keep track of time when there was nothing to gauge its passing. There had only been the single ration pack they'd given me to eat and my stomach had been growling ever since.

The brief wave of nausea that had passed over me told me that the ship had blinked at least once. Where the devil were we going?

I worried about Sheila. She had seemed genuinely shocked when I told her about the inter-colonial war, but how would she know? Fleet was probably keeping a close control on the news that filtered back to Earth, trying to keep up the illusion that the colonies were backwards worlds struggling to survive. Maybe the people on Earth were too tied up in their internal politics and too used to living off the wealth they got from us.

I felt my stomach clench and my head throb—another blink. There better be a medic wherever Spratt was going. My burns were really starting to hurt.

There were two more blinks and another sleep before the cabin door opened. "About bloody damned time," I complained.

The grim-faced crewman at the hatch motioned with a stunner. "This way, capper. Spratt says he needs to chat wit ya."

He didn't look very intelligent. Well, I couldn't expect Spratt to choose from the best and brightest, could I? Maybe if the man were as dense as he looked there might be a chance to wrest the gun from him. I stepped into the corridor, braced for a chance to spring, but two other crewmen grabbed me from either side. "Lead on," I said gloomily. As we walked along I noted a change in the air, the smell of a station.

"Ah, Hart. I trust your accommodations were up to your exacting standards?" Spratt said cheerfully.

"I've seen worse," I bit back. "As will you, no doubt."

Spratt ignored my promise. "I hear the Fleet jails are much nicer than ours, a fact you should keep in mind should you have any ideas of escaping."

"Escape to where? I don't have a drive up my ass, so where would I go?"

That got a laugh. "I always liked your sense of humor, Captain."

"Lieutenant," I corrected him. "Did you buy your rank, or steal it like you did my ship?"

Spratt shook his head. "Don't insult me, Hart. After all, I did rescue you and Sheila. Besides, I'm not doing anything illegal. We're just honest merchants doing what we can to help the Fleet."

I shook my head. "Nobody's going to believe that line, Spratt."

Sheila glared at me from the hatch. "So we should believe a blasted pirate, instead? *Pfaugh*, as if anyone should believe a word y'say."

"I never lied to you," I said, turning to face her. I noticed that she had on clean clothes and had done something nice with her hair. I guess she had better accommodations than me. Damn, and here I'd been worried about her.

"No? Have you forgotten that people have records? Captain Spratt showed me his papers from when y'signed him on, Captain."

Damn, who would have thought Spratt would keep a freaking memento of the brief time he was my second-in-command. But that was before the war, before a hell of a lot of other things happened between us, and before I was recruited. "That was a long time ago," I said.

Pitr never did anything that wouldn't get him a nice return, so why would he tell her that? I failed to see how he could benefit from promoting me.

My answer came when, a moment later, a young Fleet officer and one of his sailors stepped onto the bridge. He wore a shiny gold ensign's brassard and had a few hairs toward a youthful beard on his chin.

Spratt smiled broadly and, so help me, rubbed his hands together in glee. "Ensign Wright," he said as he shook hands. "This is the Captain who stole the *Elvira*. I found him and Captain Foster near death, floating near a transfer point."

Wright scowled at my disheveled clothing and wrinkled his nose. I wasn't surprised. It had been over a week since I bathed. "Are you sure you just happened upon them?" Smart kid, I thought. You didn't have to be a genius to guess that Spratt had been tracking the pursuit, waiting for a chance to grab the spoils.

Spratt spread his palms wide. "I was on my way to another place, Sir, and felt a merchant's obligation when I spotted them. It was just my good fortune to find them before they expired."

"That's not quite true," Sheila said. "But Captain Spratt did rescue us, and for that I am very grateful." It hurt me that Sheila was thankful to Spratt for anything.

"I'll see that you get the bounty," Wright said as he handed Spratt a chit. "The more of these rebels we put away, the better."

So that's why Spratt wanted everyone to think I was still a Captain. Fleet wouldn't pay bounty for a junior lieutenant, so I had to be promoted. Still, the bounty wasn't that much. What was Spratt's real angle?

"Come along, you," the young officer said.

"I'm no Captain, youngster," I said. "That's just Spratt's little joke."

"Sorry, but I know differently." He nodded to his crewman to push me along.

"Been nice knowing you, Sheila," I smiled. "Maybe we'll meet again some day." Right, as if I was ever going to get out of a Fleet prison before the war was over. That is, if Wright didn't space me along the way. I've heard stories.

"Better I never see y'blasted arse again, y'damned lying pirate," Sheila spit. "Maybe honest merchants'll be safer with y'gone." She smiled at Spratt as if he were one of them.

"But I have to bear y'out for a few more days," she continued. "Much as I hate to do it, they're taking me to New Caledonia to pay off my debts."

"This way, Sir," the crewman said politely as he turned me toward the hatch. Wright took Sheila by the arm.

"One moment, Sir," Spratt said. "I'm not so sure it would be wise to have just one guard. Hart's a desperate and violent man. I'll send a few of my men along to help. Just until he's secured on your ship, of course."

Ensign Wright raised an eyebrow. "I hardly think..." he began.

"Tut, not another word, Sir. It would be my pleasure. In fact, I'll even walk along so I can bid a proper goodbye to Captain Foster." He smiled ingratiatingly. Sheila shot a glance at me, a wary look on her face. Something felt wrong here and she felt it.

"Oh, very well," Ensign Wright replied, "but I doubt they'll give us much trouble. Where could they possibly go?"

We walked by rows of empty cargo bays. The place look abandoned. I took a good look at my escort. He was quite a bit older than Wright and had that hard-edged look combat gives a man. The name Quince was emblazoned on his pocket.

"So tell me, sailor," I asked conversationally. "What's your job when you aren't escorting prisoners?"

"I'm engines," he replied with a trace of a colonist's accent. Could he be sympathetic to the cause?

"Heavy cruiser?" I asked. "Commanded one of those years ago...before, I mean."

"Naw, it's just a boat," he replied with an embarrassed grin. "They won't let us expats on the warships."

"Are they afraid somebody's going to steal them?" I joked. "What about your boat?"

Quince laughed softly and looked to see if Wright were out of earshot. "Naw, he's not worried about me. But he says we have to guard it whenever we're transporting something valuable." He bit off the last of his sentence as Wright glared at him and then whispered, "Stupid regulations, if you ask me."

Quince's ship turned out to be a Corvette, one that was a fraction the size of my old ship and as heavily armored. Corvettes were half drive, one-quarter cargo, and usually carried a crew of five, which explained why there was only Quince, Tag, and Tiger.

Corvettes were fast couriers with little crew space so, with Sheila along, there wouldn't be room for me. I supposed I'd be shoved into the cargo bay. Well, at least I wouldn't have to wait long to get to wherever we were going. These little boats could eat up the light years quickly.

Wright waved our entourage to a halt as we neared the Corvette's hatch. Quince pulled me to a stop short of everyone else. "Gotta follow protocol," he sneered. "Ensign's a stickler on rules. Says Tiger's not suppose to open the hatch without him giving the all-clear. Stupid, but the kid's a real prick about stuff like that."

When Wright pulled out his radio and barked something, I suddenly realized what Spratt was about to do. I shouted a warning as the hatch swung open, but it was too late. All hell broke loose.

Spratt shoved Sheila aside and pushed the muzzle of a blaster into Wright's ribs. One of the other crewmen snatched the stunner from Quince and threw him to the deck. The rest rushed into the ship with blasters. There were a few brief flashes of light from inside and then one of them poked his head back out. "We got both of them," he said.

"You can't do this," Wright protested as one of the crew pushed him toward us. "That ship is Fleet property."

"Shut him up," Spratt ordered and glanced around. "Where in hell's the girl?" I'd been so intent on the action I had lost sight of Sheila as well.

Some more crewmen showed up with a transporter. "You two, find the woman," Spratt yelled. "The rest of you get the cases unloaded so we can get out of here."

"What's so important about your cargo," I asked as we were herded together and out of the way. A Corvette can't carry much.

"Twenty billion in credit bonds destined for New Caledonia," Wright said through gritted teeth. "Bearer bonds for Fleet operations."

That would be the money Fleet used to pay for fuel, repairs, and supplies from the friendly colonies. It didn't make a great deal of sense to travel all the way back to Earth whenever you needed toilet paper so they lived off the local economies when they could. Twenty billion was a huge haul for Spratt. It would finance the Consortium for years if he took it back, and that was a big if.

"I'm really going to get in trouble for this," Wright groused. "There goes my career," as if that was his only concern. He'd be lucky to get out of this alive.

Two of Spratt's crew were holding their guns on us while the others began transferring the boxes containing the twenty billion. What was the value of each bond—one, two, or ten million? I tried to get my head around how many boxes it would take to hold so much wealth. Twenty billion was such an enormous number that I couldn't do the math.

One of the crewmen Spratt had sent after Sheila came out of a corridor. I had just noticed how ill-fitting his clothing was when...

"Charlie, where's..." one of our guards started to say when the newcomer shot him. Two more bolts quickly followed to drive the others into the hatch. It was Sheila with a blaster in each hand.

"Grab their guns, y'blasted fools," she yelled as she sent a couple more bolts of compressed energy toward the hatch. "Let's go!"

I didn't need much encouragement and neither did the others. We scooped up the weapons and ran after her.

"Did you get both blasters?" she asked once we'd gone a ways down the corridor.

I looked back. I could hear them yelling, but no one had come into sight as yet. "There was only a blaster and a stunner."

"Damn." She led us through an open hatchway. "We don't have much time. I expect they've alerted their shipmates already. Any ideas?"

"We need more firepower," I said. "Three blasters and a stunner aren't enough to overcome the few back there, let alone Spratt's shipmates." I pointed at Wright and Quince. "Do you both have experience with blasters?"

"Everyone in Fleet does, Sir," Quince said at once.

"Just a minute, sailor," Wright protested. "Why are you listening to him?"

"Because a pirate's the best man for the job, y'daft fool," Sheila said.

Staying alive and out of Spratt's hands was certainly my first priority. "Listen, they could take both ships and abandon us," I said. "We need to take the battle to them before that happens."

Quince was keeping one eye on the corridor while we talked. "They're not following us."

"Good," Wright said. "Cowards."

"No, bad," I replied. "It means Spratt isn't worried about us. Sheila, how did you manage to knock out the two crewmen who came after you?"

"When they found me I just told them I was frightened and ran away," she said. "Then I kicked one in the balls, grabbed his blaster. and shot the other one." She paused. "I shot the second one after I took his clothes."

Wright looked shocked. "You shot an unarmed man?"

Sheila looked him straight in the eye. "Damn right, and I might do it again if you don't shut y'fucking blowhole."

"We need to get back to the Corvette." I said. "Spratt's going to be concentrating on moving the bonds, so he might not leave a guard there."

"We've got to get those bonds back," Wright said. "I can't allow some damn colonist to steal..." His voice cut off quickly when Sheila twitched the tip of her blaster in his direction.

"Can we catch them in a cross-fire?" I asked.

"There's another corridor," Quince said. "That's the way we came earlier."

"All right. You two go that way. We'll backtrack from here." I felt around. "Here," I tossed the second blaster to the Ensign and kept the stunner for myself. "Good luck."

Sheila and I waited for them to get to the other corridor before we started back. "All we have to do is take over a guarded ship with four people, a stunner, and three blasters," I said, feeling considerably less confident than I hoped I sounded.

"Surely that's no problem for a real pirate," she replied. After seeing her in action, I wondered who the real pirate was.

There were three men guarding the Corvette. Two were armed with projectile weapons—nasty things that threw metal slugs instead of stuns or bolts. "Spratt means business," I whispered.

"Oh, y'be afraid of a slug thrower?" she shot back.

"Being hit by one of them is just not something I might enjoy."

"Argh, yer a blasted coward, I think. Is that why y'chose the damned stunner? For myself, I think I fancy one of theirs." She pointed toward the guards. "Y'shoot the one on the left and I'll do the right. Then we both shoot the middle one." Sounded like a sound strategy to me. "On my count," she continued.

I let off my first shot before she finished saying "Three." My first went wide but the next was dead on target, as was Sheila's. Both men fell to the deck just as the third's shot hit the drum beside me with a nasty ringing sound.

"Down," Sheila yelled as she sent a few more bolts at the guard. I shot twice as I dropped to the deck. No further projectiles came our way.

"I'll take a look," I whispered over my shoulder and peeked around the drum, only to see Sheila kneeling to retrieve one of the rifles. Just then, two crewmen came through the hatch.

"Watch it!" I yelled, stood, and shot wildly. I must have winged one, for he yelped and dropped his blaster. The other swung his toward me, ignoring the kneeling Sheila, who swung her rifle and cracked the guy across the knees. He let out a scream of pain as his shot went wild. She reversed the rifle and pointed it. "Get their weapons," she shouted.

I retrieved the other rifle and both blasters. "What do we do with them?" I pointed at the two guards.

"Don't be daft. Didn't they teach anything pirate school? Shoot them... or I will."

I didn't doubt for a moment that she'd do it. I stunned the two conscious ones, figuring that knocking them out was the better alternative. That would keep them out of action for a couple of hours.

Some of Spratt's men remained on the Corvette. "They can pick us off if we try the hatch," I warned.

"Argh, no time to be shy," she said and made for the hatch with her rifle at the ready. A shot hit the deck by her left foot.

I pulled her back out of the line of fire. "Don't be a damn fool."

This was bad. With armed men on board there was no way we could overcome the odds when the rest of Spratt's crew showed up. But, seeing her beside me with a slug thrower in one hand and a blaster in the other gave me confidence that we might stand a chance.

We heard a ruckus behind us. Wright ran out of an adjacent corridor with Quince behind. Both were firing bolts over their shoulders. There was some return fire.

"Crap, looks like Spratt's men have arrived," I said.

Sheila pulled one of the drums around and rested the rifles on top. "Pull the others around us to make a fort," she shouted as Quince and the Ensign joined us.

"We shot at the transporter crew," Quince said breathlessly. "I got two of them before they started shooting back. Eight men left."

"Why aren't you inside the Corvette?" Wright asked.

"Shooter inside," Sheila barked. "But go ahead and try if you want." She sent a slug ricocheting down the corridor. "That should make them a bit more cautious."

It was only a matter of time before Spratt overwhelmed the four of us. Not only did he have more firepower and men, but he could wait us out.

"Do we rush the ship?" Quince asked. "With enough firepower we might get lucky."

"Sure, and they'll get some of us in the process," I answered. "Is there another way into the ship?" I asked Wright.

Only he was nowhere to be seen. "Oh shit," Sheila said and pointed at the hatch. Wright was kneeling unprotected to one side at an access panel. A second later, the hatch slammed shut.

"Jesus, he's cut off our escape route," Sheila said and swung the rifle around.

I was afraid she was going to shoot and knocked the barrel aside. "What's he doing," I asked Quince as a white frost began to appear around the seal where the Corvette snuggled to the station.

"He's accessed the maintenance override!" Quince said admiringly and explained. "He's venting the air."

So the frost was air being propelled from the interior. Tough on those inside, but that was their problem.

A bolt passed so close that it singed my hair. I heard two pops from Sheila's rifle before Quince and I turned and sent a few bolts in return. "Get back here," Quince yelled at Wright.

In the next few minutes there was a fierce exchange of metal slugs, blaster bolts, and stun charges between the corridor and our little fort. I think we got a couple of them, for they pulled back momentarily as a hideous scream sounded. It dropped in a moment to a low roar of rushing air. The hatch was slowly opening and letting the station's air rush inside.

"Oh my God," Quince said. Wright was lying in a pool of blood. I grabbed a rifle, pulled Sheila along, and threw her through the hatch before I turned around to see Quince struggling with Wright's body. "I'm not leaving the kid," he said gruffly enough that I had to help him, if only to speed things up.

We closed the hatch. The inside was a mess with the two asphyxiated crewmen, and Tiger, Tag, and Wright's bodies. As we placed them all in the cargo bay I noticed that there were still two of the eight bond boxes inside—five billion at least.

"Can you get this thing fired up?" I asked Quince. He sprang to the engine console and began waking the Corvette's engines and drives.

"I'll take the con," Sheila said and dropped into the leftmost seat.

"Not on your life," I said as I slid into the right. "Fleet are traditionalists: Pilot's seat is always on dockside." She cursed as I started activating the controls, but I was too busy to listen.

In the bowels of the Corvette I could hear the blink drives starting to spin up as we moved away from the station on our steering jets. Quince was getting us ready to blink out of here.

When we were a hundred meters away, I used the steering jets to guide us across to where Spratt's ship was docked and maneuvered directly behind it.

"What are you doing?" Sheila asked. "We need to get away from here."

"I am not about to let Spratt get away with fifteen billion," I replied. "I'm going to make certain he stays put."

With careful use of the steering jets I ran the armored hull of the Corvette along the other ship as I gently goosed the engines. There was a terrible, grating, metallic sound as we scraped along, snapping off the steering nozzles and anything else sticking off the hull.

At the end of the run, I flipped the ship around and went in to opposite direction, paring away anything that we'd missed on the first run. "The first rule of pirating," I explained, "is to make sure your target can't maneuver."

At the end of the second pass we sat off the stern, where the huge reaction engines sat on their outriggers. I pointed the Corvette at the nearest boom and goosed the main engine. It hurt me to use the small ship as a battering ram, but it was the only weapon I had.

There was brief resistance before the boom twisted under the pressure and the nozzle was pointing back toward Spratt's ship. Then I did the second one.

"That should keep him here for a while," I said. "Now, let's get out of here." I was about to set the coordinates for home when Quince poked a blaster in my ribs. "I hope you're setting up for New Caledonia. Fleet would like to get their bonds back."

"That's exactly what I was thinking," I lied and quickly changed the settings. "You know what that means for Sheila and me—prison and lawsuits."

"Well, I'm sure that they'll consider all you've done when..." Quince never finished the sentence as he slumped to the deck.

"Well, I guess these things have their use," Sheila said as she turned her stunner toward me. "I just hate ungrateful people," she said with a glance at the sleeping Quince. "Besides, I was wondering what my life might be like with a ship like this and a few billion in bonds." She cocked an eyebrow. "Unless y'think of taking it all for yerself?" The tip of the stunner was unwavering.

"Of course not," I said.

"Argh, don't lie," she said. "I know y'got the balls to take it, Hart."

"As I've been telling you all along; I'm an officer, not a pirate. The Alliance desperately needs money and ships."

She kept the stunner on me. "I've insurance, banks, and a life of debt facing me back home. I can't walk away from all this with nothing." She hesitated and then put the stunner away. "Aw, the hell with it. Do y'think the Alliance would take another pirate Captain?"

I smiled as I engaged the drives. "Always. And we'll even give you an eye patch."

DERELICTION OF DUTY

A Chronicle of The 142ⁿᵈ Starborne

Patrick Thomas

DAMN IT TO HELL," YELLED MAJOR HANS BENEDICT. EVER SINCE HE HAD ASSUMED command of the *Colossus*-class warship *Behemoth*, he never seemed to receive any good news in his ready room. Today was not about to change that.

"Too late," replied Captain Shana Morales, with a faint smile.

"This intel is solid?" Benedict asked, obviously hoping that it wasn't.

Morales nodded.

"So the entire post simply abandoned the people on the planet below. Did they even try an evac? The crew is barely five thousand. That sky station can house half a million. That's a quarter of the population of Ozark," said Benedict.

"Not from what Shodon and the rest of our people were able to send out before Colonel Hastings took them prisoner," said Morales. She hesitated for a moment. "She also refused to recognize your authority."

Benedict shrugged. "Some days so do I. I can't believe she would cut tail and run."

"Sir, it is in the manual. In case the reanimated..." The military refused to officially call them zombies even if everyone else did. "...go rogue, procedure dictates to secure military facilities from outside contaminates."

"That's meant for the battlefield. Hastings is in a god-damned satellite three miles above the planet. No way for a zombie to get in there." Benedict was a simple, direct man who called a zombie a zombie and a vampire a blood sucker.

"Unless she brings them in, Sir," replied his second in command.

"She has docking bays with full surveillance. Quarantine the lot for thirty hours, give each a cot, rations, and a field pot. Tell them anyone who leaves their assigned area will be shot. In hour thirty one she'd know if they were human or not. Snipers could take out any of the infected. While she's being lazy and a coward, people are dying below her, which is only feeding the monsters' ranks. If it continues unchecked, the entire population will be turned and the only option left will be to nuke the planet."

Morales cringed at the thought. Humans who were clever enough to avoid the zombies would be killed with the monsters. Then she cleared her throat. "Sir, not to be indiscrete, but there are rumors regarding your past...relationship with the Colonel."

Benedict smiled wearily. "Captain, stop pussyfooting around. Yes, we slept together. We were even an item, but that was a lifetime ago. By refusing to assist the people she was assigned to protect she is giving aid to the enemy. She will be treated no differently than any other traitor to mankind."

"I never doubted that for a second, Sir. My concern is that your emotional attachment may impair your duty. I still feel it is improper every time you take point on a mission. In this case that feeling is doubled."

"Morales, I started my career in the Host more than thirty years ago as a sapper. I can get into any ship or station, space or planetside, and put it out of commission. If you can honestly tell me we have someone better than me in this command, I'll consider it. Otherwise, I take point." Benedict, whose crew cut had more gray than black, lifted an eyebrow making the scar on the left side of his face stretch out. It was an offer of a chance to speak. The small brunette declined. "Besides, if I don't make it back, you'll probably do a much better job of command than I have."

"I doubt that very much, Sir," said Morales.

"Let's hope you don't have to find out."

The battlestation *Kyklopes* orbiting the planet Ozark was *Medusa*-class and could drop five hundred *Harpy* attack ships in less than six minutes. It had enough armaments to hold off a small fleet or destroy a city on the planet's surface.

A *Colossus*-class warship, of which *Behemoth* was the only one known to have survived the conflagration, had the firepower to destroy a *Medusa*. It could just as easily be damaged or even obliterated in a fair fire fight. Benedict wanted to take the station intact. It was the best solution to retake the planet, if it wasn't already too late. The reanimated spread their infection quickly and exponentially. Every hour counted.

The job of the sapper had changed much since its start by the French military. Then a sapper had to take out a fortress' cannons. Now it was a unit in the Host that specialized in taking out enemy ships, stations, and fortifications.

A station was relatively easy to get to, at least compared to a starship. Although it moved through orbit at thousands of miles per hour, compared to something traveling between systems it was practically standing still.

A *Harpy* cruised on minimal power to within five thousand miles of *Kyklopes*. Any closer raised the risk of detection too high. The approach was made in transports designed to mimic debris and meteors, affectionately referred to as coffins. It was an apt term as there were no active systems for radar or other detection methods to pick up. Even life support was supplied by old-fashioned pressurized tanks that had to be adjusted from within by hand.

The *Harpy* had missile tubes made to launch the coffins and that momentum was how they approached their target. It was the technological equivalent of shooting someone out of a cannon in an attempt to hit a mark thousands of miles away. Each sapper was responsible for programming their own trajectory. That way if someone missed there was no one to blame but themselves, which explained why most sappers had at least a working engineering and physics background, in addition to explosives and special ops training.

Sapper teams were traditionally kept to five members. Much more and there was the chance that the systems would note an abnormality. Any less and there wasn't enough manpower to get the job done.

Benedict was a sapper legend. There were rumors that he wasn't human, but no one had ever figured out what he was supposed to be. Nor had it ever been mentioned to his face after he broke the jaw of the first man foolish enough to say it. Benedict reviewed the plan with the other four members of his team. Those spots were evenly spilt between the genders and the ranks. Private Ricco Jonas, Corporal Sheila Barnes, Captain Ami Chang, and Colonel Leon Westminster.

Westminster technically outranked Major Benedict, but it was not an issue. When the orders came to return to Earth during the conflagration, they arrived with dark details and statistics. 66.6% of the planet's population had died the first day. The message that finally reached them was not sent until day five. The only known free survivors were the upper-level bureaucrats and politicians that had summoned forth the darkness and managed to conceal their self-important hides in shelters. The planet the *Behemoth* was stationed around was under attack by the monsters. The *Behemoth*'s leaving would have doomed one hundred million to save thousands who had a hand in their own doom and that of billions of dead.

When General Dailey issued the order for the 142nd Starborne to leave, Major Benedict ordered it rescinded with his side arm cocked and pointed at the General's head. It was a bloodless takeover. The Sway had been mistreating the soldiers in the Host for years, risking their lives without rhyme or reason. Benedict's actions had the benefit of having both and the major quickly earned the crew's loyalty. Most of them. There were still a few diehard hold outs, Dailey among them. Those that decided to serve recognized Benedict's authority, but he steadfastly refused to grant himself a higher rank. It would have smacked too much of a coup.

Benedict had a habit of calculating all five trajectories and posting them. The team always made sure to double check their own results against his and to adjust accordingly. Benedict had over a 96% success rate for getting the coffins within spitting distance of the targets. Average outside of the 142nd Starborne was about 82%.

Sapper tradition dictated a last meal. In the early days of the sappers in the Host, the number of sappers who made it to retirement after twenty years was pitifully low. As training and selection methods improved, so did the life expectancy, but the tradition remained.

So did the writing of a last will and testament before each mission. Once that was complete, the five sappers climbed in their coffins and launched themselves at sky station *Kyklopes*.

A trip in a coffin is a singularly isolated experience. The coffins had limited propulsion systems, mostly pressurized gasses that could be released to steer. With no radar, all navigation was done visually. The windows had built in layers of magnifiers, much like old fashioned bi- and trifocals, with each smaller circle being a higher level.

The smallest was the equivalent to a powerful observatory caliber telescope. If something was not visible through a window, there were mirrors that were manually adjusted.

Every coffin contained a radio, but traditionally they were only used to give a suicide order. Since even a sapper didn't want to throw away his life on a useless kamikaze run, the coffins were laced with enough explosives to punch a hole in almost any armor plating they could make impact with.

The sappers had their individual ways of passing the time in the void. Jonas sang opera in five languages. Barnes composed poetry. Chang wrote out calculations for pi. In her eight years as a sapper she had filled over a thousand pages. Westminster crocheted.

Benedict studied scans of a very old tome, the very one that was alleged to have been used to summon what now ruined the Earth. They had been smuggled out at great cost prior to the conflagration. Benedict had acquired them since taking command. He studied it in small pieces, using a non-sequential pattern to stave off the madness that claimed the last two people to read it.

So far he remained perfectly sane. At least as far as those around him had been able to tell.

Kyklopes soon loomed. The calculations were dead on. Each coffin launched a pair of grapple lines. The end of each contained a sac filled with an adhesive. Contact with the *Kyklopes'* hull burst the sacs. The adhesive hardened and the coffin was reeled in slowly until it lay flush with the station's armor plating. An airtight seal was formed and a combination of energy and mechanical tools cut though it in less than a half hour.

Each sapper had their jobs. Systems control, life support, sensors, power. Benedict had his own tasks, but because of his new station in the 142th's hierarchy they were made easier than ever before. Control panels were positioned throughout the station and he made his way to the closest one. Using a master override code, he subtly altered the station's programming. With luck, it wouldn't be noticed until it was too late for anything to be done about it. If not, at least *Behemoth* and the 142nd Starborne were in good hands with Morales.

On a station the size of *Kyklopes*, not every soldier knew everyone they were stationed with. Five thousand was a lot of faces to get lost in. For that reason Benedict didn't bother with things like crawl spaces and maintenance tubes. Those places were filled with sensors and alarms because that's where the brass expected saboteurs to hide.

After thirty-three years in the Host, Benedict oozed military. No one would ever think he wasn't a soldier. All he did was change his division patch on his right shoulder from the 142nd to that of *Kyklopes* Station and he had all the camouflage he needed.

Common areas were no problem. The hard part was getting into a secure section. Soldiers knew who they served with, who relieved them and when. Any change in the regular grind would raise suspicions.

Benedict didn't bother to try any of the usual tactics, instead opting for the bull in a china shop option. He walked right up to the guards at the brig and saluted.

"I'm here for the interrogation," he barked.

The guards, a pair of corporals, returned the salute, but did not stand aside.

"Begging your pardon, Sir, but we have not received word of any interrogation," said one.

"I just left the command center. I haven't had to interrogate a prisoner in ten years. I found it distasteful then and more so now, but the Colonel ordered me to try as she hadn't gotten everything she wanted from them. Apparently the old lady believes new blood is the answer. Personally, I doubt it. Please check your orders. I just left her and she sent them before I left." He held up a card key that was supposed to be coded for the cell locks on one end and genetically coded for the card holder on the other. "Call her if you need to verify."

The last part was a bit of a gamble. Corporals tended to be wary of their COs and were fearful of bothering them. If the order was good they would be scolded or worse. If they called and learned Hastings didn't send it, his secrecy was blown and things would get bloody.

They checked the comm. "The orders are here, as is Colonel Hastings electronic signature seal. You're clear to go in, Major." They motioned and searched him for weapons. He only had one and it wasn't something that they would be looking for. "Go in."

"These are desperate men and women. It is possible they may escape. If they do somehow manage to get out, don't hesitate. Shoot them." Another gamble. No decent rescuer would encourage the guards to shoot people he was trying to save.

"Understood, Sir," said the corporal on the left.

Benedict smiled. "Of course, do whatever you can to avoid hitting me."

"We'll keep that in mind, Sir," he said, as he and his partner turned keys ten feet apart. The door to the brig slid open.

"I appreciate it," Benedict said and walked through with the authority of a god among men.

There were a dozen of *Behemoth*'s crew imprisoned. Captain Shoden, who had led up what was intended as a diplomatic mission, was in the first cell.

Shoden stood confused and looked behind Benedict, but kept his silence.

"It's fine, Shoden. You can speak freely," Benedict said.

"Have you settled things with Hastings?" he asked.

"Not yet," said Benedict.

"Are you here to rescue us?" asked Shoden.

"It's coming," said Benedict.

"If you don't mind me asking, Sir, then why are you here?" asked Shoden.

"I figure sooner or later, Hastings will notice I'm here and want to talk," said Benedict. "I could have made it to the bridge, but the Colonel would probably assume the worst and have me shot on sight. This way she'll just have me escorted at gunpoint to her." He didn't mention he was also a distraction for his fellow sappers. The cells were wired for sight and sound and this entire conversation could be being monitored.

"I'll trust your judgment on this, Sir. How long until your plan works?"

"Hastings is slipping. She should have already noticed," said Benedict. "They treating you okay?"

Shoden shrugged. "Could have been better, could have been worse."

Benedict nodded and looked at his watch. "I don't have all day." He inserted his card into Shoden's cell lock and the bars slid into the walls. Benedict waited. "That should have set off an alarm. I only programmed it with the most basic pass code. They've been real sloppy. Please step out of the cell." Shoden did. Benedict timed off thirty seconds. "Okay, you can go back in," said Benedict, using the card to put the bars in place. "No reason for them to shoot you when they come in. Or me either." Benedict put his hands out and up and stood waiting.

The outer brig doors opened and six armed men entered using standard Host procedure, each soldier moving in as the others covered them and repeating the pattern until Benedict was in the sight of each solider without any of them being in another's line of fire.

"Do not move," ordered a sergeant.

"Took you long enough. My arms are getting tired. Can we move this along?" said Benedict.

He was unceremonious secured, again searched for weapons, then had his arms cuffed behind his back. "March."

Benedict listened, but not until he looked back at Shoden and the rest of his people in the cells and winked at them.

It took them a relatively short time until they reached the bridge. Two soldiers preceded him onto the command deck, took up positions on either side of Colonel Hastings and trained their weapons on Benedict.

"Still can't trust your self-control if you are left alone with me, Andie?" said Benedict.

"Hans, what the hell are you doing on my station?" Hastings demanded.

"I would think you'd be more concerned with how the hell I got on your station," said Benedict.

"In time. I can't believe you were stupid enough to come here. The fact that your people didn't come back should have been a clue that you are not welcome on *Kyklopes*."

"You're actions say no, but your eyes say yes," said Benedict. "And the status of my diplomatic team is something I want to talk to you about."

"Diplomatic team? They arrived and told me that *Kyklopes* was now under your command. Forgetting the fact that I outrank you…"

"Only because you slept with a general and his staff. Or was that you sat on a general's staff?" said Benedict.

"Why is it if a man is promoted, it must be because of merit, but a woman had to spread her legs to get ahead?"

"Or she could just give some," said Benedict. The major knew full well Hastings had earned her rank, but he also knew the rumors were a sore point with her. It would be safest for his people to have her angry and not thinking straight.

"You have no authority to order me or anyone else. You disobeyed direct orders," said Hastings.

"I left a few old doffers to stew in a mess of their own making. They betrayed humanity. Unlike the rest of the dead, they got what they deserved," said Benedict.

"That sounds very noble, but you are a soldier. Soldiers obey orders, not lead coups."

"Not ones that would leave millions more to die. And it's not a coup. I did not take over control of any government body."

"Just the 142nd Starborne, which has enough firepower to take over an entire system," said Hastings.

"Not our job or goal. Our job is the same as it ever was—keep the peace. Just a little more difficult now that the monsters aren't even pretending to be on our side. Even harder than that when those in charge of the forces meant to protect the people abandon them to the monsters. Which is worse, I wonder?"

Benedict's words practically drew blood. "So you're a philosopher now? We did not abandon the citizens on Ozark. We did everything by the book," said Hastings. "I followed orders."

Benedict chuckled.

"You think that's funny?" demanded Hastings.

"Only in the most tragic of ways. For you to stand there and tell me of all people about how you always follow orders. We went through the academy together."

"Pranks and breaking curfew hardly constitute disobeying orders," said Hastings.

"We've served together. You made captain for breaking orders. The only reason you weren't court-martialed wasn't because you did the right thing. It was because the right thing brought victory," said Benedict.

"That matter is classified," barked Hasten.

"By a government that no longer exists. Tell me, when did you stop being a real soldier and become a bureaucrat? What did they give you for your soul?" asked Benedict.

His answer was a sharp slap which left his left cheek only slightly redder than Hastings' entire face.

"I could have you shot for treason," said Hastings.

"I was about to say the same thing," retorted Benedict.

Hastings' laugh was a harsh, brutal sound. She walked to the sensor station to verify there were no ships in the Ozark system. "You're in my house, Hans, unless you're going to magically produce the *Behemoth* and try to take away my station."

Benedict's answer was a shrug. "I'm hoping that won't be necessary. All you have to do is admit you made a mistake and start correcting it. There are still untainted humans on Ozark's surface. Evac and quarantine them before it's too late."

"I am not going to risk my people or my station. It's too late for the people down there and for that I'm truly sorry," said Hastings.

"So am I. So, does anyone else on this bridge have the balls or breasts to stand up here and tell your CO that she's wrong?" asked Benedict, making eye contact with each of the bridge and security officers. One man, a Lieutenant Shaker, looked as if he was about to speak, but ended up just looking down at his polished boots. "Pathetic. Colonel Hastings, you and your officers are hereby relieved of both your duty and command. I will ask you to peacefully bring yourselves to the brig to await your sentencing."

Benedict had spoken with such subtle conviction it was several moments before the laughter and mocking began.

"Hans, I hadn't believed the rumors about your losing your mind were true, but I guess they are," said Hastings, sitting in the command chair. "It's so very sad. Take him to the brig to rot with the other traitors."

When Benedict didn't move, one of the six security men tried to move him. Benedict took his gun away in one swift move, cocking him in the jaw with the butt of the weapon. The man fell unconscious.

"Sad when a soldier has never actually seen combat, isn't it?" said Benedict.

The other five tried to fire on Benedict, but none of their guns were in working condition. Before they could move to restrain the Major physically, Benedict had moved so he was sitting on Hastings lap in the command chair.

"Jericho," he said and the safety systems flared to life. Armored plating snapped down from the ceiling, reinforced by energy shielding. The bunker was a failsafe built to protect the commanding officer of a station or starship in the case of a mutiny. Only command-level officers were supposed to even know about the lockdown, or the fact that all operations could be run from inside the bunker, with enough life support and food to last one person three months.

"How the hell were you able to trigger my command bunker?" demanded Hastings.

"I've told you—It's no longer your command. I even gave you a chance at redemption, which you wasted," said Benedict, standing up in the cramped space around the command chair.

"I'm putting an end to this." said Hastings. "Joshua." The code to open the bunker was ignored. The Colonel said it three more times with no more luck than the first.

"*Kyklopes* no longer recognizes your authority," said Benedict.

"You don't have the authority to do that. Only a five-star or above with a thimble controller could..." Benedict waved his index finger, and then touched it with his thumb. A sleek, grey metal cap appeared, revealing the failsafe device the upper brass held over the fleet. One allowed the user to override all other commands over any computer in the Host. There were rumored to be thirteen in existence. The praetor had one, as did the twelve highest ranking members of the Host. "How in the hell did you get a thimble? Forget how you got it. How'd you program it to your DNA?"

"Not your concern," said Benedict.

"So you shut down the handheld weapons before you let us capture you in the brig," said Hastings. Benedict's face stayed stony. "You could have taken command without us even knowing where you were, couldn't you?"

Benedict said nothing. There was no reason to tell her that total control of the station could only be achieved after the wearer had been on the bridge at least once, even with a thimble. True he had laid the groundwork at the first console he had come upon, but it wouldn't begin until he spoke the codeword on the bridge. He had chosen Andie. Benedict knew he'd have no problem working the Colonel's name into conversation. Once he said it, all weapons, both personal and station wide, were rendered useless.

"You still won't be able to take this station alone," said Hastings.

"Andie, you should know never to bet against me after having faced me in over three decades of war games. You know damn well from in here all I have to do is shut down life support outside and I win," said Benedict.

"That would be murder!" shouted Hastings.

"No worse than what you did to the people planetside. If anything, it's quicker, more humane," said Benedict. "No one is forced to eat human flesh or feel their mind slowly stolen away. And I'm not alone. *Behemoth* is in weapons' range." The last could have been a bluff. Benedict didn't know for sure, but he was working under the assumption that Barnes had indeed knocked out the sensors that otherwise would have picked up his ship.

"You'd kill your own people," said Hastings.

"I can affect every section but the brig," said Benedict. He didn't bother to pretend not to notice his former lover reach behind her back to slide out a hidden blade. "Andie, you really should have changed where you hide your knives. The thimble has a built in weapons system." In reality it had a one shot electric blast that would probably knock her out, but if he fired too soon it would be an hour before he could use it again. And she'd still have the knife. Plus there was the very real risk the surge would end up frying the thimble. It was too valuable a tool to risk. "I'd prefer not to kill you, if for nothing else for what we once meant to each other. Please drop the knife on the floor and kick it to me."

Hastings did as instructed.

"This would be much easier if you helped by ordering your people to the second docking bay," said Benedict.

"What are you going to do to them?" asked Hastings.

"Punishment by way of a mission, not execution," said Benedict.

"Not spacing them?"

"I'm fighting the monsters, not looking to become one," said Benedict.

"Your word?" said Hastings.

"Yes." Benedict handed her the microphone.

Hastings did as she was asked.

It took several hours until the five thousand crew members were rounded up. There was some question of whether or not everyone had arrived, but security teams from the *Behemoth* were doing a thorough search of the station for stragglers. There were relatively few problems.

Benedict stepped up to the walkway that stood far above the docking bay. When he got to the center, he paused and looked out over the five thousand soldiers below him. Then he shook his head.

"For those of you that do not know me, I am Major Hans Benedict and since the destruction of Host Command on Earth, I have assumed command of our remaining forces." Assorted grumbles and mumbles rose up from floor level. Benedict lifted a hand to quiet the assembled. "The opinion of grunts has never mattered in the Host. That much has not changed." A couple of half hearted "ha's" acknowledged the dark humor in the comment. "I am ashamed and disappointed in the behavior of every single person serving on *Kyklopes* from the CO down to the lowest grunt. Your mission was to protect the people of Ozark. When the zombie threat reared its rotting, flesh-eating head here, the Host turned away, abandoning every man, woman, and child on the planet below. That is unacceptable and that kind of dereliction of duty is punishable by death in times of war. And make no mistake, we are at war all across the galaxy." Fearful chatter filled the air. Hastings was screaming very unkind things about her former lover, the mildest of which was calling him an oath breaker.

Benedict again raised a hand. "Execution of soldiers who made a mistake, soldiers who let their fear rule them instead of the other way around, serves no good purpose. The Host still needs its soldiers. Ozark still has people in danger. Here is what will happen. All of you will be split into five hundred teams of ten and dropped at various points around the planet. You will all have trackers which will let you search for life signs and drop points to bring survivors to. You will also be given working weapons and ammo once planetside. As of this moment, all of you are rankless." Shouts rose. Rankless soldiers had less than no rights. "To regain first rank, each soldier must rescue at least ten humans. If you lose a member of your team, their duty falls upon the survivors." Benedict had been in enough combat situations to know that some soldiers would betray honor to save their own skins. He did not want the soldiers fighting or killing each other.

"Anyone who completes this mission will be taken back into the Host, this incident forgiven. You may choose your own teams and move toward the *Harpies* for transport. Also, we will need officers. Teams that go above and beyond will be promoted at my discretion. The playing field is level. I plan to have at least the same number of officers on *Kyklopes* when this is done. Good luck."

With that, there was some enthusiasm. Now everyone was either dreaming of rising up through ranks that were formerly denied them or scheming on how to hold on to what they once had.

Benedict met quickly with his senior staff. "I need quarantine plans for at least fifty thousand, but plot out up to full capacity. Have *Harpies* standing by for rescue and evac at all times. I also want bombing solutions for the largest concentrations of the enemy. Start broadcasting on all frequencies that we're coming for them and include where the drop points are. Now let's get those people out of there."

In less than two hours, the *Harpies* had deployed all but one hundred soldiers. Hastings was in that last party. Benedict came to see her off.

The former colonel was trembling. She ran up to Benedict. "Hans, I'm fifty-two years old. I'm not fit for combat conditions. Don't make me go down there."

Benedict looked into her eyes. "Don't. You're better than this."

"Don't send me. Please, I'm begging you."

"There is only one other option..."

"Yes, I'll take anything," pleaded Hastings.

Benedict unholstered the side arm he was now wearing and pointed it between the eyes of his once lover.

"If that is what you want. I'm sorry it had to end like this," said Benedict. "Goodbye."

Hastings fell to the floor, crab walking backwards up the *Harpy* ramp, screaming with every hand and footstep. Benedict stopped a half smile and motioned for the hatch to be closed.

"That was very wrong," said Benedict.

"That Hastings disgraced herself or that you pointed a weapon at a former officer and friend?" asked Colonel Westminster.

"That I enjoyed it," answered Benedict.

PERSPECTIVE

Tony Ruggiero

WHY DO YOU THINK THEY CALL THEM COFFINS?" LIEUTENANT KEEFE COULDN'T HELP smirking as the statement flowed across his lips to the new ensign who just joined the ship.

"But it's not in the literal sense of the word . . . is it?" The ensign asked in an unsure voice.

"Of course it is," Keefe said and then chuckled. "Well not exactly," he admitted. "These coffin-shaped canisters are an older version of an ordnance carrier converted to transport the vampire to target, hence the new name of coffin."

"Oh I get it," the ensign chuckled hesitantly, "But, Sir, don't you ever get nervous about . . . well having them around?"

"The vampires? Nah. They're loaded into the containers in the safe area. Once inside the container it's locked, then we shove them in the torpedo launch bay and shoot them out. Think of it like loading a cartridge or bullet into the breach of a weapon and then firing it.

The ensign appeared to struggle with the analogy but Keefe went on. "The container doesn't open until it reaches the surface of the planet—hopefully intact—I hate to lose these containers they're such a pain in the ass to refit."

"But how do they get back here to the ship?"

"When their mission is done—or when the sun comes up—whichever comes first, they have to return to the coffin.

"Why don't they just escape?" asked the ensign.

"Ah . . . good question, Keefe said. "You see, each vampire has a little cylinder imbedded in their bodies. The cylinder contains a tracking device and a small amount of liquid which is poison to them. If they don't follow orders, such as returning to their coffin, a signal is sent and releases the poison."

"So they follow orders . . . or else."

"Exactly. Later we send a pickup vehicle which magnetically latches on to them from several miles out. By using a strong magnetic field they are able to catapult the ships from the surface and back to the ship."

"What if something happens and you can't get them?" the ensign asked.

"Then they just sit there and wait. If they have to, they can go into an extended hibernation period until we can get to them. As long as their coffins stay sealed from the sunlight, they're okay."

"Must be one hell of a ride."

"You bet. The G's would cause sever damage to the body of a normal man, but the vampire body has amazing recuperative powers, plus the fact that the majority of the organs are no longer used anyway which makes them perfect. So any injury to organs still functioning, mainly the heart, repairs itself by the time they are back on board the main assault craft."

"What about surface fire?"

"What about it?"

"It still might hit the pickup vehicle or some of the coffins on the way back."

"Yeah—it might. But so what? The pickup vehicle is unmanned and it's not like the vampires are alive or anything. They are just tools—another weapon, nothing more."

The young ensign remained silent as he appeared to contemplate what he had just heard.

Keefe pointed and said, "The status board is completely green. That means that all the torpedo tubes are loaded. That's 150 coffins ready to go. Call the bridge and report that we're ready."

The ensign did as instructed. A few moments later the order came to launch the coffins. Lieutenant Keefe pressed one button and the green indicators for each coffin went from green to black, indicating a successful launch.

"Well that's all for now," Keefe said, "nothing left to do but wait for the pickup order."

"Is that all of the vampires?"

"From this ship it is every single one. But don't forget we have several transports in orbit, all carrying their own contingent of vampires—must be a big mission to send them all at once. Maybe even a complete annihilation of the planet populace."

"Can they do that?"

"The brass can do anything they want."

"No, I mean the vampires—can they kill an entire population?"

"I don't want to know if they do," Keefe quipped back. "I don't want to dirty my hands that much. Whoever's down there on the planet is the enemy anyway. Besides—"

Lieutenant Keefe was cut off by the communication system as an announcement began.

"Attention all hands, this is the Captain speaking. There has been an . . . event on the United Planet Ship *Excalibur*. The cargo of vampires they are carrying have somehow managed to break free of their confinement area and have taken over the ship. It appears that either the crew was unable to activate the poison cylinders or there was some form of malfunction. It is our understanding that the majority of the human crew has been killed in the process. Our orders are to destroy the *Excalibur* before the vampires try and escape. I know that many of you have friends and ship-mates on the *Excalibur*. I just want to assure you that if they are alive—killing them now will be for the best. I know if I was there, that is what I would want. Stand by all batteries."

"Kill the bastards," Lieutenant Keefe growled as he prepared to fire. "I know many of the officers on the *Excalibur*." Keefe switched on a video monitor which displayed the exterior view of space. He played with the controls until the image of the *Excalibur* filled the screen.

The Captain's voice came over the announcing system, "Standby. Standby. FIRE!"

Lieutenant Keefe pressed the fire button and held it down as if the additional pressure would result in a more intensive burst of energy. On the screen, the fire from multiple ships came to bear on the *Excalibur*—in a few moments the vessel was engulfed by the rays and exploded.

Five Years Later

"I just want to drop the scum off and be rid of them," Captain Priestly said to his executive officer. "I don't like their kind—damn blood suckers—vampires in the mili-tary—what's next!" He paced the bridge nervously as if by doing so his actions could somehow make the vampires go away.

The XO, Commander Keefe, wholeheartedly agreed with the Captain. He wanted to mention the operation that resulted in the destruction of the *Excalibur* years earlier, but it had been classified and the story altered, attributing the loss of the ship to enemy fire—It was better for morale.

Captain Priestly sighed deeply and continued pacing, ensuring that each footstep echoed loudly off of the steel deck plates.

Keefe recognized the Captain's mood and knew it was best to stay out of his way. The Captain could be explosive when he was not in complete control—the standard type "A" personality. This was one of those moments when the bridge of the ship, the United Planets Ship *Lexington*, seemed extremely small.

Keefe gazed up at the chronometer to check the arrival time at the target; the dis-play indicated less than two hours remained. The information regarding the mission was unknown to both him and the CO. The ship's computer had received the pre-pro-grammed coordinates from the Joint Chiefs so they were truly flying blind on this one.

He looked at the Captain and shrugged his shoulders. "Who knows?" he said. "But the fact that we won't have to send any of our men down to the planet has its benefits. It must be pretty messy if they are sending them in first."

"I suppose," Priestly agreed reluctantly. "But I still don't like this. I feel like I'm car-rying the black plague or something. And what if these creatures should get loose on my ship? I don't like this—none of this. What the hell are the JCS thinking about this whole concept of starving them for the op?"

Keefe could understand Priestly's concern all too well. The memory of these crea-tures relying on the blood of living beings, and the friends he had on the *Excalibur* mixed together like oil and water.

"In theory," Priestly began, "well . . . in military theory that is, it's probably a good concept to have them operate at peak performance, but from the rumors I've heard, the problem is that their hunger is not specifically predictable or controllable. If pushed too far, too fast, the creatures will attack anyone, including us."

Keefe looked at him curiously. He wondered how much the CO actually knew in regard to these vampires. "What else have you heard?"

"The scuttlebutt is that this breaking point, controlling their hunger, has some problems. Supposedly, they once managed to escape their captivity and they slaughtered the crew on the ship that was transporting them."

"Wonderful," Keefe muttered and then said to himself, *If only you knew it wasn't a rumor but the truth.*

"After that event, the control over the creatures was made supposedly foolproof," Priestly continued. "Nevertheless, even with all these risks, the end result of the effectiveness of the vampire units warrants their continuance in service. They have brought a tumultuous peace to the galaxy."

"Based upon fear," Keefe added his voice full of sarcasm.

"True," Priestly said, nodding his head. "I say send them all out of the airlock, jettison the whole bunch. If they aren't human, then they shouldn't be allowed to live."

"As much as I might agree, skipper, I don't think the Joint Chiefs would," Keefe said. "I just think I would feel better—safer—if they were somewhere else."

"Me too. But, the platoon is under extremely tight precautions with redundant security measures and perimeters maintained. Their commander assures us he has positive control of them."

"I still don't like it." Keefe scoffed. "Taking risks with the crew and ship. If something should go wrong . . . it could get messy."

"Well, they have been used successfully the past few years," Priestly said, "and apparently with much success as a fighting force."

"Yeah," Keefe agreed. "What's the buzz statement? A self-sustaining unit, as long as there is a warm-blooded enemy available. They're good-to-go under any conditions, minus the few exceptions of daylight, being blown apart, or being staked through the heart."

"And positive control," Priestly added, "the human-vampire hybrid controller. More of an abomination—blending species—such bullshit. You know what they are trying to do—create the ultimate killing machine. Abominations, I say—playing with creationism is a dangerous game."

The door to the bridge opened and a Navy Commander wearing black fatigues stepped onto the bridge.

"Speak of the devil," Captain Priestly said. "Here's their esteemed leader."

Commander Keefe turned in the direction and saw Commander Reese, the leader of the vampire unit. A hybrid: half human and half vampire, he appeared mostly human with the exception of the red pupils of his eyes and the pale skin. But unlike the men he led, he experienced no detrimental effect from sunlight—the benefit of the mixture of the two species.

"Commander Reese," the captain said, "please join us."

The commander strode over to where the CO and XO stood.

"Gentleman," he said in greeting.

"Tell me, Commander," Captain Priestly began, "seeing as how we are so close to the destination which even I was not informed of, where the hell are you taking us?"

The Commander hesitated, a look of confusion momentarily passing over the features of his face and then he spoke. "According to intelligence, this planet is at a stage of development that may pose a risk to our civilization due to their violent and destructive nature. Our mission is to infiltrate the native population to . . . " he paused as if he was carefully choosing his words, "to affect a change in their development."

"You mean kill them, don't you?" the Captain said. "It's a little late to be mincing words, Commander, isn't it?"

Commander Reese showed no emotion as he answered, "If that is what it takes to ensure survival, then yes, Sir. But there are always possibilities."

"Such a diplomat, Commander . . . your careful choice of words. And they call this war. Such bullshit—this is as dark ops as they come."

"The preservation and the security of the United Planets is our main concern," Commander Reese said plainly.

"That's a rehearsed answer if I ever heard one," Commander Keefe chimed in, "even from one of your kind."

Commander Reese looked sternly at the XO. "You don't approve of my kind."

"No. No, I don't, and with good reason," Keefe said, wanting to blurt out what happened five years ago. Instead he took another approach. "I can understand the creatures you command for they are an alien race which existed on another world. They are what they are and they can't help that. But I have issues with what you are; when we start altering the ways things are by using them in a way that perhaps they were not intended to be—or when we start playing the game of altering the species, I don't feel comfortable about that." His tone softened, "But at least you have some human inside of you, unlike your . . . men. They have no human in them. Hell, by all logic and legal standards, they are not even alive anymore."

"Definition is not always the accurate way to approach some situations," answered Reese.

Keefe ignored Reese's comment and continued, "It's such a wonderful ploy . . . they, these creatures, can't be held accountable under law because a dead person cannot commit murder. Nor can anyone scream forced servitude because dead people can't be slaves or used against their wills because simply stated they have no will to be concerned about. So the military gets off scott-free in terms of any liability. The lawyers have been and will be spinning for years over this one."

"But I am one of them," Reese said, his red pupils glowing strongly in the dim light of the bridge. "I possess characteristics of human and vampire. I accept what I have become because there was no choice."

"That's right," Priestly began, "you were part of the reconnaissance team that discovered them—they tried to kill you but your body reacted in a different way."

"One in a billion . . . they tell me," Reese added. "The odds of this type of mutation happening. I have no choice but to accept this living death."

"But you are still alive," Keefe countered, "not completely dead like the rest."

"Perhaps," Commander Reese said and offered no further explanation on that subject.

Keefe continued, "I'm curious, Reese, your men—the vampires, they were found on the devastated world on the edge of the system?"

"Yes," Reese agreed, his voice tentative sounding, as if he wished to avoid the subject.

"The chain of command had to be concerned about their destructive nature . . . " asked Keefe. "I mean after all—look what they had done to their own world."

"From what we were able to ascertain," Reese began, "after years of coexisting with the human colonists, there was a war of the vampire factions on the planet. Because vampires cannot reproduce in the normal sense, the only way to increase their numbers was to turn more and more of the human population into vampires so that they could fight each other. By this over-multiplication, the vampires destroyed their own food supply, which led them to the point of their own extinction. There was only a few hundred left out of thousands when the world was discovered."

"Perhaps that would have been better," Keefe said. "Maybe some other lives could have been spared."

"The extinction of a race?" asked Reese. "That's a bit cynical wouldn't you say?"

"Not really," Keefe snapped the defiance evident in his voice.

Reese continued, "Have not our own world and civilizations been on the brink of destruction several times? Have we not almost destroyed our race by war?"

"Not the same," Keefe scoffed.

"Why?" Reese countered. "Just because you do not agree with the way in which my kind live or survive."

"Like you said, Reese," Keefe retorted, "they destroyed their own food supply, which included the human inhabitants. That's murder."

"Is it that different than what some of the animals on our own world do to survive? Is that not the law of natural selection that the stronger species survives and the weaker perish?"

"But not at the expense of the human race?" Captain Priestly interjected.

"Exceptions to the rule, Sir, isn't that a double standard?" asked Reese, "The picking and choosing of who shall live and who shall die?"

"So you side with them?" Keefe asked.

"I side with what I am," Reese said casually. "Is that not what we all do? My race did not ask to be removed from the home world, as has been done. Maybe they would have perished and maybe not. The rules of evolution are never specific beyond the fact that the fittest part of a race will survive where the weakest shall perish. But by removing them from the planet—everything has changed. Perhaps for the worse. "

Keefe thought about what Reese said and could not avoid the fact that there was some logic on his stance.

A beep emanated from the communications console, followed by the announcement, "Communication for the Captain's Eyes Only," the computer voice said, "orders clarification."

"It's about damn time," Priestly said as he went over to the computer and retrieved the message.

Commanders Keefe and Reese stood together alone—the silence after the debated conversation seeming to haunt both of them, evident by their restless and fidgety movements.

Reese broke the silence. "It's happening all over again."

"What? What's happening?" Keefe asked.

Reese looked intently at Keefe and spoke, "An element of society has decided what the proper requirements are for those who shall be first-rate citizens and who shall be the dredges of society, who shall be trusted and who shall be feared, and who shall live and who shall die."

"What are you talking about?" Keefe asked. He stared at Reese quizzically as if not sure how to interpret the man's ramblings.

"History, Commander Keefe," Reese said as he smiled sardonically, "we never learn. We just keep repeating the same mistakes over and over."

"What the hell are you talking about?"

"Wait a minute," the captain interjected as he stepped back toward Reese and Keefe with a piece of paper in his hands. "I'm to ensure that your landing craft is permanently disabled? This is a one way? You're not . . . coming back . . . ?"

"No Captain, we are not coming back," Reese began. "Unfortunately, the rest of our so-called civilized world agrees with your position. We are a threat and an undesirable element. We are the last of our kind and we are to be deposited on this world and left to our own ends as to whether we live or die."

"So what you said earlier . . . that the life on this planet was a threat to our civilization was all just bullshit?"

"Yes," Reese agreed. "This planet is some backwater world with very little technical capability. I understand that the culture is still entrenched in myth and legends. We are to be deposited here and left to our own devices."

"But you . . . you're not like the others . . . Why you?" Keefe asked.

"I still require blood to survive, so I too am considered a risk. I am the only one of my race. And I also am a threat of polluting the human gene pool."

"And what about the other vampires?" asked Keefe.

"They were all killed with the exception of me and my group. We are the last of our kind. We were spared by the fact that I was able to convince the Joint Chiefs of my argument of survival of the fittest. So we are being left on this planet where there is no chance of space travel for a very long time. The odds suggest that we will not survive that long, but this way the conscience of mankind is not completely blemished by the destruction of another race."

"Orbit established," the computer said.

"View screen on," Priestly said.

As the screen initialized, a planet loomed in the main viewing screen. They all stared at the blue oceans, the land masses of brown, gold, green, and white which were accentuated by the assorted shapes of clouds that spotted the atmosphere.

After a few moments of silence Captain Priestly spoke, "Well let's get to it then. Commander, join your . . . men in the shuttle launch and we'll get you on your way." The captain then turned his back on Commander Reese in a dismissive gesture.

"Good luck," Keefe said, the words flowing across his lips before he had a chance to consider what he was saying.

"Thank you," Reese said and departed the bridge.

Captain Priestly and Commander Keefe stood in silence as the computer counted off the time to shuttle departure. Finally Keefe spoke, "God help them."

"Who?" Priestly asked, "The people on the planet or the vampires?"

Keefe smirked and said, "You know, I'm not sure anymore. Some of the things that Reese said made sense. He has some valid points."

"I suppose," Priestly added, "but it's still hard to figure where it fits into the grand scheme of things."

"Some say we evolved from apes," Priestly said. "It sounds so foolish, doesn't it?"

"Scientists, some days you don't know who or what to believe," Keefe added.

This last statement hung in the air as the two men remained silent. Minutes later they received confirmation of the landing and the destruction of the shuttle engines which would prevent escape from the planet.

"We're done," Keefe said.

"What the hell is the name of this place?" asked Priestly.

"The information blackout should be complete by now," Keefe said. "Let's see what information the computer has on it. Computer—state planet designation and location of shuttle launch."

The computer responded: No formal designation in library. Intelligence reports only local designations."

"They must really want to hide this place," Keefe said, "they won't even name it."

"Apparently," Priestly agreed. "Computer, what are the local designations and location of shuttle?"

"Planet is locally designated as Earth. Shuttle has landed in one of the major continents called Europe in a region known as Transylvania."

"What was it that Reese said," Keefe said aloud, "that the inhabitants of this world believed in myths and legends—well I guess they will have a new one to go on now."

SHORE LEAVE

C.J. Henderson

"It is upon the navy under the Providence of God that the safety, honour, and welfare of this realm do chiefly attend."
Charles II

"God help us all."
Anonymous

THE HUMAN SAILOR'S FIST SMACKED AGAINST THE SIDE OF THE EMBRIAN'S HEAD FOR THE fifth time, making a loud and juicy sound. The noise seemed to please the sailor mightily; the Embrian, not so much.

"Keep it up, Noodles," shouted a much taller sailor, also human, one dressed in much the same uniform as the other. "We'll crack this coconut yet!"

The two sailors were part of the upstart human fleet from that far end of the galaxy into which most reputable races did not bother to venture. It was a fearsomely cluttered area, one filled with debris from the great space wars of the elder races, all of whom disappeared so long ago. The whole place abounded with black hole snares, meteor whirls, nebulae pits, all manner of mines and traps as well as system-wide sargassos of wrecked armadas just waiting for the chance to befoul modern travellers.

Of course, the Embrians being heelstomped in The Cold Bone Cellar—which by the way neither contained a particularly gelid temperature, nor found itself situated beneath the surface—did not care what race the sailors were, nor where they were from. They only wished for respite from the heelstomping and the continual thumping of their conga-like heads. Luckily for them, the unmistakable sound of approaching law enforcement began to filter through the riotous din enveloping the tavern at that moment.

"Rocky," cried out Noodles, he of the keener hearing, "sounds like the shore patrol." Holding off his next punch for the moment, Chief Gunnery Officer Rockland Vespucci cupped a hand to his ear, confirmed his friend's assertion, then shouted;

"Men of the *Franklin*—time for a strategic withdrawal!" To which Noodles, more officially known as Machinist First Mate Li Qui Kon, added most vocally;

"Run and live!"

Tossing the soldiers, sailors, and officers from the other ships with whom they had been brawling into a central pile, the sailors in question assumed a semblance of a formation, heading for the back door on the run as they sang;

"Oh, we're the boys of the *Franklin*,
We fly in outer space,
We wipe our asses with moonbeams,
We know how star dust tastes.

"The boys of the fighting *Franklin*,
The best ship in all the fleet,
Say a single word ag'in her,
And we'll pound ya 'til yer meat!"

When the military police did arrive they seemed in a particular lather, one not quite in line with a simple barroom bare-knuckler. The MPs were, as was standard at any port where different cultures docked together, a mix of the five great races of the Pan-Galactic League of Suns. That meant, of course, there were no humans among their numbers, which is why those warbling the thirty-some odd verses dedicated to the virtues of the Fighting *Franklin* were so quick to make their exit. And, with their usual precision, within only five blocks at top-speed exit, the group of some twenty-seven original roughhousers had split up into some eleven groups of two and three, all eleven striving mightily to pretend not to know one another and to walk in opposing directions.

Now calmly walking through the streets, Rocky and Noodles assumed the innocent pose of two guileless gobs out for a stroll in an exciting new port of call. And, to be fair, they were very good at doing so. Indeed, so shamelessly naive did they appear, the grifters, hoodwinks, and typical bottom leeches one found in any such hub city allowed them passage, feeling it beneath their dignity as thieves to go after pigeons so utterly tender.

"I don't think we should have run for it until we found out if that place validated parking."

About to give out with a snappy rejoinder, Rocky suddenly noted that he and his partner were being followed by four rather large and singularly dangerous-looking Danierians—pasty, bulbous beings known far and wide for their quick tempers and all-around lack of social skills. Noting that they had been noted, the quartet began to pick up speed, not slowly, but switching from a quick walk to a supersonic lurch with one quick whoosh.

This motivated the sailors to take the opportunity to test their land-legs by cranking their own mobility up to the ultimate, racing down one oddly shaped back alley and then the next. By this point the Danierians could no longer actually be seen due to the great, bilious dust cloud their pursuit was raising. Availing himself of this advantage, Machinist First Mate Li rummaged through his pockets, examining one discovery after another until coming across a temporal spanner bar.

Setting it for what he imagined were the appropriate amount of seconds, he tossed it down in front of himself and Rocky, kept moving forward, then nodded with appreciation when he first heard the tool, normally used for re-aligning warp engines, "klik" back into standard reality, then heard the expansion field open just in time to trip up their pursuers. The welcome sounds of beings falling against one another and the somewhat harder surface of the street, as well as the unwelcome ozone-frying smell of shots being fired, came to the sailors, bringing a laugh to their lips as well as added speed to their retreat.

Finally, several blocks and random turns later, the two slowed down, picking up their conversation where they left off. Assuming the Danierians were simply part of the house security for the house they had helped make so less secure, they put the creatures out of their minds as Rocky asked;

"So, Noodles, tell me, exactly what did you park that you wanted a validation for?"

"It's the principle of the thing," responded the machinist. "Storage of future information."

"Where do you get these ideas," asked Rocky. "I swear, you're the kind of guy who proposes polkas for national anthems."

"And you're the kind of guy who steals miniature aliens when running out of a bar instead of a couple of spare bottles." Needless to say, Rocky was indeed puzzled by his friend's comment. Not that part about the bottles. No, the gunnery officer was certain Noodles had managed to palm two or three fifths on his way out the door. That would certainly explain the slight "klinking" sound emanating from his duffle.

Indeed, it was the part about stealing aliens—miniature or otherwise—which had him perplexed. Scratch his head as hard as he might, Rocky could not remember a single instance of doing such. Questioning Noodles on the subject only brought the equally inscrutable rejoinder;

"Don't look at me, I certainly didn't steal them."

Rocky's confusion only lasted another moment, however, mainly because at that point the gunnery officer followed the assumed trail leading from the end of Noodles' directional finger to the objective being speared by such action, namely the nine small fry following behind the pair of sailors.

"You crazy git," shouted Rocky. "I didn't steal them. They're followin' us. And," he added, after taking a closer look, "I don't think they're small aliens."

"You think they're human?"

"No, goddamnit—I don't think they're human. I mean, I don't think they're small aliens." Scrutinizing the troop now standing still behind them, obviously ready to start moving once more as soon as the sailors did, Noodles said slowly;

"I don't know . . . they look small and they look like aliens to me."

"I don't mean they're not small aliens, I mean yes, they're small, and yes, they're aliens, but I don't think that's all they are."

"What else could they be?" Noodles looked the silent contingent over again, then asked, "Robots?"

"Not robots—why is everything robots to you machinists? No, I think they're kids."

"Who cares if they're kids—why are they following us?"

"I don't know."

"Then, you should ask them."

"Why me?"

"Because, I spotted them first, you're closer to them, and I don't like children or small aliens, unless of course they're robots." Against such thunderous logic, the gunnery officer found himself without choice. So surrendering, he dropped down on one knee and asked;

"All right, who's the ring leader here? I want to know what you bunch are doing followin' us. Com'on now . . . speak up."

One plump melon of a creature dressed for all the world in what seemed to be a scouring pad stepped forward and announced in the squeakiest voice either sailor had ever experienced;

"We grateful orphans. Follow you to happy safety. We know you kind kipkips. Not sell us to be chowder."

After a painful amount of conversation with the alien, who did indeed turn out to be a child, the two sailors learned that the nine tykes, all of different species, were orphans purchased from a galactic state home for a Representative Brummellig'ic for the purpose of being turned into a type of outer rim gumbo. Somewhat suspicious, Noodles used his com to check what the orphan they nicknamed Melon had told them. When he looked up from his labors, Rocky threw an all-encompassing;

"Well?" at him, to which Noodles replied;

"Like always, translation between Earth Basic 9.8 and Pan-Galactic's a bit rough, but the little zucchini might have something. There is a Representative Brummellig'ic on planet right now, and he's got enough power to keep all information about himself off the low class bands. The kid's right, though. I found a mention of him on some kind of society page—he is throwing a big party tonight."

Rocky and Noodles looked suspiciously, then sternly, then helplessly at their new litter. Finding no recourse there, they walked away several paces, then looked at each other, lips pursed, eyes narrowing. As one they turned and stared down at their three-times-three tag-alongs, and then turned back to look at one another again—lips tighter, eyes down to slits. Finally, on the verge of choking and going blind, Noodles offered;

"This can't be happening to us . . . "

"I know; we ain't had shore leave in sixteen months—"

"We don't know anything about taking care of kids . . . "

"And this Brummellig'ic creep, he's certain to have a lot of muscle—"

"It's not like we can go to the authorities . . . "

"No, no—even if there weren't no spotter cams in that bar we just helped redesign, they'll be lookin' for everything in blue and white to invite in for a chat—"

"MPs will only be worse . . . "

"Even if we weren't in trouble, guy like this Brummellig'ic could have people bought off anywhere. If we was to even talk about this to anyone, if word got back to him—" Rocky drew a finger across his throat, with an accompanying dreadful sound to get his point across. Rolling his eyes, mostly in fearful agreement, Noodles said;

"This is not fair . . . "

"I know that," agreed Rocky. Turning his head, he stared as hard as he could at their nine new companions, trying to ignore their pathetic demeanors and large imploring eyes—those that had eyes, of course. Turning back to his friend, he whispered;

"Elvis Corkin' Presley, all I wanted was to drink and fight, dance some with beautiful girls, see a couple shows, do a little gamblin' . . . not play nursemaid."

"You're absolutely right. This is not our responsibility. By Buddha's Mint Julep, for all we know, maybe they sell orphans all the time to make into bouillabaisse out here. We're not home, you know."

"And another important factor," added Rocky, his voice dropping to an even lower, more conspiratorial level, "we're a lot bigger than they are—"

"Our legs are longer . . . "

"We could most assuredly run much, much faster than them—"

And then, the one that looked like Shirley Temple, if Shirley Temple had been the offspring of a seal and a geranium, started to cry. She had a beautiful crying voice, not—that is—one melodious to listen to, but one perfectly designed for fetching sympathy. So utterly loud, shrill, and trembling was it that windows began to open, and even passing motorists started coming to a halt. With the speed of politicians placing blame, the pair of gobs emptied their pockets, searching desperately for something they might just happen to have on their persons which would placate a caterwauling alien five-year-old.

Luckily, Noodles just happened to have a 9/10s galvanized securing bolt which caught little Shirley's eye. Throwing out a purple tendril, she snagged the five-point-eighteen ounces of steel and happily began chewing. Wiping perspiration from their now freely beading heads, Rocky with the edge of his tallywacker, Noodles with his bucket cap, the two shrank against the closest wall as the oppressive reality of their situation began to dawn on them.

"You know," said Noodles, his eyes now constantly scanning for authority in all its varied guises, "we're in trouble."

"Oh, ya think? Listen, Edison, we gotta start cogitatin' on what we're gonna do here." With that statement, Rocky turned to look over the kids. Noticing they were near a type of public park, he rounded up their reluctantly-accepted charges and got them all off the street and out of the main public view. Finding an alcove large enough to house them all, and discreet enough that they could talk freely, he posted Noodles at the leafy entrance to keep watch, positioned the children on the ground, then sat down in front of them and asked;

"All right, let's figure some stuff out. First off, how many of you understand what I'm saying?"

Melon screeched out a reply detailing that he, Shirley, and three others whom the gobs immediately nick-named Curly, Snip, and Poodle could understand basic humanspeak. The others, whom they designated Bubbles, Fork, Creepie, and Poindexter, did not speak anything close to Earth 9.8, but Snip could apparently translate for

Bubbles and Creepie, Creepie could then straighten out Fork, and Poodle could get across enough to Poindexter to keep him in the loop. With this established, Rocky immediately explained the buddy system, telling the group that if things were going to work at all, everyone was going to have to help everyone else. And at that point, Shirley asked the question that sent our boys from merely falling over a cliff to rocketing over it.

"What things are going to work?"

Her question could be taken in any of a hundred ways, and both swabbies felt the twisting knife of each possible one. Cutting through the selfishness of their desire to throw away their paychecks on dice, dames, and drinks, her query focused the small fries' plight perfectly—abandoned by Rocky and Noodles, the nine of them were bound for a soup pot. Boiled alive with celery and onions to feed the decadent rich.

"Noodles," said Rocky of a sudden, "if you'd like to take off now, and go back out to have some fun, I'd be real understandin' of such an action."

"What," responded the machinist, "and let a loose propeller like you get our kids baked up into won tons? No way I'm going anywhere, you crazy wop."

The gunnery officer smiled. All right then, he thought, it was settled. They would help the kids. But, the back of his mind questioned, help them to do what?

A quick interrogation gave the gobs the following facts. The kids had all come from the orphanage. None of them had anyone on the outside to whom they could turn. The beings who were going to sell them to be soup were to meet those wishing to make them into soup at The Cold Bone Cellar. The merry disruption caused by Rocky, Noodles, and their shipmates had rendered the kids' sellers unconscious, giving them the opportunity to escape along with the still conscious combatants. The buyers had been the ones they eluded outside the tavern.

"All right," declared Rocky. "We gotta get off the street, and back to the ship. We get these kids to the captain and he'll make sure they're taken care of." Melon and the other English speakers looked a little worried, but Noodles added;

"No, the captain's a good egg. Honest. He'll protect you all. But," the machinist indicated with several complicated eye movements both the idea of direction and extreme distance as he added, "it's a hell of a long way back to the ship. You got any ideas on how we're going to get there?"

"Actually," answered Rocky, his face rearranging itself into a mask of lopsided smugness, "I think I do."

"This is ridiculous," muttered Noodles. "This is something they only do in cartoons."

"And tell me what part of today hasn't been a damn cartoon, would you—please?" Looking over the pair's three new companions, the gunnery officer added;

"Besides, I think they look pretty good."

It had to be admitted, for a totally outlandish and completely improbable kind of stunt, their nine charges did look "pretty good." To shorten a frenzied search through numerous clothing stores, plus a great deal of pushing, guessing, prodding, a bit of cutting and sewing, and some emergency work with baling wire and extra-strength duct tape, what the sailors had done was stand the kids one atop the other, taking into account their different shapes and abilities, then dressed them as adults. The results made them—especially when attempting to walk—appear more like drunken zombies, but they looked far less like children, and for the moment, that was good enough for the boys.

"So now," whispered the machinist to his partner-in-absurdity, "what do we do next?"

"We get inside somewhere where we can find some guys we trust. Then, with some help on our side, we get back to the ship, get the kids placed somewheres where they won't get fricasseed or barbecued, and then we try to get back to enjoying ourselves."

"And where exactly would we be able to do that?" Staring across the street at a garishly lit nightclub, one promising gambling, female companionship, and beers from across the galaxy, Rocky pulled at his chin and answered;

"Yeah, where indeed?"

Moments later, the five were crossing the street, three of the quintet bouncing and rocking as if they were in a quake zone, the other two attempting to hold them together while talking loudly about how ashamed they were of their friends for drinking to excess. This continued up the stairs of the entrance to Ping's Dingled Showplace, through the doors, and down the stairs into the main ballroom. Following a waiter to a table for five, the oddly moving party waddled along as best they could, all of them gratefully collapsing into their chairs.

Instantly Snip began wailing because, as best the gobs could figure out, either Poodle was standing on his face, or Creepie had farted and the duct tape holding the two of them together had begun to melt. As quickly as it could be managed discreetly, the sailors got the kids as comfortably arranged as possible, ordered two pitchers of Gullyfoyle Malt Liquor, three of SweetSweet BugJuice, and then sat back to peruse their surroundings.

Ping's, at least at first glance, seemed a perfect place for the swabbies and their charges to try and get their bearings. If nothing else, every table received a complimentary revolving platter of treats, one with enough variety that it held something all the kids could ingest. The fact that the club was dark enough no one at the other tables would notice the extra hands, tentacles, flippers, claws, and so forth extruding from the three non-humans at their table was certainly a bonus.

Beyond that, it seemed like the kind of place where people were only interested in those at their table, or what was going on up on stage, which at that moment was an act labeled as Tina Dillfreb and her Titanic Tower of Terriers. Feeling somewhat secure for the first time in some forty-nine Earth Standard Minutes, the swabbies began to relax. And, after finishing their first pitcher, Rocky and Noodles found themselves as relaxed as house cats on a hot day. Finding the kids content with their BugJuice, assorted treats, and the ever-toppling tower of dogs on-stage, they were just about to begin planning a strategy when suddenly the already dark interior went positively ebony.

The darkness lasted but a moment, and then a bright orange spot focused on the center stage. In that brief moment Tina and her hounds were removed along with all of their props and one embarrassing accident, and replaced with startling efficiency by a Golblacian Master of Ceremonies. Drumming up a more-than-deserved round of applauds for the departed Dillfreb and associates, the creature best described as a seven foot blue/green penguin then dropped its voice to a lower, throatier range, and said;

"Now, gentlebeings, all you flippers and floggers, you squasheads and bipeds, everything out there with the strength, enthusiasm, and moral turpitude to do so, let me get you to make some deep, loving tribal noise for the seductive, the lovely, the incomparable, Miss Beezle Uvi!"

A pink shot of butterfly lights were sent dancing through the white spot framing center stage. All the orphans made appropriate "ouuuuuhhhhhhhhh" sounds, except, of course, for those stuck in the middle of their costumes. At least, for that moment. Responding to the appreciative sounds of their fellow tureen escapees, those in the mid- and bottom sections of the costumes abandoned their stations to congregate around the center pole of their party's table and peek out from under the tablecloth.

As they did so, the curtains began to part and the orchestra began to warble, all of it timed to both the movement of the lights, and the entrance of a creature so entrancing, so curvaceously shimmering, so delightful in movement and gesture that Rocky would have fallen out of his chair and out onto the main floor if Noodles had not fallen over at the same moment, the two of them smacking into each other, then propping each other up as their insides dissolved into jelly. The darkness hid their antics, of course, as it was meant to do, keeping all eyes focused on the approaching Uvi.

Strolling calmly toward her spot, the singer moved her charmingly antique voice amplifier to what apparently served as her mouth, and in a slow, sultry voice began to release the lead-in lines of her song to the already raptured audience.

> "When intelligent beings first went into space,
> And met creatures from another race,
> It was, of course, one of those great, historic finds.
>
> "The galaxy didn't worry so much about war,
> Intolerance wasn't even brought to the floor,
>
> But . . .
> There was one . . .
> Burning question . . .
> On alllllllll . . . inquiring minds . . .

And then, the house lights blazed up, whites becoming yellows, pinks becoming reds, the band shifted from a quiet respectful background accompaniment to a raucous blast of hot horns and sibilant strings, and Uvi hit her mark, threw back her head, and in a voice higher, louder, stronger, and twice as shot through with promise as before belted out;

> "What is that, and where does it go?
> Should it be inserted, fast or slow?

"Does it like to be licked?
Does it like to be grabbed?
Does it like to be twirled?
Does it like to be stabbed?

"Oh, just what is that, and where does it go?"

Bouncing off each other, their heads banging together like empty spittoons, Noodles and Rocky at first found themselves instinctively trying to cover the ears of their many charges. They gave off on this futile endeavor for, first off, they had far too few hands, second, they did not have the slightest idea where most of the orphans' audio organs where positioned, and third, to be perfectly honest, the childish tittering coming from all their charges, except well, of course, for Poindexter, cued them that they were far too late to protect this particular interstellar nine from the facts of life.

That being established, the swabbies looked at each other helplessly for a moment, then simply surrendered to the obvious and went back to enjoying the show. All of this happening within a handful of seconds, they had their chins firmly placed within the palms of their hands, their elbows on the table, and the sappiest of grins plastered on their faces as Uvi hit the second go-round, belting out;

"Oh, what is that, and what does it do?
Is it there for both of us, or just for you?

"Does it get much bigger?
Does it reach out and scratch?
Does it remain a solo, or
Can you grow a batch?

"Baby, what is that, and what does it do?"

At this point, alarms were going off back aboard the gobs' ship in the medical bay, alerting the ship's physician-on-call that two shore-leavers were close to coronary arrest. With the flip of a few switches, however, the doctor ascertained the two were merely staring at a choice piece of stimuli. Wishing he were fifty years younger, he mentally wished them both luck and cancelled the alert. All in all, a good thing, for the meter readings were only going to get worse.

As that stanza ended, the Dingled Showplace Dancers joined the club's star on stage, backing her up for a repeat of the chorus, making all the appropriately rude gestures of licking, grabbing, twirling, and stabbing, while Uvi kicked up her heels, mesmerizing the crowd with the way she could move her many and varied appendages with such flawless synchronization, all of her coming together just in time for her to re-enter the center spot and warble;

"Tell me, what is that, and how does it feel?
Like the mushroom we first saw, or some eventual eel?

"When our races met,
I thought it was just another find.
Now all I can think of is,
Your place or mine?

"Oh lover, just what is that, and how does it feel?"

Noodles set about "shushing" the orphans, whose giggling had attracted the attention of more than one waiter. Rocky, in the meantime, could offer no assistance. Alien in every way as the singer was, he simply could not tear his eyes from her. And, it had little to do with the woes of Earth navies of elder times. His ship was one of the most modern in the fleet; its complement was completely integrated with members of both sexes.

No, Rocky's problem had nothing to do with not having seen any females for too long a time. The particular sailor's problem was that he had never seen anyone like Beezle Uvi—anywhere, ever—except in certain dreams, the dates of which he still marked the anniversaries of with a boyishly wistful fondness. Thus he did not even notice when Noodles slipped from his seat and fell to the floor with the kids, his eyes locking with Uvi's as she sang;

"The cosmos is shrinking,
The boundaries are changing,
And I think my pelvis is in . . .
For a slight . . . rearranging!

"And so I challenge . . .
Our greatest scientific minds . . .
To somehow find an answer . . .
To that one burning question . . .
That IIIIIII . . .
Just have to know . . .

"Oh, just what is that . . .
And where, oh where does it gooooooooooooooooo?"

The full regular house lights went up then, and applauds thundered from the audience with a force so powerful some of the chorus girls were forced to take a backward step, or slither, or whatever. Rocky's own hands were contributing a massive amount of the audible appreciation, as were Noodles'. Melon, Poodle, and Curly were in for a round as well, Bubbles, Snip, Fork, and Creepie were all wrestling over the last items on the appetizer tray; Shirley, having finished her bolt was working on a corner of the table, and Poindexter, well . . . you know.

What startled Rocky, Noodles, their menagerie, and most of the occupants of Ping's Dingled Showplace, however, was what happened next—an event so unexpected, so unprecedented, that the *Galaxy Today* reporter permanently stationed in the club would have written it up and sent it across the waves immediately if the shock of it had not sent her stumbling backward into an unfortunately extremely large and heavy ice sculpture. What stole the breath, ability to speak, and common sense from those gathered was the fact that, defying precedent, good taste, and well, common sense again, Beezle Uvi had left the stage and was walking for Rocky and Noodles' table.

"L-Little buddy," stuttered the finest gunnery officer in the fleet, "I-I-I d-do believe she's . . . comin' this way."

"You might be right," agreed Noodles. Ducking his head under the table, he hissed quick orders to the orphans, getting them to reassemble into their pretend persons before the singer could reach them. Doing his best to help, Rocky stared forward, attempting to keep his eyes from falling out of his head, rolling around on the table and growing their own tongues with which to blast wolf whistles.

"Mind if I join you?"

"Geezzzz," asked Rocky seriously, "do I look that foolish?" Uvi giggled, an undulating action that made several seemingly unconnected body parts shimmy. Signalling her favorite waiter to bring her a Cosmic Laugh, she turned and focused her attention on Rocky. After he introduced Noodles, she pointed a finger, moving it from one of them to the other, asking;

"You're human, aren't you?"

"Ah, well," Rocky answered honestly, "yeah—last time I looked."

"I've read about humans," she admitted. "Heard a lot of good things."

"Gosh, I don't know what to say," responded Rocky. "I don't even know what species you are. Not that that matters or nothin'."

"I was impressed by that attitude," Uvi admitted. "You stare with such charming hunger. Tell me, are you myopic, or were you just enjoying the show?"

"I don't want to seem forward or nothin'," the gunnery officer said, "the show was okay and everything, It's just, there's somethin' about you, ma'am, somethin' . . . and I know this must sound crazy, but it's like I'm fallin' in—"

"Ix-nay on the ov-lay alk-tay," hissed Noodles, poking his pal hard in the ribs. Rocky turned, mightily disturbed for having been interrupted at that particular moment, but then, he saw what the machinist had noticed. All around the club, police officers and MPs had begun to take up positions. Worse yet, the quartet of Danierians they thought they had left in temporal disruption had somehow gotten themselves undisrupted.

"Great jumpin' jackasses," blurted Rocky. "How could they all have found us—at the same time?"

"A good question," replied Noodles. "Rhetorical, I'm hoping?"

"The cops," asked Uvi, "those Danierian creeps? They're all looking for you?" When two forlorn nods were given her as answer, the interstellar diva asked the galaxy's most popular one-word question;

"Why?"

The swabbies took turns filling Uvi in on what had happened to them since leaving The Cold Bone Cellar, one explaining this or that section while the other looked to the orphans, seeing if there was any way possible they might be able to get all nine of them out of the boiling pan and away from the fire once more. Hearing everything the pair had to say, the singer asked;

"So all you want to do is get these kids to your captain to help you protect them?" When the boys nodded sincerely, Rocky tying Poodle's shoe for the fifth time, Noodles wiping what he hoped was Creepie's nose, Uvi's facial area seemed to melt with genuine affection. She was just about to speak when a whistle was blown from somewhere in the back. Leaping to his feet, praying there were more sailors within earshot than he could see, Rocky bellowed;

"Pie fight—*Franklin* style!"

And at that moment, chaos exploded throughout Ping's Dingled Showplace. From twenty different spots, pastries, dinner plates, flower pots, beer mugs, chairs, and anything else not nailed down was seen flying through the air, most of the flight plans registering an authority figure's head as its destination. As per standard *Franklin* tactics, the second fusillade was launched at the lights. Clutching Rocky's wrist, Uvi shouted;

"Grab the kids and follow me."

The sailors did as ordered, scooping up their charges and following the singer onto the stage. As their fellow sailors, and quite a number of innocent patrons, fell into a pitched battle with the police and MPs, Noodles noticed that the Danierians were still heading straight toward them. Reaching the up-stage side of the curtains, Uvi pointed out her dressing room, telling the others to meet her there. When Rocky protested, she hissed;

"This is my world; I can deal with them—go!" Then, turning to the chorus line of Dingled Showplace Dancers, she shouted;

"Rubes rushing the stage, girls—make them sorry!"

Giggling, the chorus girls waved Uvi on, then prepared for battle. Dropping the curtain on the heads of the Danierians, they then wandered from lump to lump, flattening them with heavy objects to what looked like heads and kicks to what looked like groins. In her dressing room, Uvi held out bundles of clothing to both Noodles and Rocky ordering them to get into them immediately. The pair protested, but she shouted back that they had no time to argue, and unless they had a better plan than hers, that they should simply shut up and do as they were told. Pulling his jersey off over his head, Noodles mumbled;

"I think she may be related to the lieutenant." To which Rocky responded;

"Awwww, just shut up and help me adjust my bra."

"Is that what that is?"

"I think so—for like maybe, three?"

Pulling, pushing, and experimenting, the two managed to get themselves dressed in only a handful of minutes. Checking themselves over in the room's full length mirror, they did make better females than the kids had made adults, but not by much. In the meantime, Uvi and her wardrobe assistant had removed the last remaining scraps of the kids' disguises and replaced them with new ones. Having cut apart several throw rugs and her own fur coat, the orphans had all been converted into what could pass for dogs if the inspection was not too strenuous. Looking again in the mirror, down at the kids, back to the mirror, and back to the kids, realization hit Noodles' mind.

"I get it," he exclaimed. "We're supposed to be Tina Dillfreb and her Titanic Tower of Terriers."

"Machinists are so smart," cooed Uvi. "I'll bet you know about robots and everything." Noodles beamed at the mention of his favorite topic, barely noticing the sour look Rocky was throwing his way. Getting in front of the pair of gobs before anything could come of it, either, Uvi said;

"All right, now we're going to just march out there right past them all, just a big happy bunch of girls and canines, right everybody?"

Rocky and Noodles agreed, as did Melon, Shirley, and the others as translation spread through the pack. With the last pseudo-terrier nod, Uvi opened the door and the lot of them poured out into the hallway. The diva led the way, throwing her ample self in front of the first curious eyes of authority they met. A slight chill ran through her as she saw the enormous extent to which curiosity was running that day.

Flipping the "flirt" switch within her head, the singer sauntered, doing the best she could to attract all license-to-hurt attention to herself. Rocky and Noodles, doing their best to herd the orphans along, trying at the same time to keep up a light and breezy falsetto chatter, followed behind, keeping their all-too-stubbly faces averted from the police, military and otherwise, filling the hallway. As they approached the exit, they found two disagreeable officers arguing with one another.

"I don't understand the problem," growled the one. "We know they're from an Earth ship—the *Franklin*. You should have the bio-reads of everyone from that tub by now."

"But, Sir," answered the other, "I keep trying to tell you—we checked every registry in port. There's no ship, Earther or otherwise, called the *Franklin* in dock. The closest name is the *Felkinsku*, but that's a Saurian wine merchant freighter, methane breathers." As Rocky and Noodles smiled to one another, the superior of the two officers growled;

"And what do you, ah . . . ladies, find so funny?" Trusting his chances at making female sounds better than Rocky's, Noodles cocked his wrist limply and tittered;

"Ohhh, you big, strong man, you—I knew there was someone out here just dying to take me to dinner. Rocklina, be a dear and take the puppies out on your own. The general here has eyes for me."

Taking a good look at the eye-batting, lip-pursing Noodles, the officer blanched, practically knocking his underling over in his haste to clear a path to the door. Sticking his nose in the air with as offended an attitude as possible, Noodles sniffed appropriately, then followed the others out the door. Once outside, Rocky laughed;

"Didn't know you made such a good dame, little buddy. I'll have to keep that in mind for those lonely nights once were back out in the black." As Uvi hailed a passing cab, Noodles glared at Rocky through his eye makeup and snarled;

"And I'll be certain to let everyone on board know this new fact about you. There are more than a few members of the crew with enough 'alternate' wardrobe choices to keep you happy for years, I suspect."

"Bet they're all machinists, too."

The pair were about to contemplate taking things a step beyond the playful when a cab willing to risk nine hounds stopped for them. Piling inside, the kids all giggling with glee as they threw themselves onto the floor, doing their collective best to bark in their nine different accents, Uvi gave the driver a destination then turned to the boys. Settling her various appendages around her, she asked;

"Not that I'm not grateful, but why is it those two at the door couldn't find your ship?"

The swabbies smiled once more. As Rocky's laughter attracted Fork and Bubbles who both piled into his lap, soon followed by most of the others as he started tickling and growling at the first pair, Noodles explained;

"Our ship is really the *Roosevelt*. But, those what named her never said which Roosevelt she was named for. You see, back on our planet, there were two great men, Franklin and Theodore Roosevelt. On ship, there's those of us that say she was named for Teddy, and others who insist it was Frank. So, whenever we hit a new port, we Teddies cause as much trouble as we can pretending to be Franks, and then they do it to us." The machinist laughed shortly, then added;

"I guess it sounds a little stupid."

"Whether it is or isn't, it saved your bacon back there."

"They got bacon on this planet," asked Rocky with the mention of his favorite dessert. About to answer, Uvi suddenly went silent as her eyes caught sight of something out of the back of the cab. Squinting to make certain of what she had seen, she turned around to the driver, shouting;

"Triple the meter if you can outrun what's coming."

"What you are seeing and I am seeing," the driver asked, his fingers already implementing a speed shift, "this thing we are seeing, it is coming for you?"

"It's coming for 'us,' darling, and it's probably coming with the idea of shooting first and talking about it later. So unless you were thinking of jumping out at the next corner . . . "

"Your meaning is clear, good lady."

Turning around as one, Rocky and Noodles got a gander at what Uvi and the driver had already seen. As the cab blasted forward, nearly doubling its speed, Noodles offered;

"Make that quadruple—I've got money, too."

"Me, three—and I want to live to spend it," added Rocky. "By the blessed blue suede shoes of the King, what's goin' on around here?" Looking down at their charges, Noodles mused;

"Must be one damn good soup they were going to make." Rocky glared at his partner, who shrugged his shoulders, protesting;

"What? I'm just saying . . . "

Further talk was obscured as the first of the Antagonizers let loose a shot which tore large sections of street up behind their cab. The ships were a matched pair of Danierian design, a fact not lost on anyone in the cab. After a few more shots were fired, each barely missing their vehicle, the driver said;

"Luckily these are some very bad shots, yes?" Shaking her head, Uvi replied;

"No such luck—they're herding us."

Rocky and Noodles looked at each other grimly. Both the machinist and the gunnery officer knew she was correct. Rolling up the crushed silk sleeve of his blouse until the tattoo of an anchor on his upper arm showed, Rocky said;

"Well, little buddy, I'm thinkin' this is it."

"We all have to go sometime." The pair nodded one to another, touched fists, then Rocky shouted to the driver;

"Get ready to slow enough to let us jump out. We're gonna try and stop those mugs." Uvi started to protest. The orphans all started to squeal. The driver hit the brakes.

"I didn't mean for you to come to a complete stop, ya boob!"

"No sir, I am certain you did not," answered the driver. "But, I am thinking that they did."

Following the directional path of the cabby's pointing digit, the swabbies found their path blocked by more firepower than that possessed by many small planets. The Antagonizers rounded the same corner, saw what awaited them, and attempted to break off pursuit. One was vaporized, the other was sent crashing into a billboard advertising the great deals to be had at Lapine's Luxury Liquors. Poking his head out of his hound disguise, Melon asked;

"Is this where you jump out to save us, Rocky?" Staring forward into the oncoming armada, the gunnery officer asked;

"Noodles, can we improvise some weapons here?"

"What were you thinking," asked the machinist. "Wet towels? Pictures of their ex-wives?"

And then, the approaching ships came to a halt, the lead cruiser actually dropping to the street. As all in the cab watched, a panel slid open in the side of the personal dreadnought, and a figure in a business suit came out onto the extender reaching for the ground below, one surrounded by more than a score of heavily armed soldiers.

"Kids," said Noodles. "You go on and make a run for it. We'll hold them as long as we can."

"Yeah," added Rocky sourly. "That should give you two, maybe three seconds."

"If they're lucky," said Noodles with a grin. Smiling back at his partner, Rocky nodded, and then the two reached for the door handles, ready to do their best, when Melon suddenly shouted;

"Daddy!"

It was some time later when everything had finally been straightened out. Sitting in the offices which had been given over to representative Brummellig'ic and his staff, Rocky and Noodles, finally back in regulation dress, sat quietly at attention as their captain, Caldo Bippdi, the mayor of the port town, and the representative tried to hash out all the particulars.

"So," said the captain, hoping to nail the whole thing down, "if I have this correct, you, Mr. Brummellig'ic, slipped on-planet quietly for an inspection, looking for signs of Danierian mischief." When the big alien nodded, the captain continued, saying;

"But, unknown to you, the Danierians, having discovered your plan, kidnapped your son's class while on field trip. They were attempting to force you to turn a blind eye to their chicanery, when my boys here caused a diversion that allowed the kids to escape their captors."

"A diversion?" Mayor Bippdi began turning an array of exotic colors, several which drew appreciative "ahs" and "ohs" from the former orphans. Before he could continue, however, representative Brummellig'ic cut him off with a wave of his hand, saying;

"Yes, Captain, you are correct on all counts. And, please, Mayor, all damages will be taken care of by my office."

Noodles and Rocky smiled at each other upon hearing the representative's pronouncement. Still sketchy on some of the facts, however, Rocky asked;

"You'll forgive me, gentlemen, and all, but I was wonderin', Melon," he called out to the ringleader sitting on his father's desk, "why you give us that story about orphans and soup and all?"

"An idea of one of my officers," answered Brummellig'ic. "The children have been taught this cover story. You see, most species in the galaxy would sell their own mothers for a box of mints. We've found that whenever someone is lost, if they claim to be running away from us, most anyone who finds them will turn them into whomever they say they're running away from expecting a reward."

"Yes, Mr. Vespucci, Mr. Kon; it seems you two have done great things for the human race, intergalactic relations-wise. Would you agree, representative?"

"It's rare we of the inner circle of the Pan-Galactic League of Suns get such an opportunity to measure a race's true worth," said Brummellig'ic to the captain. Turning to the gobs, he said, "You two might turn out to be fine examples of humanity, or tremendous exceptions, but you have given the league something to think about."

There was more chatter back and forth after that, but it was the usual circular palaver of politicians. Finally, even that was cut short as the rest of the high-powered parents of the supposed orphans forced their way into the meeting to reclaim their youngsters, and to shower Rocky and Noodles with praise, well-wishes, and gifts. Seeing Uvi waiting in the outer office, Rocky left Noodles to soak up any remaining goodies, hurrying out to the diva.

"So," he said, a trifle nervous, "they kept you here, too?"

"No, you silly," she said, her voice still delightfully in full possession of all the gunnery officer's faculties. "I was waiting for you." Rocky blinked hard, barely able to believe his ears. Smiling as wide as humanly possible, he answered;

"Oh my, I know I'm just a mutt, and I don't know how we could, er, I mean, what we'll have to, ummmm . . . I'm just sayin' I don't care about nothin', not so long as I can be with you."

"Oh," said Uvi in response, her voice a thing filled with apologetic surprise. "I'm sorry—I get so comfortable in this thing I forget I have it on."

And, so saying, office Beezle Uvi of Earth Intelligence slipped out of her bio-infiltration suit, revealing all one hundred and fifteen pounds of green-eyed, red-headed, well-proportioned loveliness which was the real her. Quickly explaining that she had been placed onworld in preparation for representative Brummellig'ic's inspection, she explained that she had spotted Melon in Rocky's care, and had moved in to recover him.

"Everyone was on alert. Normally I would have just stunned you and Noodles, taken the children into protective custody, and you two would have been taken away, but . . . "

"Yes," grinned Rocky, "but what?"

"Well, you do have such nice eyes . . . "

And then, the two came even closer together. Eyes closing, they were just about to kiss when suddenly, the door slammed open and a Embrian came in at a run, shouting;

"Mayor, mayor, big trouble! There are human sailors tearing up another tavern. Much fighting, much damage!"

"What ship are these from," growled the mayor, to which his aide answered;

"The *Theodore*."

"Oh well," sighed the captain. "There goes all that good will."

Representative Brummellig'ic scowled, but then Melon laughed, and his father laughed back. The other parents went back to hugging their children; Noodles asked the mayor if he had ever thought of using robot police; Uvi and Rocky finally kissed.

And outside, the port sirens shrieked In glorious futility as the boys of the "*Theodore*" continued their mayhem.

Jack Mc Devitt

CRYPTIC
_____

BLACK TO MOVE

Jack McDevitt has been on the final Nebula ballot 11 times, but has never won. *Omega* was named best novel and given the John W. Campbell Memorial Award in 2005. He has received the Phoenix and SESFA awards for lifetime achievement, and twice won the SESFA Award for best novel (*Deepsix* and *Seeker*). He has also won the Locus Award for best first novel (*The Hercules Text*, 1986) and the UPC International Prize for best novella, "Ships in the Night." McDevitt is a former naval officer, an English teacher, a customs officer, and has trained managers for the US Customs Service. He lives in Brunswick, GA, with his wife Maureen.

John C. Wright

PETER POWER ARMOR
_____

FORGOTTEN CAUSES

John C. Wright is a retired attorney, newspaperman, and newspaper editor, who was only once on the lam and forced to hide from the police who did not admire his newspaper. His works include a number of short stories in such publications as *Asimov's, Absolute Magnatude,* and several editions of *The Year's Best SF.* In addition he has eight novels to his credit published with TOR Books, including his first, *The Golden Age,* and the forthcoming *Titans of Chaos.* He presently works (successfully) as a writer in Virginia, where he lives in fairytale-like happiness with his wife, the authoress L. Jagi Lamplighter, and their three children: Orville, Wilbur, and Just Wright.

Mike McPhail
_____

WAYWARD CHILD

Mike McPhail's lifelong dream was to join NASA and become a mission specialist. He attended the Academy of Aeronautics in New York, as well as enlisting in the Air National Guard. Among his works are a number of stories, including "Chimera", in the anthology *No Longer Dreams*, based on the *Alliance Archives*™ series and its related Martial Role-Playing Game™; a manual-based, military science-fiction that realistically portrays the consequences of warfare. To learn more about his work, visit www.mcp-concepts.com.

James Daniel Ross
NOT ONE WORD

James Daniel Ross is a native of Cincinnati, Ohio who first discovered a love of writing during his education at The School for the Creative and Performing Arts. While he began in simple, web-based, vanity-press projects, his affinity for the written word soon landed him a job with Misguided Games. After taking a large part in writing and designing *Children of the Sun*, he continued as a freelancer on various contracts with BBRACK productions. After a slowdown in the gaming industry made jobs scarce, he began work on his first novel: *The Radiation Angels: The Chimerium Gambit*.

Danielle Ackley-McPhail
IN THE DYING LIGHT

Danielle Ackley-McPhail has worked both sides of the publishing industry for over a decade. Her works include the urban fantasy, *Yesterday's Dreams* and its upcoming sequel, *Tomorrow's Memories*, an edited anthology, *No Longer Dreams*, and contributions to numerous collections, including *Dark Furies, Hear Them Roar, Sails and Sorcery,* and *Bad-Ass Faeries*. In the past, her work has been nominated for both the Compton Crook Award and the EPPIE Award, but sadly, she has not yet won. She is a member of both EPIC and Broad Universe. To learn more about her work, visit www.sidhenadaire.com.

James Chambers
KILLER EYE

James Chambers "writes stories that are paced fast enough to friction burn a reader's eyeballs," says Horror Reader.com. His tales have been published in the anthologies *Crypto-Critters, Dark Furies, The Dead Walk, No Longer Dreams, Sick: An Anthology of Illness, Weird Trails,* and *Warfear*; the chapbook *Mooncat Jack*; and the magazines *Bare Bone, Cthulhu Sex,* and Allen K's *Inhuman*. His tale "A Wandering Blackness" received an honorable mention in *The Year's Best Fantasy and Horror, Sixteenth Annual Collection*. His first short story collection, in collaboration with illustrator Jason Whitley, is *The Midnight Hour: Saint Lawn Hill and Other Tales*. For more information visit www.jameschambersonline.com.

Jeffrey Lyman
COMPARTMENT ALPHA

Jeffrey Lyman is a mechanical engineer working in the New York area. In 2004 he attended the Odyssey Fantasy Writing Workshop for six weeks in New Hampshire. His first publication came in 2005, in the anthology *No Longer Dreams*, followed by a short story in the anthology *Bad-Ass Faeries*. Upcoming publications include a novella in the anthology *Blood and Devotion* and a short story in the anthology *Sails and Sorcery*, both by Fantasist Enterprises. Jeff was recently married and is now beginning the search for a house and a dog.

John G. Hemry
(a.k.a Jack Campbell)
DEAD END

John G. Hemry (a.k.a. Jack Campbell) is the author of the best-selling *Lost Fleet* series under the pen name Jack Campbell (*Dauntless* July 2006, *Fearless* January 2007, other volumes to follow). Under his own name, he's also the author of the 'JAG in space' series, the latest of which is *Against All Enemies*. His short fiction has appeared in places as varied as the latest *Chicks in Chainmail* anthology (*Turn the Other Chick*) and *Analog* magazine (which published his Nebula Award-nominated story *Small Moments in Time*). John's nonfiction has appeared in *Analog* and *Artemis* magazines as well as BenBella books on *Charmed, Star Wars*, and *Superman*. John is a retired US Navy officer who lives in Maryland with his wife (the incomparable S) and three great kids.

Bud Sparhawk
BROADSIDE
ALLIANCES

Bud Sparhawk began writing science fiction stories in 1975 and, after two sales, stopped writing for thirteen years. Since again taking up the pen, his stories and articles have appeared frequently in *Analog, Asimov's*, and other SF magazines as well as anthologies. Bud has been a three-time finalist in the Nebula's Novella category in 1998, 2002, and 2006. More information may be found at http://sff.net/people/bud_sparhawk.

Lawrence M. Schoen
THRESHER

Lawrence M. Schoen holds a Ph.D. in cognitive psychology, with a special focus in psycholinguistics. He spent ten years as a college professor, and has done extensive research in the areas of human memory and language. His background in the study of behavior and the mind provide a principal metaphor for his fiction. He currently works as the director of research and chief compliance officer for a series of mental health and addiction treatment facilities. He's also one of the world's foremost authorities on the Klingon language, having championed the exploration of this constructed tongue and lectured on this unique topic throughout the world. Among other writing endeavors, he is currently expanding "Thresher" to novel length. He lives in Philadelphia with his wife, Valerie, who is neither a psychologist nor a speaker of Klingon.

Patrick Thomas
DERELICTION OF DUTY

Patrick Thomas is the author of over 75 published short stories and more than sixteen books including seven books plus two spin-offs in the popular fantasy humor series *Murphy's Lore*.

Patrick co-edited *Hear Them Roar* and the upcoming *New Blood* vampire anthology. He has edited for *Fantastic Stories* and *Pirate Writings*. His novellas appear in *Go Not Gently* from Padwolf and *Flesh and Iron* from the Two Backed Books imprint of Raw Dog Screaming.

His stories have sold to many anthologies including *Until Somebody Loses an Eye, Hardboiled Cthulhu, Dark Furies, Clash of Steel 3: Demon, Unicorn 8, Jigsaw Nation, Crypto-Critters Vol. 1 & 2, The Dead Walk Vol. 2 & 3,* and *Warfear*. Patrick is penning three issues of a comic mini-series with artist Daniel Horne. His *Graveyard Angel* series is currently being serialized in *Cthulhu Sex* magazine. He has a short story collection coming out from Elder Signs Press as well as a novella in another Two Backed Books collection centered around Kali. Terrorbelle, The Daemor, and the DMA will also be getting their own collections in the near future.

Patrick continues to write the syndicated satirical advice column *Dear Cthulhu*.

Please visit his website at www.patthomas.net.

Tony Ruggiero
PERSPECTIVE

Tony Ruggiero has been publishing fiction since 1998. His science fiction, fantasy, and horror stories and novels have appeared in both print and electronic mediums. His published novels include *Team of Darkness* and *Aliens and Satanic Creatures Wanted: Humans Need Not Apply*. Tony is also a contributing author to *The Fantasy Writers' Companion* from Dragon Moon Press. Other collaborative work include the anthologies *The Writers for Relief Anthology* and *No Longer Dreams*.

Upcoming novels from Dragon Moon Press, *Alien Deception*(2006) and *Alien Revelation*(2007).

Tony retired from the United States Navy in 2001 after twenty-three years of service. He and his family currently reside in Suffolk, Virginia. While continuing to write, Tony teaches at Old Dominion University, Saint Leo University, and Tidewater Community College in Norfolk, VA.

C.J. Henderson
SHORE LEAVE

C.J. Henderson is the creator of both the Jack Hagee hardboiled detective series and the Teddy London supernatural detective series. He is the author of some forty novels and books, everything from *The Encyclopedia of Science Fiction Movies* to *Black Sabbath: The Ozzy Osbourne Years*. A professional writer for some thirty years, he has also had published some thousands of non-fiction articles as well as hundreds of short stories. In the wonderful world of comics, he has worked with everyone's characters—from Archie to the Punisher and from Batman to Cherry Poptart. He tries to finish at least 10,000 words a day, but often will settle for 80 or 90, especially if an episode of Hercules or Xena is on.

Now Announcing
The First Annual

MILSCIFI.COM™
Reader's Choice Awards

Interested in participating? It's easy . . .
Read *Breach the Hull* and/or *So It Begins*
and let us know which story was your
favorite from **each** book!

Prizes
The author of the story with the most votes
will receive a commemorative trophy.

Five randomly selected respondents will
win a selection of five patches based on
the artwork from *Breach the Hull*.

Rules and Regulations
One vote per person and address.
Duplicate or repeat votes will be disqualified.
Those directly involved with either publication and
their families are barred from entry.

To vote by email send your name, address, the author's name,
and the title of the story to RCA@milscifi.com
To vote by conventional mail write the above information
on a 3 x 5 card and mail to:

**MilSciFi.com Reader's Choice Award
PO Box 493
Stratford, NJ 08084**

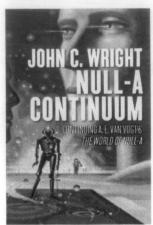

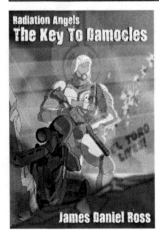

From Ace Books

Jack Campbell's
THE LOST FLEET: RELENTLESS

After successfully freeing Alliance POWs, "Black Jack" Geary discovers that the Syndics plan to ambush the fleet with their powerful reserve flotilla in an attempt to annihilate it once and for all. And as Geary has the fleet jump from one star system to the next, hoping to avoid the inevitable confrontation, saboteurs contribute to the chaos.

ISBN: 978-0-441-01708-9

Watch for Book Six . . . **THE LOST FLEET: VICTORIOUS.**

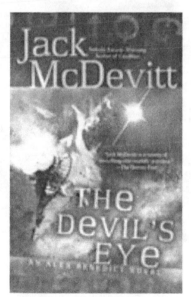

ISBN: 978-0-441-01635-8

Jack McDevitt's
THE DEVIL'S EYE

"Why read Jack McDevitt? The question should be: Who among us is such a slow pony that s/he isn't reading McDevitt?"
—Harlan Ellison

Interstellar antiquities dealer Alex Benedict receives a cryptic message asking for help from celebrated writer Vicki Greene—who has been mind-wiped. The answers to this mystery lie on the most remote of human worlds, where Alex will uncover a secret connected to a decades-old political upheaval—a secret that somebody desperately wants hidden, though the price of that silence is unimaginable . . .

Watch for . . . TIME TRAVELERS NEVER DIE

Finally, There's Something We Can All Agree On.

It's something we've all said many times. And it does seem to be one of the few things that Americans unanimously agree on. But it takes more than agreeing with each other. It takes the USO. For more than 60 years, the USO has been the bridge back home for the men and women of our armed forces around the world. The USO receives no government funding and relies entirely on the generosity of the American people. We all want to support our troops. This is how it's done.

Until Every One Comes Home.

Help support our troops.
888-USO-5566 / www.uso.org

Printed in the United States
153085LV00003B/1/P

9 780979 690198